THE ROAD

Echoes: Classics of
Hong Kong Culture and History

The life of Hong Kong has been described and explored in many books, literary, historical and scholarly. The purpose of *Echoes* is to make the best of those books available and accessible in order to bring their insights and reading pleasure to a new and wider readership.

———————

THE ROAD

AUSTIN COATES

With a Foreword by
Peggy Cater

香 港 大 學 出 版 社
HONG KONG UNIVERSITY PRESS

Hong Kong University Press
14/F Hing Wai Centre
7 Tin Wan Praya Rd
Aberdeen
Hong Kong

First published by Harper & Brothers, New York, in 1959
Republished with a new foreword by Oxford University Press in 1987
This edition published by Hong Kong University Press in 2009

ISBN 978-962-209-078-1

Secure on-line Ordering
www.hkupress.org

Printed and bound by Pre-Press Ltd., Hong Kong, China

Foreword

Peggy Cater

Among the small eclectic group of Colonial Cadet officers, considered by themselves and others as the elite, which led the post-war Government of Hong Kong, Austin Coates stood out as a most unusual, multi-talented addition to their ranks. Coming from a famous family and having served as an Intelligence Officer in the RAF, he found himself in the early 1950s posted to work to KMA Barnett, acknowledged leader in the halls of academe, in particular Sinology, in possibly the least sophisticated area of Hong Kong's population as a District Officer, New Territories (Islands).

This job was a pure gift to Austin, giving him a small kingdom of his own away from more pedestrian colleagues some of whom were not entirely comfortable with his sexual orientation. He in turn considered their stronghold, the Secretariat, to be a sort of nursing home where none of the patients ever recovered and when in town contrived to spend time elsewhere especially at Government House where Lady Grantham sought his advice on interior decoration, recognising that here was a man of taste and discrimination. He began to write when most of the despised denizens of the Secretariat limited their talents to memos in the files.

The Road, written when Lantau, now the site of Chek Lap Kok International Airport, was still an unspoilt island, larger than Hong Kong Island itself, where the greeting was 'Which hill have you come from?', where the only transport was an occasional sedan chair for those who couldn't make the steep gradients on foot to Shangri-la (Ngong Ping), and there was one horse who had his own sampan (literally three planks tied together) upon which to ford the stream in the village. Such wonderful memories, nostalgia and, yes, regret. It is wonderful that *The Road* is being reprinted.

Foreword

WHEN I was in New York in the autumn of 1956, my publishers, Harper & Brothers, suggested that it was time I wrote a novel. I had already written a travel book, *Invitation to an Eastern Feast*, which had received a warm critical welcome. My second travel book, *Personal and Oriental*, was about to come out to, as it transpired, an equally warm welcome.

Not caring much for the prospect of writing a novel, I decided on a tactic.

I replied: 'It's interesting you should say that, because I was thinking of writing a novel about a road. It might even in fact be called *The Road.*'

I calculated that this would put them off sufficiently to make them drop the subject.

To my consternation, they said that it sounded very interesting. By my tactic I was trapped.

The road which I had fired off at them at random was a road which had figured in my own life. Over the previous seven years I had been a civil administrator and magistrate in the Government of Hongkong. For part of this time I had been in charge of the Southern District, which had a population of about a quarter of a million, and consisted of a fairly large section of the mainland, including Tsuen Wan, Saikung, and parts of Kowloon, and nearly all the islands except for — providentially — Hongkong itself.

Lantao Island — largest of the islands, larger than Hongkong — was roadless in those days, as indeed was most of the district. Along its southern coast it was almost impossible to put a boat out to sea during the five summer months when the prevailing wind blows from the south. Several villages lay along this coast. In the distance, within view of most of them, was the little island of Cheung Chau, where there was a hospital. For five months every year these Lantao villagers could not get their sick to hospital, although they were in sight of the island on which the hospital stood. The vision of being sick in one of those villages during the summer — the time of sickness — haunted me as being something peculiarly dreadful. I decided to build a road.

It would lead along the coast, linking all the villages, and then, running over a frighteningly steep piece of mountain (but I reckoned we could just do it), reach Silver Mine Bay at the eastern end of the island, from which there was a regular ferry service to Cheung Chau, and the hospital. Get a few small trucks over to the island (and a garage mechanic) and the immediate problem would be solved, after which ... well, one thing would lead to another.

It did; and this, a year later in New York, was what interested me about it. I had left the road as a completely designed and costed scheme approved by the Government, but with the finance branch thinking of every possible reason to stop it being built. At that point a new phase in Hongkong's near-perpetual water crisis began. A huge new reservoir was urgently needed, and the only possible place for it was on Lantao Island, at Shek Pik, the village to which my road design led.

Water! That impossible south Lantao coast! A road must be built from Silver Mine Bay to convey the cement mixers and other heavy equipment to the reservoir site. A complete design for such a road existed! The finance branch was ordered to find money instantly. It found money instantly. Work began. In an amazingly short time the villagers were getting their sick to hospital, but in the reservoir people's trucks, no other vehicles being allowed to use the road for the first two years or so.

The road, it had to be admitted, was a sensational local success, fulfilling its designed purpose. Yet its nature had entirely changed from anything originally contemplated. It was this that intrigued me: that an inanimate design, still no more than a drawing on paper, can change in its nature, becoming something quite other, yet remaining the same.

I did not see the road being built. I had been appointed Chinese adviser and magistrate in Sarawak, today part of East Malaysia, in those days a colony. A friend wrote from Kuching warning me to bring with me all the clothing I could possibly need for years to come. 'Nothing, nothing can be bought or made here', he wrote, and he was not exaggerating. It was a far cry from

Hongkong. Banana trees and jackfruit grew in my garden, the turtle eggs were excellent, and the country was claimed to be the world's third largest importer of brandy, which on occasion did not seem to be an exaggeration, though it probably was.

But gazing at banana leaves I was bereft of ideas for my road novel, irked by a letter now and then from my New York editor enquiring how the book was getting on. I think that in my mind I must have abandoned the idea, because I remember how, after some months, a wise old European friend with whom I sometimes discussed writing problems, came to see me, and I said to him: 'What on earth am I going to write next?'

He was a very intuitive old man, what some people call mediumistic. He ignored my question, and talked about other things. Then, half an hour later, when he was leaving, he turned in the doorway and said: 'Write a book about a woman who is cleverer than her husband.'

I did not pay any attention to this until some days afterwards, when Sylvia arrived. I had not met her previously; I still have not met her. She was a persistent caller, however.

In those days I used to write in bound volumes of manuscript paper. It was a precaution against the vagaries of loose paper when writing under an electric fan or in the breeze from ever-open windows. I took out a new volume and began to write down what Sylvia was trying to tell me. She was very fluent on the subject of herself, presenting no obstacles. In fact, she talked so fast that I nearly finished an entire chapter before realizing what she was driving at. It was my road.

At the Court House and the Treasury, in lovely old buildings designed in the homely elegance of style of the Brooke Rajahs, I was running three government offices simultaneously. In the busiest of them we were ordering heavy equipment from abroad, for building a road into secondary and primary mountainous jungle, in the most difficult part of Borneo, which is an island of mud, and which in this particular bit has the highest annual rainfall on earth.

Then there was my Chinese magisterial work, to be conducted with minimum delay to the public. On top of that, I had at my own request taken on the 'metropolitan' district, extending from the sea to the Indonesian border, and which included the capital, Kuching. I was reasonably busy, in other words.

Yet somehow the book was written in less than three months.

It came out in New York early in 1959, and in London in June of that year. None of the characters were based on real people. The book came so quickly, in fact, that I really only became familiar with the characters after the book was finished, when I could lean back and take a look at them.

By accident, one sees quite a lot of Hongkong in the book, as it was in those times. It was much more 'British colonial' than now, although never unbearably so; one could live outside it, as Sylvia and Richard both did. Servants and servants' quarters were encountered more frequently then than now. There was almost no air-conditioning, nor did anyone feel the need for it. No one drank wine except at dinner; it was hard liquor throughout — very colonial, although as all liquor in China is hard anyway, it did not seem so. Chinese manners today have more of a Western gloss; in those days, without the gloss, they were more distinct. The clearest moment comes at the music party towards the end of the book; that is absolutely Hongkong as it used to be. Women's lives have changed for the better. Women like Frances Lau were very rare indeed; a woman had to be frightfully careful what she did if she was not to get a bad name in Chinese society. In a purdah society it would not have mattered, but educated Chinese women found it very restricting. And then we find Interpreter Leung living in a *floor* of an old Wanchai building, enormous by today's standards. One could still do that — just. It did not last much longer.

Twenty years passed before I first saw and travelled on 'my' road. It was a pleasant experience because all my Chinese companions fell asleep *en route*, and I was able to look at it undisturbed. It was built by one of the foremost engineers in the East, a man for whom I had the greatest respect. He started at Silver Mine Bay by an entry different from mine (I should have spotted my error, but failed to, and he had corrected it), but as soon as he made it to my route he followed it the whole of the way — from him, a nice compliment.

I sympathize with drivers who dread that hill. It is a demon; and now that Lantao has many more roads, there are a few more similar demons. It is not an easy island to build roads on.

Macao–Hongkong
December 1986

Austin Coates

4

Part One

I

SYLVIA, an intelligent woman, stretched herself out indecisively in a canvas chair, and wondered why the Acting Governor had invited her to the launch picnic. The dullest possible wives of colonial civil servants could be invited to launch picnics—as the Acting Governor obviously understood, having included Mrs. Webb, the wife of the Deputy Director of Public Works. A launch picnic was one of those occasions on which one could dispose of the otherwise unentertainable. There were diversions. It might be rough, in which case one could discuss stomachs and medicines. Someone might fall down one of the inconveniently placed hatchways in the Governor's launch, in which case the unentertainable could be clever with bandages or damp napkins. When halting for lunch, one could gaze out upon the sea and talk about fish. It was a little break from the suffocating social atmosphere of the government servants' enclave, with its never-ending discussions about salaries, leave, the weight of new-born babies, and the swearwords so shockingly used by the neighbours' children, who learnt them, of course, from their parents. At Government House, the influence of the people from the enclave quickly became overpowering round the table, introducing among the royal portraits and crown-studded plates the horrible incongruity of the semi-detached villa. The best arrangement was to invite the enclave members in small numbers, and only in the company of other more amusing people, whose chatter kept them hushed, either with awe or with a brave show of superciliousness.

The Acting Governor understood these things. His parties were usually among the best. Somehow today he had misjudged the situation. The enclave was dominating the launch picnic.

5

Mrs. Webb, in a print that resembled the bathroom curtains at a seaside house Sylvia had once spent an English summer in, was explaining how much cheaper it was to buy frozen fish from Scotland than fresh fish from the Chinese market, and the air of vindictiveness against circumstances in general—the air indispensable to the maintenance of harmonious relations in the enclave—was oozing over the deck, as far as the handrails, where the azure brightness of a perfect tropical noon checked it spreading any further. Between the handrails and on the deck, however, in a restricted space, it hovered like one of those patches of mist that cling to the sides of the drenched mountains in spring: though to be in it was unpleasant, it had no effect upon the drier air beyond it, either to the right or to the left.

Usually, when the Acting Governor invited Sylvia, he did so on occasions with a cultural flourish to them. The visit of another famous author, the passing through of a more than usually interesting foreign ambassador, this was the type of evening on which he liked to surround himself with a selection of the intellectual bright lights of the colony. Of these, Sylvia, since the success of *The Chasm of Love*, was unquestionably the foremost. Important visitors, knowing she lived in the colony, invariably wished to meet her—more out of curiosity than admiration, the passionate intensity of her book having shocked the squeamish and rocketed the sales—and in an oblique way the Acting Governor derived kudos from having her at his table, despite the passion, and despite the righteous burble of the enclave, still busy trying to recognize its members in the pages of *The Chasm*. There was nothing strange about it. His Excellency's prestige and reputation were local, hers world-wide. In colonial society, it was a scheme of things that had to be handled gracefully. Sylvia had not been a civil servant's wife for six years without learning how to manage the company of governors and other officials ranking higher than her husband. In public, always the deference due to the Queen's representative; but at the smaller private parties, at Government House or at home, the representative became Freddie, a rather amateurish collector of Chinese jade, as a government servant a man of vision, yes, but with a tray of files always piled up between himself and the view.

At the launch picnic, not only could he not be called Freddie: there was almost no subject of interest that Sylvia could mention. If she were to speak of books or writing, Mrs. Webb would report

6

around the enclave how Sylvia had blatantly attempted to control the conversation. If by chance she should mention the name of anyone famous—for fame had brought her in touch with others of equal or greater fame—this would be condemned as showing superiority. If she should make an original remark, it would certainly be misinterpreted later. There was nothing to do but keep quiet.

And wonder why she had been invited.

Since the Governor had gone on leave, the Marine Department had taken all the comfortable chairs out of the ship, ostensibly to have them repaired, actually to use them in the Director of Marine's launch. The canvas chair Sylvia sat in was one of those fundamentally uncomfortable ones, with a sense of square-ness about it, in which it was impossible either to lounge, loll, or elongate oneself. Indecisively she stretched herself out, until one of the chair's adamant ribs felt as if it were going to cut right across her back. She hoisted herself upright again, as the boy came to ask what each guest would have to drink.

Brandy and ginger ale, with plenty of ice—a fresh, pleasant drink in the tropics. How much, she wondered, did alcohol aid the self-deception in life? It freshened life at first, afterwards soothed and eased it, then confused it a little, and finally, for some people, blotted out what it was inconvenient to remember.

'But what I say is, every government quarter ought to have a drying-room. In this humid climate it's not fair to expect families to live without one.'

Possibly Mrs. Webb had nothing inconvenient to remember. It would have been pleasant, however, if she could have remembered to call Freddie something. Because of her embarrassment at saying Sir Frederick, she steered clear of any title whatever, letting her sentences loose like goods without a label, and involving herself in a series of you, you, yous which made her sound as if she were presumptuously telling the Acting Governor what to do. Titles are like spears, Sylvia thought; they point at each person, testing his social mettle, whether firm or flabby.

The confessional was another way of eradicating inconvenient memories, though in fact it alleviated the burden of them rather than blotting them out. So too with a book. Inconvenient memories could be blazoned forth in print, with exciting material results, coupled with mental *soulagement*. By taking an opposite course, by publicizing instead of concealing, the same effect

7

could be reached. The cloud passed. The social fabric had not, or so it seemed, been disturbed. The book, a separate entity, not entirely true, not entirely false, scuttled out across the world with a life of its own, written by Sylvia, but not Sylvia's life, showing Sylvia, but not Sylvia's body, breaking Sylvia's reputation, yet leaving her still a respectable married woman.

The inconvenience of memory, surely, arose chiefly in the case of memories of matters discordant with principles of behaviour accepted by society, necessary to society for its own safety. The principles had nothing to do with individuals, as any individualist in life could quickly discover. The rules were imposed by society, for society. Beyond them, in the company of civilized people, lay a world of freedom.

After writing *The Chasm of Love*, however, Sylvia had altered slightly this view of the world, because the world, though highly intrigued by, did not approve of, the story of her affair with—in her book she had called him the Indian Military Attaché in Tokyo. The world, in fact, reacted strongly. Many important newspapers refused to review the book. Others attacked it and its author mercilessly. The various Church papers in Britain and America called Sylvia everything short of a harlot. In her view, they did what might have been expected of people rigidly bound by principles of society. Frightened by the terrible ease of passion expressed in her book, they saw in it a danger to society, and struck attitudes.

Not because they disliked the book. They had all obviously read it right through, judging by the reviews. The attitudes they struck—standard ham gestures of actors in the old stock companies—were the classic expressions of the self-protection of society. No one could possibly object to Sylvia's writing the story of her affair with the Indian Military Attaché. The trouble was, she was already a married woman. After the affair ended, in the poignant way she had described, she went back to her husband, and, while living in his house, and having deceived him all along, proceeded to sit down and write the whole story in a book. Had the woman no shame? asked some of the more outraged newspapers.

To Sylvia, shame did not enter into it. Her affair was an exhilarating experience, her book a work of art, and neither had anything to do with her married life. Instead of judging *The Chasm* as a work of art, the critics had pounced on a moral

8

irrelevancy, enormously enhancing the sales as a result—possibly the last thing they wished to do.

The tendency of the world—particularly the Western world—to attitudinize had surprised Sylvia, a woman who had not struck a moral attitude since about the age of fourteen. In the schools she went to, in England and Switzerland, there was no such thing as a moral attitude. The girls discussed with mingled excitement and wonder their mothers' most recent divorces, the latest night-club incident in which one of the fathers had said something so awful that by mutual agreement the newspaper containing it was kept hidden from the headmistress, and examined at length the many problems of how to deal with stepmothers only five years older than themselves. True, there were scripture classes; but they were conducted apologetically, often by a mistress who had little idea of the Bible anyway, and was hoping one night to sleep with the man who ran the garage from which the school hired cars.

In other words, a moral code existed—with the inevitable attitudes attached to it—but it was a theoretical subject, like algebra and classic Greek. Just as one would not turn round and tell a junior girl in Greek to sit down, so one did not strike moral attitudes. In life one simply read on into the next chapter, as it were—an enthusiastic spectator, only wanting to know how the story ended. Until the publication of her book, Sylvia had ignored the fact that attitudinizers still existed. Surely they had by now entirely died out, being replaced by a generation brought up in a cooler moral climate.

As one outraged article followed another, however, she began to doubt the truth of this.

Comforting, reassuring, confounding the moralizing of the critics, were the sales. One could rely more on the public than on the critics. The public knew. The public, that vast body of receptive, sentient thought, read Sylvia's love story, read it and, by their continuing cash payments and subsequent silence, liked it.

The public, as Sylvia assured herself, though they might be less direct in admitting that life with less attitudes was more representative of the age than a life bound by outdated prejudices and taboos, recognized in her book the reality of what they themselves vaguely felt. Even Mrs. Webb, for example: were Freddie, an attractive widower, to make suitably discreet suggestions to her, would she not dismiss convention, if she could do so without her husband knowing? Or would she strike a great attitude? Perhaps, to begin with, she would strike an attitude. But Haren—the real figure disguised behind the Indian Military Attaché in Tokyo—had always said you could tell instantly which attitudes were unbreakable, and which were conventions disguising anxiety, excitement, and hope.

The boy brought her a brandy and ginger ale. The boy was Chiu, the special one, who had come to her aid late one night when her car broke down near Government House in torrential rain and Chiu was on his way home. Abandoning the car, she had taken his offer to walk her home under his oilpaper umbrella. Her shoes were ruined, and his trousers were soaked, because two under the umbrella instead of one meant that the flimsy thing gave less protection to each. At first they kept a little apart from each other under the umbrella, until Chiu, with a gesture of distinction—a masterpiece of deference and tenderness—put his arm round her. Because her arm next to him was stuck in an awkward position, she, with less distinction but something approaching tenderness, put it round him, so that, clasping each other firmly, they at last reached her doorway, with the downpour still clattering and spitting around them. At the door they released each other, and under the disapproving glare of the Pakistani night-watchman—a man with a face as black as a burnt potato—their hands touched, and Chiu's face glowed all over with an untainted love that nonetheless included something physical. They parted. Hardly a word was said. Chiu's knowledge of English was limited, while Sylvia spoke Mandarin, not the local dialect. Ever afterwards, however, at cocktails, receptions and dinners, between Sylvia and Chiu there was a special relationship, an utterly confidential, reliable relationship, which insisted that, however many hundreds of guests might be present, when Sylvia had the slightest want—a match, a cashew nut, an ashtray—Chiu was there. It was thus that he handed her the brandy on deck: with the implicit understanding that is between those who have walked with arms around each other and whose hands have touched in a particular way. The smile on his moon face, with drooping pig eyes and stolid, reliable chin, radiated in the brilliant noon the wet uncertainty of that night when Sylvia's car broke down.

Transitorily she wondered, as she drank the brandy and watched the blue-green sparkling sea, what a mind must be like that was capable of adopting moral attitudes. Had her own parents been intellectuals, she might have known, for from them she would probably from childhood have listened to argument, theory and standpoint, and would thus have acquired a standpoint of her own. But her parents, who were not intellectuals, never argued except on personal matters. Her father, a prominent wholesale draper, had an expensive apartment in Mayfair, and used to bring home, when she was a girl, people remarkable chiefly for the size of their motor-cars and their skill at golf, bridge, or poker. They floated through memory now like a generation of diamond and onyx cuff-links, insubstantial decorations in an everlasting drawing-room scene, figures from a commercial world Sylvia had neither understood nor cared for. Her mother's friends had always interested her more. Her mother, before marriage, had been a musical-comedy actress, who preferred Mayfair, limousines and anonymity to the luxurious public discomfort of stardom. Hospitable and friendly, long after leaving the stage she still kept up with her former colleagues. Actors and actresses, writers and producers, filled the drawing-room in the interstitial periods when there were no golf players around. Gershwin on the radiogram, the percussion of the cocktail-shaker. And the attitudes of the actors and actresses were invariably delightful, nearly all of them attributable to the various parts in which people had particularly praised them. What was a kiss, or even a passionate embrace, in that pleasant world?—part of a rehearsal for the next time a similar scene occurred in a play.

Came the day when someone—an actress, perhaps; she could no longer remember who it was—brought with her the distinguished travel writer, Enid Stampden. It was in the early part of the war, and Enid was returning to China, to a China heroically struggling against the Japanese invader. Enid spoke a lot about China, and Sylvia and her mother were both fascinated. Neither of them, of course, had ever read anything Enid had written. The author stayed after the actresses had gone to their theatres, into the long summer twilight. Father, evidently held up at a session in the five-pound room at the Hamilton Club, did not return for dinner. The three women dined together, Enid, in the absence of the servants, preparing a special style of raw salad for them. They talked of the fall of France.

At last Enid said:

'On this next trip to China, I shall need a secretary. Why don't you come?'

One of those crazy, never-to-be-forgotten moments in life. Sylvia felt her inside go cold with the realization of an undreamt-of future, the sudden revelation of what lay before her. She said to herself: I don't care what stands in my way—I shall go.

Which, after a good deal of parental excitement, and difficulty in obtaining a passport for such an outlandish and dangerous destination as China, she finally did, via the United States, Hawaii, Japan and Hongkong. On this immense journey, changing the entire course of her life, she became even more independent of attitudes. Though not noticing it at the time, in retrospect she could see clearly how any remaining propensity within her to assume a moral—or indeed any—standpoint was dissolved by the impact of that first year of travel, by the awareness that in each separate civilization the attitudes were different. None of them were absolute and universal.

Why had Freddie asked her to this indescribably dull launch picnic? Could it be . . .? Was he going to suggest after lunch that they swim off, while anchoring in a deserted bay, leaving everyone else sleeping in the launch, and perhaps loll comfortably, if maybe somewhat too close to one another, in the clear, shallow water, letting small fishes come up in the sand to nibble their toes? Freddie's relations with everyone were so effortlessly exact, it was hard to imagine that behind his manners might lie a seething core of inexactness. He was one of those men who, the more formally dressed he was, the better he looked, until in white tie and tails, with his ribbon and star of St. Michael and St. George, he looked truly himself. Even when he only wore a swimsuit, Sylvia could not help mentally filling in the unclothed parts of him with cuffs, collar, ribbon, medals and star.

It would be humorous to see such a man collapse into bed. But perhaps his type never did. There was the bed to think about too, that enormously hideous gold and green edifice, set with forbidding respectability in the centre of a Corinthian stucco bedroom thirty feet high, with twelve doors facing all four quarters. An inhibiting place for passion.

Freddie looked round for his A.D.C.

'Williamson, tell the coxswain to put into Wireless Bay. We'll have lunch there, at anchor.'

It all pointed to it.

The launch, after a few seconds, veered towards one of the lonely islands they had been passing unconcernedly five minutes earlier. As she swung round, Sylvia caught sight of the police launch following them, swinging round in sympathy. If they swam together after lunch, the police would not dare come too near. They had binoculars, of course, but they could pretend to notice nothing. Anyway, Freddie was a person of too much finesse to commit the least indiscretion in public.

In spite of the pleasantly fresh heat of noon, Sylvia felt suddenly chill. Pretending to go to the washroom, she left her drink behind and went aft to steady herself by the slight movement this action involved. One of the Chinese sailors smiled at her. With simple people, with the non-attitudinizing, she was popular. Everyone knew her. Fables about the excellence of her Mandarin spread around unchecked. She was one of those special exceptions to the rule about Westerners, the rule being that Westerners are generally disliked. The rule being so, the exceptions were quickly elevated to Living Buddha rank, preceded and followed by tales of many marvels. Each person had to take the place of many.

Sylvia did not want another love affair. Haren's amazing aptitude for love, the long spring-time holiday in Japan, and the gradual realization of his ingenuity in what many readers of *The Chasm* called complete duplicity, had given Sylvia an entirely new experience. For the first time, she had learnt something she had formerly thought incomprehensible: that a concubine can be happy to be no more than a concubine; that the hour of pleasure together overrides by its impulses the day of separation that follows, while he is embracing his wife, or possibly another concubine; that the self-abnegation of a concubine is a proof of love more final than any a wife can give. It had been an extraordinary discovery for her, she who had always tended to dominate and monopolize any man she came to love. She had drifted down upon it, like an eagle drifting down from a craggy height; and her heart fluttered near her mouth as she rocked and swayed, coming ever down, down from her mountain-top, falling to the lowest depths of abasement.

She had denied the sacred individuality of herself. Haren's wife was thousands of miles away at the time. It was his Japanese mistress she learnt to welcome in her heart as being part of Haren's happiness and self-fulfilment. Letting her into her heart, she drained it of herself, leaving herself soulless, lifeless, though from a doctor's point of view alive. She emptied herself of herself, becoming only a vehicle for a great torrent of emotion and physical responses, like a corpse that is somehow imbued with the capacity to make love.

How was she not ashamed? asked critics of her book. Ashamed! She was shattered þy the experience, shattered, as after the accomplishment of some astoundingly unusual vice, that leaves one sated by the very shock of the depth to which one can go, shattered by the unforeseen simplicity of that final sin: throwing one's own self away, in the hysteria and passion of perverted unselfishness.

She was cold now. She did not want another love affair. She would remain cold for a long time, until gradually recovering the self-confidence to allow her heart to go a little way, without the fear of loosing it completely, without allowing the domination of her soul by someone else, without allowing another to take possession of her, as if she were a medium at a *séance*.

In a way, there was nothing to worry about. Freddie was not like Haren—although he might be a good deal more interesting in private than he ever appeared to be in public.

The launch headed into the quiet green loneliness of Wireless Bay. Years before, a Dutch company had set up a private transmitter to keep contact between their forest plantations on the island and their head office on the colony's parent island. The Dutchmen, the plantation, and the transmitter had all long since been forgotten, but the name remained.

On every side around the bay rose steep, rocky, grass-covered hills, trackless and silent. Though it looked like a deserted island, Sylvia knew by experience that beyond the rough fringe of tough grass bordering the sand were probably some rice-fields, and behind them, at the foot of the hill, a small Chinese village, nothing but a single row of grey stone houses, occupied by people all of the same clan, with the same common tradition of where they originally came from and when. Once, when she first came to the East, she had been interested in such matters. Nowadays her only interest in islands such as this, and in the few villages hidden in the bays around them, was that they provided good swimming beaches, and that if one became too thirsty one could sometimes buy a papaya from the village.

The launch drew in past the arms of the bay. They were near

enough now to see the long grasses moving in the wind, and to imagine, above the sound of the engine and the wash, the sound the grasses made over their lonely hills.

Perhaps, she thought with a kind of willing reluctance, if it has to be, it has to be. She turned unresponsively back to the foredeck and the other guests.

They had formed themselves into two circular groups, Freddie being seated in the more forward group, talking to Richard and the Webbs. Richard was saying something dull.

'With our population problem, it seems so baffling that we have all this wasted, empty land on islands like this, and nobody willing or able to use it.'

Freddie turned slightly, sensing Sylvia's return. His rough, silver hair seemed to catch the sparkles thrown up by the water as the launch gently came to a halt. But as he courteously rose and brought up another of the comfortless chairs for her, Sylvia noticed that their eyes were far from meeting. He was absorbed in the conversation. Before she was even fully seated, he was turning back to Richard and saying, as he leant forward for matches to re-light his pipe:

'There's only one thing to do with an island of this kind.'

'What is that, sir?' asked Richard.

Freddie re-lit his pipe, placing a matchbox on top of the bowl while he made it draw.

'Build a road on it,' he said briefly.

Richard frowned slightly; the Webbs visibly drew back in their chairs at such an unusual idea.

'A road?' exclaimed Mrs. Webb, with the faint suggestion of a titter—the titter of contempt used so often among the wives of technical officers when discussing the madcap notions of administrators.

'What kind of a road?' asked Webb.

'Any kind you like,' replied Freddie, with, on his side, a faint suggestion of the urbanity which would have so markedly developed in his character had he chosen a career in London instead of in the colonial civil service. 'But the larger the better,' he added, smacking the box of matches down on the wicker table.

'The larger the better? But who would use it?' asked the thick-set Webb, genuinely puzzled.

'Yes, who would use it?' echoed his wife. 'Almost no one lives on the island.'

Leaning forward again for the matches, and with a turn of the head that he often used when dismissing a remark—and the person who made it—Freddie replied only to the husband.

'There is never the slightest point, Webb, in asking who will use a road. Roads are the beginning of all development. Build a road, and everything else will follow.'

The anchor fell, and the launch swayed round slightly, bringing the green, empty hills into the full view of the party on deck, as if the island itself were intruding into the conversation. All five of them—the other group of guests had not heard the conversation—looked for a moment silently at the island, while Sylvia slowly took in the new thought, disconcerting and a little bleak, that Freddie had decided to have the picnic simply to enable him to enjoy dry, manly conversations with men: that, in fact, the real and inner situation between him and her was the same as the outward and apparent situation. It was a disconcerting thought, because it counteracted everything her instincts told her. In this tall, rugged figure, with the broad features a sculptor might admire, the dreaming blue eyes that contradicted the determinedly practical expression of the face as a whole, as if the latter were a mere mask concealing the vibrant being within, there was that sense of restrained strength, of a deep, inner reserve of creative energy, seldom actually drawn upon, but used as a cushion, bolstering the petty works of today and tomorrow, impregnating them with greater significance than they deserved—a quality she had found before in great men. To Sylvia this hidden strength appealed in every way: to her as a person who wished to savour life to the utmost, to her as a novelist, to her as a woman. She could not believe that it was a reserve of energy from which she was excluded. Surely, one day, it would speak silently to her.

Yet, that today was not to be that day was in a sense a relief. As she let the unsatisfactory thought sink in, that reality and appearance were the same, she felt the influence within herself of a prim comfort. As if, instead of time and the occasion having denied her the means of breaking in upon the secrets of this man, she had herself resisted the most remarkable temptations from time, the occasion, and from the man himself, she enjoyed a brief sensation of saintly purity. As if the dawn had come for a second time, finding her refreshed after sound sleep, she welcomed one of those days of utterly new, unsmeared experience, which in fact never come except in the hopes of the repentant—and Sylvia was not in the least repentant about anything.

From this sensation, as refreshing as very cold water thrown on the face, she sat, as it were, bolt upright, facing the island, and facing too the now nearly certain fact that Freddie had invited her simply because he wanted to talk about the island, and Richard was District Officer in the area that included the island. It was Richard he had really 'invited. It was he Freddie wished to entertain.

Richard, parenthetically, was Sylvia's husband.

2

'YOU nearly died of boredom, my darling.'
There were moments when Sylvia hated Richard, and of these none were more intense than occasions such as this, when he stood behind her, his hands close to her breasts, and interpreted with effortless understanding all that she had with such conscientiousness attempted to conceal.

They had just returned to their apartment at the conclusion of the launch picnic, and Sylvia, whose mood by evening had changed to the sour frustration of neglect, was looking blindly out of the windows over the colony's great harbour, spread across the view of declining light below. Pressing her closely to him, with his mouth he shifted back her hair and kissed her left ear, with a liquid intensity reminding her of darkness and midnight.

As she sighed involuntarily, and struggled to be free of him, she turned her hatred upon herself. It was Richard's peculiarly possessive knowledge of her that made her hate him. When his intuitive sense of what she was going through manifested itself —in a single sentence and a kiss—it awakened in her the shame of failing to know him as he knew her, of underrating him as he could never underrate her.

'No, I enjoyed every minute of it!' she said, breaking loose from him, opening a section of the long windows, and stepping out on the verandah dizzily perched over the craggy, shrub-tufted slope.

He followed her. Putting his hands, one on either side of her, on the balcony railing, he prevented her from moving away from him—nothing but an abyss of rock and scrub lay before and below her—while his body pressed gently against hers.

'You're telling lies.'

It was pleasant to be loved, she thought—and sometimes infuriating. From hour to hour the nature of love changed. If only it could change simultaneously in the other to whom it was directed! If only such hours could be avoided when—as in the launch—her warmth was aroused (momentarily for someone else, but no matter) during his coldness, and—as now—when her coldness was the only response she could make to his warmth.

'Don't be bloody-minded,' he said, biting the lobe of her ear.

She bent forward over the rail of the balcony. As she did so, he released his hold on her—they could not go on indefinitely falling off the side of the hill—and, without turning round, she was conscious of his looking in another direction, concentrating on something else. Even with clothes on, the framework of his body altered its tendencies in such a way as to suggest this.

'If it's the last thing I do, I'm going to do it,' he said, with sudden fervour.

'Do what?'

'Build that road, on the island.'

She turned her face slowly to look at his. In effect, as she had already judged by the sound of his voice, he was looking towards the island, visible in the distance, a black mass against the declining sun.

'Such enthusiasm!' was her only comment. It flashed through her mind that, after *The Chasm*, Richard was determined to do something on his own. Sylvia had always thought of this great manifestation (which had to come in the end) as a book—a history, possibly, of some little-known race, or a manual for the Colonial Office on some seldom-used procedure. That it might prove to be, instead, a road was an unexpected thought. Considering it coldly, she had to admit that he could do a great deal worse. Considering it in her heart, the special thought that, whatever the great manifestation was destined to be, the time for its advent had now perhaps come, was less assuring. Feeling his muscles relax behind her back and his body withdraw slightly from hers, she experienced a sense of isolation. Not that her life and well-being depended on Richard. Not that she would die without Richard's sedulous attention. She loved Richard. He was the pivot round which her life revolved. She understood and was accustomed to Richard. She understood Richard as no one else understood him, not even his various mistresses—they seldom lasted long, and, being Chinese night-club girls, had an understanding of Richard that was strictly confined to certain points. They had names like Lily, Dolly, Maisie and Connie, and Sylvia watched with total equanimity their rise and fall in Richard's esteem.

'When you get married, honey, remember one thing,' her mother had said, 'never ask questions.'

'Provided it's quits, poppet,' she replied, 'we'll be doing fine.'

It was. And one of the more exasperating aspects of reaction to *The Chasm* was that people pitied Richard, treating him as aggrieved and injured, or else—she was sure of it—thinking of him as gormless and effeminate, content to be run over rough-shod by his wife and be publicly belittled. Had the hero of her novel been a European, reaction might have differed somewhat; the story would have been more ordinary, less obviously drawn from personal experience. Her unrepentant use of Haren as the Indian Military Attaché, her patently evident knowledge of Hindu love-making, her own passionate responses—these intruded into the argument the hyena of race, combined with certainty in the minds of most of the colony's readers that the writer had actually experienced and enjoyed the love of an Indian. Indians filled the lowest rank in the colony's diverse racial hierarchy, and though, since independence, they had had a Commissioner as senior member of the colony's Consular Corps, their status, and the average British attitude towards them, had not changed. Sylvia's admission of what the Courts would call carnal knowledge of a Hindu, and her freely expressed pleasure in the matter, aroused the defensive hatred of Englishwomen to a degree which was only explicable in the context of marriage to husbands surrounded in their offices by attractive young Chinese girls and bearing with them, in many cases, remembrance of unusual experiences during the war in India and Burma. Women, so the unwritten doctrine ran, should stand together to resist male knowledge of women of other races. When an Englishwoman broke the doctrine by herself enjoying the forbidden delights of inter-racial love, and publicizing them, she became instantaneously anathema, and her husband an incomprehensible problem, almost as dangerous to society as a criminal lunatic. Both had defied the laws of colonial society.

'D'you feel like a stroll?'

She did not, and said so.

'I'll go on my own, then. Back in half an hour.'

She needed time to think—and to think alone. She stayed on the balcony after he drew away from her and the front door clicked shut within the apartment. She gazed over the blue and purple harbour and its hills. She thought uneasily about the particularly loose construction of her marriage. While Richard followed and she led—was this not the truth of the situation?—in some indefinable way there was harmony between them. If Richard was to assert himself, make his great manifestation, might not this harmony be upset? Might not a new relationship between them have to be established?

He had gone for a walk because he wanted to think about a road on that island, and from the walks encircling the hill at the level of their block of apartments it was possible to see the island, as an aid to reflexion. This she knew without words said. She knew, too, that with his special brand of intellectual concentration he would return home with a scheme in his mind, a scheme that might develop into a threat to her own happiness, in that that happiness depended on her pivoting around him in a flexible way, while he remained statically dependent on her, the Chinese girl friends counting as little more than occasional exercises.

Her relationship with Richard might have been less complex had he been the first man in her life. He was not, however, nor was she by a long chalk the first woman in his.

Sylvia had reached China in the middle of 1941. She was already disillusioned in Enid Stampden, even before they sailed into Hongkong. Enid, an ageing woman, was flattered to be surrounded by younger women. Sylvia, as became clear in New York, was to be her little disciple, her patient devotee. Enid's wants steadily increased. Whenever there was a chance of Sylvia going out on her own—even to anything so faultlessly respectable as the Frick Collection—Enid developed a headache, and had to be wrapped up, a cold bundle of nerves, in blankets, while Sylvia massaged her neck and temples. Meanwhile Enid groaned—with pain, Sylvia first thought, until she became more used to it, when she decided it was an expression of hopeless pleasure. It usually finished with her drawing down one of Sylvia's hands between her breasts, till their faces met, when she would kiss Sylvia and say:

'Don't leave me, child. I can't bear to be without you.'

Sylvia obeyed dutifully, rather as she would have obeyed her headmistress. She was only recently out of school. One of the arguments she had used with her parents to allow her to leave England was that other girls of her age were being evacuated to the United States and Canada. China was a step further, and considered more dangerous; but it would probably be safer than England during a German invasion.

As the headaches became more frequent, however, and as massage became distinctly more important than secretarial duties, Sylvia decided that she would put up with it uncomplainingly till the two of them reached Chungking, the capital of Free China, which was their immediate destination. Having come so far, she was determined to arrive there, and she could see at a glance that Enid, a very experienced traveller, was one of the only Westerners on earth capable of accomplishing the journey without undue trouble. From Hongkong they crossed to the Portuguese colony of Macao, ostensibly on a weekend visit. Thence, leaving that charted section of the world that deals in passports, visas, rules and regulations, they set out on a journey of hair-raising discomfort, by river-boat, by truck, by broken-down bus, ever onwards, and nearly always by night (in order to avoid air raids), into the depths of China. Sometimes they were escorted by soldiers ostentatiously disguised as bandits, sometimes by bandits posing as government troops. The places they slept in, usually during the day, were noisy and horrible. It was certainly the worst journey Sylvia ever made in her life, and that they arrived at all was entirely due to Enid's remarkable knowledge of dealing with Chinese people and situations.

In Chungking they lived in one noisy little room, procured for them with difficulty by a Chinese friend of Enid's, a wealthy war contractor. In many ways, it was an ideal introduction to the Far East. There was no time to reflect, no time to compare. Every day, because Enid's life was part of the life of China, into which she fitted like a piece in a jigsaw puzzle, they had to struggle like everyone else to obtain food, dodge air raids, and wait anxiously for news of the war in other places impossibly far away.

It was then that she met Bill, a young American journalist residing across the river in the foreign enclave referred to contemptuously by Enid as the ghetto.

He was miserable. So, too, after very few days, was Sylvia. Enid, relishing her ability to keep Sylvia tied helplessly to her, due to her inability to understand a word of what was happening around her, was having less headaches than before, but was making it effectively impossible for Sylvia either to escape into the foreign circle, where she could find friends, or learn to speak Chinese, to enable her to share Enid Stampden's life as an independent human being.

To some extent Sylvia fell in love with Bill. She found him physically interesting, and he was essential to her if she was to sever her connexion with Enid. In the tense and unreal circumstances of war and extreme isolation from the West, Bill talked seriously about marriage when the war was over. It gave a touch of respectability to the occasion when he first took Sylvia to bed with him. Bill was at heart a conformist. When they had done love-making he needed to lie beside her and tell her how much his parents in Richmond, Virginia, would be delighted in their daughter-in-law. It was an improbability Sylvia knew she would have to tolerate.

Bill found her a spacious room in a White Russian house in the 'ghetto', and, after an acutely embarrassing and emotional dust-up with Enid, Sylvia moved in—not quite as Bill's fiancée, but certainly not as his mistress. The very word would have made him perspire with anxiety. Enid went off with a flat-breasted Chinese school teacher whom she apparently idolized, and ended up at the Communist headquarters in Yenan. It was later said that she was doing a great deal of important work, though what, nobody knew. The West never heard of her again.

Having been introduced to China by Enid, Sylvia had learnt some unforgettable lessons in what was good and worth having there. Enid, she felt, had given her a fortune. Free of her now, she was going to take up that fortune and use it. She learnt to speak, read, and write Chinese, and after a year had progressed to a standard that made her indispensable to the newly formed British Army Aid Group to China, the token force which Great Britain maintained in China while her full strength in the East was concentrated on recapturing Burma from the Japanese. With the B.A.A.G. she worked as a confidential secretary until the end of the war. During this time she made a wide circle of Chinese friends, to whom she occasionally escaped when Bill's rigorous adherence to the belief that you can make a little Richmond in the middle of the Gobi desert, provided you got your heart in it, became tedious.

Their liaison lasted nearly three years. In war-time Chungking, as soon as they both became known in Chinese society, they were accepted socially, being invited everywhere together. Their liaison, which might well have shattered both their lives, had it taken place in the United States or in Europe, caused no excitement at all in China. Situations of this kind were just one of many to which Chinese social diplomacy had learnt over several thousand years to adapt itself, and neither of them ever suffered the slightest discomfiture.

She outgrew Bill, of course. As she became more akin to the Chinese—and she used to say this was the only way to describe the many incalculable changes that come over someone who learns to speak, read, and write Chinese—Bill began to shuffle off with increasing frequency. By 1944, if she had not dared admit it before in so many words, Sylvia knew it would never work as a lifelong partnership, on no matter what basis, legal or illegal. He could not face the truth of it. As hope began to dawn that the war would soon be won, he began to think more and more of his mother, and of the attitudes which Richmond would strike when it learnt that Bill and his wife had lived in sin for several years before they were actually married. He was nervous of the attitudes. Faced with them, time and again he did what was, according to them, the right thing. Sylvia knew she could never suffer this for long.

She and Bill stuck it together somehow till the end of the Japanese war. Before it was even declared safe to travel, Bill went on what he called an assignment to Hongkong, taking most of his luggage with him. Sylvia waved him goodbye.

Both sensed they might never meet again. Both were relieved by the sensation. When proper communications were opened, Sylvia came down to Hongkong, to find that Bill had left for the United States. It was the end of an epoch, in the world's history, and in her own life. This was when she met Richard for the first time.

Used as she was to the free and easy relationships between Europeans and Chinese in the B.A.A.G., and to the society of American and British Army officers and others whose aim was to help China as an ally, and who, though they might criticize and laugh at Chinese inefficiency and corruption, came to respect the cultural originality of the country they had come to help, she was shocked by her first contacts with post-war Hongkong.

The place was full of British troops from India and Burma, their officers having in most cases a casual, unsympathetic attitude towards the people of the East. On the other hand, there were the colonial civilians, a phenomenon Sylvia had not previously encountered. Most of these had been incarcerated since 1941 in Japanese prison camps, from which they had been released with the irrational feeling that, though they had suffered miserably, their sufferings had passed unnoticed amid the great tide of war. As a result, at all social events, they harped endlessly on their experiences and woes 'in the camp', poisoning the very air with a violent sense of racial outrage, giving an extraordinary impression of the type of inter-racial relationship which Hongkong must have known before the war, and might know again in the future, once the civilians came back to health and strength.

For a few days, before she rationalized it in her mind, Sylvia had the horrifying sensation that in China her entire mental equipment had changed, as a result of learning Chinese, and of long isolation from the West, and that the way of the Hongkong civilians and the casual troops was the way of the world, which she had forgotten, and which she had better re-learn quickly if she wished to regain her life as a woman of the West. It was as if, while she had been isolated in China, world thought had been forging on, until, like a great bulldozer, it was advancing towards her, threatening mercilessly to crush her, knowing itself invincible, its advance unalterable.

It was at this point that she met Richard, a flight-lieutenant in an obscure branch of Royal Air Force intelligence. It was at a cocktail party, and one of the former British internees was holding forth in the strain that Sylvia had heard on a number of previous occasions.

'But I can say one thing. The Japanese were tough, but at least they were straight with us. I can only thank my lucky stars we weren't in a camp controlled by Chinese.'

'Well, I see your Government is at last taking the necessary measures to ensure that you never will be,' said a young, but incisively acid, voice, a dry, intellectual voice, that yet sheltered a disordered passion. It was Richard, and, as usual, he butted in without being spoken to. As Sylvia turned her attention to him, he stood poised hawklike above the rather shorter Hongkong civilian. With a sense of having him cornered, as the man's gaze was lifted to him, Richard, not moving his head, put on a pair of glasses, holding the fellow with professorial eye.

'What d'you mean by that, may I ask?' said the civilian, with some offence taken already.

'I mean that at least you're abolishing all these ridiculous restrictions on housing. As you probably know,' he continued, turning to Sylvia, 'it's hitherto not been permitted for any Chinese to build a house or own land more than 130 feet up the Peak. The Japanese were allowed to own land on the road level above that, the Indians, Parsis, and Eurasians on the next, and continental Europeans on the next. The British, of course, reserved the top exclusively for themselves. The entire nonsense, I am glad to say, was abolished by the stroke of a pen last week.'

The civilian cocked a white eyebrow at him.

'You're glad to say, are you? Young man, what do you know about the East? We're the ones who know how things should be done here, we who've dealt with the Chinese for the best part of our lives. I could tell you what I think of you young fellows and your ideas of improvement here. You're well-meaning, all right' —this with masonic brotherliness—'well-meaning but inexperienced. I didn't expect to come through this hellhole of a camp to see victory, followed by a policy of surrender. But that's what I'm seeing now, under my very nose. Victory, and a policy of surrender.'

He walked off to another group of like-minded civilians.

Happy to have surrendered the top—and indeed also the sides —of the Peak to post-war common sense, Sylvia and Richard began to talk, with the utter enthusiasm of one adventurer meeting another and comparing experiences in the most improbable circumstances. Only in his jeep, taking her home, he remarked with his characteristic abruptness:

'I'm not interested in Englishwomen, you realize. At least, not while I'm out here.'

'Understood,' she came back. 'I'm not much interested in Englishmen myself.'

'As long as you understand the position,' he said, with a shade too much emphasis, due to alcohol.

'Oh, but entirely,' she replied, with comedy that was lost on him.

'Tell me where to turn.'

She did so, and they saw each other regularly for a few weeks, while she was waiting for a troopship to take her back to England. In the picture of his life, she occupied a rather high, spiritual place, being almost a heavenly presence, an Immaculate Conception, with Lily, Dolly, Maisie, and Connie as cherubs and seraphins floating about all too substantially in the background. She found it hard to descend from the throne he placed her on, yet the pinnacle of his own intellect was equally an impediment. Before she finally embarked for home, she knew she would have liked to see that pinnacle come tumbling down. In the sea breezes of the Indian Ocean she grew calm with the certainty that they would never meet again.

Her homecoming was not as she had hoped. The first reunion with her mother, after more than five years' absence, was exhilarating for the first hour, until Sylvia realized that, though her mother was deeply happy to see her again, she had lost the habit of having a daughter around. She was glad, but no longer sure what they should do together. With mingled amusement and sadness, Sylvia watched her mother trying to entertain her, as if she were a visitor. Indeed, worries of one kind and another had filled up her life, leaving no more of the emptiness there had been when Sylvia first went away. Of these worries, the only one that Sylvia thought about seriously was that her father had more or less—except when social occasions demanded that they be together—deserted her mother, to live with his current mistress, for whom he had taken a flat in Kensington. At the time of Sylvia's return, her father was away in New York on business, having, it was said, taken the lady with him.

Almost with a sense of surprise, as if she had discovered in herself an unsuspected capacity for being disloyal, Sylvia found that, though a woman may sympathize with, and grow angry over the treatment meted out to, another woman—even a sister— the reaction to a mother's entirely similar difficulties arouses no sympathy at all. As she listened to her mother's story, Sylvia

26

felt only a flat neutrality, a sense of apartness from her parents' lives such as she had never felt before. With life's quiet inevitability, she understood that her parents' home was no longer her home. It was the setting for a drama in which she was not even a bit player. The plot was, moreover, something it was even indecent for her to know about.

Pleased to be back in the West again, yet at the same time feeling rootless, she spent a great deal of her time outside, away from her mother. She made the discovery that in London those English people who knew China formed a sort of club without fixed address, meeting each other often, passing on news of each other's movements. The London she returned to was different from that which she had left. There were no more poker-playing business men, or actors and actresses. There were now the writers, travellers, business men with Chinese connexions (who were inclined to figure in London more as connoisseurs of Chinese art than as sellers of pig bristles or woollen shirts), senior members of the Armed Forces, diplomats and others, all with China occurring as an incident somewhere in their lives. It was a somewhat masculine world, yet one in which Sylvia had by right a well-founded place, the only weakness of the club being that it looked backwards, upon strange and happy days long since past. Its meetings were implicitly nostalgic.

As a diversion, she had an entertaining affair with a former Air Force officer turned farmer. The fascinating narrowness of the life into which she temporarily fitted herself produced in a very short time her first book, *The Revenant*. It also produced a slightly less rapid dissipation of interest. The farm was in beautiful Berkshire country. The wife, whose room she occupied, was, Sylvia concluded, a victim of her own tragic over-anxiety to marry when she was very young. Temperamentally she had little in common with her husband, whom she had met and married in the highly strung atmosphere of the Battle of Britain. He had married reluctantly; her reluctance did not occur till after he returned demobilized. She then developed the custom of spending weeks on end visiting an uncle in Cornwall. Both husband and wife were, in their separate ways, bitterly unhappy, prisoners of one another. This provided the story of Sylvia's book.

The Revenant was received politely by the Press, and with acclaim by Sylvia's friends—who were the more discerning of the two, because it was a good book. It was too hot off the mark to find real favour, except with those who, like Sylvia herself, were seeking to adapt themselves to a narrower life, and finding it impossibly difficult to do so. The reading public was still thinking of war. War books, prison camp books, atrocity books still dominated the publishers' world, together with the dying light of the fashion for poetry, one of the inalienable accompaniments of war.

Among the many people who wrote to her about *The Revenant* was Richard, and that his was, in Sylvia's opinion, the most intelligent of all the letters she received, was the reason she suggested they meet again. She had more or less forgotten her earlier ideas about him. She was, since the publication of her book, rapidly becoming another person. She expected to be gracious and condescending with him, nonetheless telling him how much she had appreciated his letter. Yet why, she then asked herself, had she so appreciated it, were it not that it provided her with one of those entirely correct opportunities (which should always be taken, on the grounds that they are fatally organized) for thinking again about an old thought, for reviewing what had not been entirely dismissed?

Richard was taking a degree at London University. When Sylvia saw him standing in an oily, dirty Air Force raincoat at the door of her mother's apartment, she was upset with herself at having wished to be condescending, because, as she now saw, condescension was socially as uncomfortable to her as it would be to him.

It was the raincoat that did it. It intruded into their already prepared attitudes to one another, something uncompromising, that admitted of no pretence. He came to her with the truth, abundantly showing, and truth begs for a true answer. As in Hongkong, so in London, they found themselves isolated by the tide on a small sandbar to which both of them had instinctively swum. The raincoat represented not so much poverty as despair, despair of a flood tide of unappreciable sentiment, despair of the drab mediocrity of war's aftermath, mediocrity in men, in thought, in aspiration.

'I'm not going to stay here,' Richard said, as they sat in an unpleasant little café on the borders of Bloomsbury.

'You didn't have to tell me,' she replied, looking at the raincoat.

She wanted a new life, too. The farm was losing its allure.

So, too, was the mental discipline of restricting oneself to the farm's regimen, to the strict hours, to the lack of view, and to the smaller things: the morning paper not read till evening, the lack of time for an embrace except within recognized evening hours when, pray heaven, all the animals were asleep, the moral importance of never being idle (so different from work in an important job, where there was no time to be idle), and the tedium of providing food each day at definite hours for a man who returned home invariably hungry, and whose taste in food was—even without thinking of China—puerile, dictated by the likes of some nanny, the memory of whose name and features had long since been lost.

'I think,' he said, looking down with unmeaning intensity at the imitation tartan tablecloth, 'the colonies are the thing.'

Again, irresistibly, she took a chance on fate. She didn't care whether she never saw him again.

'Yes, that way you can be nearer those popsies of yours in Hongkong.'

He looked up at her and laughed once, sharply.

'You remember that?—I'm really more interested in going with you.'

'Really? What a compliment!' But her breast heaved very slightly as she said it, and he noticed it.

'Don't argue with me,' he said. 'I hate argument.'

Meekly she replied: 'So do I.'

'Is it agreed, then?'

'Is what agreed?'

'That if I can get a good colonial job, we'll go together?'

'Why do you complicate your life?' she asked, searching for a cigarette case in her bag.

'Proposals, of course, mean nothing to you,' he said bitingly.

'Nothing whatever. I've already lived twice virtually as a married woman.'

His eyes met hers, as he glanced up in a reaction of admiration —for her frankness, she presumed.

'I've been more or less married five or six times,' he replied. 'But they never last, you know. Marriage—real marriage—is a mental adaptation. I can live with any number of people—for a time—provided no mental adaptation is involved.'

'Your experienced view then is, I take it, that we're mutually capable of adapting.'

Holding a box of matches in one hand and a match in the other, he spread the two objects out.

'I've never found anyone else.'

'You inspire me with the minimum of confidence,' she said, as he lit her cigarette. 'Don't you smoke?'

'Seldom,' he replied. 'But I carry matches, don't worry.'

Today, six years later, they were together, still on much the same footing, yet with, Sylvia knew, a real understanding between them, an understanding that appreciated on both sides a life of infinite personal divisions.

Was this understanding in some measure achieved by the fact of Richard's not having found himself to the extent that she had, and might not the delicate balance of their marriage be upset if he were to find himself?

She stepped back from the balcony into the apartment. They were to go to a Chinese restaurant for a quiet dinner together —the *table d'hôte*, referred to euphemistically in Chinese as harmonious vegetables—and after that to a cinema.

She took a bath, lingering before a mirror as she dried herself afterwards. The solitude and silence of the apartment—the servant was having an afternoon off—accentuated her memories of the unsatisfactory hours at the launch picnic, and what was unsatisfied in her focused upon the road, as upon an obstacle that must be removed.

She moved away the towel from her body and looked at herself.

'After all, I am beautiful,' she said aloud.

So she dried herself slowly, did her hair slowly, applied perfume with the subtlety of a Chinese bride, and instead of dressing, she lay down on her bed, which was beside his bed, letting the towel cover her slightly, in the manner of the best Italian paintings—and waited. It was Sunday, *du reste*, and at cocktail time did one necessarily have to drink cocktails? Might one not do other things instead?

He returned, sweating, pulling off his shirt as he entered the bedroom and lopping his spectacles on to his bed. He hardly seemed to notice her.

She still waited, while he had a long shower. She had waited before—and for others. To wait was not unpleasant, with some experience to use. As he came out of the bathroom the telephone between their beds rang. He came round to answer it and was about to sit down on his own bed.

'Mind your glasses!' she said.

He sat instead on the edge of her bed. The speaker rambled on for a second or two in the dialect before it became evident that it was a wrong number call, but by that time Sylvia had caught his other hand and introduced it to her body. Before the call was through, the hand responded, moving gently, securely, with knowledge and appreciation. The telephone receiver was down, and with a quick movement he had twisted round and was pressed against her.

'Don't be angry with me,' he said quietly. 'The weather's too hot. I couldn't stand it.'

She laughed very slightly and drew his mouth to hers. When she could speak again, she said with equal softness:

'Switch on the fan.'

It became dark outside without their noticing it.

A particularly pleasant aspect of Richard was his desire to continue kissing her after the climax was past. He was the only Westerner she had known who had this long, sure capacity. Haren had it to a fine art. It had endeared her to him in a special way, inexplicable perhaps by daylight or with a light on. It had endeared her always to Richard.

She did not hasten to move. They could be late for harmonious vegetables, late for the film. The important thing was that the road project, if it ever came to anything, should not displace her in any way. She had felt, after her bath, that it was imperative to make, then and there, some proof of herself and him. Now she smiled to herself in the darkness and turned her face away from him. If he could achieve his great manifestation without losing his taste for other things, then she could, she considered, afford to support warily the idea of the road. She must not, at any rate, resist it. Blunt the edge of Richard's ardour, perhaps, if necessary—that could be done. But entirely in a woman's way—above all, without words.

3

FAI, carrying a table on his head, walked happily back from Sheung Tsuen, the upper village in the valley, to Ha Tsuen, his own village, closer to the sea. It was a happy day. Dog, the eldest son of the village headman at Sheung Tsuen, had married Fai's cousin-sister. The two villages had occupied the valley, people said, for a very long time indeed, more than a hundred years—and the crazy foreign professor who once came said seven hundred years—yet, though the clan name in both villages was Liu, the people of the upper village seldom spoke to those of the lower. Today, not only did they talk together, they celebrated a wedding that united them—at least for a few hours. Fai's cousin-sister, in fact, was Chan, and thus able, according to correct custom, to marry with Liu. It was a nuisance, of course, that the inhabitants of Ha Tsuen, every one of whom was invited to the early morning wedding party, had all had to carry some furniture with them, a stool, a cooking pot, a bench, a basketful of cups, or, like Fai, a table on his head. But, coming home, jollified with locally distilled rice liquor, the stomach stinging, the body hot, the skin soft and damp, everyone felt, like Fai, happy to have brought their own furniture for the feast. It was indicative of the miserliness of Sheung Tsuen not to have enough. Ha Tsuen was conveniently contented to show how much they had. In a long file, the Ha Tsuen people followed Fai along the narrow track, everlastingly in squares, running through the rice-fields. As they went, they shouted to each other, and everyone's faces were flushed with wine. It seemed to Fai the happiest and most important day in the hundred—or seven hundred—years since the ancestors had settled in the valley, away from the mainland of China.

Fai was only thinking about reaching the village quickly and getting the table off his head. He was not paying attention to anything except the balance of his head and hands, and the direction of his feet on the narrow mud walls between each rice-field.

'Devil men!' shouted one of the older women behind him.

Wanting to turn round and look at her face, to see in which direction she was looking, Fai nearly dropped the table. He remembered himself in time to keep it flat on his head, then looked—more sensibly—for himself. There was, if he had only thought of it, only one direction from which devil men ever came—from the sea, on which they arrived in motor launches, more powerful than any possessed by the island villages, but unwieldy boats, incapable of entering the cunning shallows of the bay behind which the two villages were situated.

On either side of the valley, hills rose sharply from the flat, green fields. In front lay the sea. On the left side of the bay was the only entrance through the shallows, to a cove on the inner side of which steps led up to a small temple, set among rocks on the shore. From this temple, a path led into the maze of rice-fields. It was the only route by which people coming from the sea could enter the valley.

Along this route was approaching a file of devil people, with one or two devil women in the rear. It was an unusual sight in the valley, boding something of importance, Fai thought—unless perhaps it was simply that in the big city there was a holiday, and these were crazy holiday-makers, pretending the islands were better than the city. He had seen such people before in the valley.

Looking out to sea, he saw the Magistrate's launch, with the Magistrate's flag flying on it. Rapidly he glanced back at the group of devil people approaching, most of them clad in obscene bright-coloured shirts and short pants, even the women, with their huge legs all bare, and their arms as thick as a Chinese man's thigh. First in the group was a Chinese, but, strangely, attired in the same way as the foreigners. In the distance, Fai recognized him by his way of walking. It was the Magistrate's senior interpreter, the dreaded and respected Mr. Leung. Behind him came . . .

'Silence!' Fai shouted to the women behind him. 'It's the Magistrate!'

Being filled with liquor and good food, they continued chattering and laughing, having temporarily forgotten what the difficult and seldom-heard word 'magistrate' meant.

As the two groups, nearing each other in the criss-cross track through the fields, came within easy view of each other, however, older men at the tail end of the procession ordered the women to shut up, confirming Fai's warning that it was the Magistrate who was paying a visit to the island and the valley. The merry-makers quietened down. Solemnly the two parties approached each other, even the foreign devils ceasing their loud conversations as they drew near the alien band.

Fai was excited with wine. He was nineteen, and had never known a woman. His face was flushed with drink, but on a wedding day he did not care. He became bold with wine, and today not even his father would be able to criticize him; for today was the great day of reconciliation between the two villages. By the shadow of the table on the ground, it was nearly noon. There was time for adventure. The strength of the wine would last for several hours, during which Fai might have time to reach Mui's village. Not walking, of course—because walking would wear off the effect of the wine on this bright, hot, midsummer day. But if the foreigners' boat was returning to the big city, and could stop on the way at Mui's village, he could arrive at Mui's father's house, and talk to her in a fine, easy way, with the confidence wine gave him. And Mui's father, Uncle Cow-neck, would be equally unable to criticize him, for everyone knows that wine is served at weddings. The coming of the Magistrate was a wonderful chance, which Fai was determined to take advantage of if he could.

The parties came gradually nearer amid the fields.

'*Wai!* Going home?' shouted the wicked interpreter, with his seemingly cheerful smile.

'Going home!' shouted the women behind Fai, with giggles and clatter, as they recalled the funny things the people at Sheung Tsuen had said to them, about their reputation for this and that (the wedding party had been truly a jolly affair).

The parties met and stopped. To pass each other on the narrow bunds between the watery fields was difficult, particularly in view of the table on Fai's head. Either Fai had to descend into the mud, or else all the devil people, including the devil women, would be bumped into the mud as the merrymakers passed. This disaster Fai was anxious to avoid, being determined to beg the Magistrate to take him to Mui's village. Such a chance came only once, sent by the gods, and he must not allow it to be wrecked by any foolishness on the part of the stupid women following him.

'Stop!' he ordered those behind him, as he came face to face with the wicked interpreter.

34

Mercifully, the women behind him stopped.

'Not enough tables at Sheung Tsuen?' the wicked interpreter said gleefully.

'Not enough, not enough!' everyone shouted with pride, lapsing thereafter into a babel of succeeding remarks.

'Hey! Ah, Fai! Where are you coming from?' asked the Magistrate, as he caught sight of Fai. He spoke the local dialect, but as city people spoke it.

'From Sheung Tsuen, Magistrate, from the wedding.'

'Drop that table and come back with us to Sheung Tsuen. I have something important to discuss with you all.'

Fai's heart sank. If there was to be a discussion, it might last for hours, and he would never reach Mui's father's house before the effect of the wine wore off and he began to feel sleepy and timid. Still, there was no alternative. Unless he stuck to the Magistrate, there was not even a chance of reaching Mui's village, which was the best part of a day's journey on foot. Carefully he lifted the table up off his head and swung it down so that it stood incongruously in the rice-field, with its four legs descending into muddy water.

The wicked interpreter asked something of the Magistrate in devil language, and when answer was given, the interpreter ordered all the old men in the rear of the procession to drop what they were carrying.

'Now, all you old folk!' he shouted. 'Come back with us to Sheung Tsuen for a meeting!'

Everyone looked puzzled and stupid, partly because they could not understand why the Magistrate should want them to go back over the way they had just come, and partly because they were fuddled with liquor.

'No, not the women!' said the interpreter angrily, as some of the women also started dropping their loads; and the interpreter laughed with the Magistrate, showing his laughing face to the old men, who also laughed.

'No, not the women!' some of them said, not knowing why they said it, nor why anyone thought it was funny.

So the merrymakers' party divided into two, the women carrying on to Ha Tsuen, the men going back to Sheung Tsuen with the Magistrate.

'*Wai!* Woman! Carry this too!' shouted one of the old men to his wife.

'Yes, carry this too! Woman! Did you hear? Carry this!'

They dumped their burdens on the edge of the bund, and were in some measure happy not to have to carry them any further. Their women, having carried their first loads to Ha Tsuen, could come back to this point and collect a second load each. This also solved the problem of the two processions passing each other on the bund. The women all stepped into the mud, with their burdens on their heads, or tied like babies on their backs, and allowed the devil people to pass.

Fai, too, stepped barefoot into the mud—he seldom wore shoes—and followed in the rear of the last devil woman. He was interested in the different smell of foreign people. Behind the last of the women he sniffed discerningly at what he decided was a mixture of sweat, beef, and butter. He did not exactly like the smell, but he wanted to know more about it, because it might reveal why foreign people had such big bodies and could obviously make large babies. Unfortunately, when they reached the village and sat down in the small school building, the women took very small bottles of scent out of their handbags, and all the odours in the schoolroom were changed.

There was plenty of beer in the village, due to the wedding, and Old Liu, the head of the village, insisted that the whole of the devil party join in drinking with him. Dirty old glasses, seldom used in the village except when officials visited it, had to be found and rinsed clean in hot water, a tablecloth was fetched to cover the schoolmaster's table, a pot of imitation flowers placed in the midst of the table, in front of where the Magistrate sat, and the beer bottles had to be set out equidistant to each other down the centre of the table before any could be opened. Teacups were then brought, and wild hillside tea was poured out for each guest. Only then, after all had taken a sip, could discussion begin.

No sooner had it begun, naturally, than the beer bottles had to be opened, slightly dirty cups and glasses had to be sent out for a second rinsing, and the chatty confusion was prolonged a further few minutes. Fai was beginning to grow desperate. Old Liu, very fuddled, was giving beer to the devil women, when they had asked for soft drinks; the wicked interpreter was scolding him and exchanging glasses from one person to the next; the devil people were talking loudly among themselves in devil language, occasionally laughing like buffaloes howling;

36

the children of the village were murmuring excitedly at the door of the schoolroom; everyone was becoming very hot; and time —precious time—was passing.

'Ah, Fai! What's wrong with you? Are you drinking nothing?' asked the Magistrate in the dialect. He used to single out Fai to joke with whenever he came to the valley.

'Yes! Ah, Fai! Here, this is yours!' cried Old Liu, filling up a spare glass. 'Drink, everyone! Drink, Magistrate!'

Fai drank with the rest, but more deeply. He knew his face was red. Under his eyes his skin felt hot and puffy. He knew too that Old Liu grudged giving him any more liquor, only filling another glass because the Magistrate wished it. Still, he did not care any more. He was going to drink all he could get, then go in the Magistrate's launch to see Mui.

'How would you like a road from Wireless Bay to Sheung Tsuen?' asked the Magistrate suddenly.

Old Liu exposed his five teeth in a stupid grin.

'There already is a road, Magistrate,' he said.

Everyone roared with laughter, one brown old face nodding to another, while, behind the men, the women cackled at the Magistrate's not knowing that there was a road already.

With them, however, the wicked interpreter was also laughing, louder and longer than all the others.

'You old dunderhead!' he said to Old Liu at last, when he could make himself heard. 'The Magistrate isn't talking about the old stone footpath. He means a big motor road, wide like this, like in the big city—you know, poop-poop!'

The laughter and chatter dwindled away into silence. Nobody could understand what the interpreter meant.

The Magistrate continued: 'All those old deserted fields on the hillside could be used again. If you had a motor road you could grow vegetables and get them through to Wireless Bay in time to catch the early ferry into the big city. Your vegetables would reach there in time for the morning market.'

Old Liu wiped the beer off his lips and laughed stupidly again.

'But we don't grow vegetables, Magistrate,' he said.

'I know,' replied the Magistrate. 'But you could, in the future, if you had a motor road.'

Old Liu looked embarrassed, turning to the other old men in the hope of finding another laughing expression that would

37

give him courage to tell the Magistrate how funny his idea was. But all the other old men's faces were blank with liquor and incomprehension. Timorously, he turned back to the table.

'No one in the village knows how to grow vegetables,' he said.

The wicked interpreter chuckled. The Magistrate said: 'We can teach you.'

Old Liu shook his head, then looked down and scratched it. Fai could understand how it was that the old fellow could not explain to the Magistrate, for he himself also could not have explained it. People from the city could not easily understand the village and the valley. How could anyone teach them to plant vegetables? And why should vegetables be connected with a motor road to Wireless Bay? A larger boat might be useful for transporting their fish catches. Yet, even with that, would the dealers on Little Island, where they traditionally sold their fish, be any more lenient with credit? In any case, most of the fish caught was eaten in the valley. Only a small portion was sent to Little Island.

'There's so much land wasted and unused,' said the Magistrate.

People wagged their heads, smiled at the Magistrate, and looked emptily at one another.

'If I can tell the Government that each village on the new road will contribute free labour, there's a chance the Government will agree to giving the money for it,' the Magistrate went on. 'Otherwise, I'm afraid they'll say it's too expensive.'

Like everyone else, Fai was completely confused by this talk about vegetables. The city people always talked in a mad way, all upside down and back to front. The meeting began to vibrate with loose chatter.

The interpreter grinned round at everyone.

'Do you want a road?' he asked, holding his glass in his hand and drinking from it rapidly. 'A good road, maybe with a bus, so you can get quickly into Wireless Bay—in twenty minutes, maybe—then into the city by ferry.'

People ti ttered, because no one knew quite what twenty minutes was. It was possibly something good, by the way the wicked interpreter spoke, but it was meaningless.

'Do you want a road?' he asked again, banging the table with his now empty glass.

The old men in the front row of the school benches began nudging each other and giggling.

'Yes, Magistrate!' one piped up. 'We'd like a road!'

Everyone laughed with relief, because it was better to be with the Magistrate than against him, and the meeting had been so hard to follow that unfortunately they had all put themselves in the wrong position of being against the Magistrate, which was improper—at least, at a public meeting it was.

'But we'll believe it when we see it!' shouted Old Liu, suddenly regaining confidence; and there was a big roar of laughter from everyone, including the Magistrate.

'If you promise to give free labour, you'll see it all right!' he replied with a sharp laugh, like gunfire.

'We'll give the labour all right, when we see the road coming!' Old Liu returned.

There was another burst of laughter.

'All right! It's agreed! We must be going home,' said the Magistrate, rising.

Others rose as well, laughing and joking with others; and Fai was sighing with happiness, because now they could be off towards Mui's village, when Old Cow, Liu's wife, came in with a round, tin tray, on which were at least twenty-five hard-boiled eggs, which she laid with a toothless, wrinkled, and actually a little drunk, smile on the table in front of the interpreter and the devil visitors. This time Fai was so angry he walked out of the schoolroom. Some of the eggs would have to be eaten by the foreigners; this was etiquette. How could Old Cow be so foolish as to keep the eggs to the end, only delaying everybody? He stood outside in the hot sun, his body trembling with worry, his thighs tensed as sometimes when in sleep he dreamed he was lying with a girl, physically helpless, beyond control, cold in the hot sun.

After a few moments, while laughter and chatter continued within, one of the devil women came out—Fai thought it was the Magistrate's wife—and spoke to him. He was scared at first, but when she repeated what she said, Fai realized that she was speaking, not in devil language, but in some kind of Chinese he could not understand. Listening more carefully, he knew it was Mandarin, and that the lady must therefore have come from Shanghai—all people from the North were from Shanghai.

'. . . eat eggs,' was all he could catch of the first sentence.

'I don't like to eat,' he said, in the dialect, hoping she would understand.

'Nor I. Very hot inside.'

She was obviously a good woman. In spite of her large brown eyes and wavy brown hair, in spite of all the things about her which, from the Chinese point of view, were ugly and rather frightening, she clearly had a good heart, or she would not come and speak to Fai. Even so, she should have learnt the dialect. It was not polite to speak in the proud Northern way.

'You are the Magistrate's senior wife,' he said.

'Yes,' she replied, not looking at him now. 'You must all learn to plant vegetables. The Magistrate is wise in what he says. This way, the villages in the valley will become prosperous, selling vegetables to the big city.'

Fai shook his head.

'We cannot,' he said, thinking how unfortunate it was that the lady could not speak the dialect, because to her he could perhaps explain what it was difficult to explain to the Magistrate at the meeting.

'You should learn, and teach the others.'

'There is no time,' he said lamely, then with a tense fear, a mad courage: 'May I please come with you in the Government boat to Wireless Bay?'

She hesitated, possibly not understanding exactly, and began: 'My husband——'

The party was breaking up within. The Magistrate and other visitors were rising from their places. As he came to the school doorway, he exchanged a few words with his wife.

'Yes, come to Wireless Bay with us, Ah Fai. We can stop there and put you off.'

Excited by a mixture of wine and emotion, tears came into Fai's eyes as he heard this. His plan had succeeded. He would see Mui before nightfall and speak bravely to her. It was all working out as he had secretly hoped. Indeed, that he was being helped by the Magistrate himself, and would arrive in the Government boat, indicated that his luck was extremely good. Heaven was in favour of his design. The way was clear.

4

THOUGH Mui usually went barefoot, she was generally reputed to be the most beautiful unmarried girl living in the east end of the island. Her father, Uncle Cow-neck—as he was known throughout the island—was rich, but he was far from being the richest man on the island. For the richest man one would have to look among the seven or eight city people who had built themselves summer resorts in the vicinity of Wireless Bay.

Compared with them, Uncle Cow-neck and his family were bumpkins. Compared with the other villagers, however, there were certain distinctions about Mui's family which accounted for Fai's entirely devoted admiration and humble hope of marriage. Firstly, the family lived in an old stone house, like an ancient fort, set in the midst of the valley. It was the only house of its kind anywhere on the island, and was a distinction in itself, being antiquely Chinese. Secondly, Mui played the p'ipa, the Chinese mandolin of classic elegance, celebrated by the greatest poets. No other girl on the island could play the p'ipa. Few girls in the big city could play it. Thirdly, there was Uncle Cow-neck's reputation for once having been a person of importance in South China during revolutionary times. Certain older men from outside the island still called him Colonel Cow-neck. He was a square, shrunken man, with pig eyes, and a mouth that opened and shut like a box. His hands were large and bony, the knuckles being as large as the claws of the dragon in the temple of the God of the North on Little Island.

'You should have stayed in your village,' he said irritably, when Fai reached the house.

As this was perfectly true, Fai said nothing. Uncle Cow-neck was talking to a group of rich men from outside the island, and Fai was able to pass through the stone living-room to the kitchen beyond it, where he found Mui and Uncle Cow-neck's two concubines. Mui was washing rice for the evening meal, and Fai was glad to find her working, so that he could watch the movements of her body as she bent beside the stone water-runnel, which conveyed water from the mountain direct to Uncle Cow-neck's house, depriving three entire clans of any easy supply of water. Uncle Cow-neck, since retiring from the Chinese Army and coming to live on the island, had become the ruler of the island's eastern valleys. Mui was his only heir, the princess. Sons he was reputed to have, in China; nobody knew for certain. Nobody knew very much at all about Uncle Cow-neck, the principal reason being that his life belonged to an outside place, beyond the island's experience. As Mui washed her rice in the water which could have irrigated the fields of three entire clans, Fai watched her with pride he dared not express or show. Her fair skin, without a line or blemish on it, was fairer than that of all the women in his village; her hands were long and narrow, meaning that she could make love well; and her body was thin in spite of all the good food she ate, meaning that she would have little difficulty in childbirth. She was without a doubt the most marvellous girl on the whole island.

'Why didn't you stay in your village? Isn't there a wedding there?' quacked the older of Uncle Cow-neck's concubines, a flat-faced woman of forty-five with a duck voice.

'I came with the Magistrate, in the Government boat,' he replied.

'Why, how important! We shall have to wear silk whenever you come in future,' she said mockingly.

'Only if there's a wedding here too,' he answered, with a quick glance at Mui.

The concubines laughed at his repartee, but Mui, suddenly embarrassed, stamped her bare foot on the stone.

'Why do you come here to talk rubbish?' she said angrily to Fai, and took her dish of rice out beyond the kitchen door.

'Ho, ho! my fine girl!' the duck-voiced concubine called after her. 'And how do you propose to spend your life? Will you go into a nunnery and grind beancurd?'

'At least I shall only marry as a senior wife!' Mui shouted back from outside, at which the duck-voiced concubine's flat face swelled with anger, and there would have been a flaming row between them had not Uncle Cow-neck shouted just then for more rice wine. The junior concubine, a quieter woman, with the remains of what had once been a florid, rustic beauty—large eyes, large lips, large breasts—went instead to the kitchen door.

'Daughter,' she said with authority, 'if you don't control your

42

tongue, no man will love you, and you will drink only vinegar all your life.'

Mui's eyes turned red, and a tear spurted out from one of them into the dish of rice. As Fai saw it, he could hardly control his excitement, for the tear bursting out showed the strength of Mui's body and the extent of passion she had within her to give to a man. He wanted desperately to touch her, but dared not in the presence of the second concubine. Mui, furthermore, was upset by his presence, and if she were not to be angry with him, the best thing was for him to withdraw for a little, hoping she would remain in the house, so that he could speak to her when she was happy again. He rejoined Uncle Cow-neck and the rich men in the main room.

'So, you bigshot, you came in the District Officer's boat?'

The speaker was Dirty Joke Wong, so called—behind his back, of course—because he was reputed to keep dancing girls and to be over-interested in what people referred to as the secret thing—meaning sex. He was a large, pale man with fish eyes and a fish mouth; he wore foreign clothes and a big purple ring on his left little finger. His real name was Harmonious Virtue.

Like most city people, he referred to the Magistrate as the District Officer, the correct title used in the city. The country people preferred to use instead the older Chinese name.

'Yes, Mr. Wong. He allowed me to come with him.'

'So you're a friend of his—must be,' Dirty Joke said with interest. He was a business man with many pieces of land at Wireless Bay.

Meanwhile the duck-voiced concubine had returned to the kitchen, where the women could be heard shouting angrily together. Fai's heart fell. He had set so much store by this meeting today, and unexpectedly it had all gone wrong. The concubines were angry and Mui probably miserable—and angry with him, too. The kind fate that had brought him to Wireless Bay seemed to have deserted him.

'Why should the District Officer go to Sheung Tsuen on a Sunday?' Dirty Joke was asking.

Fai passed his thoughts back into the room he was standing in.

'He held a meeting there.'

'A meeting? Why?'

'To talk about building a road.'

Uncle Cow-neck sniffed acridly.

'Always planning something or other, these officials! Nothing ever comes of their plans. Drink!'

He raised his winecup, and the rich men drank with him. Some of them ate dried prawns, biscuits, and other miscellaneous small dishes which had been served as a prelude to a full meal.

But Dirty Joke Wong was not satisfied. He had only recently made money—in gold smuggling—and had less knowledge of government officials and the way in which their boldly announced plans failed to materialize.

'What kind of road, Ah Fai? From where to where?'

'From Wireless Bay to our valley. He said it would be a motor road, like those in the big city.'

'A motor road? Hey, son, come here! Sit down beside me. How would it be possible to run a motor road through to your valley, and what would be the purpose of it?'

Fai shrugged his shoulders and stared at the floor.

'None of us can understand it,' he said.

'It must be a military purpose!' announced Dirty Joke, putting on a very fierce and proud expression. 'Soldiers will come, and camps will be set up!'

There was quiet now in the kitchen. What had to be said had been said, and the women were working again. Fai's only prayer was that Mui would not go out somewhere, lest he should no more be able to find her before the time came to start on the long walk home—up and down the gaunt, rocky hills, across streams, and slowly along the soft sand beaches, far into the night.

'It is very probably a military purpose,' Fai replied, pursuing the correct Chinese style of contradiction. 'When he was there, the Magistrate talked about all of us growing vegetables.'

'Vegetables? In Sheung Tsuen? Too far from the city!' exclaimed Dirty Joke, with the speedy assessment of an expert.

'He said we must have a road,' said Fai sadly, incomprehendingly, 'if we wanted to grow vegetables. We tried to explain to him we don't want to grow vegetables, so he could spare himself the effort. But none of the foreigners understood us. You know how it is.'

Dirty Joke was no longer paying attention.

'Vegetables!' he said to Uncle Cow-neck, with dreamy significance. 'In fact, it's a good idea.'

And Fai realized that Dirty Joke Wong had lived so long in

the big city that his way of thinking had become as foreign as that of the Magistrate and the other devil people who had come with him. They saw nothing strange in the men of Sheung Tsuen and Ha Tsuen growing vegetables. Neither, evidently, did the rich Dirty Joke. Not even he could understand.

As soon as he politely could, Fai left the table and returned to the kitchen. He no longer wished to drink wine. Within, though probably for no more than a moment, Mui was alone, cooking food in a big pan.

'I have to start home now,' he said, feeling stupid because he did not know what to say. The awareness that they could only be alone for a minute placed a tension within all that was said.

From her cooking, she looked up sharply at him.

'Why do you speak of marriage in front of me, when you know it's not possible?'

Fai was silent, his liver cold. Of course Mui would know that he had a betrothed wife already; someone would have been bound to tell her. When she spoke openly of it for the first time, it was nonetheless a surprise.

'The crowning has not taken place,' he replied quietly and obstinately, referring to the ceremony which would transform the betrothal into a formal state of marriage. 'I don't want it to take place. I don't want her.'

'So you will put loss of face between your family and that other. How can you do that? Nobody will allow it in your village.'

'Nobody in the village can force me to marry whom I don't want,' he answered sullenly. 'That is why I speak of marriage here, in front of you. That is why I came today.'

He had said so much, he felt he had just finished making a speech. After all, it had been as he had hoped. He had wished to make it all plain to Mui, but had despaired of doing so. Now it was done. She knew.

The concubines returned from outside, carrying vegetables. Mui was at her cooking again. By her very haste in turning back to the fire, her assiduity in shifting about the chopped-up morsels of chicken and onions in the big pan, Fai knew for sure that, if he could settle the affair of his betrothal, she would be willing to go with him. Whether they would have to flee from the island and try to find work in the big city, he could not foresee. He foresaw difficulties ahead, but what kind he could not specify. In any

45

case, the first great difficulty was past. Mui, shifting the chopped-up chicken, wished him to have her, and would give herself to him.

'I am going now,' he said.

There were the usual platitudes with the concubines, Uncle Cow-neck, and the rich men.

'Thanks, son! Your information is very interesting,' said Dirty Joke Wong, with a wave of the hand.

In another moment Fai was out on the sandy path leading away from the sea and through the rice-fields, up towards the first steep hill on his long walk home. He was happy, although worried for the future; worried, although feeling secure in the future. There would be troubles, inevitably; but in the end Mui would be his.

5

I T HAD been one of those paradisal days, for which the colony was famous, when, in unutterable azure calm, tropical summer first allowed autumn to tell of its coming. The heat of day, the majesty of summer, still remained; but the shadows were growing darker, the atmosphere indefinably sharper, the colour of the sea changing towards a composition more blue, less green; and in the shadow it was beginning to be cool.

Sylvia had spent the whole day at home, darning Richard's socks, listening to the radio, and from time to time pausing altogether to think about a new novel she was planning, until, her eyes drawn to the long, low window of the living-room, she would stop thinking about anything except the sheer beauty of the view, over the islands, mountains, and sea that lay all around.

The District Officer's residence was on Little Island, situated on a small hill that gave a commanding view in every direction, over Little Island itself, a flourishing fishing town with rocky hills at either end of it, and beyond to the granite peaks of Great Island, where Richard was hoping to build his road. West and east lay many other islands, large and small, populated and unpopulated, one of the larger and higher ones to the north-east, about twelve miles away, being the island of Victoria, the colony capital. The shadows were lengthening, and in the cooler evening air Sylvia had brought her chair out on the long verandah fronting their modern house, where she lay stretched out in comfort and spiritual peace, at the close of a day without commotion or desire, with nothing but nature at its finest to admire, accompanied by some good music on the radio. The radio was off now, and Sylvia listened instead to the small sounds from the town below their house: the distant clatter of clogs in the narrow, cobbled alleys which were all that Little Island possessed in the way of streets, having neither cars nor bicycles; the hooter of a small factory dismissing its workers for the day; the tin bell of the hospital calling the nurses to take their evening meal; a sudden burst of cracker-firing, as some family aboard a junk in the harbour celebrated a birth, a wedding, or a death, or warded off a particularly malevolent spirit whom they felt to be around. Through these sounds came the chugging of a ferry starting out on its return trip to Victoria, and soon the ferry-boat itself could be seen heading out into the waters of the harbour, turned grey and sparkling gold by the rays of the descending sun. She gazed down on the sea, looking for the small, black speck with a bolster of white foam before it, which from afar she knew would be Richard's small launch returning home. A smell of simple country Chinese cooking swept up, mingled with thin grass-fuel firesmoke from the hundreds of houses below.

An unruffled day such as this, with autumn coming, made her look back over the past, and think how equally interesting life could have been had she always been demure and chaste, living a life without commotion, without passion, a gentle observer instead of a violent protagonist. The thought passed, however. She knew it was useless to wish for such a life, and equally useless to regret she had not wished for it. Even with her one caller during the day, the affluent but highly nervous Wong Tak-wor, she could not resist the faint indication of a polite flirtation, pressing his hand as she said goodbye to him. He was so terribly nervous, he fascinated her; and when she pressed his hand and said something in Mandarin with a fearful double meaning—which, as she reflected afterwards, mercifully Mr. Wong did not understand—he came out in perspiration all round his eyes and on his temples. People—it was really people who interested and intrigued her more than anything in life. She could not resist probing into them, discovering their weaknesses, utilizing with men that innate knowledge which had been hers long before she was anything but a little girl, with women employing other tactics, but arriving at the same end of unveiling human frailty—and sometimes unexpectedly discovering human strength. She was not in the least interested in Mr. Wong. Had he been a bandit chief who had captured her in some lawless part of China, she could have slept with him contentedly. He was a pleasant man, and clean. Only in such circumstances would such a development have been possible. Circumstances, in Sylvia's life, were the essential in everything. In any circumstances it was pleasant to tease poor Mr. Wong Tak-wor.

All the same, it was extremely courteous of him to have brought the wild pig and the quails. Richard always delighted in the meat of these wild pigs from the mountains, and Chow knew exactly how to cook them—very slowly and mixed with a little yellow Shaoshing wine. It was still too early to prepare the quails in Chinese style; there were no lettuces yet on Little Island, and a lettuce or two was required. Chow would have to fix them in Western style instead.

That was, indeed, a joy about living amongst the Chinese: these small courtesies and gifts, that eased life along in a peculiarly friendly manner. The friendship was not deep. Where an official was concerned, there was usually some small request concealed behind the gift, unless it was in return for some service rendered in the course of duty, or for an act of personal assistance. There were strict government rules against civil servants accepting presents, but such rules could not be taken seriously by anyone in close touch with the less sophisticated run of Chinese people. The presentation of small gifts to officials had long tradition behind it, and to refuse was rude, being merely an abrupt way, in Chinese etiquette, of indicating that the gift was not costly enough, and that something better should be offered. Accordingly, whatever the rules might say, provided the gifts offered were not valuable, Sylvia and Richard had agreed they should, generally speaking, accept them, unless there was any chance that they might be in the nature of an inducement—and to present such a gift was a Chinese mistake committed only by the socially ignorant. The simple country gifts, like the quails and the wild pig, made the relationship between an official and the people he administered warm and personal.

Then into the harbour bay sailed Richard's launch, flag flying. So occupied had she been with her own thoughts she had not noticed it rounding the other side of the island before appearing on the harbour side.

Involuntarily, her heart sank slightly. Nobody was coming to dinner, so they would spend another long evening with Richard returning time and again to the subject of the road. He had always been intense about his work, being a person with a natural tendency to be intensely interested in whatever he was doing. But, as she had originally foreseen, this road was different. For the first time he was about to undertake a large project which was entirely his own, which he was certain would benefit all the villages along its route, which would earn him the gratitude of hundreds of people and the praise of the whole colony for his foresight in taking seriously Freddie's chance remark, and wisely choosing a route that would benefit the greatest number. Hitherto he had been restless and dissatisfied. Now that he was about to achieve something distinctive—distinctive from his colleagues, distinctive (it could not be avoided) from his wife—he was personalizing the matter. The road was scarcely a Government undertaking any more. It was his road.

Since their visit together to Sheung Tsuen, she had a foreboding about the road. Perhaps this was too strong a word. In any case, she disliked it. She had said hardly anything to Richard about her feelings, because of her initial realization that it would be unwise to resist him in the matter, and partly because, with cool self-analysis, she wondered still within herself whether the real reason she disliked the project was precisely that it was so much Richard's, that she had grown accustomed to being the better-known and more active member of their marriage partnership, and reacted inwardly against something that might, at least in the eyes of the colony, rectify this disbalance. Yet, recalling the village meeting, and her few words with the young Chinese lad outside the schoolroom, she found herself assured that she was right, in a way impossible to define. It was an excellent idea of Richard's to encourage the villagers to plant vegetables. With a road to Wireless Bay they could send them to the city in time for the morning market, and greatly improve the economy of the villages. Yet they did not seem to want this improvement. It was so completely unlike Chinese people to be in the least dubious about a road, or indeed about anything affecting their own betterment, that she felt there must be something wrong—something neither she nor Richard understood.

He climbed up the hill as dusk fell, entering the house as usual in a hurry, sweating even at this hour—poor Richard, did anyone sweat more?—he simply never looked tidy, his clothes always crumpled with it, his head poised forward as if he were about to burrow or dive into something more (in addition to all his worries as District Officer), and carrying a knapsack full of paraphernalia, a change of underclothes and shirt, a tape measure, a compass, notebooks. She could never understand why he daily victimized himself with these unnecessary loads. Someone else could do the measuring, when it was required, and someone else could carry the knapsack, with clothes only in it.

Seeing at once that he was more worried than usual, she said as little as possible. With only a brief word, he went to bath and change.

Later, when they were both seated on the verandah, watching the last vestige of day depart over the mountains and the sea, Chow brought drinks and set out small tables.

'The price of land has gone up at Wireless Bay,' said Chow, who took a personal interest in being the District Officer's servant, and occasionally came out with interesting information, 'from twenty cents a square foot to as high as ninety-five cents.'

'How d'you know?' asked Richard.

'Wong Tak-wor was here this afternoon. He told me.'

'Oh, Richard dear,' Sylvia broke in, 'I completely forgot. That nice Wong Tak-wor came and brought us a magnificent wild pig and three quails.'

She might have stopped earlier, could she have seen Richard's reaction, but the low light of dusk prevented this. He turned on her hotly.

'Did you accept?'

'Yes, dear.'

He stood up in a sudden fit of temper.

'Oh God! What have you done?'

'It's a very good pig, sir,' said Chow softly.

'Oh, go away, Chow! Go away!' he said angrily, pushing him slightly on the shoulder. 'Haven't I told you,' he went on, turning

back to Sylvia, 'not to accept anything without consulting me?'
Chow pretended to return to his kitchen.

It was hard to be angry in the approaching dark. A humble
reply seemed to be called for.

'Yes, my dear, I'm sorry. But it seemed a very harmless
present. It never occurred to me you'd object.'

'Harmless, indeed! You fool, nothing is harmless!'

Sylvia sighed.

'Darling, don't call me names in front of Chow. You know
he doesn't like it.'

'To hell with Chow,' he said, but dropped his voice and
sat down again. He very nearly, with an automatic movement,
took his glass again. In the dark Sylvia could see him check himself just in time. Then, realizing he had fallen for her quiet way of
settling him down, his irritation returned.

'It must all be sent back tomorrow!' he said.

'It can't be, dear. The pig's already being cooked now. We're
having it for dinner.'

He put his head between his hands and looked down at the
now completely black verandah floor.

'Sylvia, you don't seem to realize the importance of what
I'm doing.'

'Don't be stereotyped, dear. Of course I do. But you're
working too hard and worrying too much. You're quite jittery
with nerves, you know. Maybe you don't realize it. If I have to
check with you every time some kind villager brings half-a-dozen
eggs, we'll never get by. And what else would you like to be
consulted on? When that poor Mr. Wong came today, I squeezed
his hand, you know, and he perspired all round underneath his
eyes. It was most intriguing. Incidentally, he has eyes and a
mouth exactly like a fish.'

But Richard ran his hands round the back of his head and
whispered deeply to himself and to the ground: 'You women!
Why won't you leave well alone?'

Sylvia noted this as an indication that Richard must be in
trouble with his latest mistress in the city. As always, she said
nothing on that subject.

'You say that about women, dear, but that's exactly what
I say about men. Why can't you leave well alone? This road
project, for instance. Ever since you had the idea, you've been
worrying yourself sick about it. I've never known you worse

company. On top of that, we don't even know whether anyone really wants a road. Willie Rogers says those villagers have lived there in peace for seven hundred years, and some probably even longer. Why do you want to stir things up for them now by bringing a road there? Why not do just what you've said, and leave well alone?'

'You don't understand. This thing's got to succeed!'

'Oh, I understand that all right,' she said suavely, almost to herself, wondering whether she caused Richard as much upset as this when she was writing *The Chasm*. 'If you start it, it must go through to the end. What I mean is: need it really start at all?'

Richard leant right back in his chair. As far as his tense nature allowed, he relaxed.

'Now that you've accepted that damned pig,' he said quietly, 'I really don't know whether it should.'

'Could we have the lights on, d'you think?'

'Yes, of course. Chow! Lights!'

The lights within the living-room were lit, throwing a gentle glow over the verandah. The lights of the town, now that night had fully come, were exerting their influence from the other side.

'More drink, sir?'

'Thanks, Chow. I'm sorry, old chap,' he added, patting Chow's arm. 'Too much work.'

'Never mind, sir,' Chow replied with his ugly but friendly grin. 'D.O.'s life always one big headache.'

'It's true, Chow, it's true.' Chow departed, as he continued dreamily to himself: 'You're leading people all the time, thousands of them, but where to? You never really know.'

'What has my friend Mr. Wong been up to?'

Richard crossed his feet and stretched himself out.

'I only found out today, in fact, so you couldn't really have known,' he said, with the innocent superiority Sylvia had for long learnt not to be roused by. If she wanted to know about something happening in the district, she could usually discover it in advance of Richard. 'He's somehow found out—from my office staff, I suppose—the route which the road's going to take; and he's doing his utmost to buy up all the private land along the route. Now he's put in to buy by auction a large piece of Crown land, which I'm refusing to sell. It's right on the future road, and would be of great value. It's near the Long Sands, and ideal—when

52

the road is through—for building bungalows for city people to enjoy their weekends in. In addition, he'll be able to claim compensation from the Government for surrendering part of his land for the road. If the road had been decided on and publicly announced, I could refuse the sale on grounds of speculation. But as it hasn't been approved yet, there's nothing I can do but delay the file, without giving a decision one way or the other.'

'Couldn't you refuse?'

'After your accepting that infernal pig, it'll be difficult,' he said coldly. 'Now do you understand?'

'Yes, of course. You don't want individuals to profit from what is meant to be a road built for the benefit of the general public.'

'It's far worse than that. Don't you realize what I mean when I say he's buying up all the private land? He's buying *all the land* of every village he can contact. The villagers are ignorant. They know their land has never been worth more than one or two cents a square foot. Now here is someone coming offering them ninety-five cents or a dollar. They're not going to think twice. They're selling to him, selling away their entire village lands. They'll be left with nothing but to disband the village, and go into the city to work as hawkers.'

'Can't you stop it?'

'It's too far gone already. As you know, I check the sales of land each week. I had noticed a slight rise in the number of sales in the area; but I thought nothing of it. Only this morning I found out that all these different purchasers' names in the land registers—they're all concubines or relatives of Wong Tak-wor. He's buying up the entire route.'

'Dinner ready, sir.'

Sylvia said: 'Serve it out here, Chow.'

Chow moved on and off the verandah, setting out all they would require for dinner on a cluster of small tables. Richard continued his thoughts aloud, as if Chow were not there.

'Why is man's greed so insatiable,' he said, his hands once more about his head, 'that they won't allow any good to be done for others? I'm so sick and tired of selfishness and dishonesty in that District Office, the never-ending grab for wealth, power, privilege, prestige. . . . Nothing can be done honestly any more. Before you know where you are, it's twisted into something dishonest and mean, the last thing you expected to happen.'

53

'If this has happened in the case of the road, what I said already: why go ahead with it?'

There was a long silence from him. She smiled slightly to herself, feeling like a tormentor in some antique hell, administering a subtle test to a wretch in her clutches. If he answered one way, he escaped. If he answered the other way, he was doomed.

'The road must go ahead,' he said quietly. 'It is progress.'

Sylvia spread out a table napkin and leant back slightly.

'Then why do you worry about it? You can't do good to all of the people all of the time; and if progress is to be the aim, progress destroys as much as it inaugurates. Eat your food, my dear.'

The aroma of the freshly cooked wild pig permeated the air around them. Richard looked at his plate.

'No, I'm not going to eat that,' he said, taking the plate in both hands and handing it back to Chow. 'Take it away, Chow. Give me something else.'

'Richard, really! Do eat it! It's delicious. Just try a little.'

'It's like the flesh of a blood sacrifice,' he said darkly. 'Chow, give me something else.'

'What you like, sir? Omelette?'

'Yes, an omelette will do. Anything; but not gifts from the hand of Mr. Wong Tak-wor.'

Chow smiled slightly as he went into the house, and Sylvia smiled as she saw it, for even Chow knew that a wild pig is a wild pig, its meat either tasty or bad.

'Do you think Wong Tak-wor will ever know whether you ate the pig or not?' she asked.

'Of course he'll know!' he said, draining his whisky glass. 'Chow will take care of that. The whole town will know by tomorrow, and it will be a good lesson to Wong.'

'It'll teach him nothing,' she said drily—there were moments when she felt her surer touch in matters Chinese, due to her longer stay in China and deeper knowledge of the language. 'It would be in Europe. But not here. When Wong Tak-wor learns you refused to eat his wild pig, he'll think either you're going insane due to overwork, or else that the meat was bad. If it's the first, he'll laugh at you, because the situation will amuse him. If it's the second, he'll be very upset, and probably send us another pig. Whatever happens, he won't understand the slightest

54

thing about your feeling that it's the meat of a sacrifice. For goodness' sake, dear, change your mind and have some.'

'Sylvia, I'm not in a mood to sit listening to you being right all the time. I don't want to eat that meat. I don't want to eat anything! God, I must take some fresh air. You suffocate me.'

He rose as he said this, jolting one of the tables as he did so. His glass slid off it and broke with a wet sound of crushed ice on the concrete verandah floor. Noticing nothing, he walked out into the darkness, away towards the gate leading down to the town.

Sylvia did not move. The crushed ice melted, the water oozing towards her sandalled feet. The iron gate clanged somewhere round the other side of the house.

Chow, who had heard someone pass near the rear of the house, hurried out to the verandah. He looked seriously at Sylvia, at the empty chair, at the broken glass.

'Master not want omelette?' he said.

'No. Master's gone out,' she replied, her voice shaking a little.

Chow leant down to pick up the fallen pieces of glass and mop up the water. As he rose and walked in again, Sylvia noticed in him an attitude she had not observed since she and Richard were first married: that Chow was Richard's servant, not hers, and that if things went wrong between them, Chow, in immemorial Chinese tradition, would lay the blame entirely on the wife, never on the husband. She for an instant wondered what would happen if Richard never came back, after which she half-smiled to herself at magnifying a small incident. He had often walked out before, sometimes in far more trying circumstances, when she had had to ring up and plead sudden illness as an excuse for not attending a dinner party half an hour later. She disliked these temporary separations—usually of not more than an evening's duration. They produced in her a reaction of desiring to assert complete independence. Her insistence that their marriage was a partnership of equals looked unexpectedly false.

She calculated now that Richard could do one of two things. He could remain out, calling on friends, till it was time when most people were going to bed, after which he would have to return home, Little Island providing few places for him to stay out all night in. Alternatively, he might take the launch and return to his haunts in the city.

She stayed calmly on the verandah, awaiting developments. At first, she passed the time checking the household accounts. After this, she read a few pages of a novel by another woman writer, an affected creature whom she had met on their last visit to London. Later still, she stopped reading, and simply waited. It was nearing eleven o'clock. The lights in the town were out, except for a few along the waterfront, where the open-air cooked-food stalls were evidently still doing a little business. There was no sound of the launch leaving. The only engine heard was the steady chugging of the old-fashioned machine that supplied the island with electric light.

Around half-past eleven, when the remaining lights were going out, and the electricity plant had transferred to its quieter and smaller nocturnal engine, she began to conclude that there must be some third alternative to Richard's whereabouts, which she had not foreseen. Reluctantly, with a slight sense of disquiet, she began closing the windows on the rain side of the house, preparatory to retiring for the night. Passing into the kitchen to check that the lights were off, she found, to her surprise, the lights on and the back door wide open.

'Chow!' she called.

There was no response.

Going out through the back door, and standing near the window of Chow's quarters, she called for him again, this time more softly.

'He's gone out,' snapped Plum, Chow's wife, wide awake within, and as if waiting for this.

'Where's he gone?' asked Sylvia, using some of her gradually acquired knowledge of the dialect.

'How should I know?'

Sylvia controlled herself, knowing that, in the colony, Chinese of this class were apt to be unintentionally rude when they were uneasy about anything. As she re-entered the house and bolted the back door, however, she wondered whether this could explain such a degree of rudeness as Plum's remark.

For a second time, the old traditions came back to her, which she had learnt amongst the families whose personal tragedies she had first witnessed in Chungking during the war. She was not only in the wrong. From Plum's viewpoint, she was to be jeered at, almost openly, and despised.

She hesitated before locking the verandah door. Should

Richard decide to return in the small hours, had he a key with him? She looked into his dressing-room. There was a certain disorder in it, which was unusual, because Chow generally put everything straight before retiring to bed. A clothes cupboard stood open, a coat-hanger lay on a stool, and a small drawer was ˜open, from which dangled a tie and a handkerchief, apparently taken out in haste and subsequently left there.

Still more disquieted, Sylvia opened the door to Richard's bathroom. No sooner had she turned on the light than she saw that Richard's toothbrush and shaving gear were not there, though they had been earlier in the day. It became plain that Chow had taken them to him, knowing where he was.

Sylvia's heart began to race, until, with an intellectual effort, she checked herself. What was the use of anxiety? The morning would show. Returning to the verandah door, she shut it, locked it, turned out the remaining lights, and went silently to bed.

6

HAVING spent a good deal of his time with Europeans in the administration, Ronnie Cheng had acquired some of their prejudices, amongst which was dislike of the loud percussive noises which leave most Southern Chinese unmoved. Involuntarily, as he sat with Professor Wen in his small, whitewashed bungalow half-way up the more southerly of Little Island's two hills, Ronnie wondered how on earth anyone as sensitive as Professor Wen could stand the appalling din of mahjong-playing from the inner room, the savage clatter of pieces rapidly banged down as hard as possible on a table with the hardest and noisiest surface, and the shuffling of the hundreds of plastic pieces, during which conversation in the outer room, if it was to continue at all, had to be carried on in shouts.

The gentle and kindly professor, however, paid no attention at all, while his wife, with two of the island schoolteachers' wives and the matron of the hospital, battered along with their game. With the hospital doctor (a rotund, jolly man wearing shorts),

Ronnie, and one of the teachers, the professor discussed the different types of birds in China whose eggs are good to eat, and how each kind should be prepared.

Ronnie Cheng could not fully understand why, every time he came to Little Island, he went to see Professor Wen. He was not interested in statistics, on which subject Wen had formerly been professor in the University of West China, nor did he have much to say to Wen on any subject when he called. Ronnie worked as a clerk in the Postmaster-General's Office. At present he was enjoying his annual leave on Little Island, staying with another postal clerk who had a house there, and who made a little extra money by his wife selling vegetables, grown on their small plot around the house. Having worked for a number of his youthful years with an English Postmaster-General who was a considerable scholar in the Chinese language, Ronnie's ideas were slightly less shallow than the average Chinese born and educated in the colony. Whether he understood it or not, he knew it was the proper thing to respect learning; and though often Professor Wen made statements Ronnie could not follow, he continued to visit him, as if in some way he derived benefit from such visits. Professor Wen, a refugee with his wife and family from Chinese Communism, lived quietly on the island, going into the city each day to run an export-import business. His small bungalow was a jerry-built structure, with doors that did not fit, and a concrete floor that was already crumbling away after less than a year, the Little Island contractors being crooks sharper than most. In a typhoon, water was apt to spurt through the cracks in the front door, and the floor was always flooded. As this was only for two or three days a year, the Wen family made no complaint to the owner, being philosophically happy to have found a small home away from the deathly mental asphyxiation of Communist China. The walls were of plain whitewash, with two carefully selected pieces of Chinese calligraphy of great merit hanging in couplet form on either side of an old mirror with carved blackwood frame.

As he prolonged the conversation, deliberately, drinking more of Professor Wen's beer, and leading him on from one rare bird to another, Ronnie had almost a sense of guilt. In truth, the professor was probably glad to see him—and was far too much of what the English called a gentleman to show it if he was not—but whereas on most former occasions Ronnie had called to give respect and wile away time pleasantly, this evening he had come definitely, and with a certain sense of shame, to waste time. Usually, when he had leave, he tried to go away from his wife and children. His wife was happy, not having to bother about him for a couple of weeks; and he was glad to slip back, in thought at least, to his carefree bachelor days, staying with friends of those times, temporarily forgetting the everlasting restrictions that society, and life itself, impose on the Chinese middle-class family man. Once, each time he had leave, he tried to have what he described as a bit of fun—a night with a woman other than his wife. This evening, on Little Island, this was the night. Women of the slightly higher class, whom Ronnie preferred, did not come over to Little Island very often, where the clientele were chiefly fishermen, about the roughest element in Chinese society. The Mid-Autumn Festival was approaching, however, when fashionable city people came out to the island to hire boats and sail around on the night of the full moon—'enjoying the moon', as the Chinese saying was. At this time, one or two enterprising women yearly came out to Little Island; and this evening Ronnie had booked the best of them for the whole night, at a price much cheaper than it would have been in the city. She was tied up with other customers till eleven o'clock at night, so, until that time came, how better to spend it than with Professor Wen? With the beer inside him, and the pleasing anticipation of an entirely safe adventure in front of him, he had become rather more mellow than he usually allowed himself to be in his attitude to life, being now prepared to wax intellectual with the best of them, due to the certainty that all flights of intellectuality would later be laid to rest in a satisfyingly sensual bed.

'But there must be references in classic poetry to all these famous dishes,' he was saying. (Because they all spoke different brands of Chinese, friends calling at Professor Wen's house spoke usually in English.) 'Are there no T'ang poems on the subject?'

'Certainly there are,' said the professor quickly, until, remembering the teacher on his left, he turned his thin face round to him, smiling with his eyes only, through his steel-rimmed spectacles. 'Isn't that so, Mr. Wu?' he asked, with courtesy whose weightiness only Ronnie noticed; the hospital doctor regarded it as a genuine inquiry.

'Oh yes, oh yes,' said Teacher Wu, and shook his head knowingly, clearly not having the faintest idea about anything to do with T'ang poetry.

There was a knock at the door. (The door, usually open until people went to bed, had been closed on account of stray dogs wandering in and out.)

'I shouldn't have shut it,' said the professor with a laugh, getting up to open it.

Outside stood a tall foreigner, rather pale, with a slight stoop, piercingly intellectual eyes, from which he removed his glasses as the light shone on him, and rather loose hair receding slightly at the sides of his forehead. Professor Wen, with an expression of surprise and pleasure, invited him in deferentially.

'Hey! How good! Come in, come in!'

The doctor and the teacher both stood up, broad grins on their faces, and began rearranging the positions of the chairs round the table. Ronnie, not to be the only one left sitting, rose also.

At this juncture, the periodically deafening clatter of the reshuffling of mahjong pieces suppressed all other sounds. The foreigner shouted something friendly to Professor Wen, and crossed the threshold. The professor yelled something back. All was lost.

From the inner room, as the noise died down and the Great Wall of China was reorganized on the excessively hard and noisy little table, some of the ladies quacked an appreciation of the foreigner's arrival. He waved to them cheerfully, and sat down next to the professor. Everyone sorted themselves out in new positions.

The professor reflected for an instant.

'I don't think you know Mr. Cheng,' he said, pointing at Ronnie.

'No, indeed. How d'you do?'

'The District Officer,' said Professor Wen.

Ronnie stiffened slightly. As a government servant, he knew where he was now. He might even have guessed, if he'd had a little less beer and was less interested in the evening's entertainment before him. He appropriately added 'sir' to all his sentences.

'You will drink beer, because in the evening it is good for the bowels, isn't that so, Doctor?' said the professor, who always liked to have support for his more *risqué* statements. The doctor laughed heartily, agreed, and slapped his thigh. The teacher smirked nervously. Ronnie watched for the District Officer's reaction. It was favourable. The conversation moved from birds' eggs to laxatives, each root and herb mentioned becoming more and more unusual as the subject held.

'Drink more! We don't often have the honour of your company,' said the professor, filling the D.O.'s glass again. Ronnie, fresh from the city, where social calls are not made without a purpose, wondered why the D.O. had come. Professor Wen, possibly wondering just as much, gave no indication of the fact, being apparently prepared to drink through till dawn—or until the wives and the matron stopped playing mahjong.

Ronnie, with his knowledge of Europeans, could see that, though the District Officer joked freely, he was a serious man, with some deep matter on his mind. As he drank, and as the evening drew closer to the time when Ronnie's lady would be free of other engagements, the District Officer grew more serious, until Ronnie, who had had a good deal too much to drink by this time (which, he said to himself, was stupid because it would spoil things later on—yet he still went on drinking, with occasional sorties to the back compound to ease himself), could only vaguely follow what was happening.

'The great problem of life——' the D.O. was saying, and at that moment there was another ear-splitting explosion from the inner room. He shouted hard at Professor Wen, but Ronnie heard nothing. He doubted if either the doctor or Teacher Wu did, either.

'That's difficult,' the professor said meditatively, as the noise abated somewhat, to be replaced by the sharp click-click of individual pieces smacked down hard on the table-top. 'Also, from the Chinese viewpoint, we don't like to give judgment on a theoretical problem, as it were, at random. No problem in life is quite like the next, and there is no set of rules for dealing with problems beforehand. There are moral rules, of course, but in each case the moral values of a problem have to be contrasted and weighed beside one another. It is in the weighing that the individual's decision lies, and the weight of contrasting moral values is something which every human being will assess differently. Then again, you are a ruler, an administrator; and a ruler's view is in some ways deeply at variance with that of other people. The ruler's needs, after all, are different. He is playing a bigger game. Furthermore, in the interests of the State, he is not necessarily concerned with right and wrong—at least, as individuals understand what is right and what is wrong.'

'Oh, you old cheat!' shouted Mrs. Wen to the matron, in the inner room. All four ladies burst into peals of laughter.

'Then what should be the overriding moral attitude of the ruler?' the District Officer asked—Ronnie was quite out of his depth in the midst of this extraordinary conversation.

Professor Wen smiled self-deprecatingly.

'This is not my subject,' he replied. 'I have never had to rule anyone except a lecture-room full of students—oh, and my own family.'

The doctor and Teacher Wu laughed heartily, glad to find something in the discourse which they could definitely understand. Ronnie laughed too, then thought of his wife, and wondered why he had ever been fool enough to obey his parents and get married.

'But, if I may say so, in keeping with Chinese classical tradition,' the professor went on, 'I would say this: the ruler has the most power; he should therefore be the most merciful. That is a case of *yin-yang*, the positive and negative principles.'

The doctor looked up at the D.O., then down at his feet.

'Yes, that is very sound. The ruler should always be merciful.'

The D.O. slipped his spectacles on again.

'But what, when to be merciful means there is no progress?' he asked.

The doctor, baffled, hastily refixed his eyes on the floor. Teacher Wu and Ronnie exchanged looks that were so elaborately contrived to hide each from the other his incomprehension that in effect they just stared at each other for an instant like lovers. Professor Wen alone appeared calm. After a moment's thought:

'Is the progress you speak of something which it is in the interests of the Government to see come about?'

'Certainly,' the District Officer replied. 'It means, in this particular case, more food production. At least'—he faltered—'it *could* mean more food production, if . . .' and with that he bowed his head slightly and covered his high forehead with his hand.

Everybody looked embarrassed, including the professor, none of them knowing what would happen next.

Another explosion broke forth, throughout which the four ladies quacked at each other with such shattering vehemence that the professor turned slightly round to see if he could not catch the eye of one of them, to entreat them to mute themselves. But it was no use. The ladies were totally absorbed in their game.

The District Officer slowly raised his head again, his eyes looking as if he had been lost for hours in remote thought.

'If there is a doubt in your mind,' the professor said gently and kindly, almost as if he were discussing a personal problem of the D.O.'s, 'perhaps it would be better to halt and consider.'

'No, actually there's no doubt about it, Dr. Wen,' he replied with a sigh. 'An increase in food production there will be. But if it benefits those it was not intended to affect, and ruins those it was intended to benefit——'

'Ah!' the professor laughed. 'That is a riddle the Government must solve. It's too hard for me!'

Ronnie saw the professor had had enough of this heavy conversation, and wished to change the subject.

'Ah! Very hard!' the doctor laughed, slapping his thigh again. Teacher Wu laughed half-heartedly. The District Officer rose and took his leave.

'I've kept you up too late, Dr. Wen,' he said with a sad smile.

'We're all very happy you came,' he beamed in reply, taking him to the door.

The District Officer passed outside, turning back to wave good night to the ladies, who shouted back in the dialect 'Walk carefully!'—the equivalent of good night—and carried on their game without pause.

'And remember,' Professor Wen concluded at the doorway, 'be merciful. Consult your clever wife. I'm sure she will say the same.'

'Yes! Consult your wife!' echoed the doctor with a belly laugh. 'If we all had wives as clever as yours, we'd stop working!'

There was a big laugh, in which Ronnie joined. The doctor was a decent, human chap, with no odd corners to him.

'Oh, she'd agree with you all right,' the District Officer answered, a trifle seriously, Ronnie thought. ' "Be merciful." I know. To whom? The stupid or the intelligent? And what about ourselves? Are we never to think of ourselves? Or do we show ourselves no mercy?' He spread his arms, then let them flap against his legs.

'Life is full of problems,' said the professor with a gay smile. Everyone smiled.

'Good night, Dr. Wen.'

'Good night, sir.'

Ronnie said good night with the rest. The D.O. stepped out on to the hill path and walked off downhill, towards the town. Slowly the professor closed the door.

The doctor frowned as he sat down again.

'They take themselves so seriously, these foreigners,' he said, 'all the time making mountains out of molehills.'

'Their morality makes it difficult for them,' the professor conceded, as he too sat down and served more beer. 'Their values are abstract, and they attempt to make them all-embracing. In the process, the values become inhuman, impossible to follow. How much easier it would be for him in his problem, whatever it is, if only he had been born a Chinese! He would not then be in this difficulty.'

'Very true,' intoned Teacher Wu. 'The Chinese way is greatly superior.'

'Yes, indeed,' agreed the doctor.

Ronnie felt obliged to say something.

'The two ways are, of course, very different,' he said with deliberation, brought on more by the beer than by the depth of his thought.

With nods and grunts, they all agreed.

'Let's drink,' said the professor.

They drank. Ronnie's being the last word before the toast, he felt he had acquitted himself well in this august company. How pleasant it was to be on holiday, to become a man again, instead of a time-grinding clerk!

'Have you any idea, incidentally, what his trouble is?' the professor asked the doctor.

'It's difficult to say. The D.O. has so many functions. But I can guess it may be his office.'

'His office?'

'Yes. You know—the staff. It's always had a bad name, that office.'

'In what way?' the professor asked mildly.

64

The doctor stroked his thumb against his first two fingers suggestively.

'Oh, I see! Well, I suppose all governments are alike. I remember in China before . . .'

Ronnie's fuddled mind did not take in the details of the involved anecdote of governmental corruption that followed. He had his eye partly on his watch and partly on his stomach. It was nearing the time for his rendezvous, and he had drunk far too much to be an effective lover. Before eleven o'clock he must go down to the town and eat something to steady the beer in him. Once unleashed on the subject of corruption, the conversation was likely to exceed in length even the mahjong game, which, unless the men stopped it, might well go on till dawn—unless the matron was on duty the following morning, in which case it would break up around midnight. After two long anecdotes, he made a move.

His farewells were lost in another screaming clatter of mahjong pieces, as the ladies reshuffled. In a few minutes he had passed down the narrow hill path, between other small bungalows like Professor Wen's, into the cramped old town, with its labyrinth of overhung alleys and lanes, along which, even at this hour, men were running with poles slung between them two and two, carrying a pig in a long tunnel of a basket, or else a crate of wet, freshly cut vegetables, being taken down to catch the night ferry to the city, to be first at the morning market next day.

At the entrance to the small eating-house he usually frequented he ran into Interpreter Leung, a former classmate, who stopped him with his curiously wicked smile.

'*Wai!* Ronnie! Where are you off to?'

'Well, well! Long time no see. I'm going to eat a bowl of noodles.'

'Not there, man! That place is no good. Come with me.'

Leung led him to another eating-house a few doors away. It looked no better than the one he usually went to, but Leung insisted. Possibly he got credit there. In the country these District Office clerks did well. They knew their way around.

Ronnie relaxed, letting things take their course. The cool evening air, after the heat of Professor Wen's house, had made him feel even more drunk, and he was in no position to resist Interpreter Leung's friendly accosting—provided it did not make

65

him too late at the little hotel near the ferry pier where he had his rendezvous. He watched glassily while Leung, opening the refrigerator just within the entrance, selected a crab, the tail end of a pomfret, and some sliced chicken livers. Yes, he thought, that will do me a power of good.

'Anyhow,' said Leung, putting an arm round his shoulder as he led him into the inner part of the eating-house, lit by fluorescent lights and overlooking the dark harbour, in which here and there moved the faint yellow lamps of sleepy junks, 'my boss is in the next one, and if we get stuck with him, everything becomes too solemn.' He gave his big, cackling laugh which, Ronnie had heard, made villagers frightened of him. 'So you're becoming a young dog again,' he continued with another cackle, as they settled at a table overlooking the black water. The nearly full moon was hidden in cloud. The eating-house was empty.

People said that, since joining the District Office, Leung had become affluent. Certainly he was fatter than he had been in their student days. He was also older, his face more lined than Ronnie's, lined with the marks made by that curiously enticing laugh. To talk to, though, he was just the same. They discussed their other classmates, the positions they now held, the incomes they earned, the number of their wives and children. Leung, it appeared, had only one wife.

'One's enough!' he snapped like a friendly puppy.

Ronnie agreed. He was having a more than expectedly pleasant evening. He was feeling bigger, as a person, than he had felt for a very long time. He began to talk things he could not remember, but which were probably pontificate nonsense.

From this happy state he was stirred by the awareness that his old friend was no longer paying attention to him. A man had come in, wearing only a singlet, underpants, and clogs, a fleshy fellow whose ugly face was vaguely familiar to Ronnie.

'Your Honour!' he said deferentially to Leung, 'may I have a word with you?'

Leung turned round, just as Ronnie recognized the man as the proprietor of the other eating-house, his usual one. With so much beer inside him he was losing his grasp on things.

'What is it?' asked Interpreter Leung.

'It's the Honourable Magistrate, Your Honour,' the fellow began, and stopped, looking guardedly at Ronnie. 'I think I had better speak to Your Honour alone.'

'Oh, nonsense, man!' the interpreter rattled out. 'This is my very old friend. Isn't it so, Ronnie?'

'Yes! Very old friend!' Ronnie replied gaily, raising his glass.

'What is it?' Leung asked the man brusquely.

The eating-house owner fell back a little in awe. Ronnie was frankly amazed. He himself earned about the same as Interpreter Leung, and whereas he was treated as a postal clerk, Leung was treated like a high official of the old days. People trembled in front of him, calling him Your Honour. He began to wish now that he had chosen to work in the country instead of in town.

The fellow fumbled for words, until like an actor on the stage, he leant down near Leung's ear and said in a voice loud enough for Ronnie to hear (but this he considered the politest way of doing it):

'The Magistrate wants me to find a woman for him for the night.'

Having delivered himself of it, he stood upright again, rather prim and pleased with himself.

Ronnie gave a guffaw of laughter. The District Officer didn't know the ropes like he did in Little Island!—and he quickly glanced again at his watch. Time enough yet. Only as he looked up again did he take stock of Leung's reaction, which was not in the least a reaction of amusement. The interpreter's face had hardened into the lines of his famous wicked smile, but with all sympathy or humour drained out of the eyes. He was like a busy man, keeping people waiting at his desk with a mechanical gesture of goodwill, while checking an important account or sealing an urgent document. He was, thought Ronnie (much impressed by the poetic fancies the beer had given him), like a chess player about to make a critical and decisive move.

'Don't be afraid,' he told the man quietly. 'Tell him you have fixed everything, and that exactly what he wants will be ready in, say, half an hour. And don't tell him you have spoken to me.'

'No, Your Honour. Thank you,' he said, backing away quickly.

'Stop!' Leung commanded. 'Repeat what you have to say to the Magistrate.'

'Yes, Your Honour,' he replied placidly.

'I said, repeat it!'

'What? Me?' he said, pointing one finger stupidly at his own nose.

'Yes! What must you say?'

He grinned.

'I must say I—myself—have fixed a real whacking good what's-it for him, and he'd better do his best because she's his for the whole night!'

This time Leung laughed, his usual high cackle, and Ronnie laughed too. The eating-house owner was a simple fellow, a good fellow. Leung slapped him on the bare shoulder.

'That's a good man!' he said gaily. 'Say just that! It'll stimulate him,' he added, aside, to Ronnie, and again, as the fellow walked off, they laughed together.

The laugh was no sooner off Leung's lips, however, and the last drop of beer drained, than he became his sober, active self once more.

'Time is short. I must go,' he said. 'You stay and finish your drink. I must run. And please pay nothing. This is all on my account.'

Ronnie made the conventional protestations, rising and pulling Leung back as he did so. But the interpreter insisted.

'You must excuse me,' he said. 'This is serious, and I must deal with it.'

'You've got to rescue him, is that it?' Ronnie asked.

'If possible, if possible,' he answered perfunctorily. Ronnie thought how troublesome it would be if he had a Postmaster-General to deal with like this District Officer, for whom the interpreter became a sort of father-confessor, or even a warden. Bidding Leung an over-friendly good night, he collapsed once more on his stool, with his back against one of the posts supporting the ceiling. After some minutes the boy brought a bowl of soup.

'With His Honour's compliments, and please take,' he said, ladling it out.

Maybe it was not ethically very proper to be enjoying a classmate's hospitality quite to this extent. It was a delightful change, however. It put him in an ideal holiday mood.

He finished his beer, drank as much of the soup as he wanted, and sauntered out of the eating-house feeling a million dollars. Everyone saluted him respectfully as the friend of His Honour the Interpreter. To think it was only old Leung! What a joke!

Passing along the main street—ten feet or so wide—and across the now deserted covered market area, he reached the hotel, just about on time—five minutes late, to be exact. Instead of going, like a newcomer, to the front entrance, and mounting up through the brilliantly lit barber's shop on the ground floor, he opened the door into the public latrine next to the market, and walked carefully in the darkness through this noisome place to the far end, where he drew open a small wooden door in what appeared to be a blank wall. Through this door he stepped down into a stone yard, where the hotel-keeper's wife washed her family's clothes, and thence to the back door of the hotel itself. The door was not yet locked. He slipped quietly into the absolute blackness within. He knew the way well enough to locate the bottom of the stone steps leading to the first floor. Half-way up these, light could be seen from the office and general reception room (if it could be so distinguished) on the first floor, and his way became clearer. Reaching the first floor, he continued up the stairs, without the advertisement of entering the reception room, where the owner and his wife stayed apparently awake day and night. Taking, not the main staircase, but a small, straight stairway leading to one door at the top—known, for its discreet location, as the bridal chamber—he came quietly to the top, and knocked softly on the door.

A sensation of silence within made him wonder if his watch was wrong and he had come too soon, while a second later confusion started on the first floor, and the proprietor, bald and clad in a vest and long, pale blue Chinese pants, came to the bottom of the staircase. On his face, as he gazed up into the darkness, was a desperate, a catastrophic, look.

'Mr. Cheng!' he whispered loudly up the stairs. 'Is it you, Mr. Cheng?'

Ronnie came slowly, curiously, down, on his guard lest the old rascal be trying to cheat him.

'What is it?' he asked coldly, when he was a step or two above the proprietor.

'With limitless apologies, Mr. Cheng, I have been placed in a most difficult position, sir. Someone—a gentleman of importance —a—I have been obliged to reserve the bridal chamber for someone else.' He appeared partly distressed, partly thrilled with unsuspected excitement. 'But everything has been alternatively arranged for you, Mr. Cheng, in this very inferior little room, which I know you will dislike, but which I beg you will accept.'

He led Ronnie to one of the tiresome cubicles on the first floor, where the light never entirely went out all night, and every sound could be heard from all the other cubicles, as well as the transactions being conducted in the reception room (all night) by the indefatigable proprietor and his wife, both of whom sported large crucifixes round their necks.

'Free?' Ronnie asked, with impertinence induced by drink.

'For you, Mr. Cheng, free,' he replied, as docile as a dove.

'She's here?' he asked apprehensively.

The proprietor beamed broadly.

'Everything has been arranged, Mr. Cheng. Rely on me always.'

Ronnie pushed open the door slightly. With relief, he saw his girl was there, waiting for him. He closed the door again.

'Who's having the bridal chamber?' he asked.

A look of solemnity crossed the proprietor's face.

'Interpreter Leung told me not to say, but, in fact, to you, Mr. Cheng, I know I can say privately . . .'

'Naturally.'

'It's reserved, sir. Reserved for the Magistrate!'

Having said which, the solemnity left him. Bursting into a hilarious grin, he doubled down and smacked his thighs with a big whack, all the while swaying backwards and forwards in silent laughter, like a comic scene in a silent movie. He shook, rippled, inflated himself, with laughter.

Ronnie wasn't all that amused. This was not exactly how he would have looked after the Postmaster-General if he'd got drunk and started talking stupidly about wanting a girl. The D.O.'s launch was in harbour. Why hadn't Leung taken him there, anchored out, and put him quietly to bed? Goodness knows, in his young days before the war, Ronnie himself had had to do it often enough with his European superiors.

'Who's he with?' he asked. 'A girl from the city?'

The proprietor raised his eyebrows and drew his lips into an O of admiration.

'Oh, Mr. Cheng! There! There's a girl! But, in a class on her own. *The* best! But then, nothing but the best would satisfy Mr. Leung. I will tell you who she is,' he continued in a lower voice. 'You've probably heard of Mr. Wong Tak-wor of Wireless Bay.'

Ronnie nodded; he knew him by sight.

'She was his favourite—kept her for several years, which is good going for him. He gets through many. In fact, they say he's still keeping her.' He sighed. 'But she's really a beauty.'

70

'Well, you've done your best. Thanks. Good night,' Ronnie said, opening the door again.

'Thank you, Mr. Cheng, and again my deep apologies.'

Ronnie closed the door behind him, glad to be in the semi-gloom of a private room. As the door closed, she rose with a quick movement from the bed and came to him. He embraced her senselessly, drunkenly, for a long time, until he had recovered from his relief at discovering that the District Officer had not taken her for the night. He was welcome to someone else's semi-discarded concubine, but not to this special girl, whom Ronnie knew, and who understood him through and through—that is, when he was in a holiday mood.

Happily assured that she was his for the rest of the night, he transferred his attention to the cubicle walls, usually peppered with tiny holes, through which spies from other cubicles could take various vicarious enjoyments. As he examined the walls, she giggled and whispered:

'I've taken care of that already.'

Indeed, she had. Each hole had a small wad of dirty paper stuffed into it, so that if it were moved, it would fall into the cubicle with a little plop, warning them they were being watched.

He too giggled. He found one hole she had not spotted—there were twenty or so on each wall—and teased her, till she quickly made another small pellet of paper and sealed the space up, after which he went on teasing her in delightful silence, undressing her meanwhile, until they collapsed together on the bed, whereupon Ronnie, after a vigorous attempt to enjoy himself, accidentally fell sound asleep.

7

CHOW brought coffee as usual the following morning, keeping his thoughts and looks to himself. Later, Sylvia ordered the food for the day, before settling herself in the living-room, delightfully cool in the mornings, in a position from which she could watch the comings and goings of boats in the harbour. It was useless asking anything of Chow or Plum. They would tell nothing; and to question them would be merely to humiliate herself. It was the first time Richard had stayed out so long.Usually he came back before going to work, even if only for a very late breakfast. The disappearance of his razor and toothbrush put an unusual touch on this particular escapade, and Sylvia was on her guard.

Sure enough, at about ten-thirty in the morning, Richard's launch left harbour, with the pennant flying at the bow, and thus with Richard aboard. After it was hidden by the northern hill of Little Island, Sylvia waited for it to reappear on the other side of the hill, which would indicate he was heading for the city. The launch did not reappear, however, and Sylvia was left to guess where it had gone, since the way northward led to many other islands, all of them possible destinations for Richard in the course of duty, and none of them visible from Little Island. For a time she considered telephoning the District Office, situated in the city (which was the natural centre for all the various islands), to see if they had any record of Richard's travel schedule. Then she frowned wrily at her own unwisdom, forgot about the entire thing for the present, and went down the hill to call, in turn, on the doctor and his wife, the English police inspector and his family (the only other Westerners resident on Little Island), the headmaster's wife, and the jolly but very pious Buddhist wife of the island's richest gold smuggler. The day passed pleasantly enough —but the launch did not return. She spent a gloomy evening and slept badly.

Early the following morning there was a telephone call. As she picked it up and heard the high hum of the radio-telephone system, she realized it was a city call.

'Darling, I'm ringing up to know how you are,' said the anxious if somewhat affected voice of Brenda Macpherson, a fairly close crony of Sylvia's, with pretensions to being an artist.

'How very unexpected of you! I'm quite well, thank you.'

'Then it isn't true—the news, I mean?' the breathless voice asked.

'What isn't true? What news?

'Oh darling, never mind. Maybe Julie Holliday got it all wrong.'

'Julie Holliday? How does she come into it?'

'Well, it was she who told me, dear—I mean, about Richard.'

There was a silence. Sylvia's heart dropped like a stone.

'What about Richard?' she asked coldly.

72

'Oh, then it is true! He really has left you?'

'Brenda, what are you talking about? Where has all this gabble come from?'

'Well, darling, I don't exactly know, but—then it's not true?'

'Of course it's not true. I never heard such nonsense.'

'Is he with you there on the island?'

'Not at present. He's out travelling for a few days.'

'I see. Oh, well, that's just wonderful, dear. Then there's nothing in it. Any chance of seeing you in town in the next few days?'

As the conversation continued, a uniformed police constable, a young Chinese lad, came to the open front door and saluted. Without breaking what she was saying, Sylvia took the letter he was delivering, smiled acknowledgment of his salute of withdrawal, and opened the note with one hand. It was a short message in pencil, in the big, bad handwriting of the island's police inspector.

Madam,

Two newspapers telephone this morning asking if you was on the island. I had to say you are. It seems they wish to come and see you. Thought you'd like to know.

B. Smith.

'Brenda, on second thoughts, I think I'm coming into town this morning. Could we meet for coffee?'

'Darling, I'm afraid not. I'm having a hair-do. Could you make it lunch?'

'Yes, that'll suit me fine. Shall we say the Budapest Inn at one? I'll book a table.'

'Wonderful. You really are all right, are you?'

'Why not?'

'Well, I've never known you have second thoughts before.'

'Old age, my dear. See you at one o'clock.'

She put the phone down and sat back in a chair. Like a delayed reaction, she remembered how Richard had quietly walked out into the garden with that foolish remark about her always being right, and was deeply disturbed. Something serious must have happened, involving Richard; yet, since he was fairly certainly still in the district, it was hard to imagine what incident of importance could have occurred. There was nothing else for it but to go into town as soon as possible, and find out what it was that Brenda knew—and Julie Holliday, for that matter, too—that was causing the excitement.

At first she thought of going in just for the day, until, reflecting on Brenda's casual invitation—delivered while she was opening the letter from the police inspector—to attend her 'enjoying the moon' party that night, the night of the full moon, she decided she might wish to stay the night. After breakfast, therefore, she packed her usual small plastic bag of toilet articles, and walked down the hill, cheered up by the calm serenity of another slightly autumnal day, to catch the ten o'clock ferry.

She seldom carried much luggage when travelling between Little Island and the city. Her country clothes she kept on Little Island, her town clothes, evening dresses and so on, in town, at the apartment high up overlooking the city which was one of the luxuries she had been able to indulge in since the success of *The Chasm*. Though there was no real distinction, it was tacitly understood between them that the bungalow on Little Island was Richard's, while the town apartment was hers. Richard's man-servant kept his wife, Plum, permanently at the bungalow, while, in town, Sylvia kept an old amah who had turned up as a refugee in the colony, having worked for Sylvia in Chungking in the days of Bill.

It would have been a great deal less inconvenient if she could have asked the police inspector, or his wife, or the doctor's wife, or anyone on the island, what had happened to Richard—for they surely must know, the strange report having presumably started from the island. But in her position as wife of the District Officer this was not feasible.

'I shall be back either this evening or tomorrow morning,' she told Chow as she left.

Great Island looked faintly pink in the morning sun. Flecks of cloud hung motionless around its peaks. Brown-sailed junks glided quietly in and out of the Little Island harbour. She started down the hill, losing the view, immersing herself in the descending lane of small bungalows with brightly decorated gardens, finally sinking to the stone alleys and cheery squalor of the town. Good morning to this person, good morning to that. Everybody seemed disposed as usual towards her. At the quay she bought her ferry ticket. Broad smiles from the ticket seller, a rough joke, a laugh, a reply conceding the inferiority of women to men, happy smiles all round at hearing a foreigner speak Chinese, everything normal. What in heaven's name had Brenda got hold of?

Sylvia always enjoyed the ferry ride. When the weather was fine, and specially now that autumn was coming, she sat in the stern, where it was all open, with no windows, and the strong breezes disarranged her hair, making her feel clean, healthy, and very young again. When the ferry rounded the head of Little Island, passing between it and the tip of Great Island (so vastly larger), new currents clashed, the ferry rocked and swayed for a while, till it settled on its clear course, unimpeded by rocks or islands, towards the island of Victoria. The buffeting of the sea and the heaving of the vessel made Sylvia redispose herself on her bench. While doing so, glancing casually northwards, she saw Richard's launch approaching, pennant flying, evidently returning to Little Island.

She had an instantaneous, vivid picture in her mind: Richard entering the bungalow, finding her toilet things gone, questioning Chow—a hideous misunderstanding. She must telephone him as soon as she reached her apartment in Victoria. She had not walked out on him. She had simply gone to town to find out what was at the bottom of this ridiculous rumour. Why could he not come over in the evening to join the celebration of the Mid-Autumn Festival? A reconciliation. A gay evening party on a ship with bright lights. A heady return home. Bliss.

She began to fidget with impatience, glancing often at her watch. It would take more than an hour from here to the city wharves. There were few passengers on the ferry, and none in the stern. She paced about with her hands behind her back, like a worried sailor.

Until another idea occurred to her, and she sat down again. Richard, determined to be free of her, seeking for an opportunity to take legal action, returning to the bungalow to find she had deserted him. Chow not explaining she was coming back, and she unable to telephone Richard, since in the mood he was in, whatever she said would be interpreted by him as a change of heart, a capitulation, an admission of foolishness. He would never believe she had simply gone into town for the day.

Looking down at her plastic travelling kit, she felt so furious about it, she could have hurled it into the sea. What crazy whim had driven her to drag away with her the one proof that she was only on a day's outing?

Until uncertainty returned. If only she could know exactly in what frame of mind Richard was coming back to the island! If only someone else, there and seeing him, could tell her! But the choice of Chow (disloyal to her), Mrs. Smith (a simple Devonshire woman with no valid judgments about anything except when her husband had drunk enough) and the doctor's wife (a volatile Cantonese, liable to jump to the utmost length of any conclusion) was not encouraging.

Thinking of them, and of the absurd predicament she had let herself into, she broke out of it and laughed at herself. She had, without knowing it, put herself into a theatrical situation. Soon she would be striking attitudes with the rest of the players, she who had always unerringly avoided such nonsense. The play was, in some peculiar way, closing in on her. She could not escape from it. She was on the stage, with the lights on, the curtain up, escape to the wings barred, and no way of leaping over the orchestra into the merciful neutrality of the audience. She was famous. The least hint of a break-up in her marriage would set the international news agencies buzzing with trite versions of some idiot's assumptions about her married life. The versions would go out according to the principles of the play, which were that one party was right and the other wrong. After *The Chasm*, she would be wrong, and Richard immaculately right. Not that that mattered much. God knows the last thing she wanted to do was to cast any blot on Richard's name on this vast, international network. Far better that she should be blamed. People would say it was so completely in character.

How nice, she thought off-hand, if she were now in a position to strike a tremendous attitude! 'I loved him, but he wouldn't have me.'—'He deceived me. I am black as pitch; he is blacker than hell.'—'Love in me demands greater things than can be given by a member of Her Britannic Majesty's Colonial Administration.' (That would appeal to America.) 'At last, I am free to tell the truth about my marriage. And I shall tell it as freely as I told the story of my love for a gallant Indian officer.' There were several possibilities.

Life is easy for those who strike attitudes, she thought in an unsubtle way. Such people can be easily understood. The public can pity them unreservedly, or knock them down pop like Aunt Sallies. Though an attitude was, of its very nature, false, certain attitudes in the public mind as influenced by holders of the

76

appropriate qualifications earning their living writing copy for news agencies and papers were obviously false, while others appeared deceptively genuine. The truth—that every attitude was indicative either of moral cowardice or a mental incapacity to face facts—might have adherents among a handful of philosophers. Few else would even be aware of when exactly an attitude was being assumed.

Sylvia, as usual, had no attitude. She only wanted to know in what humour Richard re-entered the empty bungalow; and concerning this, by the time she reached the city wharves and took a taxi up the hill to her apartment she was something near desperate, sensing that, if she did not know, and if she made a false move in this entirely unreal game, she would be drawn into the very type of involvement she most heartily disliked, into that play, under the glittering lights of which every move was a sham.

Juen, her old servant, in her customary white smock and black silk pants, with her grey hair faultlessly combed into a neat little bun—such a clean, orderly, dependable old thing, Sylvia thought every time she came back: like a rock in a storm—met her at the door of the apartment.

'Oh, Honourable Mother, how fortunate and praise Heaven you have come back!' Juen began. (Since Sylvia's marriage she was always the correct Chinese form of Honourable Mother with Juen, despite there being no children.) 'Really, I haven't known where to put my head this morning. The telephone has been ringing and the doorbell going from early morning, and everyone wants you. I told them all you were in Little Island, but when those bad-mannered young men with cameras came they refused to believe me, saying they knew you were here, and I had to threaten them with the police.' In her grave, modulated voice, speaking Mandarin somewhat like an old aristocrat of West China, Juen recounted a long series of small incidents, all of which had combined to make the morning an unusual one for her. If she knew of any reason for the excitement, she made no reference to it. Together they walked into the apartment, Juen a few feet behind Sylvia—slowly, reflectively, into the beautiful, long living-room, with its panoramic view over the colony's great port, and over the mountains and islands beyond.

'Thank you, Ah Juen,' she said simply, at the end of the recital, sitting down to put a call through to Little Island. She was quickly connected. 'Hullo, Chow, is that you? Is the master home?'

and at the far end, over the high-pitched hum, the same hint of disloyalty as Chow replied: 'No, Master not come back yet.' 'All right, Chow, thank you. Please tell him I telephoned.'

The doorbell went.

'There they come again,' said Juen, going to the door.

'Don't open it!' Sylvia interposed quickly, adding, as she saw Juen's face fall with some loss of mental equilibrium, 'You've gone to the market.'

Juen brightened up again. 'Yes, I'm at the market,' she said, trotting off with Sylvia's plastic bag.

Sylvia drummed her slender fingers on a glass table, while the bell went on ringing and ringing.

8

WILLIE ROGERS, the Assistant Lecturer in English at the colony's somewhat anaemic university, was one of those intellectuals who, due to the perverting influence of too much education, coupled with the wish that he had been born to a title, was unwilling to associate with, or think well of, anyone except aristocrats and celebrities on one side, and the roughest of rough peasants on the other. He had pale skin and light brown hair that had once been golden, when he was a boy. He wore thick-rimmed, high-powered spectacles and, with monotonous frequency, the tie of an Old Etonian. In taking a university appointment in the colonies, he was thankful to have come to one of the few colonies where there was at least some semblance of elegance in social life. Since his schooldays, he had always moved in an elegant circle. In winter he wore peculiar waistcoats, some of which looked as if they might have come out of the property box of an Edwardian pantomime; and he regularly visited the city's most elaborate hairdressing establishment, where he could have a manicure.

Willie Rogers did not like Brenda Macpherson, but he accepted her invitations. Her husband was number two in one of the largest British firms, one of the highest-paid men in the colony. Willie appreciated a table on which there were good wines and well-chosen dishes, and, since he was asked chiefly because he was smart and amusing, he felt little obligation, as a bachelor, to repay their usually lavish hospitality. If it suited them that way, it suited him, too. Brenda he considered a silly woman and a frightful snob, while her painting was methodically plebeian. He appreciated that she wanted to make her parties different from other people's, that she couldn't stand drabness of any kind anywhere in her life. Too often her inventiveness, in Willie Rogers' view, ran away with her into vulgarity.

The party she gave annually on the night of the Mid-Autumn Festival was an example of this. The festival was entirely Chinese, the only Europeans who participated being those invited by their Chinese friends. Yet every year Brenda Macpherson not merely gave a party of her own, but actually had the nerve to hire a Chinese junk (complete with the family of fishermen whose only home it was) to give it in. She then decorated the junk with coloured lanterns, and invited Chinese guests to attend, which, most of them being business associates of her husband, they reluctantly did.

This year lived up to the last, although, as Willie Rogers stepped aboard the junk at the wharves at nine o'clock in the evening, he noticed some innovations. As a result of veiled complaints last year, the boat had been thoroughly scrubbed, for one thing. The fishing family's dog, a mangy beast, had been locked up somewhere (or had perhaps died). Decorations more magnificent than usual had been erected; and in the centre of the deck, surrounded by the guests' chairs, stood Brenda's easel, with some canvases ready. Willie groaned.

Since Macpherson had risen to the position of number two in his firm, their parties had become more representative. That is, the guests were selected in rather the same way as the guests to Government House dinners. Balances had to be contrived, different interests and facets of society represented. The Macphersons, in short, were beginning to inflate themselves, the only mitigation being that Macpherson himself came from a Scottish family of distinction, being related to two earls and (though distantly) to a duke. He had some inherited right, therefore, as Willie Rogers put it, as well as a commercial reason, for entertaining on this somewhat formal basis.

'Willie, how nice of you to come!'

It was Brenda, in a tight-fitting black evening gown, walking forward to the bows of the ship, as two of the fisher family's elder sons helped him aboard along a narrow ladder. She was wearing three heavy rows of misshapen pearls—in fashion that year—with ear-rings to match, and her soft auburn hair was brushed upwards in a slightly boyish way. By any standards, she was certainly one of the best-groomed women in the colony, and among the most beautiful.

'How pleasant, Brenda! I see you've invited Sylvia Gracechurch.' He could see the famous writer, in a pearl-grey evening dress with yellow orchids, talking on deck to the Garrison Brigadier.

Brenda shivered theatrically.

'Be careful what you say, Willie,' she said swiftly in an undertone, as they advanced towards the other guests. 'Richard's left her.'

He looked abruptly at his hostess.

'I hadn't heard anything.'

'It's a very hot cake—only just happened. Now then, Willie,' this in a louder voice as they came within range of the brilliant kerosene lamps in the centre of the deck, 'you know everybody, don't you? Brigadier, you know Mr. Rogers?'

'Yes, of course. How are you, Rogers?'

A tall, thin man with hair parted in the middle and plastered down with water, following the system he had used when a schoolboy; an enormous black moustache; a monocle; a caricature. A reality.

Willie Rogers greeted the novelist, and stuck to her. Around her was a peculiar atmosphere of freedom. The Brigadier, discussing Debussy with her, was speaking, as it were, out of a mental straitjacket, created by his convictions and prejudices, and tightened by his military career. Across the deck Mr. Szeto, the huge, fat owner of the colony's largest bus company, looked narrowly out on the scene through his large, round, expressionless eyes, that were like microscopic windows through which alone he could perceive reality. Dumpy and ever-hungry Mr. Hillary, the Government's greatest Chinese scholar, talking to the Honourable Edwin Lau, a member of the Legislative Council, was tracing each word of Chinese spoken between them to its remote historical antecedents (like lightning, as the conversation proceeded; one could see him doing it). Edwin Lau himself was honestly interested in nothing except the value of the gold dollar and his race horses.

Each, in other words, was a person enclosed in a tight frame of his own making, into which it was necessary to penetrate slightly before any human contact could be made.

Sylvia Gracechurch was different. Each time they met, it relieved Willie Rogers to be with her, while also disturbing him, in that he was unable to define what was the nature of this peculiar air of freedom about her. Was it that she was a sexual libertine, and took no pains to conceal it? She was a modern, less torpid, version of a Burne-Jones beauty, with her luxurious, curling brown hair and large features. Under the safe disguise of his thick spectacles, Willie Rogers let his eyes ramble greedily on her breasts. She was well made, almost bosomy, a type Willie Rogers liked, but was nervous of, having unusual fantasies now and then about being smothered or emasculated by women physically of larger proportions than himself. He attributed it to a nurse who had hugged him when he was a small child, and made him fascinated by, though frightened of, women with large breasts.

Or was it an attitude of mental freedom only, a fundamental independence, that made Sylvia Gracechurch different? She was not enclosed by any conventions. There was something fresh and airy about her. Certainly, he was not interested in her as a writer. Her novels were slick nonsense, with probably far more invention in them than most people realized. How could she have resumed her married life, if the affair with the Indian Military Attaché in Tokyo had been true? Unless . . . and it brought him back to his original posit that the basis of the sense of freedom with her and about her was sexual.

Hell, he'd warmed up since stepping aboard! He glanced down at the glass which a boy had put in his hand the moment he reached the deck.

'Brenda, this rum punch is a darned sight stronger than I thought,' he called across the deck.

She flashed a smile that disentangled itself from a fifteen-minute discourse of some solemnity by the sinologist Hillary, who was a crashing bore.

'We start them rough,' she replied. 'The next bowl will be gentler.'

Gongs crashed, drums beat, and with fearful din a volley of firecrackers exploded as the junk moved slowly away from the wharf, using its motor engine.

'Oh, no!' exclaimed Brenda Macpherson. 'Brian! I said no

crackers! Darling, the shocking things, they kill me!' After which, she hurried round from one group to another, apologizing about the crackers.

'Don't worry, Mrs. Macpherson,' said the enormous Mr. Szeto in his high-pitched voice, 'we Chinese are used to them.'

'Yes, of course. How silly of me!'

'And so are we soldiers,' added the Brigadier, *basso profundo*.

Brenda Macpherson shivered all over with laughter. (What a fright of a woman! Willie Rogers thought.)

'Oh, Brigadier! You put me utterly to shame. But utterly!' she repeated to Sylvia Gracechurch.

'Darling, it's a lovely party,' the writer replied softly, taking the hostess's hand in hers.

'Is it really? You're looking wonders, darling, and you're *being* so wonderful'—this with pointed, intimate stress. 'Well,' she continued, to the group around her, 'I can't do without my one evening a year in the Chinese style. After all, what's the use of living here if we don't take part sometimes, just the littlest bit?'

The description of the degree of part-taking, Willie Rogers thought, was scrupulously exact. Dreamy with rum punch, his eyes wandered over the deck, vaguely registering the uncanny scene: the junk, hung with paper lanterns, moving out into the harbour, as the miraculous lights of the city rose up and around them; the coarse shouts of the big junk family; the barking of a dog (it was not dead, then); young men in short pants moving here and there amid the rigging; a naked boy dashing up a rope to attend to a lantern catching fire; and in the brilliantly lit deck centre the small group of Western and Chinese high society, all the men in black dinner jackets, the European women in long gowns, the Chinese women in full-length *cheungsams* of dark, formal tones; and in the very middle, the easel and canvases. What madness was it?

'But what I can't understand about these damned Chinese,' the Brigadier was saying to Sylvia Gracechurch, '—mind you, I shouldn't be saying this to you, ma'am, you're an expert—but to a simple man like myself, and to my men also, anything about the Chinese is so impossibly difficult to explain! For instance, my orderly only this morning was asking me why it's called the Mid-Autumn Festival, when the autumn hasn't even started. And, dammit, I couldn't give him a proper answer. I don't know myself!'

'In China, further north, it is now the middle of autumn,' she replied quietly.

The Brigadier's mouth fell open. He made a sound faintly resembling a hiccough.

'By Jove! How astoundingly damned simple! You amaze me.'

Boys were beginning to serve small delicacies to eat. The junk was by now well out into the harbour. The glittering rock on which the city arose was looking superb. All the dark water was a mass of gaily lit craft—junks, launches, ferries—moving here and there with a hundred cheerful toots of their sirens to warn someone or other of their approach; and as Willie Rogers looked upwards, the clouds cleared away, and the enormous moon, yellow-gold and vibrant, shone out above the dark hills, above the sparkle of innumerable lights, the most splendid light of all. A great yell of joy went up from the junk family in the stern, and everything was atrophied by cracker-firing.

'Brian! Darling!' Brenda screamed. 'I can't bear it! I specially said *No crackers!*'

Macpherson chuckled into his glass of punch. No one paid more than perfunctory attention. Willie Rogers, who had begun to feel positively pleasant to other people, whoever they were, now woke up to the fact that this was a situation, a great dramatic moment. Here he was, standing beside the world-famous author of that horrible trash *The Chasm of Love*; and her husband had just deserted her. It would be front-page news all over the world.

He tried to speak to her, but she was talking rapidly in what sounded like Mandarin with Mrs. Edwin Lau, a svelte, ivory-skinned Cantonese beauty, with whom the authoress seemed specially friendly. Mr. Szeto, of the bus company, wandered heavily across to them.

'I understand that husband of yours has some plan to put a motor road on Great Island,' he said in high-pitched English, breaking in on the Mandarin conversation, which he apparently did not understand.

'Yes, surely. D'you like the idea, Mr. Szeto?'

'I like roads, Mrs. Fairburn, I like roads,' he said airily, rather as if he ate roads for breakfast. 'The more roads there are, the more people want to travel. The more they want to travel, the more buses people ask me to provide. Now, my dear, you tell that husband of yours, the moment he's got that road ready, I want to have my buses on it! Maybe only one to begin with. Let's see how it goes. I have to be cautious. I must see how it goes. But if it's a success, then there's no knowing . . .' He switched to Willie Rogers. 'There's no knowing, my dear sir.'

A sudden onrush of self-importance impelled Willie Rogers to take Mr. Szeto aside.

'I think I should warn you, sir,' he began quietly. . . .

'What's that, Mr. Rogers?' the magnate asked loudly, against the noise of tooting launches passing them.

'I want to warn you, Mr. Szeto. Mrs. Fairburn is, it appears, estranged from her husband.'

The enormous Mr. Szeto stepped back a pace, his thick lips compressed into a pattern that made him look exactly like a vast bullfrog.

'Impossible!' he piped dramatically.

'It's true. Just the last few days.'

Mr. Szeto adopted a deeply confidential manner.

'Does Edwin Lau know?' he asked, his voice, by an effort, dropping as low as it could reach.

'I don't think so. Very few people seem to, yet.'

'I'd better warn him. Thank you, Mr. Rogers. I hope I didn't put my foot in it.'

The great bullfrog (who had very large feet) moved off to contact the suave Edwin Lau, who was discussing the last race meeting with Brian Macpherson. The news, in fact, travelled round the company within a few minutes, during which time the entire character of the party changed. The Chinese male guests, as Willie Rogers quickly realized to his discomfort, were placed unexpectedly in a social quandary. If the Fairburn marriage was going on the rocks, they found themselves this evening in an embarrassing false position, which not even the socially shrewd Brenda Macpherson had considered. Richard Fairburn was a government official of fairly high standing. Although he was out in the country now as District Officer, he might at any time be transferred back to the city. He had served in the Secretariat before; he might again. He was the right seniority to be appointed fairly soon to one of the key posts, Development Secretary or Deputy Financial Secretary, the latter post controlling licences, all large Government contracts, ferry and bus franchises, together with other matters of vital interest to Chinese big business. If Richard Fairburn might be given such a job, he was a person to be kept on the right side of.

Had the party this evening been given by a government official, the situation of the Chinese bigshots would not have been so serious. That it was given by a British business man suggested unmistakably that around the Fairburn family dispute two parties were forming, one supporting him, the other supporting her. It would have been hard to determine who was the more disconcerted, Mr. Szeto or the Honourable Edwin Lau, to find that he had unintentionally joined the wrong party.

Within a few minutes, with finesse that made the movement imperceptible, all the Chinese guests had left the centre deck and were standing amid the rigging, gazing out at the moon and the crazy galaxy of lights. The group at the lower end of the deck was reduced to the Western guests, gathered around the last arrival before the junk left the quay, an American Senator on an 'inform yourself' trip round the East. At the upper end of the deck, Sylvia Gracechurch sat alone.

With a premonitory twinge of embarrassment, Willie Rogers saw she was looking fixedly at him.

'Do you enjoy gossip, Willie?' she asked with an inviting smile, as he moved over to her again.

'It depends what kind it is,' he said limply.

'I hate intellectual dishonesty'—this with a subtle hardening of the voice that gave the remark a knife's edge.

'But surely, life would be quite impossible without some forms of dishonesty. Social dishonesty, for example—white lies, previous engagements when invited to dinner by people you don't like.'

He was longing to ask her what had happened between herself and her husband, but dared not approach the subject directly, not knowing her more than casually, at parties such as this. Confident in his social dexterity, he was planning in his mind how to come nearer to the subject, when, with another knife-edged variation in her way of speaking, she looked across the largely empty deck, and said:

'You're a silly young man, Willie. You've broken up this party, and Mrs. Macpherson is not going to love you for it. But you're right about social dishonesty. Would you mind going over to Mrs Macpherson and telling her I'm not feeling very well and would like to be landed somewhere where I can find a taxi home?'

It took a good deal to shake Willie Rogers, but not much to needle his tender vanity. From a first moment of wounded *amour propre*, as he heard her begin to speak, his fluid mind switched to a

85

feeling of utter malevolence. He thought she must be having a singularly unfunny joke.

'Are you serious?' he asked. 'Are you really feeling ill?'

'Not in the least. Will you please do as I ask?' she said quietly.

He looked down at her with a quick access of admiration. No woman had ever dared treat him in such a way before.

'I don't accept your criticism,' he said, cold with embarrassment. 'I was trying to help you.'

'A great mistake. Never try it again.'

In confusion he did as he was told, crossing to where Brenda Macpherson stood in a group round the Senator. Speaking to her in a low voice, flushing as he did so, he played the part the writer had designed for him. Brenda broke away at once from her other guests, crossing to the solitary figure at the end of the deck.

'Darling! I'm desperately sorry to hear you're not well.'

'I feel such a fool, Brenda. I'm so sorry.'

'What is it, dear heart?'

'I've suddenly developed a splitting headache. I can hardly see straight.'

Brenda put her fingers on what must have been the writer's cool brow.

'It's the reaction, my dear,' she said quietly. 'It's nothing but the reaction. Quite unavoidable, unfortunately. I always get them after the least domestic upset. Brian! Poor Sylvia's got a splitting headache and would like to be put down somewhere where she can find a taxi.'

After expressing his regret, their host looked round the harbour to see where they were, called the head boy, and gave an order, which was delivered aft to the junk family controlling the engine.

'We'll put you down at Drake Pier. We've a car waiting there, which can take you home.'

'Would you like to take something, darling?' asked their hostess, looking anxiously through the contents of her evening bag. 'There now, I've got nothing except cough lozenges.'

'No, I shall be quite all right,' the novelist assured her, leaning back with a deep sigh and throwing her head slowly up—revealing in the intense light of the kerosene lamps a neck that made Willie Rogers shiver as he looked down on its picturesque pre-Raphaelite beauty. 'Thank you both so much for your kindness. I'm so sorry to be a nuisance.'

'Darling, you couldn't be that,' Brenda Macpherson replied with a lilt of insincerity.

Everyone was kind. The junk swung round, heading for the brilliant lights of the shore. Mrs. Edwin Lau left her husband for a short time, coming over to have a few final words with her friend. They spoke hastily in Mandarin, none of which Willie Rogers could follow. One phrase only he caught. This was when Mrs. Lau, looking towards where her husband was standing with the enormous Mr. Szeto, said in English:

'He's being quite impossible.'

This divorce, Willie Rogers thought—if divorce it proved to develop into—was capable of shaking the social life of the colony to its foundations.

Mrs. Lau rejoined her husband. After a few more awkward moments of suspense, the junk came to the end of Drake Pier. Brian Macpherson was insistent that his sick guest should not move till all was in readiness for her comfort. A boy was sent to tell the car driver to bring the car on to the pier. When it arrived, the host at last indicated to her that he was ready to escort her. The Chinese turned round, smiling good night but not leaving their outer position near the rigging. The Westerners parted to both sides, each in turn saying how sorry they were Mrs. Fairburn was not feeling well. The Senator, when it came to his turn, felt obliged to make a short speech, saying how greatly he had looked forward to meeting such a famous writer, and how sorry he was that it should turn out to be in these circumstances—a phrase the implication of which he did not appreciate, though it made Willie Rogers and Brenda Macpherson, and several others in the party, exchange vivid glances. She was, the Senator said, a great new figure in that important group of people whose aim was East-West understanding, and to this she had made a notable contribution—like hell, thought Willie Rogers, thinking of the Indian Military Attaché. The Senator could not let this proud moment in his life pass, he said, without drawing attention to it.

The novelist smiled sadly. Her pearl-grey evening dress blended strangely with the dark browns and deeper tones of the gloomy pier. Turning slightly, she bid everyone a final good night, before being escorted along the perilous ladder again by Brian Macpherson and two of the almost naked Chinese fishermen.

There was a hiatus before the mental ramifications of the party were reasserted. One had to admit—and Willie Rogers wondered how his hostess would like it—that far and away the most interesting guest had left.

Ashore, the car door clicked and the car backed off the pier. Brian Macpherson returned to the junk; Brenda switched away to Willie Rogers. She hunched her shoulders and shivered.

'What a harrowing party this is being! I feel like doing my face all over again. How could I have been so silly as to invite her?'

The junk moved out into the harbour again, over which white clouds were reflecting mysteriously the brilliant moonlight, while hundreds of gaily lit craft were roaming about, hooting and honking and letting off volleys of crackers. Mr. Szeto pulled himself slowly into the centre of the deck again, the Laus rejoined the Senator and the Brigadier. Mr. Hillary, eating cocktail nuts, expounded on the derivation of the word used in Chinese for divorce, contrasting it with that used for a legal separation.

'Oh! the air seems so much fresher!' Brenda Macpherson was saying. 'Ah Fong, is supper ready? —Willie, I think perhaps now I can do some sketching. Those clouds thrill me!'

9

SYLVIA reached her apartment to find waiting for her a letter in Richard's handwriting. Bearing no postage stamp, it had evidently been delivered by an office messenger. It bore the rubber chop of the District Administration. Turning on a single reading light, she opened the huge floor-to-ceiling windows of her main room. As she did so, the distant tumult of jollification in the harbour mounted up, filling the dark apartment with lively sounds counteracting the solemn silence of moonlight. Seated beside the reading light, she opened the letter.

Little Island,
Wednesday, 5 p.m.

Dearest,

I am very sorry I walked out on you at dinner the other evening. I was being brash and stupid. But I have, as I think you realize, been working under a hell of a strain these past few weeks,

88

trying to get things moving for the new road. It is such a revolutionary idea to most people—the Government has never built a road on one of the lesser islands before—and it is damned hard to get people to take it seriously. If it weren't for H.E., I don't think we'd ever get it.

I understand from Chow that I just missed you this morning. I tried to phone you lunchtime, but you were out. That's why I'm writing this.

It occurs to me that perhaps, after all, what has happened may be in a way providential. I hope you will please not misunderstand me, but I know I've been pretty impossible to live with this last month or so, and I'm going to be impossible probably for the next few months, until the Budget is passed and we know where we are. It's been on my mind since last week that it might be easier for both of us, during this time, if we took a spell of living separately, you in town, where you've got all your interests, and I here. I hadn't liked to mention it before, but now things have turned out as they have today I wonder if you would consider it. I sincerely hope you won't misunderstand this. It's you I'm thinking of primarily in writing like this. Please let me know what you think.

I understand from Ah Juen that you will be out with Brenda and Brian tonight. I hope you enjoy yourself.

Your loving
Richard.

Sylvia leant back and closed her eyes. She had a feeling of complete inertia. She envisaged, like a long, cold tunnel in front of her, a future period of telephone calls, long, formal explanations to news agencies, written statements to lawyers, arrangements with shipping companies, packing, dealing with poor old faithful Juen, going away. . . . She was not afraid. Financially independent, she could go where it suited her. Only the inconvenience of it worried her, having to start a new life. At one cold glance, she knew that this letter meant the end of her marriage. Human relationships cannot be temporarily broken and re-set. The members evolve new joints. When the time for re-setting comes, they no longer fit.

Then, damn it! there was the interference this whole thing was causing her. She was just settling down to write the next book which her publishers were agitating for. She needed peace and calm, and the assurance that tomorrow would be like today. And here were all her hopes of achieving something completely thwarted, all her ideas of writing sent scattered and trembling to the edges of her consciousness, while she was forced—by Richard and her own nervous make-up—to concentrate on this ridiculous personal problem which need never have occurred.

She stood up, crossed the room, and kicked off her high-heeled evening shoes. Men! she swore. Men! How had anything ever been achieved in the world by an animal so incapable of comprehending anything except as it affected himself?

She paced up and down for a time in her stockinged feet, trying to assess what her life would be like if she agreed to Richard's juvenile imbecility. How old was he, for goodness' sake! Or—she stopped in her stride—was he, too, aware that what he was suggesting was the end?

Opening a carved ivory cigar-box, she took out and lit a small, slender Dutch cheroot, such as she sometimes smoked in private when writing. Going to her bureau, she took out a pen and letter-paper. Her hand was trembling so much, however, that she could not write. She turned for the typewriter, put on some more lights, and slowly, with long silences, wrote in reply, while the harbour revelry dwindled away to stillness, and the moon moved over into the west.

> *12 The Heights,*
> *28 September.*

My dearest Richard,

> *Your letter was here when I came back from Brenda's junk party, which was just about as awful as usual.*

I am desperately upset—and it would be meaningless for me to deny it—by your suggestion that we should deliberately plan a spell of living apart. My dear one, I have realized all along that you were working under a great strain, and for that very reason tried my level best to make you feel absolutely at ease and relaxed whenever you were at home. I don't think perhaps you can fully appreciate what a sense of my own shortcomings your letter has given me, showing me, as it does, how I have failed *you, failed to give you the home, the comfort and sympathy which it is my first duty as your wife to provide.*

You know very well that I have never forgotten our private promise to each other when we married, that neither would ever try to bind the other. God knows that if you want to be absolutely free and on your own for a few months, I must not stand in your way.

90

But I cannot see any purpose in making so solemn a pact in the matter. I should hate to think, for instance, on any occasion when you wanted to come into town, that you would hesitate to come, because of an agreement that we should temporarily live apart. It seems to me madness for us to agree that you should not stay here when in town—because this is what it amounts to. All your things are here, your dress clothes etc.; and when you are in town, and people know you are here, we are bound to be invited together. Also, in the opposite sense, I would hate to feel that when coming to Little Island I had deliberately to avoid our lovely home there. I really don't think this is sensible.

I'm not sure, also, whether you quite realize what's been happening at this end. Somehow—and I cannot find out how it was—a rumour came from Little Island that we had separated. It was very quick. Brenda had heard it the day after you left the house—it was to see her about it that I came into town. The outcome, which has been perfectly maddening, is that the international news agencies have been pestering me to death trying to get a story. The flat has been all but besieged by photographers, and this afternoon they were so persistent that I even had to disconnect the telephone. I have had to come and go in daytime by the servants' entrance.

John Winnington telephoned this morning from the Public Relations Office and was extremely understanding. Apparently a report of a rumoured estrangement—those were the exact words used—has gone out, and he asked if I wished to make a statement. I said (I hope this was right) that as his was a Government department I felt it would be more appropriate if any statement made came from you, and not me. He agreed, and said he would discuss it with the Chief Secretary. He also said that he had asked all the local papers not to touch the story, and they have all agreed not to, which is a relief. But foreign papers coming into the colony will carry it, and everyone is certain to know about it soon.

I do think it is most important that we should scotch this rumour completely, and as soon as possible. What I have in mind particularly is your career. You have so often said how bad it is for a colonial officer to have any scandal attached to his name, since it will almost certainly hinder his promotion. It would be the worst possible thing for the Government now to get the idea that our marriage was a shaky affair. Great things may come along for you as a result of this road, and I would hate to think that any mischievous nonsense about us should stand in the way of your chances—

91

because it is only mischievous nonsense, as I told John Winnington.

What I would like to suggest now is that you come into town as soon as you conveniently can. We can then talk thoroughly over the question of your staying alone for the time being on Little Island; and I think it would be a good thing if we could go out together at least once, in the evening, somewhere where we shall be seen by plenty of people—the Ritz, or else a cinema. Or perhaps you might like to come to my British Council lecture on Thursday. It's at 6.30. By all means let us say that for the time being your headquarters will be on the island, while mine will be here; but surely we should both be free to come and go when it suits us, just as we have always done.

With all my love, dearest,
Sylvia.

Too long, perhaps, she thought afterwards. It was hard to say everything in a shorter form. She had never written so contrite a letter in her life. Leaving it unsealed, to re-read in the morning, she went to bed and slept like a child.

For—and she became trenchantly aware of it next morning as she finally sealed the envelope—she had become, in contrition, unexpectedly like a very young girl again. She was mentally standing with her hands twisted ruefully in front of her, before some dimly remembered governess. Haren was forgotten—had she yet reached that time in her life? Perhaps he was a premonition of the future, not a remembrance of the past. All her adventures were forgotten. All the pulsating energies of her nature had been shaken down by the cool shock of Richard's letter and all that it implied for the future, until she was left with nothing but her small, worried heart, the heart of a little girl, which dictated to the rest of her as if her body had never before known what passion was. This probably wouldn't last, she thought. But it undoubtedly simplified certain aspects of life while it did last.

With bells and telephones ringing all day long, and Juen padding about in a state of anxiety, she set about preparing her lecture on the Contemporary Novel. As there was liable, she reflected, to be a more than usually full house, she might use it as an occasion for saying some of the more outrageous things which she had for long wished to say on the subject, but which she felt would be lost on a small audience.

During the next days, there was further correspondence between her apartment and Little Island.

Little Island,
Thursday, 8 p.m.

My dearest Sylvia,

Your letter has just reached me. Of course I agree with everything you say. You make my proposition sound too much like a legal writ, my dear. I only meant it as a casual understanding between the two of us, such as we have had before so often on so many different matters. Nothing must stand between us. Nevertheless, I don't want to stand between you and whatever you may wish to do. Ours is not an ordinary marriage. Most wives are dependent on their husbands, and things work themselves out on that basis. I am not much of a leader and protector to you, I am afraid. You can do without me. We both have to face that reality squarely.

By all means, let us meet and talk things over. My movements at the moment are rather uncertain, however, and I am not sure what time would be convenient to you. I'm afraid I shall not be able to come into town for your lecture. I hope it goes well. I have to visit Saipaw and Tungpaw on that day, staying the night off the coast there.

I am very sorry you have been caused so much trouble by the reporters. I will give a statement to Winnington tomorrow morning first thing.

As ever, my dear,
Your loving
Richard.

12 The Heights,
30 September.

Richard my dear,

I received your letter safely. I quite understand it's difficult for you to fix a definite date for us to meet. Should I come over to the island on Sunday? I could come on the morning ferry and we could lunch together. I'm sure we can settle everything so simply if we could just have a really good talk.

John Winnington has just phoned to say he cannot release your statement. The Chief Secretary has said that it would be improper for his office to issue anything on the subject, either from you or from me. In this case I propose to send a written statement of my own to the four principal news agencies. This awful persecution by the Press continues. I have had no peace from them.

Please let me know if Sunday will be all right. You could phone me up tomorrow evening. I shall engage the telephone after 8 p.m., the time the reporters usually stop bothering me.

Please try and make this date, my dearest. ·

Your loving wife
Sylvia.

Little Island,
1 October.

My dearest Sylvia,

In great haste. Am just leaving for Great Island. Greatly regret I shall not be here tomorrow (Sunday). Would it not be better for us to meet in town?

Yours,
Richard.

12 The Heights,
2 October.

Dearest Richard,

Your note arrived just as I was about to take the ferry. I'm terribly sorry you couldn't manage to be there. But I agree it might be better to meet in town.

Could you spend the night here on Tuesday or Wednesday? Or else perhaps you could come in for lunch on Wednesday?

Your loving
Sylvia.

There was no reply to this last letter. Tuesday and Wednesday came and went.

Part Two

10

'I'M SURE it will all be quite all right,' said Henry Winterley, the British Council Representative, trying to sound as reassuring as he could, though actually of fainter heart himself than the novelist, who was going through some last-minute qualms about whether or not she should appear to give her scheduled lecture. He sighed as he put the phone down, and, opening a bottle on his desk, swallowed a pill, with half a tumblerful of water, to steady himself. The entire occasion filled him with foreboding and distaste. If only he had been more sensible, he would never have asked the woman to speak. What could she possibly have to say of interest on the Contemporary Novel?

The British Council lectures over the past winter season had not been well attended. A faithful fifteen to twenty adherents of British culture had attended the entire series, except when one of the talks clashed with a visit by Cardinal Spellman, when the numbers dropped to five. Apart from them, possibly ten casual listeners, and a few of the speakers' friends, turned up. Henry Winterley, who had been in the colony a year and was beginning to be confident in his judgments, decided that the next season's lectures must strike a note likely to appeal to greater numbers. Forsaking his high aesthetic principles, he would be obliged to descend a little closer to the mental level of his public. With a tremor of shame, he invited a young and attractive British business man, popular locally as an amateur broadcaster, to give the season's first lecture, on the subject of jazz bands—with demonstration records. It was a nauseating occasion, the lecture room being filled to capacity with bobbysoxers of the Chinese variety (pleasanter than the American, certainly, but most unsuitable as an audience for a British Council lecture). It did attract publicity, however. The local reporters turned up in force, there were flashlights, and good coverage in the papers next morning. The second lecture was more in keeping with what Henry Winterley considered about the limit to which the Council, and a highly cultured man like himself, should go in wooing the public: an excellent colour film of Angkor, taken by one of the professors at the university, and presented with a commentary and introduction.

How he had conceived the unfortunate idea of asking Sylvia Gracechurch to give the third lecture, he could no longer remember. Having read her book shortly after arriving in the colony, he had thought fit to explain to her over the telephone, when extending the invitation, that the lectures were intended to be serious studies of their subject. To his surprise, she suggested speaking on the Contemporary Novel. At the time, Henry Winterley was worried lest the subject be too serious. Letting his pill take effect, he smiled wanly to himself at his foolishness. As things stood at present, it probably wouldn't matter if she were to talk about combine harvesters: the effect on the public would be the same.

From the morning when the announcement of her lecture appeared in the papers, there had been well over a hundred telephone calls from members of the public, asking if they could reserve seats, and how much reservations cost. Reserved seats! At a British Council lecture! It made Henry Winterley feel faintly sick. It showed, too, the type of people who might be expected to attend: people with no culture, whose only interest was in vulgar pretences at literature, or else in sensational sex stories; people who knew nothing about the British Council and what it stood for, and who had never been near it in all the years it had been established in the colony. He was particularly upset by the excitement among his own Chinese staff, whom he had hitherto regarded as such charming and sensitive young boys and girls (some of them were married with kids, but they *looked* like boys and girls, specially to one like Henry Winterley, who was an authority on Arabs). The staff were quite beside themselves, running in now and again to say which Chinese grandee or his lady had just telephoned—names that meant nothing to the Representative, who had not yet learnt how to remember Chinese names. Finally, he went into the outer office, and said petulantly:

'Will you all stop bothering me about this lecture tonight! Please behave like grown-ups. This is a very ordinary lecture, by a

96

very ordinary writer, who *happens to have had* a great success, which is entirely transitory and almost completely undeserved. She is a woman of no importance,' he continued, as one or two of the young people reading magazines in the reading-room outside looked up to see who was speaking—and the sight dried him up. 'The Council has to be absolutely impartial,' he said in a quieter, more moderate, tone. 'We have to allow the lighter and more lowbrow elements of culture to have their say. The fact that they attract the mob should not make anyone lose their sense of perspective. Miss Sylvia Gracechurch has no place in world literature.'

With this he went back into his little office, leaving his engaging, smart, and anxious-to-please Chinese staff fixed in their places like wax statues. As he regained his seat, the telephone rang.

'Mr. Winterley? This is White, Central Police Station. I shall be sending a few constables down to keep the way clear for people attending the lecture this evening. Just a minor precaution. We don't expect an incident, or anything like that.' He laughed at his own humorousness. 'But when celebrities appear, you know . . .'

Henry Winterley issued sibilant nothings of acquiescence. Putting the instrument down, he leant back in his chair and covered his face with his hands. It was all utterly ghastly. Police at the door! The whole thing was like the time when that French film actress crossed the street, and all the traffic was held up by the hundreds of people watching her. Police constables! Holding back people from crowding the entrance to the one place above all where everyone was welcome, free and for nothing, if they only wished to *learn*—instead of gaping vapidly at some romantic figure of their low imaginations. He could do no work all the afternoon, these thoughts occupying each of his attempts to study a file or compose an essay for the next issue of the Council magazine.

After making such a silly scene in front of his staff, he was unwilling to go again into the outer office.

Only after five o'clock, the clerical closing time, did he venture out. The staff always left punctually.

To his surprise the polite, cheerful faces of the staff greeted him in the outer office. He gave them a jaundiced look.

'We're all staying on for the lecture,' said Eldon Wong, the chief assistant. 'I could take some more letters in the meantime, if you have any to send, sir.'

'I've nothing, thank you,' Henry Winterley answered, walking out into the less congested air of the reading-room.

The reading-room gave on to the lecture-room, where chairs had already been set out in readiness for later. Once more to his surprise, as he neared the lecture-room, he heard a number of voices and the sound of feet moving here and there. Glancing in, he found the back eight or nine rows already filled with people. He was astounded. Such a thing had never happened before.

A combination of things had achieved this peculiar travesty of what he had intended, he continued to himself, conducting a post-mortem in advance of the demise. Firstly, there was the book itself—what was its disgusting title? Secondly, there was the remark by that film producer whose name he could no longer remember, who had stated in the local Press that it was a book that would make a great film. Thirdly, there was that sexy actress—the French one—who had stated it was her ambition to play the lead in the book. Finally, there was this latest rumour of an estrangement between the writer and her husband, who must surely have been the most talked-of couple the colony had ever known.

It was strange that Sylvia Gracechurch had had qualms about lecturing because she feared—it was evident from the way she put it over the phone—a hostile reception. It even changed his senti-ment to a momentary sympathy with her. It was an ordeal for her this evening. Scandalous rumours were circulating everywhere. The British community, consisting of (but why did it always seem to be the case in communities abroad?) too many thwarted, un-satisfied women, married and unmarried alike, was surpassing itself in pouring filth on the names of the District Officer and his famous wife. Fantastic stories were being told, dug out of the recesses of goodness knows whose perverted brain. It was cer-tainly a moment of crisis in the writer's life.

By the next time he returned to the lecture-room the crowd had increased considerably; all the seats had been taken, and there were lines of people standing round the edge of the room. The fans were whirring away at top speed, but the heat was unbearable. In the far doorway, more people were still pushing their way diligently in. Things were heading nicely for confusion.

It was the audience itself, however, that surprised him. The sober devotees of the Council's good works were nowhere to be seen. Confident of finding places, perhaps, they had not yet turned

98

up. Instead, a brilliant array of people, mostly Chinese, but with a respectable flavouring of Westerners, and one or two prominent Indians and local Portuguese, had filled the room. Their clothes alone indicated that they included many who must be from the colony's more expensive social circles. As theirs were pastures Henry Winterley did not wander in, he did not know many of them, although he recognized two of the Chinese members of the Legislative Council, with their wives. In the way that so many of the audience were signalling to each other and conversing *à haute voix* this way and that, the group reminded him of the one former occasion when he had seen the colony's top flight gathered together—at the Government House garden party on the Queen's birthday.

In the crowded doorway, a European much taller than the rest was steadily forcing his way in. Wearing a suit, and looking hot and slightly dishevelled after the ordeal of entering, he walked straight down the centre aisle towards Henry Winterley's office. The Representative recognized him as a police officer in plain clothes.

'I don't think your premises are going to be able to hold them all, Mr. Winterley,' he said, when they stood in the quieter reading-room. He was an educated man, with a cultured accent, and must have been of fairly high rank. 'They're still arriving in quite large numbers, and the stairways are completely blocked.'

'What? In spite of your constables?' parried the Representative, who felt he had to get his own back on somebody.

'They're only standing by. Have you a microphone and a relaying system? In that case we could settle the surplus outside in the passages and relay the talk to them.'

'British Council lecturers never use microphones,' the Representative said with a kindly smile, observing that, however educated, the officer was ignorant of certain niceties.

'Then I think there's only one thing we can do. If it's not in use—and I don't think it will be at this hour—I suggest we move the whole audience into the Public Relations Office censoring theatre, and hold the lecture there. You won't have to turn nearly so many away, and it's safer from the point of view of fire escapes. This is a large crowd, and there's a lot of brass in it. I don't want anything to happen.'

Henry Winterley, who was by now somewhat battered, was nearly prepared to do exactly what he was told without a quibble.

At the mention of his enemy, the Public Relations Officer, however, he stiffened. That man had always ridiculed the British Council, giving it the minimum co-operation, sometimes even thwarting it entirely. He seemed to think he was the only person entitled to speak to the public, or know anything about the public. On one occasion, he had actually presumed to give orders to the Council to withdraw certain posters from an exhibition, on the grounds of political unsuitability. Henry Winterley had appealed to the Chief Secretary, who had of course upheld his P.R.O., and the posters had had to be taken down. The Representative had sent a very stern report to his headquarters in London, from which there had been no acknowledgment.

It had consistently irked him that the two institutions should be situated next to each other, on the same low floor of the massive ten-storey building that gave them their address. They used the same lift, too. On occasions when Henry Winterley was accidentally late, he sometimes had the misfortune to ascend in company with the redoubtable Mr. Winnington. To avoid him was one of the reasons for Winterley's scrupulous punctuality. The Public Relations Officer was always late.

And now, as if confirming the inadequacy of the Council, there was not even enough room to accommodate people coming to this unimportant little talk. They had to turn for assistance to *that* man!

'There's a light on in Mr. Winnington's office. I think if you put a call through now, you'd catch him.'

The Representative was trapped. When the officer mentioned fire escapes, he knew he would have to give in. It was like those rules of the Lord Chamberlain printed at the bottom of London theatre programmes—something one had never read and would never understand, yet something statutory and absolute. When a police officer talked about fire escapes in relation to an audience, that was it.

Nevertheless, he could not—no, he could *not!*—be the one who had to crawl on his hands and knees to the Public Relations Officer! He signalled to his assistant, Eldon Wong, to do the job.

'But I don't think I can,' said Eldon, a master of the protocol involved in dealing with the Government. 'A head of department, sir! I don't think it would be quite proper.'

Speechless with emotion, Henry Winterley turned his back on

100

him and marched to his office. Biting his lower lip so hard it nearly bled, and feeling cold all over, despite the heat of the evening, he dialled the number he knew so well. Mr. Winnington had already left for home. Another attempt. The familiar voice, infuriatingly self-confident. Henry Winterley bungled his request, putting it all back to front. At the other end there was a swell of magnanimity.

'I'll put a call through, old boy, right away, telling them to open the theatre. Perhaps I'd better come down myself.'

'I hardly think that will be necessary. Please don't disturb yourself.'

'It'll be a pleasure. I'd like to hear what that sexy bag's got to say. We've had quite a dose of her these past few days.'

In a faltering voice, referring apologetically to the unexpected popularity of the lecture, Henry Winterley made his announcement. With groans, laughter, and much chatter, the audience rose and headed itself by degrees away through the far doors, where the police officer stood as an usher, directing everyone where to go. The Council staff thus scored a strategic advantage, trotting out through the rear entrance of the office, across an iron fire escape, and into the back entrance of the Public Relations Office. By the time the first of the grandees were being admitted to the little theatre, the Council boys and girls were seated, modestly, half-way up the gently rising block of stalls. While the seats filled up, the air-conditioning plant began to operate, the gentle coloured lights, concealed in the oval white roof, were switched on, and the scene assumed a general aspect of comfort and elegance. A button was pressed in the operators' room at the rear, causing the screen to drop out of sight, revealing a small shell of a stage, capable of accommodating a six-piece band. A table and chair, a carafe of water and a glass, were rapidly provided by the competent stage management. In a few minutes the hall was full, the aisles jammed with men and women standing, mopping their brows and fanning themselves while the air-conditioning gradually took effect.

Henry Winterley, standing between the stalls and the stage, could have sobbed aloud as he looked about him. The conditions he had always dreamed of! The ideal setting for his British Council activities! And here it all was, on a plate, presented to him by his smiling, confident enemy, for an occasion unworthy to be headed by the Council's name!

Eldon Wong hurried in from the fire-escape entrance.

'A telephone call from Miss Gracechurch, sir! She's on her way!'

Oh, what protocol! the Representative thought, with a shudder. The fellow even remembered not to call her Mrs. Fairburn! He hurried out with his assistant, dashed round through the now empty Council lecture-room, and started easing his way gently along the corridors, where a fair number of hopefuls were still waiting for word whether more could be accommodated in the theatre. At the entrance to the lifts, he was halted by a pitiful sight. Serried together like oysters, just beside the lift doors, were the faithful—abject, disillusioned, leaderless, unable to advance, sullenly determined not to retreat. Henry Winterley was deeply moved. He looked at them for a loving, hasty moment, before one of the lift doors opened, going down. He knew them all so well. The girls with their straight black hair and faces like pudding basins, the young men with close-cropped hair and round glasses, all of them looking like voracious paper-devouring insects, but!— the real beneficiaries of British culture!

'Wait there! I will do something!' he said, plunging into the lift. Indeed, he thought, as the lift's rapidity made his stomach rise, they did not look as though they would move. Like himself, they were mentally paralysed by what was happening.

At the street entrance, in the soft, evening sunshine, he had a few breaths of fresher, petrol-fumed air, amid the confusion of trams, buses, and aggressively driven cars, before the taxi bearing the novelist came to a halt opposite the wrong entrance further up the street. Darting a way through the ambling pedestrians, he almost collided with her, so great was his anxiety. She was wearing a full-skirted black evening dress, ornamented only by a diamond clasp between her breasts and a spray of yellow orchids near her left shoulder. With her was Mrs. Edwin Lau, cool and gracious.

Preoccupied with desperate plans for the accommodation of the faithful, he was more or less incoherent in his greeting of the lecturer.

'It is not a bit as I expected!' he sighed, wiping away big drops of perspiration from his forehead.

'Is anything wrong?' she asked, with calm wariness.

'I hope not! Oh, I hope not! But there's such a crowd! Such a crowd. And none of the regulars can get in.' This was in the lift. As his stomach sank and the lift boy said 'Third floor!' (meaning the Second, what a confusing place!), he realized what to do. 'Do

102

you mind if people sit behind you while you speak, Mrs. Fairburn?' he asked.

'No, I suppose not,' she said, puzzled and amused.

'Get a chair, each of you!' he ordered, bundling out of the lift in front of the ladies. 'Round the back way! Over the fire escape! Eldon Wong will help you. Come along! Each of you take their own chair! There are none inside.' He hurried into the Council premises, again preceding the ladies, while the oysters timorously separated into a string of intellectual pearls, picking up chairs (their usual chairs, where they customarily sat on less disturbed evenings, when the tide was not so high), and followed the Representative and the two ladies round the exterior iron stairways to the theatre.

'Put them up there, Eldon!' the harassed Representative ordered.

And thus it was. Each of the faithful mounted the stage, placing their chairs round the edge of the shell, behind the speaker's chair and table, and sat down. The shell, in fact, was the perfect size, exactly accommodating all fifteen of them. Their installation caused a hush of expectancy in the buoyant audience, followed by a laugh as everybody realized that the fifteen were not what their appearance had suggested—a choir.

As the last pudding-face settled herself devotedly down, Henry Winterley sighed again, looking up at them with pride— and with sadness, too, to think that even they, the intelligent ones, could be so easily misled by momentary success.

They did not look particularly misled, however. They stared at the audience. The audience stared at them. Intellect versus society; but with intellect in the more honourable position, seated round the stage like a group of minor deities in a neon temple.

Meanwhile, the speaker had been spotted outside on the fire escape, and a ripple of applause started. The Representative hastened outside, begging his lecturer to stand a little further back, where she could not be seen, just as the obese Mr. Winnington, manager of the showplace, lurched himself along the stairway. After no more than a brief glance at the group outside his theatre, he signalled for a private word with the Representative.

'Are you introducing her, Henry?'

'Yes. I shall have to. It's my duty.'

'Well, for God's sake, boy, she's in evening dress. Aren't you going to put even a tie on?'

In fact, he had forgotten all about his own appearance! If only Winnington had had the slightest sensibility he would have realized what a terrible time he had been going through. Instead, he understood nothing, except how to get the better of him in cheap ways, disguised under a veneer of sophisticated *savoir vivre*. Without a word, he hurried back to his office, and opened the cupboard in which, for emergencies just such as this, he kept a spare coat and tie. The coat smelt musty, and the gold silk in the tie had all been eaten out by some small creature with a liking for gold—a sort of connoisseur. He was adjusting the wretched thing round his damp shirt-collar when the telephone rang. Merciful heavens, what now? He picked up the receiver brusquely.

'Yes?' he said, vibrating with aggression.

A quiet Chinese voice at the other end.

'Mr. Winterley?'

'Speaking!'—again with aggression.

'This is Government House, sir. His Excellency will be attending the lecture at the British Council this evening. He will be arriving in—in four minutes from now.'

They used to say in the Chinese classics that, when the Emperor spoke, great officers trembled. Only the telephonist at Government House made Henry Winterley tremble, from the instant the terrible words came over, with their quiet assurance and exactitude. His Excellency would arrive in four minutes! Not five; not three. He would arrive, ye gods, in four minutes! The Representative, motionless, his heart fluttering, his hand on his coat, his mind having forgotten why he should require a coat, awoke with a sudden, horrified start. Dragging on his coat, he rushed out through the outer office, through the reading-room, into the empty lecture-room, half-way down which he stopped dead in his rapid pace. There was nowhere in the theatre for His Excellency to sit! Turning round, he hastened back on his tracks with even greater urgency, out on to the fire escape once more.

'The Acting Governor is coming!' he said hoarsely. He was losing his voice in the agitation of it all. 'Eldon! Clear some chairs in the front row!'

'But, sir! How can I? They're all taken.'

'I don't care, I don't care!' the desperate Representative whispered. 'Get the two best seats emptied. Do it how you like!'

'Leave it to me,' said the Public Relations Officer, with the calm of obesity, striding into the theatre. He bent down to speak to a Chinese husband and wife in the front row. What he said could not be heard, but they suddenly broke into lavish smiles, rose, and came to stand at the side of the theatre. Having escorted them thence, Mr. Winnington stood guard over the empty seats, glaring, like the fifteen minor deities, in defiance of society. From outside, Eldon Wong handed in two collapsible chairs for the couple who had vacated theirs.

'Does the Acting Governor often attend these lectures?' Sylvia Gracechurch asked the Representative.

'He's never been near us before!' he replied, with a shrug of the shoulders that unintentionally gave the writer the impression that he could not understand why there should be this interest now. Having again bungled things, this time even with his lecturer (who, he noticed, had become pale and nervous), he said no more, but hurried down for the second time through the vaguely moving groups of people in the corridors, down in the lift, and out to the street entrance.

He was only just in time. A roar of escort motor-cycles, the appearance of policemen on the streets from various directions in which they had till then been unnoticed, cars and buses veering to leave one side of the street clear, pedestrians stopping with blank faces, and the Governor's long, black limousine, flying his personal standard on the bonnet, came slowly to a halt exactly in the centre of the main entrance, exactly four minutes after the premonitory telephone call.

Henry Winterley was in such a paroxysm of nerves that he was momentarily rooted to the spot. Instead of opening the door of the car, he watched, as if hypnotized, while the uniformed driver quickly performed this office. The Acting Governor, wearing a tropical lounge suit, stepped out on to the empty pavement, followed by his A.D.C. and, from the front seat beside the driver, a plain-clothes Chinese bodyguard. Feeling alone and insecure, the Representative moved out to meet him in the unaccustomed emptiness created by the constables keeping back passers-by on both sides.

His Excellency was gracious, in the faintly literary, faintly amused, way which usually made others nervous of him. At the lift doors the high-ranking police officer was waiting—Henry Winterley, unaccustomed to police escorts and security precautions, was baffled by the way the officer and his men came and went, inconspicuous, yet always contriving to be just where they were wanted, as if by some prescience they knew it would all turn out in exactly this way.

They reached the theatre by the back entrance. When he saw the group standing outside on the iron landing, the Acting Governor gave a humorous smile. With a word of encouragement to the speaker, he walked into the theatre, preceded by the Representative. At once he was recognized. There was a thumping of bucket seats from various places as people rose to their feet. Others looked up and about them. The sound of upturning seats increased until the entire audience was standing.

'We've kept two for you, sir,' John Winnington said, inviting the Acting Governor to be seated.

'Thank you, Winnington. This is a nice theatre you've got. I see now where all the Government's money goes.'

The Public Relations Officer gave a facetious grin into the wads of fat round his mouth and neck, and for a second Henry Winterley was pleased. Winnington had been choked off; the British Council was one up. Glancing at the clock above the operators' room, he saw that it was exactly 6.30, the scheduled time for the lecture. The realization shook him. If anyone had told him it was 9 p.m. he would not have been surprised. With heavy heart he perceived that it was now time for him to reap the fruit of his foolishness.

Stepping to the doorway, he signalled to the speaker.

'Shall we . . .?' he said wanly, extending a clammy hand to hers, which was covered in a long, white sleeve-glove. He led her into the auditorium. A long thudding of applause covered their movement, as he handed her up the narrow steps to the stage, hastily followed her, and held the chair for her to sit on, with her back to the faithful. The crudity of the demonstration made him want to faint with shame. Even the faithful were applauding in a most uncritical manner, quite unworthy of them.

Somehow, order—a sense of propriety—had to be imposed. He came to the edge of the stage to address the gathering.

'In this, the third lecture of the current British Council series, we are presenting someone who needs no introduction. Miss Sylvia Gracechurch is, in fact, the colony's most famous name in the literary world.' ('To thine own self be true!' his heart whispered to him as he heard the dry tones of his unlikeable voice—not even he liked it—bounce deadpan off the mass of

106

heads lining the back wall.) So ashamed was he of even this drab compliment, that he made another of his classic bungles by beginning the next sentence, 'Whatever one's personal view of her writing may be . . .', whereupon sweat burst out all over his forehead, and what last vestiges of colour remained in his face vanished. He stammered another word or two until he reached '. . . and I'm sure we all agree, no one begrudges anyone a great success.' There were signs of restlessness in the audience. Desperately setting a smile on his lips, he raised his voice, already pitching itself high due to his nervousness, and concluded: 'So, now I've said enough. And I call upon——'

He never said the rest. As he turned back towards the speaker, and she rose, the applause broke out again, drowning his voice. He sank back into his chair on the left of the carafe of water.

The clapping stopped. A musical voice filled the silence:

'Your Excellency, ladies and gentlemen . . .'

The Representative could have covered his face in his anguish! She had reminded him that, when speaking, he himself had omitted the unimportant but gracious handle to his words. He had found the entire experience too shattering for niceties to be remembered. Dropping his eyes away from the sight of anything that could remind him of the dreadful experience he was going through, he fixed his gaze on his own shoes, solid, black, well-known, presentably polished, the one personal certainty visible to him in the midst of the tidal wave he had created. And from his shoes, his mind travelled to assuring thoughts about the Council's future programme of lectures: the set of lithographs, with tape recordings and a spoken commentary, illustrating Brazilian folk music; the White Russian lady he had discovered who was prepared to give three talks on Andalusian dancing; his own lecture on the Elizabethan madrigal; and his wife's talk on the early works of Benjamin Britten. It was a haven of relief even to contemplate such splendid, sober subjects, after the undignified hurly-burly of this evening.

He was disturbed in his reverie by the burst of a solid roll of laughter from the audience. He looked up at the speaker, having himself missed the joke, and laughed a little in imitation of the rest. She was holding in her left hand a tiny pocket-book, in which she had her notes, and as he watched her turn over one of its little pages he understood why she wore gloves. The hard

107

points of the gloves' fingers flicked over the pages unerringly, while protecting what must have been a damp hand within from moistening the pages and causing them to stick.

Another interruption in his reverie came when he became aware, to his horror, that there was silence. He very nearly leapt up to propose the vote of thanks, thinking that she had finished without his noticing. But then a rumble of humour rose from the audience, growing steadily into one of those slow laughs of appreciation of a subtle point.

'Yes, you get what I mean,' she said. This released a great wave of laughter.

Henry Winterley covered his mouth with one hand, so that his true expression could not be seen. He groaned inwardly as he heard her professional patter with the audience. Like Saturday night at the Palladium, he thought, in an abysm of distaste.

The agonizing minutes passed. What she talked about he had no idea. He was now entirely absorbed in the problem of how he was going to explain away this dreadful vulgarity to his superiors in London. That His Excellency had been present would at first sight appear to be a useful point, indicating to the perceptive reader of his report the dismal intellectual level of the colony. On the other hand, as it was the only time the Queen's representative had ever attended a British Council lecture, headquarters might well ask why he could not have thought of something more appropriate in the way of lecturer and subject.

A silence. Prolonged applause. The novelist sat down. Henry Winterley was not conscious of anything in particular—even though he made his usual statement about the speaker having kindly consented to answer questions—until the largest and most stolid of the pudding basins behind the speaker's chair piped out in a menacing contralto:

'Would you say, Miss Gracechurch, that love was no longer a valid basis for a novel?'

He shuddered. They had all fallen for it, every one of them! It was the evening dress, the orchids, the gloves, the musical voice, the utterly false stage management of the whole thing, that held them as if spellbound. Never, never again must he make this mistake of pandering to public taste! What a catastrophe this evening had been to the prestige of the British Council!

A moment later they were down in the stalls again, with the police officer once more advising the Acting Governor to leave by the fire-escape. The outcome was that a small group collected in the deserted British Council lecture-room, chatting off the beat prior to dispersing to their homes. The A.D.C. came to Henry Winterley's side.

'H.E. would like to know if you have a few free minutes now to come up for a drink at Government House.'

'Yes, of course. I should be delighted,' he said, with a nervous smile.

'Good. D'you require transport?'

'I can take a taxi.'

'No, don't do that. Come with us.'

Henry Winterley's personality opened like a blossoming flower in the sunlight of the A.D.C.'s affability. The only time he had ever been invited to Government House was for the monstrous garden party on the Queen's birthday, an invitation which, he considered, meant next to nothing. With a sudden personal effulgence he knew this informal invitation to drinks could be the beginning of a new phase for him in his stay in the colony as well as of a new social outlook that would raise him at one stroke to the same level as his enemy, the Public Relations Officer, and possibly higher, in that he had a more charming manner than his enemy.

Discreetly, the A.D.C. circulated among the group, speaking to certain selected ones. His Excellency spoke a final word to one or two—'You'll be following us,' he said to Henry Winterley, who nearly bowed in his anxiety to demonstrate his thanks—and left with Sylvia Gracechurch, Mrs. Edwin Lau, the A.D.C., and the socially invisible bodyguard.

'Are you coming up to Government House?' the Representative asked the Public Relations Officer, with studied casualness, his voice faltering slightly.

'No, old man. But H.E. knows. I'm working on a telegram he's got to send tomorrow morning.'

Henry Winterley's cold frustration returned. How could this sluggish creature always be ahead of him?

By the time he reached the street, only two of those in the party going to Government House remained: himself and Willie Rogers, the university lecturer. Each offered the other the door of the long, black limousine waiting for them. Somehow the problem was solved and the car drove off, with the two men sitting far apart in the rear seat—Henry Winterley silent, Willie Rogers meandering on about the lecture, about how awful Mrs. So-and-so looked, and that the Public Relations Officer would be more effective if he had had some breeding. The car began to mount the hill above the commercial centre of the city, with its huge, closed banks and offices, and headed into the pleasant leafy roads crossing the hillside public gardens, in the midst of which, surrounded by yet another garden of its own, stood Government House. At the ornamental gates a policeman came to attention as the Crown car passed unhesitatingly in. A sense of elation filled Henry Winterley. This ease, this absolute surety of movement, the majestic swing of power, that manifested itself in these small things—the cars, the drivers, the saluting respect, the undeterred advance into the greatest house in the colony—made him wake to the fulfilment of an ambition. Being a good-living family man, he wished his wife could see him now. Then he crossed that out mentally, and wrote in smaller letters that he wished his wife could be with him to enjoy all this. Yes, that was better.

Preceded by a servant, they entered the white marble hall, passed between the huge oil-paintings of King Edward VII and Queen Alexandra (was there any symbolism in their still being there, in the place of honour?), and walked straight through the house to the garden terrace facing the enchanted lights of the harbour. Standard lamps cast a gold glow over the white-cushioned easy-chairs, the white pillars, the pale granite floor and walls. The Acting Governor, already seated, invited them to join him. Cigarettes from silver boxes, drinks served in fine cut-glass, freshly baked cocktail nuts, Sylvia Gracechurch looking extremely lovely in the delicate light, and Mrs. Edwin Lau too—contrasted loveliness, Oriental and Occidental—the sparkle of a diamond ring, a searchlight raying past in a sweep from a warship far below, dance music from the roof garden of a hotel on a level a little lower than the garden, the silent movement of the smart Chinese servants in their white uniforms with cuffs and collars of Chinese imperial gold, so graceful an allusion to the historic fact that the area had on various occasions been claimed by past dynasties to be part of China—and whisky. . . . Henry Winterley felt his pores open, as an anemone, sensing danger past, expands into its natural flowery state. Admittedly, he did not, like the upstart Rogers, sink relaxedly into his chair. He remained decently upright, paying attention to His Excellency's words. He felt like sitting upright. He was springingly, meteorically, alive. He could have danced across the granite and skipped round the aged magnolia tree that rose near the pillars, as if it were a close friend of the house.

'Interesting, highly amusing, and well delivered.'

Such was His Excellency's verdict.

'The public's response was certainly most gratifying,' the Representative said gaily, almost with a twitter.

'Naturally, it would be,' Willie Rogers commented, with a nuance of acerbity.

Sir Frederick paid no attention to him.

'This colony,' he said, gazing out at the small garlands of light that represented ships on the water, 'can be counted on for good taste. It has an almost infallible sense of what is first-rate. Most unusual, I should say, in my experience of colonies.'

His grin received a response of pleasant laughter. Henry Winterley laughed, of course, with the others; but he was not quite happy to think that the administration of the colony should have been entrusted to anyone—even temporarily—whose intellectual conceptions might be regarded as frivolous.

'I would venture to say, sir,' he said, 'that the colony has a sense of what has popular appeal—meaning no disrespect to our charming speaker tonight.'

The Acting Governor looked upwards at the capitals of the pillars.

'Would you, Winterley? Would you?'—then down at him—'When you've been here a little longer, I think you'll understand what I mean.'

The Representative took it without a word of dissent. As the Governor's gaze travelled down and rooted itself in him for the delivery of this dictum, Henry Winterley felt the strange impact of power itself, the magnetic force husbanded by those gifted and experienced in giving commands. It was as if the mundane words came from the lips of some ultimate oracle, to question the truth of which would be sacrilege. This was the final word, beyond which was no other. He tried to adjust his standards to fit it. He must be obedient, in his thinking, to those who really understood the colony and its culture. After all, his values were always changing, adapting themselves to new stimuli. Some of his values were possibly out of date. That this present adaptation should arise from the dictum of His Excellency gave it unusual

111

moment, comforting Henry Winterley with a sense of its absoluteness, a sense that gave him sufficient moral courage to withstand the criticism of those proud and clever people with whom he had passed his school and college days, who never did anything ordinary, never liked anything popular, never produced anything easily intelligible. They haunted him, those people, those friends of his on whose distinguished level he must always try to remain, even in this far-away colony, lest their words, poisoned with the self-accusation of their misjudgment in having drawn him up into their circle, reach him even here, bringing the terrible reminder of social inferiority.

The A.D.C. presented himself from within the house.

'Mr. Edwin Lau has called for Mrs. Lau, sir.'

Sir Frederick's eyes twinkled.

'We're in the doghouse, I see. Ask him to come in.'

The sleek Legislative Councillor, looking fifteen years younger than his age, came on to the terrace.

'Good evening, Your Excellency,' he said heartily. 'I'm coming to inquire about delivery charges on my wife.'

The Acting Governor looked at him.

'C.i.f. or f.o.b.?'

Henry Winterley noticed how, with Chinese he knew well, His Excellency's manner became more friendly, more socially alert, than it did with Europeans. There was general laughter as more drinks were served.

'In any case,' the Acting Governor continued, 'I fear you're going to lose her soon for far longer.'

'Really?' Edwin Lau queried. 'What's she up to?'

'It's Sylvia Gracechurch's influence, I suspect. They've just been telling me they intend to visit the Buddhist monasteries in the mountains of Great Island. Any comment?'

'They can have 'em,' pronounced the Legislative Councillor. 'Maybe you two can climb up there, but if anyone expects me to, they're mistaken.'

'I said monastery, Edwin, not nunnery.'

'I heard you, sir. But those monks—nothing to be afraid of. They're interested in other things.'

Henry Winterley found himself being pleased to note that this healthily Windsor Forest conversation had reduced Willie Rogers to silent disinterest. An anaemic man, the Representative summed him up. He himself enjoyed the Governor's conviviality.

'H.E., we must go home,' Mrs. Lau said, putting an exquisite pale ivory hand on his, with an intimacy everyone was intended to notice.

'Of course, Frances,' he said, rising from his seat like a man of twenty. 'Enjoy yourself with the monks!'

Amid a general exchange of goodbyes, the party became dismembered, the others concluding from the Laus' departure that it was their time also to leave. Henry Winterley, whose mother had taught him never to outstay his welcome, drained his whisky and stood humbly at the end of the row that gracefully formed to bid the Acting Governor good night.

But His Excellency was in a happy mood, escorting his guests through the house to the canopied entrance, where a series of cars waited to take everyone home. The Representative's effulgence of personality could not have been more complete. He stepped with angelic nimbleness beside His Excellency; he all but pirouetted with gaiety of heart. People went off, some in their own cars, some in Crown cars—after the whisky and glory, he wasn't worrying much. There came a sudden handshake, a sensation of the blue, hard, cynically humorous, utterly commanding eyes fixed upon him—then the darkness of a large car, the windows shut—alone—movement—a forcing back into a too-well-upholstered seat. In the change of atmosphere he shook himself into his real consciousness again. This—all this— all that his wife should have seen (he meant, should have shared with him), was the outcome of the most dreadfully low-class entertainment he had ever organized in his life.

Stunned by the reflexion, he let his head fall back on a cushion as the car rounded the circular drive. It had been a hideous experience, a memorable evening, a humiliation which he must keep utterly from his friends, a moment of personal glory he could give fifty letters to recounting, a disaster, a triumph, a catastrophe, an exaltation; he would never live it down, he would never forget it. What a horrifying, maddening, *disconcerting* experience he had had! No one would ever understand.

He glanced lovingly back at the gentle glow of lights surrounding the portico of the house. The last car was still waiting, and, on the steps, His Excellency—blessed be his name!—and the novelist. . . . Henry Winterley groaned as the car passed between the sentries at the gate. That such a fiasco should bring him to such grandeur! What, oh what! were the Council going to say?

113

The car swung out into darkness.

And it was strange, was it not? he reflected. Why should they talk so long, those two, on the steps?

II

'STAY to dinner,' he said, looking down in her eyes intently. Inwardly, she shivered.

'Why not?' she said.

They walked slowly back into the house.

'How d'you like my new acquisitions?' he asked, indicating two monstrous Chinese decorated jars standing at floor level on either side of the arched doorway to the terrace, rather as if they graced the entrance to an ostentatious tomb.

'It's no use asking me, Freddie. I don't know anything about things as large as that.'

'I bought them for the other house, really. They don't look right here.'

'Is there any news of the Governor?'

'Yes. He's having another operation next week in London. I don't expect he'll be back for quite a considerable time.'

Two chairs remained on the terrace, the rest having been withdrawn inside.

'What you drink, madam?'

It was the gentle, understanding Chiu, the special one.

'Brandy, please, Chiu.'

He hastened silently away.

'I take it everything's all right between you two,' Freddie asked, as he prepared to light a pipe.

'Not exactly,' she replied, settling down.

'Really?' he said, looking up at her without emotion. 'I'm sorry to hear that.' (He didn't look it, Sylvia thought.) 'What's happened?'

'It may sound odd, but I don't know. Freddie, may I have a cigarette?'

'Of course.' He looked angrily into the house. When he turned his head there was a rapid movement among a group of servants

114

standing about in the dining-room. One of them hurried out with a cigarette box, and lit Sylvia's cigarette for her. 'What's it all about?'

'Oh—a road,' she replied, exhaling smoke as if it were a comment on her remark.

'A road?'

'Yes. He wants to be alone, so as to concentrate all his energy and attention on this road—the one that was your idea originally.'

'It was not my idea. It's common sense. Why is Richard so bothered about it?'

'I don't know, Freddie. Please don't press me to say anything that's not fair to him. I just don't know.'

He lit his pipe, slowly, making a virtue of it.

'Can you remember which month it is when that magnolia flowers?' he asked, nodding at the dark tree.

'I think it's in May. You must have just missed it.'

'Pity. Beautiful things.'

Brandy and magnolia, she thought, as she put her glass to her lips. A strange mixture.

'Cheers, Freddie.'

'Cheers, my dear. I think when people reach that degree of concentration on their work it's time they were posted to another department.'

'Oh, no!' she said quickly. 'Please don't do that.'

'It would be better for him, and for you, too.'

'No. It would be worse—far worse. He would know I'd seen you, and would imagine I had asked for him to be moved.'

'He'll go where he's told,' he reminded her sternly.

She looked at the sparkle of her glass.

'Do you really want to help, Freddie?'

'Help you, yes.'

'Then leave Richard where he is. He's got to get through this patch somehow. This road is——'

'—the fulfilment of his personality,' he concluded mockingly.

'But just that, Freddie, just that,' she said vexedly, glancing out at the harbour lights.

'Utter nonsense! Nothing in government leads to a personal achievement. If that's what he's after, he shouldn't be a government servant. In government you throw your ideas into the organism. They get turned round and round inside it. Usually

115

they never come out again. They're never used. And where they are used, they come out in a form quite different from your first idea, something you hardly recognize, inasmuch as they are no longer yours. They have become embodied, with a whole mass of other ideas, in a government policy or line of action. At no time in my service have I been able to say, of anything: This was my idea; this was done by me. My best ideas have invariably been ruined by other people—at least, that used to be my opinion when I was a District Officer,' he punctuated with a merry twinkle, '—and when I was sufficiently senior to start ordering things to be done, the actual doing of them was providentially entrusted to subordinates and technicians. Nothing was mine.'

'It's not quite the same with Richard,' she said, blowing smoke in the direction of the ships.

'It is exactly the same, and the sooner he knows it the better.'

'No. It's not the same, Freddie. You have to take me into consideration.'

He stood up, and walked down a few of the steps to the garden.

'But I understand you published an announcement saying there was no truth in the rumours.'

'I did. Frances Lau made me laugh about that. She said it was only after Edwin heard about my statement that he would allow her to come to the lecture.'

'Yes. That was why I came, too,' he replied, adding severely: 'Why wasn't Richard there?'

For the first time in her life she was frightened of him. The lights from the terrace threw his austere blue eyes into sharper prominence than usual. There was a hardness round the mouth she had never noticed before. The thick, silver hair looked wild and rough. In reality she had only met him socially, on occasions when, if he discussed his work at all, he did so in a detached, often humorous, way. This was the first time she had seen him concentrating seriously on a matter connected with work. It made her feel suddenly small and insecure. She saw the peculiar personal detachment of one all his life accustomed to ordering and organizing large numbers of men, and how in this he was actuated by nothing except considerations of how to achieve as speedily and efficiently as possible the object in view. Her thoughts rushing too far—though, as she said to herself, in the same direction—she recalled as she looked at him that one of his duties was to confirm all sentences of death passed in the colony, or to grant reprieve. What would happen to her if Richard were debarred by this master of life and death from building his precious road?

'He said he was prepared to resume his married life after the Budget was passed. When is that likely to be?'

'It'll be laid on the table on 27th February,' he said with unhesitating, ice-cold accuracy. 'Ten days later it should be through. Then, that statement of yours: is it true or not?'

'Not—at least, not quite. The Press requires an answer that is either black or white. They don't understand anything else. So one must give it to them. My answer was white—a white lie. We haven't separated, yet we have in a way. Our marriage hasn't gone on the rocks, yet it's on the rocks more or less. Nothing sensational happened. No one in the house even raised their voice.'

'You prefer to describe it in riddles.'

'It is a riddle.'

'If you told me the truth, it might be wiser.'

'No, Freddie. You would then try to help. That would be fatal.'

'Wouldn't you wish me to help?'

She looked at him with the shadow of a smile.

'Too altruistic, my dear. Too much self-abnegation.'

He looked her narrowly in the eyes, then slowly turned his back on her and faced the harbour. She felt herself grow cold with nerves. She even shivered slightly.

Chiu replenished the glasses.

'You are not unhappy, then?' Freddie continued, still with his back to her.

'I don't think I know the meaning of unhappiness. I may have to adapt myself to new conditions and surroundings.'

'Here?' he asked, switching round.

'No, I should probably go away. That would be better for Richard's career, wouldn't it?'

'It depends what you mean by "career". Not many colonial officers these days can be said to have careers, as the word was once understood.'

'Is it wrong of me to think that he has a career?'

'Most wives do think like that about their husbands, I've noticed. It can lead to disappointment.'

'When do you retire, Freddie?'

'In five or six years, depending on whether I'm offered a

117

governorship of my own,' he said, without indicating any desire in the matter.

'This is an uncomfortable house to live in, isn't it?'—this brightly, with a glance round the granite and marble terrace.

'On the whole, yes. But some colonies have pleasant Government Houses.'

'There's a white cat out there in the garden.'

He glanced out, and chuckled.

'It's a Siamese, actually. Belongs to Lady Wellborough. They left it behind.'

'I like Siamese cats in theory, but I hate the way they cry like babies.'

He came back on to the terrace again and resumed his seat.

'You never wanted to have children?'

' "Want" is too finite a word. Not having children becomes a habit.'

He looked at her with symptoms of paternalism.

'Am I very old-fashioned in thinking that children help a marriage along?'

'If I were married to you, Freddie,' she said, with the flicker of a laugh, 'I'm sure everything would be quite different.'

He laughed outright, and relit his pipe.

'It's an amusing thought,' he said reflectively. 'I wonder what kind of book you would write then.'

'*The Fifth Man I Tried to Live With,*' she hazarded.

His smile vanished.

'You're really rather an outrageous person, aren't you? You enjoy being outrageous.'

'That's not fair. I'm not in the least outrageous. I just try to be honest with myself and with other people.'

'Is that so remarkable? I try to be the same.'

'That's what you think. I would have said you were frightfully dishonest, never letting on about anything, pretending to live up here like a monk.'

'How d'you know I don't?' he asked flatly.

She hesitated.

'Shouldn't we have dinner? They're looking anxious in there.'

His attention was diverted.

'Chiu!' he called. 'Five minutes.'

The group of servants in the dining-room scattered on their various duties.

'Chiu is a very faithful servant,' she said.

'M'm. He needs to be. He has eleven children.'

'It was very kind of you to come to my lecture, Freddie. I was expecting a difficult audience.'

'I was expecting to see your husband.'

'Oh, not before the Budget,' she sighed.

'That's a ridiculous arrangement.'

'I'm well aware of that. What can I do?'

'What do you want to do?'

'That word "want" again. Now that it's broken, I don't think I want anything in particular.'

'So it is broken.'

'Well, I suppose so—yes.' Then with mock horror: 'And I had you attending my lecture under false pretences. Please don't be angry with me.'

'I'm not in the least angry,' he said gaily. 'For once, I'm having a pleasant, happy evening.'

She exhaled cigarette smoke.

'You amaze me,' she said, without raising her voice. 'I've often wondered just how much you can relax.'

The A.D.C. came on the terrace.

'A sherry before dinner, sir?'

'Thank you, Williamson. You might be surprised,' he added in a lower tone as a servant brought decanter and glasses.

Another servant brought a third chair for the A.D.C., who remained with them till Sylvia went home after dinner. The principal topic at dinner was English water-colours.

12

INTERPRETER Leung sat at his desk surrounded by the usual confusion and noise of the District Office. In front of him at the far end of the long room a group of land agents and speculators from the city were arguing heatedly among themselves, while the land clerk dispassionately moved large bundles of hundred-dollar notes from his desk into the office safe. Nearer, on the left, the correspondence section hacked away harshly at three typewriters, and swore loudly in the dialect whenever they hit wrong letters. Next to them were a string of hawkers waiting to renew their licences, argumentative vegetable gardeners mostly, male and female, rough people with, against the world, a grudge that developed markedly whenever they had to come into the big city. In the land section, on the right, the svelte wife of a notoriously stingy millionaire was pleading with the bailiff to allow her to convert a piece of land from agricultural to building status at a specially cheap rate. The millionaire himself never condescended to come in person, always sending his wife. She was his fourth, but one of the others had died. Immediately about his desk were a group of stupid villagers whose children could not be admitted to school because they possessed no birth certificates. Interpreter Leung's temper, never smooth for long amid the stresses of a day in the crowded, complicated office, was beginning to mount. In the next group waiting to see him he identified the participants in the most exasperating case he had had to deal with in months: two women from different villages who were quarrelling over the ownership of three cows. The third of the cows was still a calf, and was growing older and more valuable as the case proceeded, with the result that, every time they came in—they had been coming about once every three weeks for the past eight months—he had to start all over again from the beginning, making a new valuation of the animals, while the two furious ladies sat opposite him, occasionally hurling invective at each other, until he, too, usually found himself in a towering rage. Nor was he the only one. On one occasion the District Officer had thrown them bodily out of his office.

One thing was certain: if the morning was to pass smoothly, he had to avoid dealing with the cow case. It was unfortunately not one of those cases he could gently punt up to the District Officer, for he, on the former occasion when he saw the ladies, had given specific instructions that they were never to be allowed to see him again. The only way to avoid dealing with them was to keep them waiting so long that they went back to their villages in disgust and disappointment at not being allowed to convert the District Office once more into the battleground of their limitless fury.

Having dealt with the birth certificate problem, therefore, he decided that the next move had better be to go over the road for a cup of coffee with his associate, the land bailiff. He rose

120

determinedly, crossed to the bailiff's desk, and said in English, with an indication towards the cow-case women:

'Let's get the hell out of here.'

The bailiff looked at the women, smirked, apologized to the millionaire's wife at his entire inability to alter the price, and went out with him.

In the corridor leading to the main entrance to the office they ran into about eight people from remote villages on Great Island. Interpreter Leung was able to identify them as coming from Ha Tsuen and another village not far off, Fa Ping. They included two older women and a young girl. He nodded to them and passed quickly on, lest they try stopping him to secure immediate attention. At the office entrance he saw yet another person from Ha Tsuen, a young man, coming out of the lavatory. As he saw Interpreter Leung he came quickly forward.

'Your Honour, may I speak to you?'

'Eh! Ah Fai! What brings you here?' the interpreter asked with his usual gay grin.

But the lad looked worried.

'May I speak to you, sir?' he said quietly.

Sensing a little genuine trouble for once, in contrast with the stentorian histrionics and general nastiness of the women in the cow case, Interpreter Leung put two fingers on the back of the lad's shirt-collar, pretending to drag him along by the scruff of the neck. Interpreter Leung, who had nine children by only one wife, was a fatherly man, who liked to help young men as a precaution against any misfortune coming to his own sons, one of whom (the tenth child) had unluckily died.

'You drink coffee?' he asked.

'Yes, Your Honour,' the lad replied, being dragged along without any proper resistance, and allowing a smile momentarily to inhabit his worried face.

The three of them crossed the wide, busy thoroughfare, to a restaurant on the opposite side. There, seated at a small table and drinking coffee, Fai followed the immemorial good manners of rural China—which were a constant source of infuriation to almost everyone in the District Office, but particularly to the quick-tempered interpreter, who, like his post-office friend, Ronnie Cheng, had been used all his life to dealing with Europeans, with their more direct, rapid way of dealing with affairs— by remaining silent for the first ten minutes, while Interpreter

121

Leung and the bailiff chatted about nothing in particular. Thereafter, Fai discussed only the commonplaces of the village: the headman's declaration that a bridge needed repairing, the removal of the shrimps to a new bed in another bay where they had never been found before, the raising of subscriptions for redecorating the temple, which Fai considered a waste of money.

'What have you brought your sister into town for?' asked Interpreter Leung, with an intuitive flash as to the identity of the young girl in the Ha Tsuen group.

Fai looked down at the white cloth.

'That's not my sister,' he said, flushing around the eyes, as if he had been drinking wine.

'Surely I always saw her before in your house,' the interpreter pressed, his memory becoming more precise as he imagined the village from which the boy came.

'Yes. But she's not my sister.'

The bailiff, a jolly, round-faced fellow, laughed.

'Don't tell me she's a child daughter-in-law.'

The lad turned towards him hastily, and, without raising his eyes from the cloth, said:

'Yes. She is.'

The bailiff suppressed a little spasm of surprise. Interpreter Leung grunted.

'For you, Ah Fai?' he asked.

'Yes, Your Honour. But I don't want the crowning to take place. I don't want her. That's why we've come today.'

Interpreter Leung calculated various things, aided by coffee and a cigarette. He did not care for *sam po tsai* (child daughter-in-law) cases any more than he cared for any other kind of case which brought to the office the unreasoning hatreds of which his own people were so characteristically capable. The cases were usually easy to straighten out initially. In the event, all four parents had to admit that there was no way of actually forcing the young couple to make a baby together if they didn't feel like it. Babies being the main object in view it was usually recognized as the wisest course, when such an unfortunate situation arose as the refusal of the bridegroom to take the child daughter-in-law as his wife, to disentangle the relationship between the two families, and make alternative marital arrangements. In the case of the girl, to find a husband after being rejected as a child daughter-in-law was difficult, because few would believe the girl

122

was still a virgin; and the real trouble between the two families, if they lived within range of each other, usually started after, not before, the dissolution of the bond between them, the girl's family considering themselves the aggrieved party, when their useless daughter-in-law was returned to them unwanted, after possibly ten or more years spent in the house of the boy's family.

Fa Ping, Interpreter Leung calculated, was a small village—not more than nine or ten families all of the same clan—and the rejection of their offspring by Fai would probably be enough to put enmity between the whole village of Fa Ping and the whole village of Ha Tsuen, which was slightly larger, being a two-clan village. Both lay along the route of the proposed road to Sheung Tsuen, Fa Ping being situated on the coast between Wireless Bay and Ha Tsuen. A troublesome tract of rocks, hillocks, and dense brushwood separated the two villages. After the road was put through, however, they would become inconveniently close to each other, and there might be violence, unless the thing could be amicably settled and the girl married to someone else. Of that, Interpreter Leung had doubts. She was a good girl, by village standards, healthy and strong; but she had a slight squint, and the village lads were more fussy these days, specially those who managed to come into town now and then and go to the cinema. It might not be easy to find her a husband unless some other family with a son owed money that it could not repay to the girl's family. Interpreter Leung considered this unlikely. The girl's family were poor, owning nothing but their few fields, a boat, and several hundred young fir trees on the mountains behind their village. Probably no one owed them anything. More likely, they were in debt to others.

There was thus the probability of some kind of trouble between the two villages, he reckoned. He always reckoned things up. He was usually right. English District Officers came and went. Some asked for his advice and ignored it. Others ignored him altogether until, indirectly, he taught them a lesson. During the régimes of the unpleasant District Officers he made more money. It always seemed to work that way. Morals were troubled less. Opportunities occurred more frequently with less sympathetic (and thus less observant) supervision. The unpleasant District Officers had unconsciously contributed a great deal to Interpreter Leung's devoted care of his children, the eldest of whom was due to enter the colony's expensive university. After reckoning things up, there

123

was usually little to do. The District Office waited on events more than it initiated them. But with good reckonings over a number of years it became possible to know the main ramifications of the teeming population in the district—about two hundred thousand people—the tensions, the struggles for land and petty power. In this way it was easier to make money. One learnt exactly where to go for it, and how.

At present a main source of income to the staff of the District Office—according to the time-hallowed custom of Chinese corruption, the proceeds were nominally shared among all members of the staff, even including the lavatory cleaner, in order to ensure silence, though in the case of junior members the shares were decidedly nominal—was Wong Tak-wor, of Wireless Bay, who was paying pleasingly regular fees for assistance in purchasing land along the route of the proposed road to Sheung Tsuen. The severance of relationship between these two families at Ha Tsuen and Fa Ping presented a possible opportunity for a further transaction, Interpreter Leung reckoned. The road would run right through the Fa Ping rice-fields, and, with an additional mouth to feed, another unproductive family member thrust upon them, the Fa Ping family might feel disposed to making some quick cash by the sale of a few of their fields.

When they left the restaurant he let the other two go on ahead, while he put through a quick telephone call to Wong Tak-wor's office. This done, he crossed over to the District Office and prepared to take the case in before the District Officer, to whom, by long custom, Interpreter Leung accorded all jurisdiction in cases of this type. As there was money involved, he made no delay, brushing past others trying to see the D.O., in order to bring his lot in first.

'A *sam po tsai* case,' he announced gloomily as, slowing down his pace, he brought them into the D.O.'s separate office, without any appearance of haste.

'The usual thing, I suppose?' the D.O. queried.

Interpreter Leung nodded.

'The usual thing. Sit down, you folk.'

While they sat in a row before the D.O.'s desk, the Ha Tsuen group on one side, the Fa Ping group on the other, the D.O. continued writing at great speed in a file. Interpreter Leung looked at him with his usual care, trying to determine how to present the case, in order to ensure that the D.O. acted as was

124

required in the interests of Wong Tak-wor and the pockets of the staff. For the best part of twenty-five years he had watched, in this same old-fashioned office in the heart of the city, a long series of Englishmen sitting at this same desk, making the same mistakes, showing misplaced benevolence and unjust anger, very largely according to the presentation given by himself or some other member of the staff, who had their special motives for requiring their nominal master to act in that way or in this. Presentation—the art of it lay in this. In the office, Interpreter Leung was the undisputed expert at presentation. He watched the D.O. now making his nervy, harassed way through the stack of files before him. He had been in a difficult mood ever since consenting to those sales of Crown land along the south coast of Great Island. He knew, of course, that he had been tricked into it, but was innocent-hearted enough not to believe that his own staff had had a hand in it. The eating-house proprietor on Little Island had kept his mouth shut, as well he might, for he and Interpreter Leung were among the very few who knew that two-thirds of his eating-house was illegally situated on Crown land for which he held no permit. That kept him obediently quiet. As for the girl, the choice proved to have been that of a perfectionist, and, in the District Office, Interpreter Leung's reputation rose to a higher peak than ever before with those members of the staff whose shares were more than nominal. Not only was the night in the little hotel an evident success: the lady was persuaded to stay right over the Mid-Autumn Festival. Mrs. Fairburn having gone to town, the D.O. had taken his new *amour* into the house, where she spent five nights. A police corporal from Little Island had reported the news to him at his home in the densest part of the city. He had received it with a rather unseemly whoop of glee. The police station on Little Island faced the District Officer's residence, on the opposite hill, and, with binoculars, all that passed in the house of large, long windows could be seen. The occasion of staging the *dénouement* had occurred a few days later, at the opening of a new maternity and child health clinic on Fork Island by the Director of Medical Services. A large number of rural dignitaries was· invited, launches being laid on to take them to the island for the ceremony. Interpreter Leung advised Wong Tak-wor to go accompanied by his fourth concubine (really, she was just his mistress, but everyone referred to her as his fourth). At the ceremony they sat directly behind the D.O.,

125

who turned as white as a sheet as Wong Tak-wor introduced her over the backs of the chairs. She behaved as if she had never seen him before. Wong Tak-wor was restrained to the point of perfection. Interpreter Leung could scarcely believe him capable of conducting the scene with such finesse. It was so frightening and exciting that he himself was shivering, and wanting to laugh. He became so disturbed that he had to leave his place and go out to the back to pass water.

The D.O. had, in fact, reacted in just the way Interpreter Leung had hazarded to foresee. With that incomprehensible European capacity for benevolence, he had—after the first shock—become deeply apologetic. At the tea-party following the speeches, he had remained the entire time with Wong Tak-wor, whose wife was enjoying herself with other lady guests. A fervent and embarrassing desire to be friendly was transparent in the D.O.'s actions. Wong Tak-wor was socially bowled over by it. He asked Interpreter Leung privately whether the D.O. would like a present of his favourite diamond ring, at which the organizer-in-chief told him the Chinese equivalent of not to be a bloody fool. A great deal of beer was drunk—it was a tea-party in name only—and deep mutual understanding evinced. Wong Tak-wor inquired whether the D.O. had enjoyed the meat of a wild pig and some quails he had sent him, to which the D.O. replied enthusiastically that the meat was delicious. Interpreter Leung had not expected it to be so easy. The following morning the land sales were approved, and sent to the Land Commissioner for permission to issue the usual Press advertisements of the date and place of the land auction. When the Land Commissioner queried the sales, with reference to the proposed new road, the D.O. and his interpreter both went to the Commissioner's office to explain the matter. Certainly, the D.O. said, Mr. Wong Tak-wor was not a speculator, but a person genuinely interested in the development of the country and the growth of more vegetables. He further reminded the Commissioner that the land was being auctioned in agricultural status. No buildings could be erected on it. The Commissioner reluctantly approved.

After which effort the D.O. relapsed into sullenness, daily unchanged. His wife, it was said, had refused to live with him any more. From Little Island it was reported that he lived like a hermit, seldom out late, avoiding all evening invitations, and visiting only his friend Professor Wen. His mood still continuing,

Interpreter Leung had come to rely, during recent weeks, on the contrary approach, if things were to be done.

'Well?' asked the D.O., looking up at him. 'Any views?'

He pursed his lips gloomily together.

'Stupid business,' he said. 'I can't see why they don't let things go on as arranged. The girl's not bad.'

The D.O. looked along the row of people in front of him.

'Why! Hullo, Ah Fai!' he exclaimed in the dialect. 'What brings you here?'

'He's the prospective bridegroom,' Interpreter Leung prompted hurriedly in English.

The D.O. assumed a more serious aspect.

'What are the facts?' he asked.

'The girl came to live in the other family twelve years ago. All the proper ceremonies were performed. The time has now come for the so-called crowning ceremony, after which they may become husband and wife. But the boy refuses to go through with it.'

'Have you any explanation, Ah Fai?'

'What the interpreter says is true, Magistrate,' the lad replied doggedly. 'I don't want her. We've lived like brother and sister. I don't want . . .' and he faltered.

The D.O. turned to the girl.

'What have you to say?'

She looked down at the ground and said very quietly, without emotion:

'I don't want him.'

Hearing this, the girl's mother began muttering ferociously, her hard, cruel face turning red as her words became clearer. While this volcano prepared itself to erupt, the boy's mother showed signs of restiveness, shrugging her shoulders haughtily and making little sniffing noises. The boy and girl sat motionless throughout these signs of danger.

Then the storm broke.

'If that slut of an old bitch had been capable of producing a son who was a real man . . .!' the girl's mother screamed out, standing up as she spoke.

'H'm! Listen to that cheating whore!' the other cackled proudly, without looking at her rival, while the lady referred to burst into a tirade of fury that drowned everything else. 'Where did she make this little squinter but in someone else's bed?'

127

shouted the boy's mother, trying to be heard. 'And we've had to feed and clothe her for twelve years! She's got her reward now all right!'

As the tumult increased, the girl's mother becoming incoherent with rage and talking a lot of things Interpreter Leung could not understand, the D.O. raised his hands for silence. To no avail. Even the husbands were now grumbling at each other, and telling their wives (with respect) to modify their speech (Interpreter Leung wondered how on earth either of them managed to keep order at home). Only the boy and girl remained still and quiet.

'You men!' shouted the D.O. at last, louder than the lot. 'Stop these women's chattering, or get out of the room, all of you!'

With this encouragement, the husbands made a slightly more determined effort, actually touching their wives on the sleeve and warning them to behave decently in front of the Magistrate.

'What the hell do we do with this case?' the D.O. asked Leung.

'There'll be trouble if they separate,' he replied with continuing gloom.

'Never mind. If the young people don't want it, who are we to interfere?' (The contrary method, Interpreter Leung noted, still worked.) 'You can none of you force this marriage to take place, when neither the boy nor the girl want it,' he said to them all. 'The two families must sever this marital connexion.'

There was silence. It was, Interpreter Leung knew, the word of authority they had expected to hear. No word of theirs could sever the connexion. Only authority could. Though they did not like it, they humbled themselves to it instantly.

'In that case,' the girl's mother said sullenly, 'they must return the horoscopes to us.'

'Certainly not!' sniffed the boy's mother, with inexpressible contempt.

'Why not, you bitch? We paid money for them, didn't we?' shrieked the other, standing up again, while her husband tugged gently at her sleeve and begged her to show respect.

The other woman folded her arms over her plain black peasant's dress and turned slightly away.

'Give us back the money we paid you then, and we will give back the horoscopes,' she said with the certainty of triumph.

As she calculated, there was consternation on the other side.

128

Twelve years ago, Interpreter Leung reflected, the sum paid for the child daughter-in-law would have been fairly high, by Great Island standards. Now it was worth considerably less. Nevertheless the Fa Ping couple would not agree to part with a cent.

'Very well,' said the D.O. 'That's fair enough. You don't give back the money. They don't give back the horoscopes. But the bond between the two families will be severed nevertheless, and written here, in this book, which is kept in this office as a permanent record.'

He produced a heavy, leather-bound book in which miscellaneous agreements were recorded. A hush fell over the group at the sight of it. Interpreter Leung received it from him, and recorded the severance of relationship in large, stylish Chinese characters on a blank page.

'This procedure has no legal validity whatever, has it?' asked the D.O. in English, while Leung wrote.

'None whatever, sir,' he replied. 'But in my experience it has never failed to impress.'

The pattern of fine characters was completed. The four parents imposed their thumb-prints beneath it, the boy his signature in Chinese, the girl a cross made with a Chinese writing-brush. The D.O. signed. The group rose, their eyes all downcast to avoid each other's glance, and walked silently out.

Fai, the last to go, turned at the door.

'Thank you, Magistrate,' he said, and, as he did so, grabbed the hand of his former relative, dragging her back into the doorway. (Indeed, he touched her as a brother touches a sister, the interpreter noted.) 'You see, she has a friend in another village. It's true, isn't it?' he said to her teasingly.

She looked down at the floor, with the slightest indication of a smile on one side of her mouth only, and nodded.

The D.O. laughed, the first time in several weeks.

'And you, Ah Fai?' he asked. 'What about you?'

'I'm still too young, Magistrate,' he said, excusing himself from truly replying by giving a conventional answer. 'Thank you, Magistrate. We both thank you for your help.'

Interpreter Leung shepherded them out into the corridor. There they were joined by the others who had accompanied them from their respective villages. The battle over, the decision given, they were calm again. The Ha Tsuen group walked ahead, evidently intending to leave at once. The two families obviously would not wish to travel in the same ferry to Great Island, nor risk the embarrassment of having to walk together for five hours along the same track from Wireless Bay as far as Fa Ping. Near the door of the District Office the Fa Ping family stopped; they could return that evening to Wireless Bay, where they could hire a room for the night, and walk on to their village by themselves next day. The Ha Tsuen group hesitated. The Fa Ping group did not move. The two groups, the men in dark brown jackets, the women in black, looked much alike. Only Fai, in a white shirt and black, Western-style slacks, introduced any contrast in their monotony of dress. The Ha Tsuen group, sensing what the others intended, moved on through the open entrance. Without a word, a bow, a look, a sign, the girl whom they had fed and clothed for twelve years in expectation of marriage stood motionless amongst her own people, whose names she no longer remembered, while Fai and his people walked out. Nor did Fai's father or mother look at her. The matter was settled, the contract annulled.

When they were out of sight and earshot, the girl's mother started to mumble again, the men stood stupidly about, staring around the busy District Office, while the girl, at last, began to cry silently, without raising her squinting eyes.

Interpreter Leung, who had been hovering around to make sure they left the building without further quarrelling, sighed as he saw the girl. He thought of his own eldest daughter, about the same age. Thank heaven he'd never made any of these old-fashioned marriage contracts for any of his children! She'd cry all right, that girl, when they got her back to Fa Ping, and that hag of a mother started venting her bitterness on her!

Wong Tak-wor, in lightweight Western clothes suited to the cool autumn weather, walked briskly into the District Office, spotted Interpreter Leung, and came over at once to him. The interpreter signalled him to follow as he made his way back, through the confusion of desks and people, to his place at the head of the general office. Well, there were compensations, he thought as he went. Money was a wonderful compensation. Perhaps that ugly young girl would marry her beau, possibly just as ugly. It didn't do to think too deeply about anything in the District Office. Over-sympathetic English D.O.s had sometimes made that mistake in the past, ending in hospital with nervous breakdowns.

In any case, money would solve this one. Even the old hag
130

should be satisfied, and his own son would enter the university without anyone else in the family going short.

'Call those Fa Ping people up,' he signalled to the messenger, while motioning Wong Tak-wor to take the chair beside his desk.

'Thanks, Elder Brother.'

The business man settled himself down comfortably, crossed his legs, and offered Interpreter Leung a cigarette from a gold case.

13

THE beautiful Frances Lau stood in the hall of her vast, ornate Edwardian mansion overlooking the city, pulled on a pair of nylon gloves, and considered whether it would be safe to disobey her husband. At the open front door, their second car, the Packard, waited her orders, driver at the wheel. It was 10.15 a.m., a fresh, sunny morning late in November, and for the first time since summer waned she had put on a short, black silk surcoat, lined with white fur, over her simple but extremely expensive dark brown *cheungsam*, with its distinctive slit skirt effect.

The house was quiet. The children were all out, the two elder ones at the university, the other five at their various schools. Edwin had recently gone down to his office. She was free till twelve-thirty, when she had to meet him at the Chinese Bankers' Club, where they were giving lunch to a woman economic expert from the United Nations. With a final glance at her tiny diamond wrist-watch she walked forward to the waiting car, the Indian watchman opening the car door for her.

'The Heights,' she said, adding, as the car twisted down the complex drive to the nearest street far below: 'If anyone asks you where we went, you took me to the Red Cross.'

'Yes, Honourable Mother.'

That was one godsend in life, she thought, leaning back and gazing out of the window: the absolute fidelity of the servants to herself. Though they all probably liked her, they were afraid of her—far more afraid of her than they were of Edwin—obeying her slightest order as if it were sacred. Within a few minutes, having descended slightly, rounded a number of dangerous bends on the steep hillside, and mounted again to a higher level, more recently built on than the site of her own house, she was stepping out at The Heights and taking the lift up to Sylvia Fairburn's apartment.

Frances Lau represented one of the most beautiful types of Chinese womanhood: the Cantonese born and bred in Peking. She had not that drooping yet subtly inviting languor of the more celebrated type of beauty, that of Soochow. Her Cantonese vitality, however, had been softened and polished by the good manners and restraint learnt in her Peking childhood. She was blessed with the best of North and South.

Edwin had often asked her why she was so friendly with Sylvia Fairburn. He could not understand such a friendship. Though he and his father before him had occupied high positions of trust and respect among the British in the colony, though he hob-nobbed with governors at dinner-parties and race meetings, and wrote cheery little notes to European officials when their wives had babies, Edwin did not really care for foreigners, or hold any good opinion of them. He was mentally unequipped to understand how his wife could have made a real friend of one.

As for Frances herself, she had never completely analysed the sources of her friendship with Sylvia. It was, of course, pleasant for her to enjoy once again conversation in her long-neglected Mandarin, which in the colony very few people except refugees could speak correctly. This was only a fraction of it, however. There was an element of showing off her latest clothes and jewellery—Sylvia was an excellent, discerning audience. There was a strong element of curiosity, about Sylvia herself, her strange, childless married life, her sometimes incomprehensible Western values—a topsy-turvy life by Chinese standards, lonely and selfish, the kind of life illicit lovers might enjoy for a fortnight or so, not a real substantial marriage, with children and the promise of grandchildren, with constant family activity, a sense of the continuity and usefulness of life.

She rang the bell and, as she did so, reminded herself that she and her English friend had two different relationships, one which operated when they conversed in Mandarin, another peculiarly different when they spoke to each other in English.

132

The very word formations of the two languages produced this difference: two separate kinds of respect, politeness and imagery; four different people speaking, two in the trembling liveliness of European thought, the other two in the everlasting tradition of China.

Somehow, this morning, disobeying Edwin, she felt like being her modern, Western personality. She wanted to escape from honourable motherhood and her place in the hierarchy of the Lau clan.

'I'm at the Red Cross just now,' she said gaily, as the old servant led her into the long living-room, where Sylvia, clad in a dark green négligé and smoking a cigarette in a holder, sat in the middle of the floor, surrounded by manuscript paper and note-books.

'Coffee, Ah Juen,' the writer said, without stirring. She looked tired and older. 'Edwin's getting difficult again, is he?' she asked, pushing the cigarette-box to the foot of the chair on which Frances had seated herself.

'Oh! Chinese husbands!' she protested. 'Sometimes I wish I'd married a nice easy-going European like yours.' She searched for words. 'With Edwin—his position as a Councillor—he has all the power and prestige anyone could want! Yet every day he has some fear of this or that, fear of putting a foot wrong.'

The writer looked down with bitterness.

'He's not the only one, Frances. I know it better than anyone here.'

Frances, whose experience of big family life had given her a warm heart combined with a sense of drama, was worried as she heard her friend's tone of voice. With a nasty feeling of social danger, she wondered whether perhaps Edwin had been right, and it would have been safer to stay away. With Europeans one could never know for certain what embroilments one might be drawn into by associating with them. In good times such experiences could be jolly; in bad times . . .

'Surely you exaggerate,' she said.

'No, my dear,' the writer answered, rising to her feet and looking out of the sanatorium-like floor-to-ceiling windows. 'They're closing in on me. They're closing in all round. I'm being forced to do what I utterly refuse to believe in.'

Frances was baffled. In Sylvia's company she was frequently baffled. She loved it. If she waited patiently, without asking silly questions—fatal with Sylvia—she was soon rewarded with some fascinating explanation.

'Edwin isn't closing in,' she volunteered. 'He's trying to draw away, and draw me away too.' (With an odd elation she realized how, since entering the apartment, she had transformed herself from Mandarin-speaking Chinese motherhood controlling a large household, senior wife in the senior branch of the clan, to her other, pert, surprised, English-speaking self. Ah! how she enjoyed life!)

'The effect is to put a vacuum round me,' Sylvia replied. 'That's what I call closing in. What with the Europeans licking round for a good salty piece of scandal, and the Chinese taking such colossal care to be the last word in neutrality, I might as well be living in a convent—or a prison. I'm not sure which.'

'But, Sylvia, there's a way out,' Frances said sensibly. These Europeans! What crises they built themselves into!

'There are plenty of ways out,' she answered. Her skin looked so uncared-for, as if she hadn't been for a beauty treatment for weeks. 'I can go back to Little Island, in which case I surrender and become his repentant slave. Or I can leave the colony, which will mean that one or other of us wants a divorce. Or again, I can stay here, which means that I refuse to admit that I was wrong to write *The Chasm of Love*—because, of course, that is the reason we are no longer living together.'

Frances was a little breathless.

'Sylvia, you go too fast for me,' she said, while the servant handed her a small, delicate cup of cream coffee. 'Oh dear,' she murmured, looking at the cream, 'I shall burst.' (For one of the facets of her English-speaking personality was an ability to keep neck and neck with Western women in their preoccupation with slimming.)

'Don't you see? It's all false! Every word of it is false! But people will never leave us alone. There was that ridiculous man from *Time* who flew all the way from Taiwan to get a story from me, and there are all the others here, infinitely, infinitely smaller, who want to tie up my life in a neat package, and who are forcing me—forcing me, Frances, can't you understand it?—to create between Richard and myself a relationship completely unnatural to both of us. I'm trapped. It's the most horrible thing, and I don't know how to get out.' Her voice softened as she opened another of the window sections and looked out on the pale blue autumnal light over the harbour. 'There's all the beauty of the world wasted, because one's wounded in the bottom of a dark pit.'

Like the movies, Frances thought with a rapidity that surprised her. Like the great actress in the luxurious, modern apartment, of which this was an imitation, giving a heartrending version of a story which to Chinese eyes was patently a dream, a romantic picture of what might be in a world of make-believe, an unreality, a delicately tinted lie. With another dive into the depths of thought—what on earth would Edwin say if he could hear her thoughts?—she grasped an even deeper weed: either Sylvia was imitating the woes of actresses in what were considered romantic movies, or, a very much more remarkable and disturbing thought, the emotional and utterly ludicrous happenings in American and English films were actually and truly how Americans and English people behaved in moments of stress. This second idea was almost too unbalancing to contemplate. With a distinctly superior fascination, Frances, as she gazed at Sylvia by the window, saw the pleasurable nonsense of the movies move adamantly, unquestionably, into real life. The entire apartment turned momentarily into a silver screen dream. Life stopped, and became the irrational chatter of those silly people who lived around the film studios, inventing stories that never happened. (Frances was familiar with the colony's film industry.) It was a disturbing moment. It broke reality. It meant that people were acting, instead of being real. It meant there was no more point in being a mother, and hoping one day to be a grandmother. It was a situation in which a belief in one's own superiority was the only answer, the only salvation at a time of madness.

'Please may I criticize, without meaning to be rude?' she said gravely.

'But of course!'

Frances hesitated again. How to define the gulf that separated them?

'It seems to me,' she said slowly, 'that Western people make life more difficult for themselves, because, instead of facing the truth in each bit of life as it occurs, they turn away from the truth and make a gesture, like an actor in a play.'

Sylvia turned on her, her eyes burning. She ran her right hand through her hair.

'You, Frances! *You* tell *me* this!'

She looked demure.

'It's only a small idea of my own. And I express myself so badly.'

The novelist left the window and strode down the centre of the room. Frances saw she was not offended exactly, but her words had produced another dramatic reaction, which again she could not understand. Turning round at the far end of the room, Sylvia faced her guest again and unexpectedly laughed, mockingly, bitterly.

'I always thought I could keep out of it, you see! So did Richard. We prided ourselves in being free of attitudinizing. It made our lives a lot easier. But what do you do in a world that simply does strike attitudes and can't help doing anything else? You are forced to do the same. Silence, solitude, keeping your own affairs to yourself—these are all denied you. If you keep things decently private, everyone is on tenterhooks, or else keeps away for fear of making a social gaffe. They wait after the crisis to know what attitude you struck. After which, they adjust themselves. They know where they are. They're happier. It's the way of the world, I suppose.'

'It may be the way of your world,' Frances said with a touch of Chinese self-righteousness. 'It certainly isn't of mine. A wife has no attitude to strike, to begin with. She *is* the wife. She owns and manages the house. She has duties towards her husband and children, relatives, guests, and servants. If her husband is fooling round with women outside, what is that to her? She is his wife. Nothing can dislodge her. She is the mother of his sons, and her name will be recorded in gold letters beside his in the ancestral temple. It is not a question of attitudes; it is a matter of fact.

'But, of course, if the wife starts flouncing out of the house in a fit of temper, or gets into a stew of injured pride because her husband has slept with someone else, then, I suppose, in certain circumstances, her position could be impaired. But she would have to be more than ordinarily foolish for that to happen. There are many adequate ways of dealing with husbands who become too feckless. Basically, isn't it easier to ignore fecklessness? There's nothing surprising about it. Men always will sleep with other women. What's the point in making a fuss about it?'

She saw she was talking to the convinced. Sylvia listened to her throughout with agreement patent in her expression.

'That is precisely how I have always lived,' she said. 'But, don't you see, now it's broken down! And I feel I'm faced with a mob of hyenas clamouring to get me, the more savage because I've eluded them so long.'

'That's because you made the mistake of walking out on him,' said Frances precisely.

'I've told you before: I didn't walk out on him!'

'Well, you didn't go back, did you?' she said, drawing on one of her nylon gloves, watching calmly as her hostess moved restlessly about.

'How could I have gone back, Frances? I didn't know what had happened. There were those rumours, and, before I knew where I was, his letter.'

Frances took a cigarette to follow her coffee. She searched in her bag for her holder.

'Personally,' she said, 'I would have ignored all that. Rumour —what is rumour? Ever since I married I have lived surrounded by it. Often it was true, too. Edwin, of course, bothers endlessly about rumours. He's by nature a timid man, only held together by his money and by me. I never care two hoots about rumours. You are his wife—what have you to worry about? As for that letter,' she added thoughtfully, 'I think I would have destroyed it, and probably afterwards denied ever having received it. I would then have gone straight back to Little Island by the first available ferry.'

She hoped she hadn't spoken cruelly, but it was so hard to make foreigners understand anything about life that it was no use labouring with minor politenesses. She watched her hostess's expression, without seeming too obvious about it, as she turned in silence from the window and sank down in an armchair.

'Well, I didn't,' she said, in a dry, quiet way. 'Where do we go from here? I'm not wanted any more.'

'No wife ever is wanted all the time. Why make a song about that?'

She meant it to cheer Sylvia up, but instead the novelist smiled with a blank expression.

'What advice can we ever give each other, Frances, that's any use? Our ways of life are so far apart,' she said sadly.

Again, this terrible European imagination! thought Frances. It was as if foreigners made pictures of themselves, looked at the pictures, and then decided what to do. Instead of being guided by reality, they were each guided by their own pictures of themselves.

'There is no difference between us whatever,' she said firmly.

'Marriage is marriage the world over. The problem of relationship —and all life is a problem of relationship; it's the basis of existence—between a husband and a wife is the same for Chinese, Americans, Europeans, and Eskimos.'

'Yes, in a very restricted sense,' Sylvia conceded, 'I suppose that's true. But look at the differences. Look at the freedom of my marriage, compared with—well, even compared with yours.'

'What freedom d'you mean?' Frances asked, and recalling Sylvia's famous book: 'Freedom for adventures?'

'If you like. It sometimes counts in one's happiness.'

'Oh yes, indeed,' Frances admitted quickly. One of the pleasures of her friendship with Sylvia Fairburn was that with her she could be very nearly truthful.

'You agree?' the Englishwoman asked, as if surprised.

'Of course. You know as much about Chinese marriage as I do. It is only after marriage that you have any chance to have adventures. Before marriage you're much too closely guarded. Afterwards, well—busy, ambitious husbands like Edwin, always out somewhere or other, make it so easy for you.'

Her heart fluttered with pleasure as she noticed signs of surprise manifesting themselves in her hostess's expression.

'Frances, you amaze me!'

'In Chinese society, though, you can't write books about those kind of experiences, and you must never let them get in the way of your married life.'

The Englishwoman leant forwards in her chair.

'You, Frances?' she said softly. 'You as well!'

(The insolence of the woman, thought Frances. She behaves as if she were the only woman on earth with lovers.)

'The most entirely satisfactory lover I ever had was, as a matter of fact, an Englishman,' she said, paying further attention to her gloves. 'A very charming man. We've had a little private understanding for years.' Ah! it was amusing, this! The great novelist with all her woes temporarily forgotten, her attention absorbed in every lilt of Frances' voice, every flicker of an eyelash. That was another reason she liked Sylvia. As with Mac, her particular friend, she could be told things without any danger of report spreading into the omnipresent net of Chinese intrigue, where such inconvenient facts could be put to such decisive use. 'Don't mistake me. I can't run two households. Sometimes we don't meet for months on end. But he's always there—so convenient, too, an old friend of the family; everyone knows him—and when both of us are bored with things . . . Dear, dear! What am I telling you? And in the morning too!' She tapped ash off the end of her cigarette, savouring her little triumph over her friend. She had done Sylvia good, as well. The novelist's expression was more lively. Colour had come back into her cheeks. It had been a most successful visit.

Sylvia stared at the harbour and said with a hint of wistfulness:

'Richard is a husband in a million, of course. I have to admit that. He's the only man I've ever met who understands all these things.'

'Yes,' Frances gave her. 'It's as well to admit that. Even a Chinese husband would have had to do something fairly drastic after that book of yours. Except, of course, that if a Chinese had written it, she would have changed it all round, and made her husband the hero and the wonderful lover and the brave soldier and everything. There's more peace that way. Those are our gestures, if you can call them that. The first of our gestures is duty.'

'No, I agree with you, Frances,' Sylvia answered, rising from her chair again. 'That's not a gesture. It's looking at facts. It's reality.' She leant against the open windows. 'Frances, could you drop this English friend of yours?'

That too, Frances thought, was another question that betrayed a failure to grasp a living situation. She was not, as Sylvia would be in similar circumstances, emotionally involved with Mac. Mac was one of her diversions, like dancing and going to the movies. Mac was even of much less importance to her than these other two diversions.

'I've never really picked him up, Sylvia,' she tried to explain, conscious she was doing it feebly. 'Edwin and the children come first. There's no actual place in my life for anyone else. Sometimes life has become dull, you understand. They haven't filled it all up for me.' She couldn't explain any more; the effort needed was too great. A silence fell.

'It doesn't work our way, does it?' Sylvia said.

'How d'you mean?'

'I mean, the pact that Richard and I made, always to allow the other to go their own way—it'll never work out that way.'

'Pact,' Frances considered. 'A pact. That's like two nations that have been at war. It suggests a fight. No, I don't think a pact is sensible in relation to marriage. The only pact, if you like, that I've ever had with Edwin is about the amount of bedclothes we each use during the winter. Oh, he's such a cold body!'

But Sylvia was dreaming. Another dramatic train of thought seemed to have taken hold of her. She would probably never learn how to live, poor thing! Frances abandoned the conversation and prepared to leave.

'We meet, then, on Saturday,' Sylvia said.

'On Saturday?' Frances asked emptily. The children would all be back for lunch.

'Yes, for our trip to the monasteries.'

'Oh!' She had entirely forgotten the purpose of her visit. 'Sylvia, I'm dreadfully sorry. Edwin says I must be at home. The children . . .'

Sylvia sighed.

'I quite realize. I never knew I could be forced to do anything I didn't want to do, or prevented from doing what I wanted, just by people—and not even people either: by a vague mass of opinion. You must of course stay at home, Frances.' (Very magnanimous, thought Frances.) 'But why go so soon?'

She looked at the fingernails of her ungloved hand, imperfectly varnished.

'I must go down to Rexine's. I hear they've a new consignment of cosmetics, just in from Paris. Then there's a very stiff lunch with Edwin at his club.'

They made their adieux at the head of the lift. The doors closed. Frances smoothed the creases in her *cheungsam* and left the exotic world in which pertness somehow did the trick. As the lift doors automatically opened, the driver, lounging against the Packard's bonnet, stiffened to attention, and hastened to open the rear door of the car.

She entered without a word, waiting till the driver had reached his seat.

'Rexine's,' she ordered.

He started the engine.

'The first car unhappily came up here, Honourable Mother. Ah Hui saw we were here.'

'If he opens his mouth, he'll be sacked instantly. Tell him,' she said coldly.

'Yes, Honourable Mother.'

They drove sedately down the hill into the heart of the city.

140

14

'I HOPE you like climbing mountains,' the Assistant Superintendent, a Britisher, said as Inspector Tung Sze-liang, wearing plain clothes, came to attention in front of his desk. 'Because this weekend you're in for a dose.'

'What's the job, sir?' asked Inspector Tung.

'H.E.'s got it into his head to climb up to the top of those flaming mountains on Great Island. There's some sort of monastery up there, I understand. You're on Saturday duty, aren't you?'

'Yes, sir.'

'Then you'll have to do a double shift. We can't change bodyguards on a trip like that. I'm putting you on from one o'clock Saturday till he gets back to Government House on Monday.'

'Yes, sir.'

'It's pretty tough going up those hills, they say. You'll need to wear your strongest pair of shoes. If they break, you can indent for a new pair.'

'Thank you, sir. . . . Do I have to wear a suit, sir?'

The bodyguard to His Excellency had orders to be dressed with unnoticeable immaculateness.

'I—er——'

Inspector Tung's face remained expressionless as his superior officer faltered, pushing in the outer end of his moustache with one finger in a fix of social uncertainty. Inspector Tung, holding a degree in economics from Yenching University, Peking, was possibly the best-educated man in the colony's entire police force, with the possible exception of the Commissioner, who had been at Cambridge but had not bothered himself—in carefree, pre-war days—with sitting for degrees. As a refugee from communism, with nothing but his wits to aid him, Inspector Tung had taken what he could in the way of employment, keeping as quiet as possible about his academic attainments and family connexions in China, particularly in the presence of British officers holding any rank less than that of full Superintendent. Even so, provided he used to its best the exterior of a flattering simplicity, he could occasionally ask small questions—such as this particular one—

which gave him the subtle amusement of demonstrating, to himself alone, that, despite all misfortunes, he still remained an educated man from a distinguished family, superior to the various churls, busy-bodies, petty tyrants, drunks, social climbers, and pseudo-intellectuals, who constituted the bulk of the officers commanding him.

'I'll ask the Private Secretary,' the Assistant Superintendent said, partially recovering himself. He lifted the phone. 'Get me the Private Secretary to His Excellency the Acting Governor,' he said, with a degree of majesty which Tung was uncertain about: was it for the telephonist or him? No matter. The face of Tung Sze-liang was one of those unreadable Northern problems that no Britisher in any police force would ever be able to decipher. It remained unchanged. Something happened at the other end of the telephone. 'The Private Secretary, please.' This was in a tone with the first signs of reverence in it—wasted really, considering it was only addressed to the Government House telephonist. The Assistant Superintendent suddenly drew himself up. 'This is Beaton here, sir. Sorry to trouble you. But—er—this trip to Great Island on Saturday—does the bodyguard need to wear a suit?' The clipped manner of speech; the fear; the desire to impress. A pause followed. Possibly even higher personages were stumped, as the English would say, by this fundamental question. Tung nearly smiled. 'He's finding out,' the Assistant Superintendent (hand over the receiver) confided to Tung, with an evidently astonished feeling of relief that he was not the only man who did not know the answer. 'Yes?' He leapt mentally to attention again. 'Yes, sir! Thank you. Thank you very much. Yes, that's quite clear, thank you.' He put the phone down, assuming, as he did so, an air of confident solemnity. 'H.E.'s orders are that you may wear what you like, but remember it'll be cold up in the mountains at night.'

'Then I have discretion, sir?'

'Yes, Tung. That's all right.'

'Thank you, sir.'

He turned to go, thankful, as always when quitting a superior officer's room, that he had been transferred to the plainclothes branch (and thus did not have to stand stiffly and salute), and walked slowly enough from the room to hear behind him the Assistant Superintendent mutter involuntarily:

'He's a good man, that.'

Tung smiled to himself as he walked away down a corridor of the massive, old-fashioned Central Police Station. Though he had run across one or two nasty characters in the colony's police force, he had no dislike of the British as a whole. What he did dislike intensely was having to wear their police uniform in public, where there was a risk of some of his refugee friends from Peking seeing him. In point of fact, drawing an inspector's pay, he was doing rather better than many of them. He preferred, however, to conceal the source of his income, lest knowledge of it expose him to shame.

Of all the jobs available to him in the plainclothes branch, these periodic attachments to the Governor in the capacity of bodyguard were about the pleasantest, and he preferred going out on excursions with the Acting Governor, who was unencumbered with wife and children, to the more sedate and domestic outings of Sir Wavell Wellborough.

As the Crown car brought them to the waiting launch at Prince of Wales Pier, and Inspector Tung followed His Excellency aboard, the day had a mournful beauty about it that made Tung sad to be travelling alone.

'Tell the boy to give you a drink, Tung,' Sir Frederick said, as he walked forward to the solitary chair awaiting him on the foredeck.

The last salute snapped out on the pier, the Governor's personal standard, the Union flag defaced in the centre with the imperial crown, fluttered out from the mainmast, the launch disengaged from the pier, the escorting police vessel swung out into the harbour to warn other craft out of the way, and Tung sat down in the lone chair placed for him aft, while one of the Government House servants brought him a glass of beer.

The sea in the harbour was blue and choppy, the sky a misty blue, the mountains pale mauve, with here and there rifts of purple shadow down their noble, bare shapes. It was good to be going out into the country, Tung Sze-liang thought, yet a waste to be going alone. If only, on expeditions such as this, he could be allowed to make up a party of a few friends, how much more enjoyable it would be! The weather was cool, calm, and fresh. It was the season for going out with friends, taking some girls along, to picnic in the hills, and, sitting in the rough grass, to tell stories and perhaps listen to one of them singing an old song. He was disturbed, too, by a letter more outspoken than usual from his seventy-three-year-old father in Peking, in which the old man explained that he had been sick for several weeks as a result of being forced to stand time and again in the cold streets to watch processions go by. It was not, his father explained, like under former governments, whose celebrations you could ignore if you felt like it. With these people, non-participation meant active opposition. Even the genuineness of his illness had been queried by the street police. Sze-liang was the youngest son of a large family, and his father's favourite. Whatever happened to the rest, when the Communists took control, Sze-liang, on his father's orders, had to leave China and never return 'till this madness is over'. But in his father's letter he sensed the old man's regret, his wish that Sze-liang could be with him as his last days approached in the increasing gloom of the magnificent old capital, where reasonable thinking—once its foremost pride—was being systematically annihilated. The thought depressed him so much that he wanted to be with somebody, to talk about no matter what, to partake of another problem. He went forward to stand beside the coxswain.

As he did so, the Acting Governor walked down to the cabins to take his lunch in the sumptuously appointed dining saloon.

'Are you being looked after, Tung?' he asked as he descended the stair.

'Yes, thank you, sir.'

No one had bothered to replenish his beer, but what was the use of saying so? One of the servants, Chiu by name, knew he was a university graduate and treated him as such. To the rest, he was just another copper in disguise. When Chiu had finished waiting below, he would see that Tung Sze-liang was properly served. The bodyguard leant on a rail and gazed out at the exquisitely calm autumn seascape, at the blue islands scattered here and there in the distance. Being a refugee was hard. It was permanent. No matter how well you managed to survive, you were no more with your own crowd. No one knew who you were. Your father's name meant—in this British set-up, for heaven's sake!—nothing. You were peculiarly, unstably, alone.

You learnt, though, to observe things with an acuteness unknown in friendlier days, and born of the refugee's independence of view. You summed things up. You assessed people. You calculated how sweet-tempered men would behave if given power at a crisis, and traced the latent hardnesses round their eyes, the unperceived slant of frustration in the line between their lips, when in repose. You became like a policeman in real life—a detective—but collecting information for yourself only, because self was all you had left to trust in. All the others, the long-known, trustworthy people, had been left behind. Sometimes he would have given anything to go back to Peking, despite his father's wish, never mind under what government. His elbows bit into the rail as he gazed expressionlessly on the dull, barren, purposeless islands, this piece of the world's offal to which Great Britain attached so much importance, this final place, this end of all hope: pitiful rocks meaninglessly defying the ocean. Like people attempting the impossible. . . .

After three hours, and having passed along the majestic northern shore of Great Island, the launch entered O Mun, the small fishing harbour from which the Acting Governor proposed to ascend into the mountains. On the pier a police country patrol, a corporal and six men, were waiting, standing at ease in smart khaki uniforms adapted for rougher rural patrol work.

'Good lord! Are they coming with us?' Sir Frederick asked.

'Yes, sir.'

'I told the Commissioner I wished to go alone. I suppose this is what he means by alone.'

'Yes, sir.'

As the gangway was set up for them to disembark, a young European sub-inspector was seen running round the coast from the police station. Tung stood at the gangway inviting the Acting Governor to go ashore. At sight of the sub-inspector, Sir Frederick deliberately paused.

'Give that fellow time to arrive,' he said, entering the cabin for no reason, while the harassed sub-inspector, reaching the base of the pier, steadied himself to a walking pace, with obvious efforts to calm himself down. Tung was impressed by the Governor's manners; a Chinese governor would have made such a subordinate lose face by being late. When the click of the sub-inspector's heels coming to attention at the head of the gangway was heard, Sir Frederick disembarked. The corporal called his men to attention as if he were commanding a mass parade, while the sub-inspector, his puppy face red with health and haste, and his lungs still activating urgently as he held himself still, quivered to a salute that was too anxious to be smart.

'Present arms!' yelled the corporal, in English. His rural

145

patrol was independent of the sub-inspector, who was from the harbour police, and he was not going to have this foreigner stealing the show. Tung wondered if the Governor understood these minor tensions of the Force. By the faint smile that appeared in his expression at the sight of the corporal, it appeared as if he did.

'Good afternoon,' he said generally.

Tung was used to these tedious arrivals at small country places, where by inescapable custom something always went wrong. How to get the corporal to end the salute? The sub-inspector was not attempting to find a way out, being as puzzled as Tung was. The Governor, not wearing a hat, had no means of acknowledging the salute. He handled it deftly.

'You're coming with us this afternoon, Corporal?' he said.

The corporal's face froze. He did not speak English. Sir Frederick turned to the sub-inspector.

'Interpret for me, will you, please.'

The sub-inspector sprang forward and gave His Excellency's words in the dialect, which he spoke with a strong English accent, without the proper tones. The corporal understood, however, beamed assent, saluted again, and commanded his men:

'Slope arms!'

But the crisis was not over. As the Governor said 'Right!' and prepared to move along the pier, the sub-inspector quivered to attention again.

'Sir, I'm sorry I was late coming down here, sir,' he began.

'That's all right, Inspector. You weren't late,' Sir Frederick replied, moving off.

'But, sir!' he insisted, trying by the tone of his voice to hold His Excellency back, 'I was receiving a message from the Royal Observatory.'

'Really,' the Governor answered, without the least interest.

'Yes, sir. Typhoon signal number one has been hoisted.'

A young whippersnapper, straight out from some small English town, thought Tung, as he contrasted the acquisitive arrogance, growing out of the fellow's subsiding puppy-fat, with his tremendous sense of importance at this moment as His Excellency's protector. To Tung's amusement, H.E.'s reaction was as unexpected to the young fellow as if a bucket of cold water had been emptied over him. He gave a guffaw of laughter.

'Good God!' he exclaimed. 'Has the Observatory gone mad?'

146

This was too deep a question for the startled sub-inspector, who replied that he was not sure.

'Tung, have you ever heard of a typhoon in the last week of November?' H.E. asked.

'Never, sir. The typhoon season finished in October.'

'Exactly,' he replied, as if confirmed in his view that lunacy had attacked the staff of the Royal Observatory. He looked up at the cloudless sky, at the film of mist resting around the gaunt peaks, now towering unusually near them, and out at the almost motionless sea. The afternoon breeze, dry and cool, continued to blow from the north, its normal winter direction. It was weather classically correct for the season. 'I think we can ignore it.'

'Yes, sir,' replied the sub-inspector, stiff with fright and fearing his chances of confirmation to the permanent and pensionable establishment might have been wrecked, while the escorting police launch gently drew up at the pier, berthing alongside the Governor's launch.

'Ask the launch if they've received the same signal,' His Excellency directed in afterthought.

'Yes, sir!' the puppy gasped, moving desperately away and all but hurtling down the gangway into the Governor's launch, from the other side of which he would be able to speak to his colleague in charge of the escort vessel.

An inspector of slightly higher seniority came on to the foredeck of the vessel, within view of Tung and Sir Frederick.

'Have you had this typhoon warning?' H.E. called out.

The inspector smiled broadly.

'Yes, sir. We got it just now. Would you like me to ask for confirmation? I think it must be a mistake.'

'Mistake!' exclaimed the Acting Governor with a laugh. 'I think they've all gone mad!'

'We always thought they were a bit off their rockers, sir. But today they're doing better than usual,' he called back gaily, while some of the crew appeared as well, grinning and looking at the peaceful sky.

'We'll go on as arranged,' Sir Frederick said.

'Yes, sir,' the inspector answered with a salute. 'We'll probably get a cancellation and apology in a few minutes.'

There was laughter from the two speakers and smiling faces all round. The Royal Observatory, in a part of the world subject to typhoons, was a sitting target for happy criticism.

'Let these men go first,' H.E. directed.

Tung quickly explained to the corporal, who dropped the bull and told his men what to do in a normal voice. Slinging their rifles over their shoulders, they ambled along in the lead, until the rhythm of their pace took hold on their minds, when they inconspicuously began walking in step. After them came the corporal; after him, two of the younger Government House servants carrying food baskets, followed by two of the assistant gardeners acting as baggage coolies (in the hope of a little extra at the end of the month), while Tung, following immediately after H.E., walked at the rear.

Just before reaching O Mun, which was some distance in from the pier, nearer the foot of the mountains, they passed a breaming beach, where six huge junks were drawn up on the shore for their hulls to be scorched with fire, fiercely kindled from fine mountain grass, cleansing them of sea slime and the living sea-creatures clinging to them. The Governor paused.

'Ask these men what they think about a typhoon, Tung,' he said, adding, as the whole cortège came to a halt: 'Let the food boys go on ahead of us and make things ready at the monastery.'

Tung gave the necessary instructions in the dialect, then called out to the breamers. Two of those nearest them turned as he spoke. He repeated his query, upon which their rough faces, reddened by fire and the sea winds of many a summer, broke into big grins, displaying missing teeth and uncomplicated friendliness.

'Typhoon? Not at this time, Your Honour. Not at this time.'

As they spoke, others looked up from their work of bundling more grass into the raging fires, and echoed the words around.

'Typhoon? Not at this time.'

Tung looked at his master.

'You can understand, sir?'

He smiled and nodded. They waved to the fishermen and walked on. When they had moved further off they could hear loud laughter among the junks, as the seafarers mocked the ignorance of those who dwelt in cities and on the shore. They passed on into the sleepy fishing town, its inhabitants preparing to take their evening meal. The hard boots of the patrol rang out from the stone-cobbled streets, among the stone houses of ancient Chinese design. The sun was still fairly high when they reached the foot of the mountains and began to ascend the rough stone-stepped path.

148

As the hills closed in about them, and sight of the placid gold-tinted sea was lost, Tung reflected on the strange solitude of his master, and on this desire of his to go away alone, to the place furthest from ordinary men, high up too, above the rest of ordinary life, where he could look down peacefully and think his thoughts. Tung did not envy him. What was the use of a life of great position and authority without a wife and family to enjoy it with? This man made solitude deeper by hardly speaking at all. Locked in his thoughts, he walked patiently, steadily upwards, without a word, without a rest, till even in the cool of the evening small beads of perspiration glistened on the back of his neck. For two hours they walked thus. The sun set as they rose above the main body of hills, with the peaks still ahead of them. In the last minutes of twilight he paused where, on a backbone of the heights, they could look down at the sea on both the north and south sides of the island.

'Where is Sheung Tsuen?' he asked, looking southward into a deep valley where a solitary light twinkled far below.

'I'm afraid I don't know, sir. I'm not familiar with this island,' Tung replied, his legs feeling stiff and tingling as their steady movement was arrested.

'Ask,' he said.

The corporal and his men had also stopped.

'Sheung Tsuen?' the corporal asked, catching the name. 'It's in the next valley. Tomorrow morning we shall be able to see it from the monastery.'

Tung translated into English. The patrol took out their electric torches.

'Would you like a torch, sir?' Tung asked, switching on his own.

'No, thank you. Yours is bright enough for the two of us.'

They set off again, the torchlight accentuating the darkness, the last light of day forgotten. Ahead, Tung could sense more than see the forbidding shape of the first of the peaks, in the side of which the monastery was said to be situated. Soon they were surrounded by trees, a sign with which he was familiar from similar walks in China. They must be nearing their destination.

The path mounted more steeply, twisting up the sides of the mountain. The line of torches scattered haphazard rays of light among overhanging branches, weirdly shaped rocks with Buddhist sayings carved on them, small pavilions and decorative archways.

149

The sound of a waterfall silenced the tramp of the patrol's boots, and filled the night with uncertainties that only morning could resolve. Tung was perspiring. Holding his torch as steadily as he could, in order to guide his master's footsteps, he carefully pulled off the woollen jacket he was wearing over his thick flannel shirt, and as he did so he wondered at himself feeling hot at this time of year. He was in training, and should hardly have noticed the effects of the climb.

Forgetting himself, he stopped.

'Torch, Tung!' said Sir Frederick testily.

'Sorry, sir!' he answered, arousing himself and hastening to close the gap between the two of them. 'Sir, d'you notice how warm it is?' he called through the hissing of the waterfall.

His master paused.

'Isn't it just us?'

'No, sir. I think the wind's changed.'

They both stared at the blackness below them, where the trees parted and left a space.

'I believe you're right,' H.E. said, continuing to gaze out. 'It's coming from the south.'

'Yes, sir.'

'That's rather unusual for this time of year, isn't it?'

'Yes, sir,' Tung answered, looking upwards. 'And there are no stars.'

The Acting Governor looked up, the torchlight throwing his face into a strange angularity. Tung momentarily switched the light off.

'Correct,' came the answering comment.

The light flashed on again, and in silence they resumed the climb. They soon rose above the waterfall, though exactly where it was Tung could not determine. It was decidedly warmer. The wind was damp and from the sea, the heavy, warm wind that sometimes preceded a typhoon.

After ten more minutes they passed under a larger and more formal arch, beyond which was a gate god in a shrine. The floor was paved. They were in a courtyard. The torch, flashed ahead, reflected the stare of glass windows in a dark building, with orange trees planted in a row in front of it, the trees rising equidistantly amid the paved court. To the left, as they drew nearer, the unshaded glare of pressure lamps rayed out from another building further back and higher up the hillside, which rose here more gently, terraced with what appeared to be ornamental gardens, with fantastic rockeries and cunningly contrived watercourses. The sound of the waterfall was less noticeable, and when the leaves of the trees shook in a long steady driving of wind that passed above them, sheltered as they were in the carefully chosen site of the monastery, their rustling, and the crack of a branch somewhere out in the mountainside forest, could be distinguished above the rushing of water.

Within the glaringly lighted room, with stone walls and red tiled floor, two aged monks in grey robes, the light glowing on their absurd bald heads, were fussing about in a state of anxiety while the Government House servants unpacked the provisions on a long, wooden table and tried to decide what would be served for dinner.

'Not meat! Not meat!' one of the monks was crying agitatedly in the dialect as the Acting Governor reached the doorway.

Both shivered and tittered with fright and respect as he stepped in. Uncertain how to greet him, they half-bowed, chattering incomprehensibly all the while, ushered him to be seated at the table where they then perceived there was no chair to sit on, hastily altered their dispositions and invited him to take his place in an old blackwood chair placed against the wall between two pictures of devils in the Buddhist firmament, spotted that the chair was covered with dust, bumped into each other (their bald heads narrowly escaping collision) as they both started in opposite directions to find a feather duster, and at last, by a sort of psychic understanding, divided their duties, one fetching the duster, while the other poured out tea into little cups and, with overwhelmed diffidence, invited His Excellency to drink. The tea, Tung noted, was tasteless.

'You know the form here, Tung,' Sir Frederick said as he took a sip of tea that must have burnt his lips. 'I'm following you from now on.'

Meanwhile, from a room beyond, the other monk was heard moaning in the dialect:

'Oh, no! Precious Buddha! Not wine! Not wine!'—which was followed by the popping of a cork, as one of the assistant gardeners carried out the acting cook's orders to make the place a bit more homely.

In a short time the baskets were cleared off the table, a cloth was spread over it, and the Government House cut glass appeared, with a decanter of sherry looking rather distinguished amongst an assortment of whisky, gin, and brandy bottles (when travelling, one tried for perfection, but could not always achieve it). Nuts were served, and shrimp crisps. This, Tung thought, was going to be a passable evening. In the absence of any nice Chinese girls, there was at least the solace of food and wine.

The grey-robed monks fluttered like dying bats around this horrible scene of festivity, but Tung did not say anything about them to H.E., because he knew of the tendency for Europeans to treat monks with respect. As usual, he reduced his face to expressionlessness and had a quiet laugh inside, all by himself. H.E. sat on the now dusted blackwood chair, between the devils.

'Good heavens, Freddie! What on earth are you doing here?'

Tung switched round to the door at the sound of a woman's voice. The door was completely circular—what the Chinese call a moon-gate, but with glass doors across it. In the full-moon-shaped darkness of the door stood Mrs. Fairburn, wearing a pair of brown slacks and a yellow polo-necked sweater. Carrying a dim lantern, she was blinking in the bright light of the pressure lamp.

'Hullo,' said 'Freddie', rising from the blackwood chair. (This was entertaining, Tung considered. The use of 'Freddie' was rather a surprise. Could it be usual? He had never heard them speak together before—at least, not alone.) 'What have you done with Frances Lau?'

She stood still in the doorway. One of her eyebrows rose slightly, independent of the other.

'You mean, you knew which day we were coming?' she queried.

'Yes,' he said, with a chuckle. 'Edwin told me. I thought I'd surprise you.'

'You do, Freddie,' she answered without amusement, walking slowly through the moon-gate door into the room. 'Edwin evidently didn't tell you that, after all, he wouldn't allow Frances to come.'

He was taking out his pipe. At her words, his movement stopped.

'You mean, you're here alone?'

'Yes,' she replied, rather as if she were speaking to a child. She was all but offensive in her manner towards him; she seemed to take extraordinary liberties. 'I'm here alone, Freddie. Quite alone.'

152

She then sat, to Tung's astonishment, in the blackwood chair between the devils. She certainly had a nerve, this woman! In the absence of the servants, all busy elsewhere, Tung occupied himself with the bottles.

'Can I serve you a drink, sir?'

Withdrawing his mind from something far away, Sir Frederick irritatedly faced a choice.

'Brandy and soda for me. What will you have, Sylvia?'

'The same, please.'

Tung fixed them up, helping himself to a whisky afterwards, and standing discreetly just outside the moon-gate door—where the police would have said he should have been—watching the increasing disturbance of the night.

'If you knew we were coming, you could at least have offered us a lift,' her voice continued. Her tone was so peculiar, it was as if she had some hold over him, Tung calculated, as he listened to the now continuous rustling of leaves. Could it be—but it seemed improbable—that she was his mistress? There had been stories about her, and he—no, Tung knew better than most people how solitary *his* life was.

'I took it you'd be coming in Edwin's launch,' he said. 'How did you come? By ferry?'

'Yes. I came up the other way, from Tungpaw.

The monks, who had retired elsewhere, returned with frightened expressions. Their fright increased when they saw that only the two foreigners sat in the room. Hastening out through the door, they imparted to Tung their dreadful news:

'It appears there's a typhoon coming!'

Tung nodded at the doddering old idiots.

'But what will you all do up here?' they exclaimed woefully.

Without words, Tung made a significant sign of drinking from a pot. Both laughed shiveringly, becoming more men of the world with every minute that passed.

The Acting Governor and Mrs. Fairburn joined them in the doorway.

'How does it look, Tung?'

'Pretty bad, sir, I'm afraid. The wind's getting stronger all the time.'

The monks were chattering apprehensively.

'Are typhoons bad up here?' Tung asked them.

'Oh, not usually. We're very sheltered,' one of them answered. The other giggled, and murmured: 'Very lucky! Very lucky!'

'It won't be much up here, sir,' Tung said reassuringly.

'I hope you're right, Tung. We're damned high up.'

Though verbally assuring, however, the monks themselves seemed to have some doubts. While dinner was being served (which Tung was invited to attend with Sir Frederick and Mrs. Fairburn) a long discussion was going on, in and out of the room, about where it would be safest for His Excellency to sleep. Other monks had joined the original two by this time, one large bull-faced one, several nervous thin ones, and some younger, more active ones, all in the same grey robes, and with shaven or bald heads. Tung paid his entire attention during dinner to this extraneous conversation which neither of his companions understood, and concealed his growing alarm as the trend of it indicated that a typhoon had never actually hit the monastery, but that, if one ever did, this entire building (the guest house), in which they were seated, might be likely to fall down. It was finally decided, after much whispered discussion, that the safest and most comfortable place for visitors of such importance would be upstairs in the new building, wherever that was. Anyhow, by the way they spoke, it sounded fairly solid.

There were titters from the older monks as wine was served with dinner. To the younger ones there was some exciting novelty about it, and they craned forwards out of the gloom of the adjacent room in order to have a better view. At one point six of the older monks, overwhelmed by this pressure from the rear, were projected violently forwards toward the diners' table. His Excellency looked up with composure, apparently expecting the movement to be a deputation of some kind. His look crumpled it up. Scolding, wriggling, and chattering, the monks pushed each other back in a minor frenzy towards the door from which they had emerged, and long after they had all disappeared voices could still be heard castigating and admonishing in whispers. The young ones were, it appeared, still far too excitable. They must learn the meaning of detachment.

'These monasteries are nothing but a big racket,' said Tung at last, in a gap in the conversation.

H.E. laughed, surprised at his intrusion.

'Is that so, Tung?'

'Mr. Tung and I will have to compare notes on this subject,

154

I can see,' said Mrs. Fairburn. 'That's always been my general view, too. Still, they make up for having no hotels in country like this.'

After dinner, commendably prepared by the resourceful servants, they were led by the monk in charge of visitors to the so-called new building, an imposing two-storey concrete edifice, painted in bright colours outside, cream, green, and red, with a flight of concrete steps leading up to it. The night was full of sound as they walked among the monastery buildings, an indeterminate sound, partly the waterfall, partly the shivering of leaves and grass, partly the wind's movement.

'I should say this isn't much more than a strong wind,' Sir Frederick commented. She was walking at his side, ahead of Tung, who found it hard to take his eyes off her. He quite liked European women, when they were intelligent and lively—not the Mrs. Webb type. To make it more interesting, he had the inescapable impression of having walked into the middle of something.

They entered the new building. The lower floor, consisting of one large room, was the monks' dining-room, with three long tables stretching right across it. At the head of the centre table, opposite the door, was an altar with a gilt statue of the Buddha in standing position, with a smaller *blanc de Chine* statuette of Kwan Yin, the Goddess of Mercy, in front of it. On either side were lecterns, from which the scriptures could be—but probably weren't often—read during meals.

Passing behind this altar, they mounted a stout wooden stairway to the upper floor, the whole of the centre of which was occupied by a vast canopied altar of the three Buddhas, of the past, the present, and the future. Here the monks had clearly concentrated the monastery's most valued possessions. The walls were hung with finely written scrolls, some of great age, and on the left of the altar was a huge bronze bell, suspended by a steel chain from the ceiling, with a log of wood horizontally suspended by two smaller chains, with two handpieces of cloth dangling from it. To sound the bell one had to swing the log to and fro by the handpieces, till it swung sufficiently to strike the outer edge of the bell. The Buddha statues were encased in glass, the canopy being made of embroidered silk, long pendants of which hung on all sides, with small bells attached to them, like tassels. As Mrs. Fairburn passed one of them, her sleeve

155

touched the silk, causing the little bells at the bottom of it to tinkle cheerfully. Two pressure lamps illumined the large room. To their harsh light was added a more friendly glow from several hundred burning wicks gleaming with a gentle golden light in flat dishes of vegetable oil set out before the altar. In the empty space between these and the windows, leading out to a balcony, were three deck chairs. The Acting Governor laughed as he saw them.

'Everything for our comfort!'

The receiver of guests, the one frightened about the typhoon, at this point brought Inspector Tung aside to a small door behind the altar. This led to a dark corridor, off which a number of bedrooms had been formed by the erection of wooden partitions, somewhat like a Chinese hotel. It was clear to Tung that on Buddhist festivals the monastery enjoyed a thriving business from tourists and devotees.

'I hope this will be quite suitable for them,' the monk simpered, thinking evidently that Mrs. Fairburn was His Excellency's wife.

'Quite,' he replied. 'But they'll sleep in two separate rooms.'

As he said it, he felt his voice falter. Was this the right order to give? A mistake in a matter of this kind could be extremely serious to him. Suddenly, after the interlude of being a gentleman again at dinner, he reverted to being an unknown, unsupported refugee. A mistake of this magnitude could cost him his hard-earned and perilously held security. Might not this unexpected meeting in the monastery be the object of His Excellency's lonely trip? Was it not, in fact, intended to turn out in this way? Might not a word of his upset this carefully prepared plan?

'Very well,' said the monk. 'Then you will have the third room. It's quite clean. I will put extra quilts out for you.'

By the way he spoke, Tung perceived that the old man had expected the two foreigners to sleep together under a double quilt. Had he perhaps been tipped off by someone what to do? By some member of the Government House staff, for example, acting secretly in the Governor's interest? He remembered the curious intimacy between the two of them, Mrs. Fairburn's lack of respect for him, a hundred small indications of a mental current between them from which others were excluded. He looked into the small wooden room. It had a double bed already prepared. Beside it a table was set with a tea-basket, a bottle of cold

156

water, and two small teacups. The monk swung his dim lantern in.

'You see? I think they will be quite comfortable.'

Inspector Tung hesitated.

'I think separate rooms are better,' he said.

'As you say, as you say,' the silly old chap sniffed. Well, thought Tung, if the monk had in fact received contrary orders, he need not obey, and the double quilt would still be there.

The old monk did obey, however. Off he went down the stairs, to order another quilt to be brought up. 'And you, Inspector,' he said, pausing vaguely half-way down, 'you will take the third room.'

'No,' said Tung hastily, 'I'll stay downstairs.' Whatever was intended to take place, he must keep well away, if he valued his future in the Police Force. He had not expected this casual week-end visit to entail so delicate and momentous a decision for him. Feeling cold and anxious, he followed the monk downstairs to the refectory, where the corporal and his men were strolling about, having a look. They had decided, they said, to stay in the guest-house, whatever the supposed dangers. There was bedding for them there. Absorbed in his own problem, Inspector Tung hardly noticed what they said.

The guest-house monks were fussing in and out disorganizedly with various items of bedding, when one of the younger monks hurried in, conducting the young British sub-inspector from O Mun far below. He was wearing canvas and rubber shoes and a not very correct assortment of regulation clothing, including a khaki pullover and a blue scarf. His torch was down to the battery's last dim glow, and his right hand, holding a walking-stick, was cut. He had clearly had a rough time making the difficult ascent at night, with the wind blowing as it was. If he had started with any headgear, he had lost it on the way. He had fair curly hair, dry and unkempt after exposure to the wind.

With no more than a couple of words between them, Tung took him upstairs to the Acting Governor. The sub-inspector having succeeded in becoming the star of the show, Tung knew that the less he himself said the better, lest it be held against him later that he tried to stand between the sub-inspector and his glory. That was another aspect of being a Chinese member of a British police force. When it came to something between one

157

Britisher and another, one was inclined to find one's seniority counting for less than one thought. Never to stand between a young ignoramus of this kind and his dream of promotion had become one of Tung's maxims. His own dreams, after all, lay elsewhere.

His Excellency and the lady were seated in the deck chairs before the three gilded Buddhas under their ornate canopy. The puppy, who evidently did not know who the lady was, showed signs of nervousness as he saw them together, fixing his eyes on the Acting Governor, and keeping perseveringly to the matter in hand. Lacking subtlety, his manner was almost rude, almost an implication. Had he even said good evening to the lady it would have made this less obvious. By ignoring her, he irritated the Governor, created embarrassment when no one—not even Tung—knew if there was cause for any, and probably ditched his chances of a commendation from H.E. to the Commissioner.

'Typhoon signal number seven has just been hoisted, sir. At least, I mean, it was just hoisted when I left the station. Seeing as how it looked a bit more serious than we thought, sir, I contacted Royal Observatory for a special appreciation. The typhoon's name is Hilda, sir'—the Acting Governor gave a grunt of contempt—'yes, sir,' the puppy faltered, 'and according to the latest it's heading directly for the colony. It's expected to strike with full force early tomorrow morning. If it keeps to its present course, sir, they expect it to die down a bit tomorrow evening, when probably the centre will pass over us. The second blow is expected some time during the early hours of Monday, and may last all day.'

'Where are the launches?'

'Oh, I forgot, sir! The Director of Marine sent a signal saying they were on no account to try to return.'

'Where are the launches?' H.E. repeated coldly.

'Sorry, sir! They're at anchor out in the harbour, sir.'

'Good. Is it blowing hard there?'

'Not too bad, sir. The harbour's sheltered from this wind. But it may change, of course.'

Tung watched with amusement H.E.'s steadily increasing bad temper at being told about typhoons.

'Are you going to be able to go back tonight?'

'I thought I'd have a try, sir, if I can get another torch. This one's conked out.'

158

'If you can get back, I'd like you to send a signal to the Commissioner of Police, telling him I propose—— No, I'd better write it for you. Tung! Paper and a pencil, please.'

Sir Frederick wrote the message on Tung's police pocketbook:

Governor to CP: Safe at. monastery Propose remain here till typhoon passes Maintaining contact with launch.

'I'd be glad if you can get that off tonight. By the way, d'you know Mrs. Fairburn?'

'No, sir. I haven't had the pleasure. Good evening.'

She acknowledged his greeting in silence.

'You'd better have a brandy before you go.'

'Thanks a lot, sir. I'm teetotal.'

'Very well. Keep me informed tomorrow as best you can.'

'Yes, sir. I'll get a man up with a progress report as soon as it's safe. It's just that one ridge, sir. If it's really full blast tomorrow, sir, it'll be impassable.'

'I appreciate the situation. Do your best.'

'Yes, sir. Good night, sir.'

'Good night.'

His arm clicked half-way up to a salute, until he remembered he no longer had a cap on. With a mixed burst of importance and confusion, he turned about, and strode quietly out in his rubber shoes, the only sound being the occasional tap of his stick on stair and tile floor.

Seeing that H.E. and Mrs. Fairburn wanted nothing, Tung followed the puppy down to help him borrow a better torch, only to find that by the time he had made his way among the gloomy buildings to where there was a light, the young fellow had gone. Rather than borrow from a member of a rural patrol, the inspector, being of the harbour police, had preferred a loan from the receiver of guests, who at sight of Tung trotted distractedly to him at the moon-gate door, his teeth chattering with anxiety.

'It's coming straight for us, Inspector! Have you heard the terrible news? Perhaps none of us will be safe! It will be a disaster!'

'Detachment, Reverend Brother, detachment!' Tung reminded him with a pat on the shoulder.

The old fellow shivered all over, uttering as he did so a long sigh.

'In effect, I forget myself. O Lotus! O Immaculate Jewel!' he cried. 'Prayers must be said!' he decided hastily, rushing into the room beyond the guest-room, lighting three tapers, and sticking them in an ash-filled urn before another large Buddha statue. 'Ah! Detachment! . . . But, Inspector, it's difficult to be detached about this building. What if it falls down and there is nowhere to house all the generous disciples who come during the winter months? We shall be ruined!' He came miserably back to Tung at the doorway, his face pallid in the harsh light. 'What do you advise, Inspector?' he asked wistfully.

Tung affected a measure of incomprehension.

'But, Reverend Brother, surely the Precious One will attend to this important matter?'

'Ohh!!' the old monk wailed again. 'The Precious One! The Pitiful! Hail to Thee, O Jewel in the Flower of the Lotus! What an awful predicament we are in!'

Tung with difficulty kept a grave face.

'I should have said personally this building was as strong as a rock.'

The old man gazed up at him in wonderment, his eyes squinting slightly, the pointed eyebrows of age rising independently after the rest of the movement of his face had ceased, like the wings of some insect balancing on the petals of a flower.

'You would, Inspector? You really would?'

'Of course! Look at these thick walls. D'you really think any typhoon could knock these down?'

'No, perhaps not. But the roofs, Inspector, the roofs! They will all be carried away! We shall be exposed, Inspector, exposed as we lie in our beds, and——'

'Weren't the roofs built by a competent contractor?'

'Indeed they were! We spent $3,127 on them only two years ago.'

'Then we're all perfectly safe, Reverend Brother.'

He looked at Tung for a second, his face forming the sweet smile of an idiot in an old-age home.

'Ah! Detachment!' he said, and more firmly: 'Detachment! It's what I spend my life trying to teach these ignorant people. Still, prayers should be said. And, by all the Noble Truths, I still haven't found you a quilt!'

160

Without more words, he trotted away.

Tung groped his way back through the darkness to the new building. The air was unnaturally sultry, not warm exactly, but as if it were feverish—certainly not the cold, dry starlit night he had expected. He walked through the refectory and quietly up the stairs.

'You're frightened, Freddie.'

He was two steps from the top as he heard her voice. Something impelled him to stop, almost to hold his breath.

'Of the typhoon, I suppose,' came the slightly cynical reply.

There was a pause.

'No. Of another kind of typhoon.'

Another silence.

'That fertile imagination of yours at work again.'

'Not just imagination. A typhoon blowing just over us—only us.'

Tung shivered slightly. He knew what she meant. She was a clever woman, able to clothe her thoughts in images easy to understand. He wondered whether he should make a noise on the stairway.

'Haven't you presupposed rather more than necessary?' he asked.

'Only what everyone will presuppose. Freddie, please stop walking up and down. Tell me I'm an embarrassment to you. It'll make you feel better. I am.'

The sound of the wind out beyond the sheltered monastery increased in volume.

'Ah! Inspector, look what I've found you! A new quilt. Quite new.' It was the monk bundling up the stairs with a quilt impeding his steps. 'Unfortunately it smells a little strange. It's this sudden attack of damp air. But, as you see, it's very clean.'

Tung slapped one hand heavily on the banister and stepped with deliberation up the last remaining stairs.

'I've already told you,' he said to the monk, 'I wish to sleep downstairs.'

'But there's no cot for you down there. All the cots are upstairs,' the old man explained. 'Really it will be more convenient if you take my advice.' He bundled on into the corridor leading to the bedrooms.

Tung followed him. There was nothing to do but make

161

himself scarce, and wish he'd been given some other duty, without being trapped in this situation in which he had no proper place, yet in which he was forced to contend in his capacity as bodyguard.

As soon as the monk had laid out the quilt and departed with more chat, Tung flung himself down on the hard bed and shut his eyes. His legs were stiff after the climb. If only His so-and-so Excellency would damned well decide to go sleep with the woman! Let the lights be turned out, and let them all pretend they were sleeping somewhere else! He opened his eyes a little. If only there had been a decent lamp, he could have used this time to write his diary. He liked keeping a diary. It was his best, his only real, possession. It was part of his trust in himself, the one safe friend to whom matters of importance could be confided.

There was not enough light—only a faint glow from the glaring lights in the adjacent room with the great altar, where they were talking still, no doubt, trapped like him, trapped in another way, though—by passion, by the need to consume each other (it was what he had felt between them as they sat at dinner), and now about to dig their nails into each other's flesh in the last hours before being trapped by a social catastrophe, the outcome that awaited their return to the city, the disaster which even that silly little foreign sub-inspector had sensed without a whisper of explanation from anyone, the downfall that was implicit in every stirring of the warm wind.

Without knowing it, he fell asleep. He did not become aware of his weakness till something produced a change in the surroundings, a change that made him realize he had woken up. What the change was, he could not tell. Everything seemed the same, yet he had a sense of having been startled. Somewhere in the distance a monk was murmuring the endless incomprehensibilities of Chinese Buddhist prayers, which doubtless neither the murmurer nor anyone else understood.

Suddenly it occurred again. A shattering vibration, a deep crash of musical sound. He sat up on the hard bed. Someone was striking the great bell in the altar-room. He was preparing to get up when His Excellency's voice called:

'Tung! Tung!'

The voice came nearer, uncertainly, in the gloom. Tung shook off sleep and leapt to his feet.

'Yes, sir!'

He stepped out into the dismal corridor, in the door of which H.E. was standing.

'Oh, Tung'—there was relief in the tone—'we want to go to bed. Is there any way of stopping this infernal noise?'

Tung walked past his master into the still brightly lit altar-room. There, at a glance, he saw that the murmurings and the clanging of the bell were controlled at the same source.

Seated cross-legged beside the great bell was an anaemic old monk, reading sutras from a ricepaper book. At the end of each stanza he laid the book down, took the cloth handpieces of the striking log, swung them mystically to and fro, and struck, with diabolic vehemence, the motionless, vibrating bell. After this, bringing the log rapidly to rest, he resumed his reading aloud to the end of the next stanza, and struck again. The bell's voice was adamantine in the high, square room. It seemed to make the entire building quiver and reassert itself. How long this had passed unnoticed in his sleep, he did not know.

'Can you do something, Tung?' asked H.E. helplessly, while the monk droned on unconcernedly, only a few yards from the deck chairs. Mrs. Fairburn was no longer in the room.

He went up close to the monk.

'Reverend Brother . . .'

At this point a stanza came to an end, down went the book, back and forth the log, and, with an almighty crash, the bell was struck.

Long before the vibrations had died away, the next stanza began.

'Reverend Brother, are you by any chance praying for the safety of the monastery?' Tung asked, standing right over the totally absorbed pale sack of anaemia, who at this juncture hunched his grey robe closer round his body—could it have been a gesture of protest? 'Because if you are, and you're at all worried about the roof,' Tung shouted at him right through the next stanza, 'I'd say that the combination of you, the bell, and the wind would just about bring it down nicely.'

The stanza rose to a rather louder, more insistent, rendering, as if barking through comments on the suffering inherent in all life were another, less cultivated, voice telling him to shut his trap. Tung folded his arms in as sinister a manner as possible over the fellow's head, and waited. Again the stanza ended, and the bell was struck. Tung was prepared to snatch the book away,

163

when the ritual changed. Instead of picking it up, the monk struck the bell again—and again—and again—ten, eleven, twelve times. It seemed to take an eternity.

He then picked up the book, closed it, dropped his feet to the ground, rose, and walked off downstairs without an indication of having seen anybody or heard a word of what Tung had said.

The Acting Governor laughed heartily. Mrs. Fairburn came out of the Governor's bedroom.

'Well done, Mr. Tung,' she said. 'You were superb.'

She had already taken her shoes off, and her hair was hanging loose. She was attractive, in the exotic manner of a European painting. Her features had not, of course, the regularity of Chinese beauty. She went back into his room.

'Where are you sleeping, Tung?' H.E. asked.

It was a forced question, Tung saw. Hadn't H.E. seen him come out of his sleeping-room? He drew in a quick breath.

'I think I'm going to find it more comfortable downstairs, sir. It's not so cold.'

In fact, it was not cold at all. He let the matter slip from his grasp as Sir Frederick walked through to the third cubicle.

'This is not very satisfactory, Tung. I think you should sleep out here,' he said, indicating the corridor outside the second room.

'As you wish, sir.'

'Come on. Let's move your bed.'

Together they carried the wooden frame out sideways into the corridor, removing the quilt and planks first, replacing them afterwards in H.E.'s selected position. When Tung shifted the bed further away from the door, H.E. moved his end a little nearer to it, crossing thereafter to Tung's end of the bed to move it nearer likewise.

'You'll get more fresh air here,' he said.

It was a kind of chess game, with all the rules gone wrong.

He next asked Tung to extinguish the pressure lamps in the altar room. It was the moment, Tung realized, for extreme tactfulness. He walked back into the empty room. There were two lamps, one on either side of the deck chairs. The first one he lowered and extinguished. The second he detached and took with him downstairs. In any case, he needed to ease himself. The piece fitted into the picture. Opening the barred door of the new building, he put the lamp down in the doorway and walked out as far as its light would take him into the ornamental court and garden directly outside. A dog barked hysterically, scenting his movement, but not daring to come near. The wind, the waterfall, the leaves, the grass, all were speaking more loudly, wildly. It was a strange sensation, to be aware of the storm's power, yet feel nothing except the sick, moist warmth of a freak return to autumn.

He loitered at the end of the garden, where beyond a terraced wall the land dropped to a lower level, to which the lamplight could not penetrate. So undisturbed was it that a spider was spinning a web between the leaves of two orange trees. Glancing at his watch, Tung saw it was already past eleven. He must have fallen off to sleep for longer than he realized. A few heavy drops of rain fell. He looked up at the stirring blackness above him. The moon had not yet risen. No glimmer of light alleviated the threatening gloom. As the rain increased, he returned hastily to the door of the refectory, bolted it again, lowered the pressure in the lamp, and went noiselessly upstairs. In the altar-room he paused, moving about to find somewhere to place the lamp, so that in an emergency he could grab it quickly. Not that an emergency was likely in this remote, peaceful place. He tested his torch, the battery of which was still strong, pointing it in the ugly, fat, golden faces of the three Buddhas, and at the writings hung on the walls.

A few of the wicks still burned gently in the dishes of vegetable oil. What gibberish was all this that those monks claimed to believe in? Did one of them have the vaguest idea of the meaning of those Sanskrit words from India, reproduced in Chinese by their sound, a crazy jumble of characters looking like the work of a compositor gone mad?

From the bedrooms there was, so far as could be ascertained above the sounds of the wind and the waterfall, silence. Unable to pretend any longer that he had something to do, Tung came to the door of the corridor, silent himself and without a light. He had hesitated in the garden, hesitated before the Buddhas; he hesitated again now. What part had they elected him to play?

As his eyesight became accustomed to the lampless corridor, he observed that his bed had again been moved slightly. Still outside the second bedroom, it was no longer near the centre of the corridor, but had been moved to the very door of the bedroom, the sides of the frame touching both doorposts, so that without stepping over the bed no one could enter the room or leave it.

As quietly as possible, he took off his shoes and lay down

under the quilt. The silence was significant. He sensed that H.E. must be in the second room, before which his own bed lay, but within, the mosquito curtain was down and he could see nothing. Nor could he hear any breathing. If H.E. was there, he must be awake. She must be still in the first bedroom, Tung thought. She too, made no sound. The three of them, in fact, Tung reflected, were lying there a few yards from each other in the near-darkness, all of them awake, each thinking of the other, perhaps, each wondering if there was a way out of the pattern in which they lay. Tung wondered whether he would be questioned by his superiors on the matter. His future would depend on what he said. He hoped that, with His Excellency in it, the Commissioner himself would handle it. That would be preferable to answering one of the Assistant Superintendents, who didn't even know when the bodyguard had to take a coat. Lying there, he wondered what he would say if they asked him where he himself had slept. How would he answer? What was he doing, lying in this particular, carefully chosen spot? Was he protecting his master from anyone entering, or preventing him from going out? Was his master even in the room?

A rush of heavy raindrops spattered across the roof, but the wind was still too fierce for any steady rain to fall. The air in the corridor was humid and stuffy, and the quilt smelt of dankness. He thought after a while of a girl he used to know in the North, and of her family's fruit orchards, where they used to stroll together. He would have married her, had his father allowed it; but for reasons of his own his father would not. Later they said she was taken away by a Russian to Sinkiang, as his mistress. She had soft hair, with a slight natural curl in it, and in the winter her cheeks turned to a pale, pale pink, like plum blossom. . . .

15

I T W A S Monday noon before Inspector Tung reached his quarters in the Central Police Station. The party had done better than was originally expected. Towards the end of Sunday morning, up at the monastery, it was apparent by the way the wind was

166

gradually swinging from south-east to south-west that they were on the edge of the typhoon. It had altered course, and would not pass over the colony. By 3 p.m. a police corporal managed to bring up a message that confirmed what they had already judged to be the position. Two hours later the wind veered and lessened sufficiently for them to risk the journey down, the second part of it accomplished in the dark. They dined and spent the night in the Governor's launch, starting back to the city just after dawn. The journey was rough. Though the typhoon had passed, its lowering aftermath still disturbed sea and sky. A mass of roughly moving grey clouds crossed a sea strewn with waste from those beaches where litter lay along the normal tideline and had now been swept into the angry steel-grey water churning hither and thither. As they reached the harbour, rain, that would probably continue for two days, began at last to fall.

Feeling a trifle unsteady on his feet and in his stomach, Tung was in a sense relieved to be back, walking through the mournful, high-ceilinged barracks (now empty) to his small, private cubicle at the end of them. There, on his table, the newspapers of yesterday and today awaited him, two in English, two in Chinese. These daily deliveries, together with *Time* and a magazine from Taipei, were one of his few extravagances—one which earned him the reputation of a scholar among the constables, his fellow-inspectors, and the lower ranks of the British officers. It was considered extraordinary to order one's own newspapers, specially English ones (so far as the constables were concerned), and to all it was scarcely credible that any fellow-member of the police could look at magazines with so few pictures in them, and hardly any of naked women.

He flicked open the English papers with a curious apprehension, as if he himself were personally involved in what he might see. The Sunday papers warned of the imminent coming of the typhoon. This morning's told the rest of the tale. 'COLONY'S NARROW ESCAPE' ran the headline, crossing the whole page, a second after seeing which Tung alighted on the thickly headed column: 'ACTING GOVERNOR MAROONED: Privations in Buddhist Monastery'. With the speed of a professional—he had a number of journalist friends—he glanced at the credit at the tail of the article, and ridiculed the fact that the colony should receive news of itself from an international news agency instead of from a local newspaperman. Even ignoring the credit, it was undisguisedly the

167

work of an international agency. It began by explaining to the colony when the colony's typhoon season occurred. It then explained to the colony who the colony's Acting Governor was. Some incorrect detail about Buddhist monasteries followed, with an explanation for the benefit of the souls of the agency's Christian readers that a visit to a Buddhist monastery did not imply the taking of any vows, or reception into the Buddhist Church, that monasteries were popular tourist places etc., the difficulties of obtaining food on top of a mountain, the unusual dangers involved, His Excellency's calm message of reassurance to the Commissioner of Police—the busy agency had left no stone unturned. 'Also marooned at the same monastery,' the article concluded, 'was the novelist, Sylvia Gracechurch.'

Knowing as he did the litigiousness of Westerners, their skill in differentiating fine points of meaning in phrases which in Chinese were identical, Tung recognized the care with which that last sentence had been composed. It said all, and nothing. It stated; it did not infer. It was an unassailable sentence, yet to the whole world, after the success of Sylvia Gracechurch's novel, it might mean something.

A rapid stride sounded in the barrack room, drawing nearer to his cubicle. He glanced up at a yokel of a Cantonese constable standing insolently in the doorway.

'C.P. wants you, Inspector.'

'Where?'

'Headquarters, I suppose. The sergeant didn't say.'

'I'm coming.'

So soon. In effect, the colony Force was renowned for its speed and efficiency. Foreign visitors congratulated them on it wearisomely. He changed into a lounge suit and went down to the courtyard.

'Any transport going down to P.H.Q.?' he asked at the office under the arch of the main entrance.

'That truck, sir.'

'Get the driver immediately. I have to report to C.P.'

Things worked well in the Force, he thought, as he climbed up next to the driver and slammed the hard metal door. When it came to delicate matters, to high personages, to great reputations, would it be the same? At least, it was the C.P. who was to interrogate him. There was a chance of—of sophistication.

As the truck twisted in driving rain around the narrow,

168

descending streets leading down to the waterfront headquarters, he tried, with something like a last plaintive despair, to imagine what the questions would be like, and how he would answer them.

'I understand about your bed, Inspector. What happened in the morning?'

—when all he could remember in the morning was how they had crawled round the side of the cavity in which the monastery lay, till they reached the bare steep shoulder upon which the full rage of the typhoon unleashed itself, and Sir Frederick, anxious to look down into the valley of Sheung Tsuen and Ha Tsuen, had advanced half-a-step too far, to be flung back by the terrifying strength of the wind into Tung's arms. Even his breath had been stopped by it. He gasped as he righted himself in the shelter of the last rock on the mountainside, round which the narrower issues of the wind screamed, the broader mass of the typhoon filling the entire sky with its merciless roar.

'Richard's right, then,' he said loudly to her. 'There are deserted fields, a whole lot of them, above the village. With some help, and with a road, all those could be brought under vegetable cultivation.'

After which he explained in breathy yells how, when these islands first became British, the Chinese inhabitants acquired the right to apply for British passports, with the result that hundreds of them migrated to other more profitable places of livelihood, to the West Indies, San Francisco, Borneo, Singapore, Madagascar, even to St. Helena. Formerly large villages were half-deserted. The old acreage could no longer be cultivated. Large tracts of hill land, the harder land to grow anything on, fell into disuse. Since then the population had increased. Pressure on the land was growing. But restoring terraced fields to their former usefulness, after eighty years of neglect, was a heavy job, and demanded capital. It was also a revolutionary idea to most villagers.

'If only this weren't going to be such a public occasion,' she shouted at him, 'how exhilarating it would be!'

He nodded, the three of them standing side by side, Tung a little above them on the mountainside, staring down at the extraordinary view below, their eyelashes twisted upwards, distorting the shape of their eyes, their hair flying wildly upwards, making them resemble the devils on the scrolls in the monastery guestroom. Below, the sea was a seething expanse of grey battered

169

foam, the water-crests being swept up into the air and hurled forwards in the direction of the wind, like a hideous mist scudding close to the surface of the sea, moved by an uncanny power to mingle with the water itself, to fall and rise again in its desperate flight. Between two of the lesser islands, a large junk dipped and twisted uncontrollably, unable to reach the shelter of either the one island or the other.

'She's lost her mast!' His Excellency shouted.

Tung nodded. The attention of all three of them had concentrated on the far-off, anonymous disaster.

The truck, swinging out into the lower streets of the city, headed for Police Headquarters.

'Inspector Tung, my information on capsized junks is adequate. Will you kindly remember in detail: what happened in the morning?'

—when in the early morning it is hard to recall that one has special police duties, hard to deny the habits imposed by generations of family custom. Like his father and grandfather before him, Tung Sze-liang rose early, always well before dawn. At the monastery, the monks were up before him. Beneath the howling of the wind in the later hours of the night, he heard their droning prayers, the vibration of their flat gongs, the rumour of their nervousness. It was 5.30 a.m. He dozed till six, then sat up, put on his shoes, and went down with the lamp to try and find a tea-basket, the sedate old Chinese contrivance for keeping a pot of tea warm all night, enclosed in a basket lined with cushioning of rice straw. Finding what he wanted, he drank two small cups of tea, released the wooden bars across the door, and went out in search of the latrine. It took him some time to find it. A dog again barked at him. Returning to the new building, he was stopped by the receiver of guests, wishing to know at what time he should bring hot water for washing, and what kind of meal should be prepared, if any, in the monastery kitchen. When he had dealt with these problems, which involved finding out how much food the servants had brought up, he returned once more to the new building to see that the lamp was no longer where he had left it, while a bright light shone upstairs. Mounting to the upper floor, he found H.E., wearing pyjamas and a silk dressing gown, lighting his first pipe. In the process, he was glancing up critically at the ugly faces of the three Buddhas.

'What happened in the morning, Inspector Tung?'

They shot in through the gates of the headquarters. The truck drew up.

'C.P.'s office,' he said at the lift.

'Eighth,' said the attendant, taking him to the floor marked '7'.

The outer office, a European woman, a telephone call. 'Inspector Tung is here, sir.' Thick carpets, quietness, air conditioning, uncanny silence with the window panes running with rain, and the certainty that vessels were hooting in the noisy harbour. A young superintendent opened the inner door—a very modern door, like something in a Hollywood film, completely different from any door in the Central Police Station. A walk over dark blue carpet to a desk, a uniform, three rows of gaily coloured medal ribbons, a face—a foreign face, humorous, but with the capacity to empty itself of expression, with the capacity therefore of ruthlessness, with blue eyes, and a slightly bald, rather small head.

'Inspector Tung, sir.'

The soft fall of a footstep on the carpet.

'Come in, Tung. Have you read the papers?'

A dry voice, like ash in which no fire remains.

'Not all of them yet, sir.'

'Your weekend jaunt has received some fairly grisly comment in the Chinese mosquito press. The Chinese papers that struggle to be respectable have been more or less respectable. *The Bulletin* has excelled itself in intelligence, as usual.'

'I saw that, sir.'

The glassy blue eyes rose to his with empty astonishment.

'You read *The Bulletin*, do you?'

'Yes, sir.'

'There's no accounting for taste. Pressure, Tung, is likely to be exerted on you in the next few weeks, by the mosquito press and others, to expand upon your doubtless fascinating experiences. To put you temporarily out of harm's way, you will be transferred tomorrow to the Northern Sector for a period of duty with the Royal Navy patrols. Report to the Director of the Special Branch this afternoon for a briefing.'

'Yes, sir.'

The blue eyes and multi-coloured ribbons receded in the safety of a tip-up chair.

'Well, Inspector Tung, did you make a calculated withdrawal

171

when the arrows of desire began to whizz back and forth, or did you feel a moral obligation to stop them heroically yourself?'

He pondered, uncertain what the question meant.

'I—I don't know I did either, sir.'

The eyes and ribbons returned abruptly to their first position.

'Well, whatever did happen, Tung, if you are asked any questions by anyone, inside or outside the Force, your answer is that you were not there and know nothing.'

'Yes, sir.'

The eyes softened. Latent humour ran like an infusion through the subtle veins and markings of the expression.

'In point of fact, what did happen?'

He could not respond to the play of humour. He knew the police too well. This was the way they tricked one into garrulousness. This was how refugees, never really trusted, lost their jobs. He felt warm in the controlled temperature of the room. Under his vest he was sweating.

'I'm not sure I know, sir,' he stammered.

The ashen voice gave a single, sharp laugh. The blue eyes and the ribbons receded for the second time.

'Damned good, Tung. Damned good. That's the stuff.'

The interview was over.

'Thank you, sir.'

16

BRENDA MACPHERSON was horrified when she heard the news. She heard it at breakfast from her unmarried younger sister—alas! a plain girl—who had come out to the colony two years ago to stay with them for a month. She now worked as a stenographer at Police Headquarters, doing what she called graded work (meaning confidential) in the Special Branch. Strictly speaking, she should not have passed it on, but in the family circle it didn't matter. As long as these things didn't leak out among the Chinese—that was the main point.

No, it would not be fair to say that she rushed round to impart it to Sylvia Fairburn. She went round fairly soon after breakfast—after her sister and husband were no longer in the house—

but to have said she rushed would have been an exaggeration. She hoped to be the first to confront her with it. Again, not true. Sylvia Fairburn was her friend—well, as far as one could be friends with anyone in colonial society—and it was her duty to pass on something that so closely concerned her. That it would be intriguing to see her reaction when she heard was putting the entire matter in an uncharitable light.

Since the immense buzz started about Sylvia and Government House, Brenda had not been round to see her. Not because she agreed with Lady Mercer, the wife of the Chief Justice, who was reported to have said she would refuse all Government House invitations while that man remained there. Lady Mercer was a dramatic, indiscreet woman whose husband's position had gone to her head. Brenda's view was simpler. If they were, as everyone asserted, in the midst of a raging affair, it was surely wiser to let them alone until—well, until something happened. Richard might divorce her, for example. It was difficult to hold a conversation with someone who might be the Acting Governor's mistress, and yet who might not be at all. One didn't know where to begin, and whichever way the conversation went one was nearly sure to say something unfortunate, out of sheer uncertainty. Besides which, Brian could not have the firm associated with anything that might possibly be a scandal. A short little unheralded call, at their once-favourite time for morning coffee together, could, however, be slipped into her day neatly, before the meeting of the Anti-Tuberculosis Association committee at eleven o'clock. Perhaps, even, reviving past intimacies, she might be able to find out—for the benefit of everyone else as well as herself—what exactly was happening. If only this had all been taking place in England, where members of people's families could be got at for precise information, and where known life-long friends abounded as a sure source of knowledge, this socially impossible position would not have arisen. In a colony it was different. Each person was a unit, without relations or life-long friends. Frequently the only way to find out something was to ask the person concerned. In this particular case, how would it be possible to do such a thing as ask? When Brenda had told Brian she had decided to do so, he had become very grave, and warned her that she must remember it was the Queen's representative who was involved, and that to utter a word on the subject was a very serious matter indeed. Brian was by nature solemn, though, and in any case the buzz was bound to be the truth. Who could possibly believe anything else?

She was driven out from their luxurious modern house high up above the open sea, facing south. A range of steep hills separated it from all rumour of the city, although it was only forty minutes' drive to the city centre. In the car, it occurred to her that there was a certain discrepancy in the popular story. In order to become Lady Stainmore, was Sylvia really prepared to ruin Sir Frederick's career, by letting him be cited as co-respondent in a divorce case, when he was within a stone's throw—so the well informed said—of a governorship elsewhere? The morning coffee drinkers in the ladies' room of the Colony Club averred that her only aim was the satisfaction of her desires, and that she would ruin no matter whom in the process. Faintly mediaeval, Brenda thought; like witches and the evil eye. The colony was old-fashioned, though.

If they just wanted to sleep with each other and call it a day, Brenda continued to herself, why did they have to be so conspicuous about it? She had been charmed by Sir Frederick's dignified gesture of turning up at Sylvia's lecture, yet a day or so later the little British Council man, Winterley, had said that he himself knew for a certainty there was far more in that than met the eye. What did he mean? Had Sylvia so infatuated Fred Stainmore that he was prepared to let his career, his reputation, his honour, go to the winds? Would it be a case next of transferring Uriah the Hittite to some far-away, dangerous assignment?

To call at their once special coffee time, and with the present shocking news to impart, seemed to Brenda the nearest thing to infallibility in obtaining a true picture of the state of affairs.

As the old Chinese maidservant let her smilingly in, she felt in the apartment a curious packed-up sensation. There were no flowers in the bowls set out for them. A carpet in the hall was rolled up. Her heels reverberated as if in an unoccupied room.

'Brenda! What a pleasant surprise!'

She was looking wonderfully smart, in a fabric that, to Brenda's experienced eye, looked very expensive—English probably, but definitely cut in Paris. Every time the heavy tropical summer came to an end, Sylvia's exquisite winter clothes came as a surprise to Brenda. She determined now, before the winter ended, to make Sylvia answer some questions about her tailoring arrangements.

'Darling, you must forgive me for barging in on you like this,' Brenda began, 'I'm sure you're dreadfully busy.'

174

It was a hook—rather a clumsily baited one, perhaps—but better than none.

'Yes, in fact. Rather more than usual,' she replied with equanimity.

Brenda did not know what to make of this. Did it, or did it not, mean something to do with Government House?

'You look wonderful, darling,' she said effusively and sincerely.

'Didn't you expect me to?' came the reply, spoken as innocently as she had ever heard Sylvia speak.

'Well, of course. But we haven't met for weeks on end, and——'

'Not since your party on the night of the Mid-Autumn Festival. I still feel repentant about that. I'm very sorry if I upset everyone, but I was feeling ghastly.'

'Not a word about it, dear. Everyone understood.'

'Did they?'

It came as a deliberate interrogation. Brenda felt cornered.

'If you mean there was any backchat after you left, I can assure you there was none,' she said, unintentionally sounding nettled. 'It was an exit in the very best style,' she added, in an effort to rectify her tone by a jest. Somehow, things were going to pieces. She was not at this rate going to reach the nice clear-cut conclusion she had hoped for.

'The trouble in this place is people's capacity for understanding more than there is to understand.'

That was a fairly plain statement, Brenda considered, surprised that it should have been made so quickly. Sylvia suspected her motives, that was the trouble. With the novelist on the defensive, nothing reliable could be learnt.

No coffee was offered. It was the nearest thing to rudeness, considering how it used to be between them.

'I don't think that applies to something I've just recently heard, and which I think you ought to know,' Brenda said, sitting down without invitation.

'Is that so?'

It was spoken with a fundamental lack of interest, while filling a cigarette case with cigarettes from a table box. Brenda didn't seem to be able to hold the woman's attention.

'Yes. I felt it my duty to tell you,' she said, with an unintended touch of piousness. She was completely 'off' this morning.

'If it won't take too long, do go ahead, dear'—this while

handing the cigarette box to her servant and adding something in Chinese which Brenda could not understand.

'Are you really in such a desperate hurry?' she asked, this time really nettled (not that she had looked forward to getting the better of Sylvia; no one could in fairness ever say such a thing as that).

'Not desperate, dear. Not in the least desperate. I'm just leaving for New York. The car will be coming in a few minutes to take me to the airport.'

For a split second Brenda doubted she had heard properly. Then, with a quiver of excitement, she sat poised on the edge of her chair, like a bird about to hop after a worm.

'You're—for New York——?' she all but puffed with the incoherence of surprise, oblivious for the moment that she was making precisely the reaction she had herself hoped to produce in Sylvia. As if running frantically up an escalator out of control and sweeping her helplessly downwards, she bounded mentally forwards to the various astounding possibilities this news might imply. Certainly, next time she went to the Colony Club she would have something to tell everyone! Even in the gripping uncertainty of the moment, she made a mental note to have coffee there tomorrow.

'Yes, it's very exciting,' Sylvia said. 'Here you are—see for yourself,' she said, taking a cable from the top of a bookcase and handing it to Brenda.

She looked at it, holding it at a distance (an affectation, but she thought she saw things better at a distance), and trying to demonstrate speed in grasping its special brand of jargon. It was from New York.

MGM INTERESTED PURCHASE RIGHTS CHASM STOP REQUEST
AUTHORIZATION INITIATE PRELIMINARY NEGOTIATION
PEARCE

'What incredibly long words these Americans use!' Brenda exclaimed. 'It looks like a bit cut off the side of a Roman triumphal arch.'

'You know the rest of the story, dear,' Sylvia continued laconically. 'In the interests of the dollar-famished novelist, my agent will allow the screen-writer to make minor alterations. The Indian Military Attaché will end up as a buck negro, and his concubine as a downtown whore played by Hollywood's latest expert in lapsed virtue, with flashbacks to innocent college days and being disappointed by a charming young man who loved only his mother.'

Brenda obtained a clue from it.

'You get more wild about your books than you ever do about Richard, don't you, darling? I'm thrilled it's going to be filmed.'

'Hold your breath; nothing's fixed yet. Get wild about Richard?' She looked at Brenda with an astonishing—almost holy—candour. 'Why should I? He's my husband.'

It was as if the pagan beauty of youth, the desire to fulfil strange fantasies with a physically perfect man whom one would (ideally speaking) never meet again, rested possessingly in the eyes and heart of the woman who should have forgotten such nonsense—though Brenda herself had not quite forgotten, or she would not have recognized what she saw. She felt as if she were dumb and club-footed before the shining, vibrating beauty in her friend's expression, like something she could not comprehend, like those awful Bible pictures of heroic Israelite women, which her grandmother had shown her when she was a child, like saints as they properly should be depicted (but never were in Roman Catholic churches).

'I realize you're devoted to him, Sylvia,' she said, abashed and ashamed of herself. (But she had never, never intended to do anything in the least shameful. She was motivated out of pure kindness of heart for her friend.) 'That's why I just had to come. Did you know, dear—did you know he was being privately investigated by the Anti-Corruption Branch?'

Sylvia was turning away as Brenda spoke—the elegant English hunting woman on a trip to Monte Carlo, with a continental lover who had never before escorted a woman wearing anything faintly resembling tweed. With the innocence that had already petrified Brenda, she reverted her glance, her body poised, from the turn of a nostril to the point of a shoe.

'What is that? A detective agency?'

'Darling, it's the police,' said Brenda with emphasis.

'The police?' she said, appearing not to understand (Brenda decided she'd had enough of this simplicity stunt; the woman *must* be pretending). 'Why should they investigate him?'

'It's on account of certain land sales, I understand. People say he took bribes, Sylvia my dear, and sold land which shouldn't

177

have been sold. . . . Well, you know how difficult these things are to understand. Anyway, it was something entirely wrong, and they say it *could* mean—dear, I thought I'd better let you know, but I had no idea I would catch you just as you were going off to . . .'

Her words died away at the sight of her friend's expression.

'We carry with us always, don't we, the inheritance left us by our forebears? Richard's grandfather was dismissed from the civil service because of suspected corruption. The family always swore he was innocent. His diary suggested he was. Never having even really thought about it before, I wonder whether they were right.' She was rolling a Persian carpet up very gently with the point of her shoe. 'What a horrible thing to say, Brenda! Please forgive me,' she said, gazing at the changing colours of the reverse side of the carpet, as her shoe pushed it slowly round and round, till it became a horizontal pillar.

The bell rang—a loud, ugly noise in the carpetless hall and gradually denuded living-room.

'Oh, I understand what you mean, all right,' Brenda admitted. 'We never quite tie up with the men we marry. How could we? Take Brian, for instance——'

The servant hurried in, saying something amid which Brenda caught the local version of the word for a taxi.

'You realize, don't you, Brenda dear, I've got to go. If I don't, the film story will be ruined.'

'I appreciate your problem, darling,' she said. In truth, she didn't appreciate anything of the kind. How could this impossible woman walk off, leaving her without the shadow of a reaction, when she had just conveyed to her the most disgraceful news that had struck the colonial government in years?

Walk off she did, though, just like that. She even kissed Brenda on both cheeks in the hall. The old servant was weeping.

'Are you sure I can't give you a lift, darling?' Brenda said. She felt such a fool, she did not know what to say.

'She's the most unutterable bitch, Brenda,' said Brian vehemently at lunch, after the Anti-T.B. meeting, 'that I've ever come across or heard of. I've always told you not to mix up with the government set, but you've never listened to me. Now perhaps you see what I mean. Government! Damn it, our firm alone— we could buy the whole damned Government out tomorrow, if

178

we wanted to. . . . What d'you call this? Welsh rarebit? The toast's damned hard.'

Mortified, Brenda pressed her fingers down near the glasses set out for her, and, to her horror, broke the nail of her third finger. Her hand was utterly spoilt, and they were dining with the Finlaysons that evening. She could have wept then and there with fury and disappointment.

Somehow she managed to control herself till Brian returned to his office, after which, before the sound of his car had died away, she shouted for her maid.

'Get Miss Ma to come!'

'Miss Ma, Missie?' the spry little thing exclaimed. 'Missie on'y see Miss Ma laas week.'

'Get Miss Ma, d'you hear! Before six! I have to go out to-night.'

With which, she stormed upstairs to her bedroom, dimly shuttered as a protection from the afternoon sun and decorated by her flowery pictures, threw herself down on her bed, and sobbed aloud, sobs of hatred and disgust, of her bitter sense of failure and mediocrity, her envy of Sylvia's unique, maddening freedom, and her utter shame that, because one nail was broken, all the rest would have to be cut short, making her look like a woman who washed her own pans, and only wore varnish when her husband took her out on Saturday evenings.

17

In the air, between
Tokyo and Honolulu,
23 December.

Richard my dear,

I thought I'd better send a word of explanation about my sudden departure. I presume it was reported in the press—heaven knows there were enough reporters at the airport. John Winnington was a help, however, vetoing questions in the most lordly manner. Really, all they got was photographs, and as I was looking all right that day I had no complaints.

Looking back on it now, the last few weeks have been a personal crisis. I didn't grasp it fully till I was in the plane. Only then I suddenly became overwhelmed with sleep and—with relief. Relief to be away. I think I said before: I don't think you quite realize what an extraordinary position I've been in since leaving Little Island (how is it, by the way? I've so wanted to see if those new trees I planted out of season have taken; I hope you've looked after them), surrounded by deceit and fear and envy, and all kinds of malice I had never suspected people were capable of. There were times, as I think back now, when I could understand what it was like in the Middle Ages to be suspected of witchcraft. It all gets back to The Chasm, *I suppose. We both of us have reputations firmly fixed in the public mind—pity for you, fear and envy of me. Some people would start laying blame here and there. What is the use?*

I suppose you must have heard that I was stuck at the Great Island monastery, the highest one, when we had that freak typhoon and Freddie was there. The lunatic. He went up there thinking (I suppose) that Frances and I were both going. It was all going to be such a jolly surprise. Or at least, that's what I thought at the time. I just don't know for certain. Anyway, Frances didn't come, I went by ferry, alone, and there were Freddie and I caught at the top in that terrific typhoon—it had some silly woman's name, as usual, but I've forgotten it. You know the one I mean.

It was the most ghastly weekend. Freddie had that frightfully handsome Yenching graduate bodyguard with him, the Northerner. It could have been delightful. But with Freddie making elephantine advance through a situation which had happened anyhow and what was the use of worrying about it, it was just turgid, everything spun out to lengths of indescribable boredom. And Freddie is so fearfully correct; the charming bodyguard wasn't even allowed to sit with us. (That characterless A.D.C. was ill in hospital.)

It would have been quite all right, of course, if the typhoon hadn't come. The Governor being marooned out of the city, a thing John Winnington says has never happened before, brought the camera-men to Prince of Wales Pier in a solid phalanx (that is the right word, isn't it?—thank goodness Pearce's woman checks my scripts, she's so terribly literary—she'll never marry, of course). There was one wonderfully dramatic moment at the pier when Freddie, pushing me back, said: 'Cameras! Stay in the cabin!' But unfortunately I couldn't stand it any more, and giggled. We were so near home at last, and it was such a joy to think that would be the

180

end of Freddie going on and on for hours about goodness knows what—it's almost fantastic to think that I haven't the faintest recollection of a thing he said during the entire time. When I giggled, the handsome bodyguard smiled, with a fearful look of wickedness. I don't know what it is about him. He's much more manly than most Chinese.

It's the middle of the night here, and I'm sitting typing on my newly bought Italian portable—perfect for air travel. Most of the passengers have gone to sleep and put their lights out. One man has complained already about my light being on too long—via the stewardess, who was tact itself, but with a New England slant. I've just got to turn it off in ten minutes, even though I shan't sleep a wink. Thank goodness it's calm for a while. How I hate this Pacific crossing! It's at least quicker by air, however.

Which brings me to the reason for the trip. What a vaguely wandering letter this is! I'm terribly sorry. It must be the astounding mixture of wines offered at dinner—the American pattern of continental European life, enjoyed at 17,000 feet above the Pacific Ocean. We even had cheese from those adorable French caves we cycled past on our honeymoon. To think that we cycled!

Dawn, just over Hawaii.

The thing is that it looks very likely that The Chasm is to be filmed, and with the most wonderful cast, to judge by Pearce's latest cable to Tokyo. It is essential that I make sure they don't introduce any frightful alterations in the story. I shall write again from New York. We're coming down.

> Love, my dear,
> Sylvia.

P.S. New England's not so bad, really. She's just given me one of those jujubes we both so hate. She made me take it. Poor thing, she's found out who I am and is sorry (!) for me.

> Government House,
> Victoria.
> 23.12.

Dear Sir Wavell,

I was very glad to learn from Murray's latest despatch that you are now considered to be over the worst, and that we can expect to see you back here fairly soon. I understand from Murray that, even though in hospital, you are being kept closely informed of what is going on here, so I hope that on your return you will have no surprises. On the development side, the road on Great Island is the one entirely new project—and even that is not new; I was shown an old file the other day which shows that a somewhat similar scheme was considered in 1923. I am suggesting that part of the cost be borne by Colonial Development and Welfare. Doubtless our main aim in putting a road through is to increase vegetable supplies, but joined with this is the interesting project of assisting the villagers to plant vegetables in their disused fields, thus improving their own economic position. It will probably involve teaching some of them about vegetable production, and I think we have to be prepared to see a small agricultural demonstration station set up for a couple of years or so in one of the south coast villages. This general aspect of the road scheme may appeal to the Colonial Office, and an attempt is thus being made to obtain a Colonial Development and Welfare grant.

A report from the Water Authority, just out today, states that within two years, with the present increase in consumption, hours of water supply will have to be restricted unless work is started on a new reservoir as soon as possible. You will recall that this accords more or less exactly with what the Chinese members of Legislative Council said two years ago, and which the Public Works Department at the time flatly disputed. I fear that, in view of the public criticism which will be aroused if, after such warnings, water restrictions are introduced, we shall have to proceed early with work on a new reservoir. I am budgeting what is in fact no more than a guesswork figure of half the cost to be spent in the coming financial year, and preliminary investigations will be started as soon as possible—in January, I hope. Murray will show you the Water Authority's report, a copy of which was sent to London this afternoon.

Those are, I think, the only significant new items of development.

There is, however, one personal matter which I would like to mention. There has been a certain amount of loose talk in the Colony on the subject of my own relations with Mrs. Fairburn (Sylvia Gracechurch the novelist—Fairburn is at present D.O., South-Western District). Whether the origin of it is malicious or merely the outcome of misinformed speculation it is impossible to say. As is usually the case, I personally heard nothing about it till last week, when it had been common gossip for some time. It so happened that, as you may already have been informed, I was caught by the freak typhoon that occurred late in November, well after the

182

normal typhoon season, while visiting the Buddhist monastery on Great Island. Mrs. Fairburn was staying there, and I naturally brought her back in the launch after the typhoon had passed. Our return together was noted by every newspaper, English and vernacular, some of them with photographs, and two of the more disreputable Chinese mosquito papers published comments on which the Attorney-General has advised that successful prosecutions could be brought.

I am of the opinion that no legal action should be taken. My view is that it will simply draw unnecessary attention to the matter. Provided the offending newspapers each publish an apology and a statement completely withdrawing their former comments, I would be inclined to say that we could let the matter rest. Mrs. Fairburn has, I understand, left today for Hollywood where one of her books is shortly to be filmed, and I imagine that this will cause all this unfounded talk to come to an end.

There is, of course, the opposite view that the best way to put a stop to rumours of this kind is to bring them to Court with as much publicity as possible. In my view, however, this method is better suited to cases where pernicious attacks have been made over a long period. In this case, nothing like this has happened.

As it may possibly be said that grave disrespect to the Crown has been offered, I have deferred giving the Attorney-General a decision, and have meanwhile written a personal letter to the Secretary of State, giving my views as above, and asking for his advice. You will no doubt be consulted, and I thought you would wish to hear from me personally as well, on a subject of this kind. I need hardly say that the association of my name with that of Mrs. Fairburn, in the sense that is intended even in the better newspapers, is entirely without substance. Mrs. Fairburn has dined here twice in the last five months.

I greatly regret to have to trouble you with this displeasing matter. It has unfortunately produced a certain amount of reaction in British circles, and I had yesterday to receive a deputation consisting of Jenkinson, representing the Civil Service, Barker, of the Chamber of Commerce, and Ludgrove, representing the Freemasons, asking me, if (as they said they sincerely believed) there was no foundation in the current rumours concerning Mrs. Fairburn and myself, to cause swift action to be taken in the Courts against the newspapers etc. I assured them that the rumours were groundless, and informed them that I was consulting the Secretary of State on the matter, and also writing to yourself. I mention this in that it serves to illustrate the degree of emotion that the rumours have aroused.

In any case, I look forward to your speedy recovery and return to the Colony, as well as—for all our sakes—an end to this distasteful business.

> *I am, dear Sir Wavell,*
> *Yours very sincerely,*
> *F. Stainmore.*

18

R EACHING San Francisco during the Christmas holiday, Sylvia entered the United States (where her *succès de scandale* had had its greatest sales) unnoticed. She travelled on by the same flight to New York, which was going through a spell of cold, grey, graceless weather, a harsh wind rushing cruelly between the immense buildings, carrying with it scraps of litter that were tossed violently here and there, as if by some powerful poltergeist in a rage of fun. Consulting the telephone book, she found that the hotel she had stayed in years before with Enid Stampden still existed, and went there by cab. It was a quiet, unpretentious place in the unimposing East Thirties. Unlike more up-to-date establishments, it had not yet taken to the prevailing fashion for multi-pastel-shade interior decoration. With its old red carpets, standard reading lamps, and an occasional ugly candelabra, it looked more European than American, and she noted that many of the guests were from Europe—impelled not so much by nostalgia as by inexpensive rates. She took a modest suite, bought three newspapers and a woman's magazine, and went up in the elevator. It was 3 p.m. By the time the Irish maid had finished putting out clean towels and taking away dirty linen to be washed, Sylvia had had enough. Kicking off her shoes, she lay on the bed with her clothes on and slept soundly.

When she awoke, it was dark, and her throat was dry from lack of fresh air. Switching on a bedside lamp, she found it was already ten o'clock, too late for dinner. She rose, undressed, took a bath, and settled herself more comfortably, in bed this time, the newspapers spread around her. She lit one of her little Dutch cheroots and glanced mechanically at the pictures in the woman's magazine.

The wonderful anonymity of being in New York was like a healing medicine to her. How appropriately The Heights had been named! she thought. Life in that now so far-away colony was pinnacle existence. Anyone in public life, in any part of the world, was to some extent exposed in the same way to the buffeting winds as were the houses and blocks of apartments perched on the sides of the colony's steep hills. In the colony itself, the degree of exposure, actually and metaphorically, was unbearable. The career of a writer, furthermore, was at odds with the rôle of a woman of society; to attempt a combination of the two was to head into almost certain misunderstanding. As Richard's wife, she had to take her place—a defined and fairly high place—in colonial society. But she was a writer first and foremost. The entertaining, the social functions: all this was a temporary fiction—Sylvia playing games on rather a larger scale than she did as a child, but the same games. As herself, she demanded personal freedom, in order to think and write. As Richard's wife, her freedom was defined, restricted to a certain place and level. Like an actress in a play, she had to speak the lines of her own part; it was not for her to invent new lines of her own.

In New York her social position in an obscure British colony meant nothing. Even lying alone in bed, with no view but of the dark building opposite, no sound but the repeated roar of engines each time the Madison Avenue traffic lights changed, she had become herself again—far more herself than she had been with Haren in Japan, for there her connexions with the British Embassy in Tokyo brought the soundwaves of her colonial social status stretching far out from the colony. Here she was utterly herself.

What a pity Richard could not be here! she thought, and at once cocked an eyebrow, surprised at herself. The thought had been involuntary, yet, analysing it, it was not as simple as it looked. It brought her back to the basis of their relationship, to the fact that, *à fond*, she had always wanted Richard to share her life. She did not mind sharing his, now and then. But Richard's life was not real. Hers was. His was a transitory life. In time he would be promoted and transferred somewhere else. In the end, when he retired, he would return to normal life, to her life. If she stuck to him, she would have her way in the end.

New York, the decoration of the bedroom, the feel of the bed, the sound of the traffic, brought this idea home. From here, for some unknown reason, she understood the problem between Richard and herself better than when he was on Little Island and she at The Heights. Here she dwelt in the midst of her own reality, waiting for the time when he would rejoin her—even if it meant waiting till he retired.

She blew out smoke and thought about growing old. In her world of reality she wanted a partner to be with her always. She wanted Richard. Of all the men she had ever known, he was far and away the best, in spite of what anyone might say about corruption, in spite of a certain weakness of character inherited from his family, who were aimless, quixotic people. In his world, she wasn't much use to him. She marked time beside him, waiting for the next period of long leave, the next return to her world. Yet, if she was not to grow old alone—an increasingly strange, increasingly angular, increasingly eccentric figure, even in her own reality—she had to stand beside him. She would never marry anyone else. She was sick of passion and its insipidities. There it all was, in the pages of her book. There it lay, extracted from her and set down apart from her, for even herself to look at.

She might not now have been so objective, she considered, had she not passed through these last three terrible months in the colony, realizing for the first time just in what way society cannot own anyone who flouts its conventions, and how it reacts towards anyone who has dared to. Her friends gone, her enemies speaking to each other in whispers, generous-minded hosts or hostesses one after another realizing too late that they had committed a social error by inviting her, her own servants despising her, even dear faithful old Juen beginning to feel ashamed that she worked for her, and deeply upset with herself for feeling ashamed—to have been insensitive to the nuances of Chinese manner and outlook would have made the months easier. To be insensitive is not to live.

The transitory, fictional world of Richard had thrown her out. It might even throw Richard himself out, because of her. Had Richard suggested, in Chelsea or Montmartre, in Hollywood or Greenwich Village, that they live apart for a few months while he achieved his self-fulfilment of building a road, the event would have caused no commotion whatever. It would have passed unnoticed. Richard had simply chosen the wrong *milieu* in which to try it on, as indeed she had realized the instant she read his first fatal letter. Such independence of each other could not be tolerated by colonial society—by a society, that is to say, without the yeast of independent, creative thought, without its artists, writers, musicians, buffoons, the court without its jester.

To attempt to apportion blame was useless. The thing was far too involved, dating back to those post-war days in London, to that first meeting in Hongkong, to an understanding fundamental to them as individuals, but, as she now knew, incompatible with what society demanded, unless one escaped to the jester's quarters in the court, to live entirely amongst other visiting jesters, with their mistresses and dancing partners, with their uninhibited and far too knowing offspring. But when age beckoned, even if only distantly, was it not wiser to compromise, with each other as well as with the jesterless society?

She flicked sharply the pages of the magazine. Was compromise even possible? What compromise, for example? Richard had to fulfil himself, achieve something he could consider his. This was the prerequisite to any reconciliation between them. Reconciliation! What a ridiculous word! They had never been in disagreement. Or was it easy for her to say that, because she dominated him, and had confidence in her power to hold him?

She accurately threw the butt of her cheroot out of the partly open window. In New York one never had to worry on whose head anything fell. If an angry pedestrian looked up, he saw only a thousand windows, all looking exactly the same.

Had she, in fact, such confidence? Sanely and sensibly, she had not. At any time, among the Lilies, Dollies, Maisies, and Connies, might appear one who, by some shrewd trick, could hold him, away from all the rest. She was a fool, in some ways, to have come to New York. He might sink into that degradation of life with which the word 'colony' was once associated—a whisky-soaked colonial, debauched by the wiles of Oriental women. While she— she always had Enid Stampden to remember. She exaggerated, perhaps. Exaggeration helped her to see the thing.

What compromise was possible? Age crept on to the failure of a life, to two separate homes that were not homes at all, by comparison with what one united home would be. Did personal independence have to be sacrificed? Was there no way of avoiding this, whatever pacts they might have between them, however complete their understanding of each other? Would not the restriction of freedom bring in its turn an evocation of old desires, the need for another Haren, or some still more improbable love, judiciously presented by life itself just when it was most inconvenient yet most desirable?

You should grow up, my dear, she said to herself.

It would all be simpler today, however, if she had once been young. She had never been young. As early as she could remember, she had found herself joined with her parents in their anxieties about money. The great slump stood out like the first terrible obstacle in her life, when suddenly disaster fell on them, and they had to give up the house they had always lived in, and bundle themselves instead into a suburban cottage, where her mother cooked and washed dishes, and she was told that she would only be able to go to a boarding school if she promised to be very, very good, and then it would still be a great sacrifice on her father's part. When she first went to school, she had learnt how, by petty deceptions, to hide from other girls the fact that she only just had enough clothes to wear, compared with others' more luxurious outfits.

The bad times passed into good. The family moved to Mayfair. They owned more, and larger, cars. Then came Switzerland. Again no youth. Why, if one really assessed it, and put make-up on the different participants, so that young could look old, and old young, it would be easy to say that the girls in the Swiss 'finishing' establishment were like grandmothers, viewing with concern, but also with benevolent interest, the madcap doings of their children and grandchildren, belonging to a different age—in point of fact, their own parents. The whole epoch was a crazy reversal, like Stravinsky's music, with the strings playing the percussion parts, the percussion section the soloists.

She had never been young. The echoes of what should have been youth had resounded against the years following, against her twenties and thirties. If she had had a first, unique, Primavera love, if she had lived and lost her youth when youth should be lived and lost, everything that followed would have been different, softened, tempered, by that first ecstasy. Instead, there had been the illicit embraces of actors, stealing a minute between bathroom and hall, wondering where they had left their hats, and automatically remembering—even when there was no audience—that the better side of their profiles must face out. The first moment of delirium had been with Bill in Chungking, for a multitudinously mixed,

188

adult collection of motives, and with the certainty of never being able to spend her later life in Richmond, Virginia.

Did it come down to it, after the hectic rampage of an unrestrained sex-life, that the Church was right in its strait-laced ideas about marriage? Both she and Richard had been baptized in the Church of England, and dutifully confirmed at a seemly age. A priest had muttered the poetically beautiful but physically unappealing marriage service over their slightly bowed heads. They had made vows in the direction of his cassock and surplice, that smelt (a sweet smell) of sweat—the lower parts of it only; they dared not look at his face—and behind him was a frame of wood hung with green cloth with IHS embroidered in gold thread in the middle of it, and a gilt cross above. They had made vows to this collection of symbols, which only a person with a detailed knowledge of the reigns of Henry VIII and Edward VI could understand, and had forgotten afterwards all but the priest's breath, which smelt of onions and cottage pie. The only reality was their private, personal agreement—their pact—and the important fact that, as experience showed, it worked. At least, it worked until *The Chasm* had its success. After that, it continued to work, but with difficulty. Both of them skated socially on thin ice. One more overt sign of defiance of society's conventions, and—in sum, exactly what had happened.

Tired of lying in bed, not feeling prepared yet to sleep again, she got up and, for want of anything better to do, filed her nails, seated on the pink upholstered stool set in front of a three-sectioned mirror and low dressing table.

It depended, she thought, looking at herself briefly in the mirror—her hair fell loosely over her forehead—what one believed in. That, too, was one of the craziest things about life, as considered in the context of churches and societies: why should it be necessary to believe in anything? Why should there be only a belief, and no more; a request for proof, followed by silence; a struggle to understand the reasons underlying the belief, with an outcome consisting only of doubt, and that green cloth with IHS on it, and a cross above? In a sense, the Church merely stated the laws of society, dressed up with some hocus-pocus of divine origin. Still, it was easier for someone like herself to bow to the Church's edict than to any judgment of society. Bowing to the former, there was at least the possibility that something greater lay beyond the symbols. Conceding anything to the latter was simply paying respect to Mrs. Webb and her views on drying rooms.

Seated before the mutually reflecting mirrors, she perceived one aspect of her life with complete clarity. Tracing back this perception to its origin, she came back to the occasion when Frances Lau told her about her particular friendship with a European. Sylvia, in spite of herself, had been shocked by this revelation—not because there was anything so terrible about Frances having a European friend to sleep with occasionally, but because it revealed to her, in an unforeseen manner, the nature of her own relationship with Frances. That Frances had a European lover merely surprised her. What shocked her was that her friendship with Frances had till then subsisted on the belief that Frances led a married life of unruffled contentment. As soon as this belief showed itself to be false, she felt her friendship with Frances evaporating, even while she watched her in the chair, pulling on those unsuitably troublesome new nylon gloves. The evaporation was caused by a sudden comprehension: that because of her own restlessness in life, her everlasting search in love, she chose for her friends those upon whom she could mentally lean, as upon pillars of stability, motionless framework amid the fluid uncertainty in which she herself had chosen to live. On the instant that she grasped the fact that they were not pillars at all—that in fact they were as fluid and uncertain as she was—she sprang away from them, like someone leaning against a wall and realizing with horror that it was collapsing over the edge of a precipice. When Frances confessed to her European love affair, Sylvia withdrew a great measure of her sympathy from her, and was shocked, utterly shocked with herself, as she perceived the extent of her own weakness: that she had been obliged to lean upon a woman like Frances, in order to steady herself in the world of her own making. It was this, her own weakness, that shocked her. She had never glimpsed it before. Here it stared her in the face.

Her own mental movement of repulsion from Frances was sufficient almost to suffocate her with the impact of the bargain she had made with life, the debt she owed it: that, in order to enjoy what she would, with whom she chose, she depended on foundations and frame liable to collapse, unworthy to be laid or mounted. The entire basis of her life was false and weak. Worse than this: the basis of her life was not even herself, but those upon whom she leaned. It was they who supplied the impetus of the

190

springboard, from which she dived heedlessly into the pool. If the suspicion prevailed that the so-called diving board was nothing but a balanced plank, without springs and unsecured, who would bother to ascend the steps to it?

Human beings, she considered, looking darkly at her tell-tale eyes, stood each on his or her own plot, alone. It was perhaps their destiny to learn to stand alone. Sometimes two might select one another as mates, resolving thereafter to stand two together. Even so, it was the unsupported effort of standing in loneliness, both of them separately, that constituted the strength of their stance in union. In their strength they stood, and without that strength, without the nobility of standing upright, they could have no unity together. In their small weaknesses, adding to the sum of human character, they might lean a little, but upon each other.

It was thus that, escaping to the monastery to reflect upon herself, she had been irritated to find Freddie there. It was thus that she had felt for him nothing but indifference. It was thus that she had silently laughed at him pursuing his masculine way through a situation he could not fully cope with. It was thus that she had faced the gossiping Brenda Macpherson with the retort given her by Frances, that she had nothing to fear: she was Richard's wife, he her husband.

If they were both to stand of their own strength alone, no longer leaning on others whom they did not so much as recognize as being the stable pillars of their life, there was no alternative to denying the delayed impulses of youth, to following the rule which the Church disguised as vows, and which society imposed in the name of respectability, and which life in terms of society, moreover, twisted and tightened into practical necessity.

True, she could have her loves, and write about them, withdrawing afterwards to some unhierarchic Bohemia. Life, society, the Church, Mrs. Webb, could not stand the truth, even in the form of fiction. Truth was wild, wanton. To live, it had to be overlaid and forgotten. Common sense gently insisted on this, and the prospect of age . . .

Noting the faintest shadow of a line she had never remarked before—a line caused by laughter, but nonetheless a line—she laid down her nail file and began to apply a cream Brenda Macpherson had recommended. So in the future she would be more distant from all people, men and women, and near only to Richard—if such a thing were possible, if Richard's hopes were fulfilled in that famous Budget. Part of the strength of standing alone lay in the distance hedged between one person and others. From girlhood, she had always preferred nearness.

Would Richard ever grasp such an idea? she wondered, smoothing the cream into her skin and walking slowly over to the window. With her elbow she pushed it open a little more—the air conditioning made the air in the room seem lifeless.

The streets were quieter. Only a late taxi or two geared up to the stimulus of the changing traffic lights. She wiped her fingers on a tissue, threw off her dressing gown, and stepped into bed again. The newspapers disintegrated, falling about unnoticed, never to be read. She thought of Haren, and—why not?—of the handsome Northerner, the bodyguard. She thought of the marvellous freedom life appeared to offer, but in fact denied. With a deep sigh she turned her cheek to the pillow, her skin moist with cream, and fell into sleep once more, with the reading light still on.

19

Pingshan Mansion,
Upper Level Road,
Victoria.
10th March.

My dear Sylvia,

We went to dine with the substitute Acting Governor last night, and I must tell you we were not impressed. He is very dull and gloomy, and walks in the room like a ghost. He is from Hongkong, which makes it more surprising. We both said coming home that we would be glad when Sir W. comes back, so you can understand our feelings, having heard us complain so often about him. Although it's really Lady W. more than him who dries things up.

I enclose a cutting, from which you will see that Richard's road is really on its way at last. When will you be coming back? Life carries on here much the same as usual. I haven't seen Richard since

192

you left—not even at the dancing places. They say he lives very quietly alone on Little Island.

Let me know your plans. Is the film fixed yet?

Yours sincerely,
Frances.

The cutting accompanying the letter read:

'GREAT ISLAND DEVELOPMENT
BOLD VEGETABLE DRIVE

In his address to Legislative Council yesterday, the Acting Governor, His Excellency Mr. A. B. Watson, C.M.G., outlined a bold new scheme for developing communications in South-Western District in an attempt to improve the colony's vegetable production by bringing remote villages more in touch with the central markets in Victoria. The programme of development includes a number of new piers on islands in S.W. District, new bridges, and the enlargement of several footpaths into bicycle tracks or—as His Excellency remarked amidst laughter—tricycle tracks. The principle feature, and the most expensive one, is the construction of a motor road along the south coast of Great Island, from Wireless Bay, becoming popular as a picnic resort, to the remote valley of Sheung Tsuen and Ha Tsuen, an area potentially rich for vegetable production, but at present neglected due to the inability of any would-be producers to reach a market. With road connexion with Wireless Bay, Mr. Watson explained, vegetables crated before 6 a.m. could be transported to Wireless Bay in time to catch the early morning ferry into Victoria, and thus in time for the early market. He reminded Hon. Members that the south coast of Great Island is inaccessible to shipping, except at great risk, for eight months out of every year, due to the treacherous tides.'

Sylvia read it listlessly, flicking it away on a table before she reached the end. As she placed Frances' letter with it, she saw it had a postscript.

P.S. Sir Frederick is still in London on 'special duty' at the Colonial Office. Edwin says he will probably be offered Trinidad. Would that be better, or worse?

193

She stretched out to take up Richard's letter, to read it through again. It was addressed to Lavinia Thomas, at whose small apartment in Tudor City she had been staying for the past fortnight. Lavinia worked across the other side of First Avenue, in the blue glass skyscraper of the United Nations.

'I've been transferred to Latin America,' she had announced over the telephone on the first day Sylvia contacted her, by which she meant that she had shifted from the nineteenth to the twenty-eighth floor, to an office on the doors and desks of which one read such names as Gomez da Costa Pereira e Mattos, Goncalves Teixeira de Silva e Souza, and Metello de Souza Menezes, culminating, in the room next to Lavinia's, in a Miss M. Silva—how was such simplicity possible?

When Lavinia read Richard's letter—Sylvia could see between the coffee cups it was from Richard—her face became stern, and Sylvia's heart beat faster than usual.

'M'm,' she said thoughtfully as she folded it up after reading it. 'I think you can cope with this, duckie. Oh, yes, I think you can.' Lavinia, a fifty-five-year-old spinster with a wide knowledge of the world, had modelled her human relations technique on some outstanding headmistress she must have encountered during her school days. 'Brace up for it,' she said, handing the letter to Sylvia. 'If you want more coffee, you do the chores. If you don't, I'll do them now.'

'I'll do them,' said Sylvia automatically, unfolding the letter. She was at first vaguely conscious of Lavinia moving about in the apartment as she prepared to go out to work. Imperceptibly she lost consciousness of everything except the letter—and of the man, her husband, speaking to someone else, not to her. Lavinia must at some point have said goodbye, and she must have responded. She remembered nothing of it.

> *District Office,*
> *South-Western District.*
> *8th March.*

My dear Lavinia,

> *Forgive me for burdening you with one more letter, working as you do in the world's largest paper factory, but in the pleasant lull that always follows the Chinese New Year, while everyone is too busy with kaifong[1] parties to worry about the woes they generally*

[1] Neighbourhood.

194

bring to the District Office, I have a blessed time for correspondence, and I need your advice and help.

As you will probably have realized already, it's about Sylvia. I cannot imagine her going to New York without seeing you, and I am hoping you are in touch with her and can put me wise on a few things. I don't know if she will have told you, but the fact is we had been living apart, for a few months prior to her trip to America. I wanted to be alone to concentrate on a very heavy schedule of work which I felt was making me rotten company for her, and I suggested we should separate temporarily. I thought for about six months, to get me over the worst in the office. At the time it seemed a reasonable enough proposition, and she more or less agreed with me. I had no idea then that it would run both of us into such a nightmare of trouble, and end now in a situation where I don't even know quite where she is, or whether she intends to come back here. She has written twice, quoting her agent's address, but—you know her—she disguises herself so much in letters, in conversation too, at all times, that I haven't any idea what is really going on in her mind. I suppose she may even be preparing to write another Chasm, God preserve us! (She writes well, though. I wish I had the same talent.)

I can't describe properly just what happened when we made our decision to live separately for a time. Out in the district one's rather cut off from what's going on in the evil-smelling colonial melting pot where careeers are made and smashed. The whole thing blew up a few weeks ago when Stainmore, the Chief Secretary, who was acting as Governor for several months—did you meet him when you were here?—was 'removed' to London in connexion with some allegations about his knowing Sylvia—you know the sort of thing. (I don't know whether there was anything in it. I shouldn't think so; he was too dull for her.) A few days later I was invited to a cocktail at the Chief Secretary's house, where Jenkinson—he's really the Financial Secretary, a pompous ass with an immense belief in his own importance—drew me aside, and, while prodding the fire with his foot and doing everything possible to avoid looking at me (even re-aligning the ornaments—nasty little black glass horses—on that hideous marble mantelpiece), more or less said that if Sylvia wanted to return here I had better ask for a transfer to another colony, or else resign. It was a matter for reflexion to hear this pillar of the Established Church advocating divorce in the name of undiluted self-interest, but there you are. He'll be in the front pew next Sunday as usual, no doubt.

195

As you can see, the situation is slightly critical. I don't know if Sylvia wants to come back. If she doesn't, I have to decide what to do. If she does, and is going to (because one thing is always certain with her, she'll do exactly what she wants), we may both be faced by a very difficult situation, so far as the British are concerned—in particular the Government set—and she ought to know in advance. But frankly—and I know you will understand this—I hesitate to write to her explaining all this when it may be that she couldn't care less and has written me off anyway. What a mess!

I regret to say that with Jenkinson I bluffed unashamedly, saying she was certainly coming back when she had concluded her negotiations in New York, and inquiring whether there was any particular Colonial Regulation under which he was making his statements. He was very huffed, and kicked the logs with more fury, saying that I realized of course, that I would be blackballed from the Club—I cross its threshold on an average once every two years; why I pay the subscription is only sheer moral weakness—and that we would both be ostracized from Western society. In other words, he hasn't a leg to stand on. He can't force me to resign, and he can only fire me for an act of insubordination. But if Sylvia does come back, we've got to face the music. She could do it, I think. With her, I could too. But it will be unpleasant, and you never know these tight European overseas groups—we might have to capitulate and go. The Colonial Office could probably fix a transfer for me, but it would be a bad loss of face with the Chinese, and, as most of our friends and contacts are Chinese, you realize that that means something to us which it doesn't mean to the average Britisher here. It would also reflect badly on the District Office, and in view of what I have been trying to do to build up the shrunken prestige of the Office, this is something I am particularly anxious to avoid.

The last few months have been difficult ones in a number of other ways too. 'When sorrows come, they come not single spies, but in battalias.' It had been obvious to me from the start that there was corruption in my office, but to what extent I had not realized till lately. It was on a far larger scale than I had thought, in land and buildings, and has been going on, if you please, for the last thirty years, organized by the same two people. The Anti-Corruption Branch have been trying to throw a net round them, but they are dealing with perfectionists who are long past the stage of making small errors that might lead them to the Law Courts. They know just how to manage their affairs. The full implications of this you will *appreciate, knowing China as you do. Naturally the entire district—with its 99 per cent Chinese population—thinks the corruption system is run for my benefit, or at least that I get the major rake-off. Even those more sophisticated, who realize that two of the clerks are the organizers and main beneficiaries, still believe I am getting something, but that I am being cheated out of my proper share by the clever clerks. It is inconceivable to the Chinese mind that corruption on this scale could go on* without *my being involved in it. Even one of our best friends here, the head of a large school and a devout Catholic, with whom I discussed the problem, doesn't feel quite sure about me. I could see it in his manner. All this has been a great strain, making most work a misery.*

When are we going to see you here again? I wanted the colony to make a bid to be the venue of the next session of E.C.A.F.E., but they're a bunch of stick-in-the-muds, they can't see the value of it—the publicity alone is worth it.

Please try and let me know about Sylvia. If you see her often, you may wish to show her this letter. I leave that entirely to your judgment of the position—if there is a position!

> *Affectionately yours,*
> *Richard Fairburn.*

He wanted her to come back. The thought was transitorily satisfying. She knew him too well, however, not to believe in the analogy of the shadow. Whatever she did, if she decided to write to him directly, she must not appear enthusiastic to return.

Nor was she. Her return presented a superb challenge, almost irresistible to her. The scene at the airport alone, touching down calmly, with every mark of being oblivious of the disaster to which she had contributed, was enough to make her heart flutter with amused vanity. Was it not Castlereagh, at the Congress of Vienna, who had said how pleasant he found it to be the most unpopular man in Europe; it was so much more dignified? Yes, this aspect of the problem—facing the music, as Richard called it—which worried Richard, troubled her not in the least. It even threatened to be the most entertaining part of it.

What worried her was that Richard had not woken up, as she had. Bothered with the technicalities of office work, and with grappling with corruption, he had not sorted himself out, as she had. He thought of resuming their life together on the same pattern as before. That could not be. Somehow he had to be made

197

to realize it. If she had been an injured party, it might be time now to lay down conditions for her return to him. But she was not an injured party. They had their pact together, and by it each had injured the other. It was no time for laying down conditions. Somehow the pact had to be annulled, and a new one—a marriage as the Church understood it—substituted in its place. As she thought it out, she felt as if she were airing clothes from an old wardrobe, and trying to put on her great-aunt's petticoats. There was no alternative. She was dry of passion, coldly renounced to the past, prepared to make the new experiment of limiting experience, of narrowing life down to a workable foundation, ignoring the cant of religion, ignoring the world of Mrs. Webb, yet trying to achieve something that would float steadily in whatever sea. It would mean a new approach to her art as a writer—this would be the hardest part of it. It would mean becoming Richard's wife in a way she had not been before—the way a tight colonial society demanded. It meant inevitably putting Richard first. But not if the régime of Dolly, Daisy, Maisie, and Connie were to continue! That would not be practical. She would not surrender on such terms. She had no intention of surrendering at all. A surrender by her would quickly wreck her relationship with Richard, for the plain reason that she would be mentally incapable of keeping it up. How to put this across to Richard with half the world between them?

She looked at her watch. She had an appointment with Pearce at twelve, followed by a literary luncheon at which she would have to speak. She had already made some notes for this, enough to steer her through.

She laid her new typewriter on the table.

> *47 Wolsey House,*
> *Tudor City,*
> *New York, 17. N.Y.*
> *14 March.*

Richard my dear,

Lavinia has shown me your letter. How psychic you are! I am actually staying with her while Flora is holidaying in England. The film negotiations have gone well, but rather slowly—American business methods are by no means as fast as Hollywood films like to make out—and I hope to sign on the dotted line in a week or so.

I really haven't got as far as making plans about what happens when the contract is signed. I was vaguely thinking of going over to London for a few weeks in April and May. After that, no definite ideas. You sound as if you're having a lot of trouble in the office, and I was much amused by your story of J. at the cocktail. So far as my coming back to the colony is concerned, I really think you ought to put yourself first. Only you can judge whether my return will make things too seriously embarrassing for you, vis-à-vis the rest of the civil servants. I would personally have said that it would be unwise if I were to return to the flat while you remained on Little Island. Besides, I am doubtful whether I would in any case wish to return to that arrangement of living. Were it not for dear old Juen, I would feel very much like determining the lease of the flat; but she has been so good, and if you were transferred to the city, the flat might be useful to you. Freddie paved his own way to downfall—or promotion?—although I think that if you had turned up on that night when I lectured at the British Council the whole nonsense might never have started. It was Freddie's unexpected appearance at the lecture that started tongues wagging later. He, poor dear, meant it as a great gesture of civil service solidarity; but, of course, when you didn't show up, the gesture misfired badly. Anyhow, it's no use holding a post-mortem on all that now. They say he's going to be made Governor of Trinidad.

Your letter asks Lavinia to sound me out about ourselves. Well, I think it's better I should write to you straight. In any case, she's got so much on her hands at U.N. it's a wonder she's still alive at the end of each day.

I have been living here in saintly obscurity, an improving existence. I am sick and tired of colonial society and thankful to be away from it. At the same time—an improper thought—I should love to come back and give it a really good thrashing for being so stupid about both of us.

Having said that, I have to admit that, judged by its own canons, it wasn't stupid. It judged us both, correctly, as being inimical to it. While we were together, it eyed us suspiciously, as a potential danger. When we lived apart, our (certainly my) every movement trod on its tender toes, so unused to barefoot life, and countered its attitudes with a perpetual scoff. I didn't scoff at it out loud. I just had to cross a room alone in public. That was a scoff. It was right, I suppose, in its own way. We are *dangerous to it. We are too much like wild animals set down among the tame.*

But in considering what each of us should do now, you must remember that for both of us the problem is different. You have your career, and if you want to keep it you are going to be obliged, I think, to compromise with the colonial set-up. You could do it in various ways. By divorcing, for example, you could put yourself right with the Club and all it stands for. They would carry you in again on their shoulders. You could then marry someone inconspicuous, much younger than yourself preferably, and devoted to you, and you would then live happily ever after and retire with as many stars and ribbons as Freddie has.

I, on the other hand, am not bound, since my good fortune in writing, to compromise with colonial life. Nothing would please me so much as the thought of never having to see Mrs. Webb again. It would not really matter to me if we did not even divorce—at least, not as I am thinking at present, in the cloistered surroundings of Lavinia's apartment—this building symbolically has a Perpendicular top, looking rather as if an enterprising contractor had bought one of those ornate tombs in Worcester Cathedral and draped it round the top of a skyscraper. This is Manhattan acquiring ye olde traditions. But for you, of course, divorce would be more sensible, because you would simply have to remarry. Bachelor existence, in your life, is most inconvenient.

The question resolves itself if, as I said earlier, you put yourself first and ask yourself, what do you really want me to do? Would you prefer me to stay away? I could do that. Would you like a divorce? It could be arranged. Do you wish me to come back and compromise with colonial life? I could do that too, but not willingly, unless you yourself compromised as well. The one thing I could not do—and I see this very acutely—would be to return to our usual, special form of living. It would take too long to say why I think this. I'm not sure I even really know. I simply feel that if we are to live together again, we have both got to make our separate compromises with the life in which you are obliged to work. Part of my compromise would be that I would consider my obligation in that respect to be the same as yours.

Would we be capable of doing that? I can say now that I would. The attitudinizers are winning over me. In the colony they win hands down. As I see it, what now remains is for you to make your choice, putting yourself first.

When I mention divorce, do not think that this is a disguised way of saying that this is what I want. I do not, unless you wish it. What I want to let you know is that, if you desire a divorce, I would be prepared to agree, and say our marriage has been a failure. Personally, I don't think it has been a failure. What I do think is that, if it is to endure, its basis must be changed.

All this is so hard to explain. I feel that, when you get this letter, you will either understand every word of it, or else find it incomprehensible.

My love to you, my dear, and don't worry too much about that office—your letter confirms what several Chinese friends had hinted to me but which I hadn't liked to bother you with when you had so much else to worry about. . . .

As always,
Sylvia.

She signed it, folded it into an envelope, leaving it unsealed, to be read again next morning, and prepared to go out to her agent's office and the luncheon.

20

EIGHT days is an eternity to wait for a reply.

'Pearce irritates me,' she said to Lavinia at breakfast a few days later—it was the only time they regularly met. 'And that woman of his—whose Christian name, *par exemple*, is Oona —is doing everything she can to probe the depths of what she is sure must be my New York love life.'

'You're pining away, duckie,' Lavinia observed, surveying her seriously. 'You'll have to go back to Richard. That's doctor's orders.'

'It would be better,' she said.

'It's essential.'

Once again, by chance, the same post brought a letter from Richard and one from Frances Lau.

'Well, here's fate,' said Lavinia, handing them both to her. Sylvia slowly folded her newspaper. 'If you want more coffee, you do the chores. If you don't, I'll do them now.'

'I'll do them,' said Sylvia.

'And for goodness' sake, telephone me at the office when

you've read what he's got to say. I shan't be able to think straight in Spanish until I know what's going to happen next.'

With slow perversity, she opened Frances' letter first.

18th March.

My dear Sylvia,

 I just wanted to add something to the letter I wrote you a few days ago and which I hope you received. Did you know that Richard is staying at The Heights? He's been there for several days. We met him today when he was taking an evening walk. He looks terribly thin and worried. I wanted to ask him in, but Edwin has been so frightfully difficult about him that I didn't dare. He doesn't even like my writing to you. So I don't know what's going on. My driver, who knows your Juen, says he's living there alone, in to all meals, but eating almost nothing. It sounds as if he needs looking after.

  Hoping to hear from you soon,

   Yours sincerely,

    Frances.

'The auspices are favourable,' Sylvia called to the retreating Lavinia.

'Good show, duckie!' she called back from the door. 'Ring me up! Ring me up! I'm late already.'

When the door closed, she rose and opened a window. Lavinia had become accustomed to air-conditioned American buildings. Sylvia still found them asphyxiating. Seating herself in Lavinia's most comfortable chair, she opened Richard's letter. That he was staying at The Heights, however, made her every movement slower, weightened by the sensation that all would be well.

19 March.

Dearest Sylvia,

 I have read your letter four—perhaps five—times, I can't remember. I believe I can say I understand it all. I hope that's true. But I still don't know what to make of everything you say. Am I to take it that you mean exactly what you have written? Or is there another intention behind it? When I read it for the first time, I felt you just wanted to settle things up, kiss and part. But now I'm not sure any more. If you really do mean all that you've written, I can only say what a tower of strength you are. If there is something else I haven't understood, will you please write and say it frankly, no

202

holds barred. We have hurt each other—unintentionally—enough to be able to stand worse still. Let us come clean now.

During these tiresome weeks I have been going through here, I have wanted your company again and again, I don't mind admitting it. But I have felt like a person incapable of speech, at any rate, of speech with you. I seemed to have lost our own private wavelength, if you like, and I imagined that you had moved much further away from me in sympathy than your letter (now that I have got over what at first looked like its harshness) implies. Frankly, I have been going through a harrowing time. Everything I've touched has gone wrong. The road has got tied up with some damn-awful vegetable project which, as we know, will bring no benefit to the villagers because of their rooted obstinacy to believing that they will ever learn how to grow them. A housing scheme which I had recommended at Long Sands, on the route of the road, has become a goldmine for speculators, and has already such a filthy name amongst people of the type who could have benefited from it—city clerks commuting daily and at present living in overcrowded conditions in the city— that I have thought of calling off the whole thing in sheer disgust at the avarice with which I am surrounded. Every piece of human goodwill is corrupted in that stinking office into some subtle scheme for making money. And to think that when I first joined it, I thought it was such a happy office, with a good staff, working well together! Now that I can see what is happening below the surface, I realize what a hellhole it is to work in, each man suspicious of the next, each trying to make a little extra for himself which the rest will not know of, and all thus indirectly battening upon and oppressing the country people. Not that the country people have ever been used to anything else! They regard government as a superimposed, irremovable evil, and think none the worse of it, whether it's British, Chinese, or what you will. In the remote places, of course, there is great confidence in the power of the District Officer to get their simple wants attended to. It's where development starts, and the tentacles of the city begin to feel their way out into the countryside, that the trouble starts. You can hardly believe the extent and depth of it. Last month, for example, I simplified a permit system, so that villagers from remote areas don't have to come into town to pay their permit fees, but can pay at their nearest market centre. This has been promptly interpreted as a means whereby I intend to evade the vigilance of the central government and collect squeeze quietly in the country on every permit issued. In one market centre the clerk from *the District Office is almost certainly collecting $5 on every permit issued, explaining that a percentage is for me, a statement which the village people, with their traditional outlook on any form of government, unquestioningly accept.*

I mention all this because it brings me to the point I wish to make. I had hoped to be able to do a lot of good in the district. Actually, I am achieving nothing satisfactory. Improvements like the permit one I have just mentioned are merely introducing new forms of corruption, while the potential big improvements—like the road— are all going awry. One can of course say that it is just my luck to have inherited a thoroughly bad District Office, and that in a place with cleaner morals these difficulties would not have arisen. That is not how I look at it. The more I have thought about it, the more convinced I have become that I am responsible for it all. There was the old belief in China that when the Emperor was virtuous, all things under him prospered. When famines, droughts, or floods occurred, it was traditional for the Emperor to ask himself—and Heaven— what he had done wrong. If he had been of impeccable virtue, the famines and floods could not have come. This is an exaggerated idea, of course, yet basically I believe it is a true one. I have felt very strongly, these last weeks, how dirty hands produce dirty work. Where the ruler—in this case, myself—is not morally impeccable in his thoughts and actions, his works cannot achieve what he desires that they should achieve. As long as one grain of moral dirt clings to a single finger-nail, the work done by the two hands will produce only disbalancements and imperfections. In the case of the family man, such imperfections will affect merely his family; with the business man, his business. In the case of a ruler, they will affect thousands of people for ill.

I have formed this idea, I suppose, as a result of my Chinese reading. I cannot dismiss it or pretend it is an illusion. It is a reality, and will stay with me in my thinking. When I realized how wrong things were in the District Office and in the district itself, I asked myself what wrong I had done, and I knew at once the answer. It was, in short, that I was living a lie, in which the two of us shared. We were married, yet our lives were a negation—to some extent—of what the world calls marriage, and in making that negation we were breaking one of the world's laws, disturbing the balance of things as they should be. I truly believe that, had I been all along obedient to this law, the rottenness of my office would have ceased, or at least have been reduced to small proportions, by the imprint of virtue (in the old Chinese sense) being imposed upon each one of those taking my orders. It is a return to the most ancient concepts of the Chinese State, as you will recognize. I am convinced, by experience, of the validity of those concepts. The moral weakness of a ruler transmits itself to those beneath him. Some consciously perceive the weakness, the rest just feel something they cannot define. But down it travels, from rank to rank to the bottom of the line. Moral weakness, it seems to me, affects judgment, and judgment is something one applies every day to all kinds of things. Thus it is not necessarily administrative weakness that produces bad administration. It can be also lack of moral virtue, which affects judgment, which in turn affects everything one does, in one's public duties as well as in private life. Life is one whole, after all, though we insist on trying to partition it.

If you really mean what you say, therefore, about the basis of our marriage being changed, and if that is your own first choice in the matter, coming long before the alternatives of divorce or separation, you will see from what I have told you that I agree completely with you; and to this I should add that I would be determined to try it—to compromise, as you say, with society. I don't even call it a compromise. I think of it as the importance of agreeing with life, and, for the benefit of all that we do, being in concord with its laws. Only in this way can any of us achieve anything worth while.

Would you please let me know as soon as you can whether, from this letter, you can say that I have understood your letter properly. Perhaps then we may begin to see daylight.

Enjoy yourself, and give my regards to Lavinia.

Your loving
Richard.

She dressed and made up with more care than usual, put on her favourite suit and smartest shoes, and descended to the street. It was a fresh, bright, gusty day, and she felt fine, a little nostalgic too at the thought of going away, as she walked up to Times Square. Pearce was waiting for her in his panelled office, his expression a counterfeit of pious worry concealing his desire to have the business settled soon. He was one of those would-be dilettanti whose waywardness had been reduced by American conformism to the wearing of a rather large gold ring with something said to be a family crest on it. He indulged his longing for freedom from the rigours of American ritualistic social discipline by becoming almost friendly with the writers who were his clients, and not (mercifully, thought Sylvia) by telling smutty jokes, like the run of business men of this particular brand whom she remembered from childhood in London.

She was informed of some fresh difficulties arising from her last proposals.

'Never mind, Mr. Pearce! Agree to everything and let us sign as soon as possible! I don't care for the book anyway. It's *vieux jeu*. My next—ah! Mr. Pearce, my next! . . .' Oona, who was collecting correspondence from a filing tray, stopped, breathless, '. . . no, quite different from *The Chasm of Love*. . . .'

'I hope written with the same gusto, Mrs. Fairburn, and with the same depth and truth,' the agent said in his deep American being-solid voice.

'Certainly,' she said lightly. Oona, not knowing what to make of this, moved on again. 'How soon can we conclude the business?'

Mr. Pearce gave a big smile of well-cared-for teeth.

'By the end of the month, ma'am, at this rate.'

'Good. May I use the outer office for making a few calls?'

'Sure, Mrs. Fairburn. Make yourself at home. Miss Melville will look after you.' He brought her to the door and gave the requisite instruction.

A call to Thomas Cook's, another to Lavinia.

'Have you a cable form, please?'

'Yes, surely we have, Mrs. Fairburn,' said Oona, producing one.

In capital letters she wrote out a cable to Richard: 'YOU UNDERSTAND SO HAPPY BOOKED TWA FLIGHT ARRIVING FROM TOKYO SEVENTEENTH APRIL LOVE SYLVIA.'

'I guess it looks like a happy ending, Mrs. Fairburn,' said Oona, as she took the cable and read it. 'The happy ending still commands the best sale.'

'How encouraging,' Sylvia replied coldly, regretting now that she had entrusted the cable to Oona. 'I don't think one should confuse novels with true stories, Miss Melville. The best true stories—biographies—end with a death.'

With which she passed the office door, to the strains of Oona's long titter of nervous surprise.

Foolish girl, Sylvia thought, feeling unexpectedly a hundred years old.

Part Three

21

WHEN he received Dirty Joke Wong's letter asking him to meet him at Ha Tsuen, Fai felt pleased and proud. Old Liu of Sheung Tsuen, returning home from Wireless Bay in a trading motor vessel, brought the letter with him, and before the evening was through, everyone in both villages knew what it was about, Fai deriving considerable face as a result. Dirty Joke was coming with a group of government officials, he wrote. Ha Tsuen laid in a stock of beer and aerated water for the occasion, and on the day of the visit one of the younger women was ordered by Fai's father to walk over the hills to O Mun to buy fresh cakes.

At the time stated in Dirty Joke's letter, Fai was waiting with his younger cousin-brother near the shore temple, at a place from which, between the rocks on the sand beach, there was a view of the open sea. It was the beginning of the second moon,[1] a dull day with a moist south wind blowing, the first warning that summer was not far off. The sea was choppy, but not unduly rough to Fai's experienced eye. He thought how sensible Dirty Joke Wong was in writing to him. In the first place, he was one of the few people in the village who could read. Secondly, in whatever weather (except during a typhoon) he could guarantee to bring them ashore safely, being himself the most expert sampan oarsman in the valley. His cousin-brother, who would hold the forward oar, was learning from him, but had not yet reached the stage when he could be trusted to handle the rear oar at the tricky twist between the rocks into the sheltered little cove in front of the temple—at least, certainly not with important visitors aboard.

[1] Mid-March.

Punctually a launch came in sight between the rocks, and the two young men ran in their bare feet to the temple steps, where they unmoored their long sampan, with its curved shape, stern high in the water, and rowed out across the calm cove to the narrow and dangerous entrance to the sea. Fai shouted at the critical moment, his brother pulled hard, and with one quick assessing glance at the rollers approaching them at a slant, Fai twisted the sampan round to face them fully, the sampan riding out easily over them, slowly seawards.

But as he looked at the launch, which was now slowing up to anchor in the deeper water of the large bay, whose arms were the hills enclosing the valley of the two villages, Fai realized the visit was perhaps more important than he thought. The launch was a large white craft, larger than any of the police launches, far larger than the Magistrate's launch. Drawing near, they saw its gleaming brass and clean appearance, its crew in a uniform of some kind, and that the cabin windows had curtains and electric fans inside. It was like the Governor's launch—possibly larger even than that. Everyone at Wireless Bay said Dirty Joke was rich. He seemed such a straightforward man that Fai had not really believed it till now.

Dirty Joke waved gaily from the deck.

'Hullo, Ah Fai! Thanks for helping us!' he called over the water.

'It's nothing, Mr. Wong!' Fai shouted cheerfully back. He felt more proud than ever, and excited. He had already thought of asking Dirty Joke to help persuade Uncle Cow-neck to consent to his marrying Mui. If all went well today, he proposed to do it. Dirty Joke was Uncle Cow-neck's friend and powerful associate at the east end of the island. His word with the old man would carry weight. If Fai could tell his own parents that Dirty Joke was supporting his request, this would give them the necessary confidence to speak to Uncle Cow-neck, whom they might otherwise think unapproachable, even (as custom demanded) through a go-between.

No sooner had he decided this, however, than he saw he would have to say nothing today, for Uncle Cow-neck himself came out of the cabin and stood beside Dirty Joke. The old man wore his usual blue village cloth, his shrunken face turned expressionlessly towards the sampan, with the hopeless look of the old men in the village. Next to him—and Fai wondered, a slight frown crossing his expression, as he noticed him—stood Old Fu, the headman at Fa Ping, the father of Fai's renounced child daughter-in-law.

'Why should Old Fu come to our village with these important people?' he asked his cousin-brother.

'Me?' he called back. 'How should I know? You are the one who knows all the great people.'

Fai laughed inside himself, for lately he had acquired this special reputation, and it made him happy. It made it all the more possible for him to marry Mui and bring her to the valley, without her father being disappointed. When the old man knew, from the inquiries he would cause to be made, of Fai's local reputation, he would more surely be content. Still, Fai was not happy to see Old Fu. It meant the possibility of something in all this which he could not understand.

They drew alongside the stately white launch, the sampan gaily rising and falling with the waves, the larger craft more steady. A rope ladder was thrown down, and the passengers began to tranship.

'Is it safe for us all to come at once?' Dirty Joke asked anxiously.

'How many are there?' Fai asked.

'Six.'

Fai and his cousin-brother both laughed.

'Can!' he replied with a confident, singing lilt to the word.

First came two unknown Chinese, clean-faced, city types wearing foreign clothes. After them came Uncle Cow-neck, lowered down with difficulty, for he was frail—Mui was the child of his old age, his favourite, in spite of being only a girl. Then a foreigner appeared, but with such terrible appearance that both Fai and his brother stared at him with their mouths open and nearly lost control of the sampan. It was not that he was a large man—he was large, but no larger than a big Chinese. What frightened Fai was the man's resemblance to a demon. His face was as red, and his eyebrows and moustache as fiercely bushy, as those of Kwan Kung, the War God, in the temple. Yet this foreigner was worse than this. His bare arms were covered with thick, black curly hair. There was hair on the backs of his hands, even on the backs of his fingers. Evil black whisps of it hung down below his eyes, above the part of his face that he shaved. Added to this, his eyes were of a penetrating blue, as uncanny as the eyes of an evil spirit, drenched of their proper brown colour, and thus drenched of life.

Fai could not take his eyes off this portentous apparition. As it passed him, he smelt, over the freshness of the sea, the aroma of a strange, repulsive kind of meat. Recalling what an office clerk on holiday at Wireless Bay had once told him about foreigners, Fai guessed that this—which his friend had described as a repulsive smell—must be the smell of sheep's meat. He became suddenly angry at having to introduce—sponsor, in fact—such a phenomenon to his clansmen in Ha Tsuen.

'Who is the devil?' he asked Dirty Joke in an undertone, as he came down into the sampan.

One of the clean-faced Chinese overheard, telling Fai importantly that he should realize it was Mr. Wai, the Deputy Director of Public Works, one of the highest officers of the Government. Dirty Joke then introduced Engineer Wong and Engineer Pang, both from the Public Works Department.

Seated angularly on the boards of the sampan, Uncle Cowneck and Old Fu said nothing. The devil, who was presumably the two engineers' boss, talked in devil language, to which they replied hastily and with deference. Meanwhile, as the sampan moved inshore, the smell of sheep's meat wafted back to Fai, making him willing to concede that his cousin-brother had enough experience to guide the sampan in through the mouth of the cove, if only it could mean being to the windward of the devil. It was too dangerous to change places, however. He smelt it, and wondered.

They swung through the perilous entrance, into the quiet water of the cove, and there was a loud shout from the devil as they did so. When they stepped ashore on the rocks around the temple steps, the devil turned to Fai and contracted his features in such an utterly horrifying way that Fai shrank back on the small aft-deck of the sampan. Then the devil bellowed something.

'Don't be nervous, son,' said Engineer Wong. 'Mr. Wai says thank you, and compliments you on your skill.' Both the engineers laughed.

With surprise and wonder, Fai saw, by watching the devil's face carefully, that the peculiar contraction of its features was an expression of kindness, a smile. Nervously, he smiled in return.

After the devil had looked at the temple, the party set out in single file inland towards the rice-fields, the main part of the valley. After a time, the devil asked a question.

'What are the names of the villages here?' asked Engineer Wong.

210

'Sheung Tsuen and Ha Tsuen, the upper and lower villages,' replied Fai.

'Which is Ha Tsuen?'

Fai pointed to his place across the level fields, at the foot of the steeply rising hills, upon which Old Fu moved forward till he was in front of the file.

'Yes, there is Ha Tsuen! There it is!' he cried, hurrying forward.

It seemed this was not where the devil Mr. Wai wished to go, for instead of following Old Fu he paused after some time and looked round at the hills, gloomy under the grey sky. Engineer Pang unrolled a large scroll of paper he held under his arm, holding the paper out in front of the devil, while he and Engineer Wong looked this way and that, pointing into the hills, pointing at the unrolled paper, and speaking short, careful remarks in devil language. Dirty Joke, who could not understand what was happening either, smiled confidingly at Fai.

'These are my very good friends,' he said. 'Specially Mr. Wai—a very important man.'

Seeing the possibility that Dirty Joke would assist in introducing the devil to the village, Fai felt more at ease.

After some more pointing round at the hills, the devil asked Engineer Wong another question he could not answer.

'Which is the way to the big stream?' he asked.

'Fai, you lead the way!' ordered Dirty Joke, and with Fai at the head they filed at a good speed along the bunds between the now dry fields. Glancing over to Ha Tsuen, Fai could see some of his clansmen watching him, perhaps wondering where they were going. After some time they reached the nearest point to the big stream, where the two villages had combined their efforts to build a crossing of specially large, flat stepping-stones, to be used when taking the cattle to graze on the hills each day.

The devil Mr. Wai again made his terrible contortion of pleasure as he saw this, talking more loudly to the engineers. Meanwhile, Uncle Cow-neck and Old Fu, who had been following more slowly across the fields, observed that the group was going no further, and turned back in the direction of the shore temple.

'Please ask the devil officer to come back past our village,' Fai asked Engineer Wong.

On having this translated to him, Mr. Wai again looked

pleased, and Fai laughed before he could stop himself, because he was becoming used to Mr. Wai now, realizing what a tame devil he was really—nothing to be afraid of. With cheerful step, he led the party down beside the stream towards Ha Tsuen.

'Hey! you two! Join us!' shouted Dirty Joke, cupping his hands together, towards the retreating figures of the two old men. At first they paid no attention, both of them being probably deaf. When Dirty Joke and the two engineers all shouted at once, Uncle Cow-neck turned round, shook his hand and wrist negatively, and continued walking away. In fact, Fai thought, Old Fu might not like to come to their village after they had sent his daughter back to Fa Ping.

Breaking away from the fields, Fai led the way across the big stream by the long bridge of disused coffin-boards, supported by tough pillars of stone and cement, which was Ha Tsuen's proudest achievement in recent years, apart from the affray with pirates, as a result of which they received the right from the Government to possess fifteen rifles, eight more than any village on the whole island. Within a minute or two more they reached the long, flat cement threshing-floor fronting the first row of the village's old stone houses with low, double-tiled roofs. On the doorposts still remained patches of red paper stuck on them for the New Year. On a table in the centre of the threshing-floor, and thus in the central and most honourable part of the village, Fai's parents had set out a jolly array of provisions.

As Fai had feared, Mr. Wai's appearance caused a sensation. Children were temporarily struck dumb, until, waking up to themselves, they scampered terrified into the houses. Women laughed openly, concealing their mouths behind their black cotton sleeves. The men alone behaved with propriety, one of them chasing away a small child who was brave enough to stay put and shout 'Foreign devil!' at the top of his voice. Dirty Joke Wong looked embarrassed, while the two engineers exchanged a secret look.

Only Mr. Wai himself, who had caused the excitement, remained entirely unconcerned by it, because, of course, Fai considered, for a foreigner with an appearance like that there were certain advantages in not being able to understand the dialect. With the terrifying smile fixed on his face he shook hands with Fai's father, and even tried the same with Fai's mother, who, when she saw his intention, shrank back with a frightened titter amongst the other women.

212

Introductions were made, and the visitors sat down. Beer bottles were opened and tea served.

'Very hot!' said the devil suddenly, in the dialect, and pulling out a towel from his pocket, he mopped his neck, covered with animal-like hair.

A fresh wave of confusion broke forth among the women, while children, anxious to know what was happening, timidly poked their heads round the sides of nearby front doors. No one else felt hot.

'Behave properly!' Fai called sternly to his younger brothers and sisters, whose heads thereupon were withdrawn amidst giggles.

'Mr. Wai is a very high officer and a very benevolent man,' Dirty Joke explained to everyone, and everyone listened with respect, because Dirty Joke was known to be rich and powerful, and since he had started buying up the Fa Ping people's land he was becoming like a neighbour—someone to be reckoned with.

Mr. Wai asked a question, which Engineer Wong translated.

'How many families are there in the village?'

'Seventeen,' Fai's father answered.

The devil nodded. There was more discussion in devil language.

Everyone waited respectfully, until Dirty Joke began chatting with Fai's father. Later, as the beer warmed up his spirit, he cracked jokes with Fai's mother and the other women, till things became cheerful, and everybody was glad the visitors had come. Fai was happy. It was particularly lucky that Uncle Cow-neck had not come to the village. In this way he would have the chance of speaking to Dirty Joke alone.

When they left the village, with many handshakes and some appreciative grunts from Mr. Wai, Dirty Joke was already on the subject of marriage, about which he had been entertaining the ladies with tales of the big city which they pretended to be scandalized at.

'And what about you, Ah Fai?' he asked, as they once more crossed the coffin-board bridge. 'Isn't it time for you to take the plunge?'

'Yes,' he replied boldly. 'But I didn't hear that Uncle Cow-neck was looking for a son-in-law.'

Dirty Joke switched round at the head of the bridge to look at him.

'Ah Mui?' he queried, adding with a thick, pale grin, 'I'd always thought she'd be fine for me!'

They walked on.

'Maybe many people are after her,' Fai said.

'I don't think so. They're too scared of her old man. You're not scared of him, are you, Ah Fai?'

'No, Mr. Wong. Why should I be?'

'Then you've got a chance, son. You've a good chance! Ah, ha! What a wedding we'll make that!'

'But, Mr. Wong, you mustn't say anything to Uncle about this,' Fai said nervously, instinct telling him this was the best way of proceeding.

'Trust me, Ah Fai!' he replied gaily. 'But I might tell Ah Mui. Ah, ha! I might, you know, you young rascal!'

Putting his hand out behind him, he squeezed Fai's hand in his. Fai observed him quietly, confidently. He himself had not taken beer, having to steer the sampan out to the launch. He saw Dirty Joke as a helper, not as a friend. After drinking beer, he would have called him a friend. Now he simply watched him, and calculated his design.

They were passing waste land near the back of the sand beach, when Mr. Wai and the engineers stopped again to talk. This time the devil was pointing at different parts of the earth, pointing with a circular motion over there, and over there, right across the valley.

'What is it?' Dirty Joke asked Engineer Pang.

'The borings,' he answered. 'Nothing can be done till we've completed the borings.'

Dirty Joke nodded gravely.

'I understand,' he said.

They all walked on in silence till they came back to the temple.

There the two old men were waiting for them, and Fai had his mind occupied with untying the sampan's rope, helping his visitors aboard, shouting at his cousin-brother to be careful, and heading the craft once more through the dangerous narrow neck of the cove and sideways into the oncoming rollers. Only when they were out in the bay, with these duties done, and Engineer Pang, the last, was mounting the rope ladder aboard the big white launch, did Fai's mind return to the small itch of doubt that had been in it ever since seeing Old Fu on the deck.

'What have they been saying, Mr. Pang?' he asked quietly, standing near him as the sampan rose and fell.

Engineer Pang looked back, as if surprised.

'The new reservoir,' he said casually, reaching with his hand for the ship's lower rail.

'The new reservoir?' Fai repeated.

'Yes,' Mr. Pang said cheerfully, hoisting himself on deck. 'Many thanks for your help.' He waved as Fai loosed his hold on the ladder, allowing the sampan to swing in towards the shore, away from the launch. Seeing the sampan go, Mr. Wai and Dirty Joke waved too, Mr. Wai shouting at Fai and holding up his hands clenched together. Only the old men paid no attention. They were talking together, and Old Fu was chuckling.

The sampan drifted in easily over the waves.

'But our reservoir is quite good and new,' said Fai aloud, more to himself than to his cousin-brother. He had been one of the ten selected to build it, with the thirty bags of free cement supplied by the Magistrate's office; and no one so important as Mr. Wai even came to inspect it.

'That foreigner smelt horrible,' his cousin-brother commented, as they neared the cove mouth.

Rain began to fall, the gentle spring rain. Fai glanced up at the gloomy sky. In a few more days it would be time for sowing.

22

WEARING a dinner jacket, Richard sat well extended in an armchair. After his third whisky and soda, prepared somewhat pungently by Juen, who was determined to celebrate the family reunion, he was mentally foggy.

'Aren't you ready yet, darling?' he called out.

'Five minutes!' came Sylvia's call from their bedroom, the colony's famous call, which every servant in a British household understood to mean anything between ten minutes and two hours.

'The fight is on,' he said to himself aloud. 'The fight is bloody well on!'

Sylvia had been back three days, three incredible days of utter relief, three evenings of alcoholic mutual self-examination, three nights of peculiarly satisfactory abandon. It had been one of those stable moments in life, which can never be forgotten, when life becomes like the full moon of the Mid-Autumn Festival, the same full moon, but at its fullest. He had not expected it, and when, too ill to go to the airport, he had seen her at the door of the flat, he had been conscious of nothing but her look of inquiry into the scarcely perceptible changes which a single winter in life can bring about. Thus, too, he looked at her—till they laughed, reading each other's thoughts, and just then he held her in his arms.

After that, everything began to go right. He ate a reasonably good dinner. Next morning, at the office, the staff were unaccountably cheerful. Professor Wen came specially to the office to invite them both to a Chinese music party—'which I am arranging because I know you like to hear Chinese classical opera properly performed—by amateurs, of course, you realize; but they are good.'

'Better than professionals, sometimes, surely,' Richard had said.

'Professor Wen searched for the word.

'More intelligent in their singing,' he agreed finally.

Tonight was the party, their first night out together. Not that either of them really cared for Chinese music. They lived through it somehow, as a means to gaining friends, showing interest, and trying to understand. And—that was a joy about Sylvia, you never had to explain a Chinese point to her—the fact that Professor Wen was giving the party in the city, when his invariable habit was to return to Little Island in time for dinner, meant that this was an invitation that could not be refused. For Sylvia, it was a party to wash the dust from the feet after a journey; for them both, it was a gesture of sincere friendship. Professor Wen, good man, was being the first to help them break the social ice that had formed around them.

He took off his glasses and swung them round and round in his right hand. The last weeks had been unquestionably the worst he had experienced since joining the Colonial Service. Their awfulness had mounted until, had Sylvia's return been delayed by more than a day, he would have had it in him to think of suicide. With her, things became more possible—a shade more possible. The fight was on: the two of them, with a handful of real friends who might be expected in these few days to reveal themselves, as

216

Professor Wen had done, against the rest of the colony. Still, two were far, far better than one. From the hour of her return, there was hope.

Secretly—it was something he would not admit even to her— he was ashamed of himself for no longer being able to face entering a British shop, with the risk of being publicly insulted by his own compatriots. If he examined those who had been the most public in their insults, or who had hurt him most, what were they? Cosgrave, the owner of a fourth-rate shipping company which for years had made trade by running whatever blockades Far Eastern politics had at various times imposed. Cosgrave counted for nothing. Yet, on the steps of the Club, while Richard happened to be waiting for a taxi, this unimpressive man, with a nose bulbous from liquor, had talked ridiculous twaddle about the colony having been founded by men worthy of the nation of Nelson, and they didn't want any in it who weren't—and behind him others had gathered, leaving the Club after lunch, telling him he'd better take the hint quick or he'd be whipped out. He had entered his taxi and been driven off without looking at them.

He knew, without looking, what type they were. They were the same as those in the gramophone shop, where the British assistant had said that, if he didn't mind, a Chinese would serve him, and other British men and women—respectable, sensible people—had said 'Hear, hear!' and 'I wouldn't serve him at all, if I were you, John.' It was that young type that he feared to meet, with its clean, hard face, too much chin, athletic physique, the cricket player, the sports club member, the yachtsman, the good fellow, the pugilistically correct young British colonial, upon whom the Freemasons had already set their eye. It was a type he had all his life, except occasionally in the Air Force, managed to avoid, the type that dares not stand by itself, that relies on groups and clubs in order to have the crazy zigzag which it deems to be its way. Faced with strength, obedient; faced with weakness, uniting to crush. Never having had the least sympathy with such men, Richard felt unable to reply to their insults, unable even to look them in the face. If they could not see what fools they would look, say, in front of a stage audience, that was just life, and he was in no position to instruct them. Wiser to do more completely what he had always tended to do, and avoid them.

Avoiding the British—thoroughly and systematically—in a British colony, even in a city as large as Victoria, was not easy.

All that the exercise succeeded in doing was to make Richard dread going out anywhere, to his office, to the lower streets, along the upper levels for an evening walk. He grew mentally unwilling to leave The Heights. From its windows he gazed down at the descending rows of roofs, under any one of which might lurk one of his enemies, the British colonials, waiting to give him another sharp, humiliating warning, before proceeding forth to their churches and cricket fields. A quality of nightmare intruded into his view of the usually normal, pleasant city.

Against this, and against the dark, unyielding fight with corruption in his office—corruption in which inevitably the Anti-Corruption Branch suspected him of being involved—came the terse announcement, in a Secretariat memorandum, that the Great Island road was to become a top priority project, that the survey for it, already being undertaken, was to be completed as fast as possible, and that it would be too slow and inefficient to use any local labour. The Director of Public Works was ordered to be ready within ten days to call for tenders for the construction of the road on contract.

A call to Webb, the officer in charge of all major public works in the country areas—and even a call to Webb was a mental effort, to hear the hardened tone of voice when the Deputy Director heard who it was speaking—revealed the outline of the plan that had suddenly hastened the road's construction.

'I don't think it'll create any hardship,' Webb had said. 'Both villages and all the fields at present cultivated will be submerged, of course, but the villages can be rebuilt on the higher levels, provided the health authorities agree, and that road of yours will be of the greatest importance. With difficulty, of course, we could land the heavy equipment on that beach, but it will be far easier when we can use Wireless Bay pier and a road right through from there. That's the reason for the priority. The road and the reservoir are really one project.'

What was the use of arguing with an engineer, intent on his well-thought-out project? What would be the use of talking about two small villages which had been in the valley, occupied by the same clans, for seven hundred years? To an engineer it was an easy matter to move a village. The economy of the people? It could be changed. The temples? The temples could be rebuilt elsewhere. Even when they were sited according to geomantic principles, and their siting was believed to be responsible for the

218

well-being of all the villages' inhabitants? Geomantic principles? What were they?—No, an engineer wouldn't know, Webb had visited the valley himself, he said, and could see no real difficulties.

Reluctantly, Richard decided that a direct approach to Jenkinson, the Acting Chief Secretary, was the only way out. In the difficulty he had to obtain an interview, it was evident that the reluctance was mutual.

'The people of Great Island have been neglected by us for a hundred years, sir. At last, we decide to do something for them— build them a road. What happens? The road turns out to be nothing but a deception. My office staff and I have been out there time and again, working like missionaries, trying to convert them to the idea of the road's advantages. From the start they've thought—and said—that our words were just lies. Now, the Government has proved them right. To them, the road is the Government's lie, the Government's way of cheating them of all they possess, their fields, their homes, everything.'

'You dramatize the situation,' Jenkinson interrupted, coughing importantly into his moustache. 'The Government will take all measures necessary to safeguard their welfare.'

'They don't believe that. I can tell you so now. I hardly believe it myself. I warn you, sir, if this project goes forward, I would be prepared to advise you formally that the entire road project should be dropped, in the interests of the country people, who will otherwise become the prey of city speculators, and will lose all they have to them. This is an issue on which I would be prepared to resign.'

'That would be a relief to us all,' Jenkinson answered, in his high, archidiaconal voice. 'Unfortunately, you wouldn't have the guts to do it.'

For an instant Richard was taken aback. It was true, he would not be able to resign just like that, on the spur of the moment. Sylvia was returning. A strange new phase in their married life was about to begin. Resignation might throw everything to the winds. Jenkinson's words hurt, though, and he was on the point of saying something rash when his intellect checked him. Why should he be tricked into taking up a cheap challenge of this kind? After which, the words came of their own accord.

'I am your senior District Officer and the only Chinese-speaking one. It has been admitted on more than one occasion that I have a closer knowledge of the country areas than anyone else in the Administration. If I submit a formal objection to the further continuance of the road scheme, with my reasons, and my absolute objection to the new reservoir being sited in that inhabited and highly fertile valley, I think I am in a position to request that the matter be brought to the attention of the Secretary of State.'

'That will depend on the opinion of the Acting Governor,' Jenkinson answered stiffly.

'Quite,' said Richard, knowing that that opinion was a foregone conclusion. It was the first time he had ever put his foot down in his civil service career. He could not have dreamed of a day ever coming when he could have put it down with such complete confidence that he was right, that he knew what he was talking about, that he was in a position of being an expert, whose word the Government would be obliged to listen to. With this he concluded the interview and walked out. Walking along the corridor and going down in the lift, he felt exhilarated. He was in fact blind to everything and everyone. Only when a taxi brought him back to The Heights did he find he was trembling like a leaf, and so overcome with nervous exhaustion that he could only fling himself down on a sofa and lie there dazed, staring at the ceiling. By evening he had a high fever and retired to bed without eating anything. The next day Sylvia arrived.

'There isn't going to be a road!' he said in a tone of something like triumph, at some period in their long evening conversation after he had explained what had happened. 'There isn't going to be one! I bet you what you like, dear. They'll have to give in and agree with me. I started it, and I believe I can stop it, together with this damned reservoir. Let them search the uninhabited valleys for somewhere to put that in! Old Webb goes out to one valley, takes a look, and that's it. That's not good enough where the well-being of two villages is at stake.'

'It reminds me of what you said about the hands, Richard,' was her quiet comment. 'If it's all true, the question that arises is: can the hands, if cleansed, undo what has been done awry?'

'Why not? It's my idea that they can.'

The bell rang, recalling him to the present moment.

'Come along, darling,' he called, jumping to his feet. 'That's the car.'

'There you are! Ready!'

Sylvia entered the main room. She wore an orange-yellow taffeta evening gown of up-to-date New York design, with purple

220

orchids, alexandrite ear-rings and bracelet, and the new diamond watch he had just given her. It was the right outfit in which to face the music—the Chinese music, too. Whatever sorrow stayed in his heart, he put it away in a remote place. Because she was doing the same thing, they were driven to the party in harmony, appropriate to the start of a musical evening.

Professor Wen, it appeared when they arrived, had come to some mysteriously Chinese arrangement about the entire evening. The party was being given in the house of a Mr. Lee, whom neither Richard nor Sylvia knew. It was a large, ornate house of Edwardian design—though probably built after the First World War, the colony being always late in its architectural styles—with heavily barred windows, a small garden, high walls with barbed wire along the top, and every precaution on the outer gate, through which it was impossible to see till the gate was opened. Mr. Lee was clearly a person of substance.

Whether Professor Wen had asked for the loan of the house in order to give the dinner himself, or whether Mr. Lee was giving the dinner but asking Professor Wen to take the host's place because his English was better than Mr. Lee's, Richard could not fathom. Both welcomed them at the door, so that no conclusions could be drawn, while at dinner the *placement* at the round table for twelve sets of bowls was one of those perfectly enigmatical examples of Chinese politeness which baffle everyone and silence all possible complaint. The host's place was set at a slight slant to the line of the room, the definite place for the host occurring in the blank space between Mr. Lee and Professor Wen. Richard sat directly opposite Mr. Lee, suggesting that, if he was the senior guest, Mr. Lee was the host. Fat Mr. Szeto, head of the bus company, however, the only other well-known colony figure, sat directly opposite the Professor, and as Mr. Szeto might have been considered senior to Richard, this may have meant that the Professor was the host. Sylvia, to complete these intricacies, sat on the Professor's left, another place of honour. Why was thin little Mrs. Szeto not put there, and as Sylvia was there, why was Richard not in the man's place of honour opposite the Professor?

In this state of accomplished uncertainty the party began—and continued. The seventh course was a fish, signalling the end of the meal; the eighth consisted of sweets and a fruit dish. Richard was wiping his face with a hot towel and thinking how nice it was not to be obliged to eat too much, when the ninth dish arrived: a duck stuffed with lotus seeds—and another series of meat courses began, culminating in a clear mushroom soup as the fourteenth and last. By half-way through this fine repast an atmosphere of conviviality had been created. Sylvia had been cordially welcomed back. The forthcoming film—and earnings—had been toasted with all winecups bottoms up. Richard nearly made things difficult at the outset by saying to his left-hand neighbour, Mr. Szeto, that he had not realized he was a music-lover. The fat magnate gave him a froggy look and in his high voice explained that Mr. and Mrs. Hsü, the architect and his wife, who were at the table, and who after dinner were going to perform, were old friends of his from Shanghai days. After this music was forgotten, until about the time of the serving of the mushroom soup, when the flint-hard strings of Chinese zithers were heard being tuned at the further end of the long room, beyond a dividing arch. How Mr. and Mrs. Hsü were going to perform after so much food and drink puzzled Richard; but as soon as green tea was served, they both rose with apologies and went beyond to supervise the preparations. A few moments later it became evident that the Hsü family was not going to begin with such ease as might have been imagined by their confident withdrawal, for two voices, one male and one female, joined the instruments tuning up, with the long, piercing shrieks of Chinese operatic music.

Sylvia looked at him across the table, with the faintest rumour of a wink, and again he felt thankful to have her back with him. The relief of having someone to share these evenings with! He thought of the countless past occasions when they had stifled desire after desire to laugh, holding themselves back till they could be alone together, hilariously going over each comic detail, or darkly working out the significance of this or that remark. No woman he had ever met seemed to know her way so surely through the labyrinth of Chinese manners and double meanings.

Now one of the younger guests rose to join the musicians. He, it appeared, was by profession an engineer. Over the tea-cups, discussion enlarged on the guests' occupations.

'And what is yours, Mr. Lau?' Richard asked.

'Actually, in a small way, I'm a contractor,' the gentleman replied, fumbling in his wallet to find a visiting card.

'I'm sure no one who sits down at a table of this kind does anything in a small way,' said Richard, amid laughter, looking at Mr. Szeto.

Mr. Lau stood up to present his card with both hands, Richard rising to take it likewise. When he read the second character, indicating the clan branch, Richard glanced up at Sylvia, who, by her expression, had also seen the name on the card.

'Surely,' he said, 'you must be related to Edwin Lau?'

'He's my older brother,' Mr. Lau replied ingratiatingly.

Again Richard exchanged a glance with his wife. A great deal of money, their eyes said as they met, is seated round this table.

The other couple, completing the twelve, were an independent financier and his wife. The husband had formerly been a general in the Chinese Army. Was a pattern forming in the choice of guests? And what was Professor Wen doing in the middle of it all?

These speculations, arousing a certain mistrust in Richard, had to be put aside as the party rose to take their places on well-upholstered sofas and easy chairs beyond the arch. Ornate urns, green and pink, stood boldly in arched recesses. Out of view from the dining-room, a grand piano occupied one corner, draped with embroidered silk. The upholstery of the chairs was pink, the carpet a large Tientsin white of high value. Mr. Lee, though not a collector, indulged only in the best. Possibly it was he who had chosen and paid for the dinner.

An abundance of liqueurs was served in cut-glass goblets edged with gold leaf. The restaurant that had provided the dinner had supplied also the bowls and chopsticks. Now Mr. Lee's own possessions were coming forth, decanters of old Venetian glass, strangely shaped Japanese saucers for nuts and melon-seeds. On the piano stood a lone and priceless vase of Ming blue and white, its colours shouting their importance against the rest of the pinks and greens.

Richard was separated from Sylvia, preventing him from nudging her, as he would have wished, at the unexpected sight of Mr. and Mrs. Hsü, standing with their backs to their audience and screaming at the wall in front of them, from which richocheted a wildly sustained blast of *vibrato* sound. More amazing still, the male voice was that of Mrs. Hsü, an expert in male parts, while the female was that of Mr. Hsü, an impersonator of the female sex. The zithers screechingly accompanied this din, though why, it was difficult to appreciate, since they played throughout the same notes as the singers sang, or more or less.

223

The room was large, but with such a *fortissimo* filling it, it seemed far, far too small. After a time Richard became oblivious to all except the speed of the *vibrato*, as if listening to some rare machine calculating sound waves. Was it love of which they screamed? Was it war? Was it of horses, or invasions, or treachery, or of imperial commands? The only impression he had was of a sustained, guided hysteria, the art of screeching to a design. As his eardrums began to feel battered and his entire nervous system weary, he experienced the reality of the meaning of the beauty of silence. Around him the Chinese smiled and nodded to each other, sipping liqueurs and splitting melon-seeds.

Others, not invited to the dinner, had joined the music party. Some of them performed after the Hsüs. When the guests tired of paying attention, conversations began. The formal business of showing interest was relaxed. Glancing back around the room, Richard saw Wong Tak-wor standing near the piano talking to the ex-general financier. Again his eyes sought his wife's.

Hers were already on his. She spoke in French.

'I think this is some sort of trap.'

'I'm sure of it,' he replied, also in French. 'What are we to do?' She shrugged her shoulders.

Professor Wen was being kindness itself, an indefatigable host —or go-between? At the dinner table he had praised each of the guests, speaking of his long friendship with them, their virtues, their public-spiritedness, their desire to serve the public and, now that they were here, the colony. It seemed so delightfully friendly until, during a gap in the screaming, while one screamer was re-placing another and the zithers were being scratched and plinked into tune (did it matter?):

'People tell me you're fed up with your job,' Mr. Szeto said, sinking down heavily beside Richard. 'Hey, have some more of that. What is it?' he asked, holding up Richard's goblet.

'Green Chartreuse,' Richard replied, as a servant brought the bottle.

'Yes,' Mr. Szeto pursued in curiously chirruping tones. 'You fought so hard for that road on Great Island, for example. Now, what are you doing for us? They say the Chief Secretary is calling the whole thing off. You're not going to let that happen, surely? Where's all that famous enthusiasm of yours gone? I want to see my buses rolling down that road. Eh?' He chortled, and patted Richard's knee.

Somehow—Richard, having drunk a good deal by now, was not quite sure about it—the music had become more subdued, or else the musicians were talking among themselves, experimenting with different themes they knew. In a wide circle around him were gently grouping themselves Mr. Lee, Edwin Lau's brother, the young engineer-singer, Mr. Hsü, Wong Tak-wor, and the ex-general, with Mr. Szeto seated always in the same place. Richard noted how, with increased affluence and more *savoir vivre*, Wong Tak-wor was choosing his suits more modestly and carefully, following the sober British shades of Szeto and the rest. In a few days it would be too hot to wear winter suits any more, even in the evenings.

'The road will be of great benefit to all the islanders,' grinned Wong Tak-wor, in the dialect, his fish mouth remaining slightly open after he had spoken.

'But now the Chief Secretary wishes to cancel the scheme,' Szeto explained to him.

Wong Tak-wor looked shocked, his mouth opening slightly more.

'If that is so, Mr. Szeto,' said Richard carefully, unsure yet what Szeto knew or what his game was, 'you are surely the man who can persuade him to change his mind—perhaps with your brother Edwin, Mr. Lau, if he's also interested.'

'Oh, no,' replied Szeto knowingly, with another pat on Richard's knee. 'What influence have I? You are the man who can get the decision changed.'

Richard wondered, as on many former occasions, at the speed and accuracy of what in the colony was called the bamboo telegraph. Obviously Szeto had learnt of Richard's threat to petition the Secretary of State for the road and reservoir project to be abandoned. Szeto's statement that it was the Chief Secretary who wished to stop the scheme was a mere politeness. He clearly knew the truth.

'Mr. Szeto has told me how without you, Mr. Fairburn, we should never have come as far as we have with the road,' said Lau. It was in keeping with Edwin's character, Richard thought, to send his younger brother on an occasion when he did not dare come himself. Since Sylvia's return, Frances had telephoned, but had not dared yet come round, because of Edwin's attitude in siding—outwardly, at any rate—with the British. 'Please, you must help us to get it through now.'

Szeto moved his enormous bulk into a new position on the edge of the sofa, from which he could look round at Richard.

'I must apologize, Mr. Fairburn,' he croaked. 'I haven't explained things fully. The fact is that these gentlemen and myself, together with some others who unfortunately cannot be present here tonight'—Edwin, thought Richard—'have formed a company to undertake the construction of this road. It's a costly affair, and I understand the Government wants a quick job. From us they'll get it. The trouble is, this latest decision of the Chief Secretary has put us all in a rather serious position. Heavy machinery has been ordered, and some of it is already on its way from London. We shan't be able to dispose of that equipment in the colony, and we are faced with a certain loss in re-exporting it. Because it's British equipment, neither the Philippines nor Japan will be interested in it. We shall be obliged to sell at a loss in Singapore or Hongkong.'

'But we wanted to build the road entirely with British machinery,' chipped in the deeper voice of Lau, while Wong Tak-wor's fish eyes roved softly from one anxious face to another, as he tried to follow what was happening.

'It was somewhat unwise of you to have ordered machinery before the road had been put out to tender, wasn't it?' Richard queried.

'Not in the least,' Szeto replied, imperturbable. 'We knew it would inevitably go out to tender, and we happen to know that we are certain to tender successfully. There is no one else at present with sufficient capital. Mr. Lau here is one of the registered contractors, and, you know how it is, Mr. Fairburn, one contractor knows another—like thieves, they don't steal from one another,' he said with a big grin. People smiled. There was a relaxation.

Sylvia's head and shoulders appeared over Mr. Hsü's chair.

'We really ought to be going home soon, Richard.'

'Yes, surely,' he replied, glad for the excuse to stand up. 'It's all very interesting, gentlemen, and the music was excellent. Mr. Hsü, you are a real virtuoso—and where is Mrs. Hsü? We must thank her too.'

But Szeto was not to be so easily shaken off.

'You understand, Mr. Fairburn? It's a certainty for us, if tenders are called for.'

'Will you please help us, sir?' said Lau seriously, putting his soft, white hands in Richard's. 'If you don't, I don't know what we shall do.'

Richard smiled, murmuring inanities, and turned away only to find the smiling Wong Tak-wor blocking his way to the outer room. Harmonious Virtue put his hands affectionately on Richard's arms, and said in the dialect the words with which every village meeting always concluded:

'We hope you help us, Magistrate. Everyone hopes you help us.'

The others, recognizing this rough country tone of speech, beamed with goodwill. Richard thought transiently of that exquisite girl he had had on Little Island, that white, unblemished perfection beside which the greatest beauty of the West seemed gross and imperfect, and remembered how one night she dangled a dark green jade ear-ring over the white taut skin round her navel.

'Yes, we must try, we must try,' he replied in the dialect, at which the whole party expressed relieved acclamation, some of them clapping their hands as well.

'If you support it, Mr. Fairburn, it's in the bag!' Lau almost shouted.

'And you'll see a good job done by these able gentlemen,' added Szeto. 'You see, we have our own advisory engineers. We're making no mistakes. I want to see my buses on Great Island, and I want to see that they're going to be safe on that road!'

With further acclaim and laughter, the party moved through the house, at the door of which Sylvia and Richard took leave of each person present, congratulating Mrs. Hsü on her rich tenor, and generally manifesting grace and goodwill, until the final moment of uncertainty whether to say good night to Mr. Lee last, or to Professor Wen—who had re-emerged after a fairly long disappearance. Sylvia decided on the professor, and Richard, aware of her judgment in such matters, followed suit. She was 'being right all the time', as he had once said. Tonight he was proud of it.

Their last glimpse was of the friendly, intellectual eyes of Professor Wen, through their steel-rimmed spectacles. Mr. Lee held open the door of his own car, which then took them home.

Without letting it be too obvious to the driver, once away from the house they both leant back deeply in their seats and gasped for breath.

'How Wen can let himself be such a stooge is beyond me,' Sylvia exclaimed at last.

Richard waved his spectacles round airily.

'He probably did it out of pure goodness of heart, thinking he was acting entirely for the best.'

'Where do you go from here?'

Silence fell between them. Richard gazed vaguely at the passing lights, their changing colours and patterns.

'Of course, it would be no loss to them at all to have to re-sell a bulldozer or two and some quarrying equipment,' he said at last.

'I agree.'

'But that's not the point, is it? It means the enmity of old Szeto, and of the Laus—Edwin and Frances as well. Has there ever been a governor they haven't been on intimate terms with? Could they not thwart everything we either of us tried to do in the future?'

The car swung round a sharp bend and began to mount the hill homeward.

'Revenge is such a powerful Chinese motive,' Sylvia reflected aloud, looking out of the window.

'Especially where money has been lost,' he added, looking out on his side too into the darkness of trees and sleeping hillside mansions.

'It looks as though it's not going to be possible for the hands to undo what has been done,' she said.

The car wound round corners and roundabouts, mounting ever upwards. He sighed deeply, a sigh of tiredness, and of too much to eat and drink.

'I was leaving it for you to say it,' he said. 'I agree. It looks as if, once begun, things go on, and we go on with them.'

The car swung round into a level drive-in. They were home.

23

'W HAT in hell's name is all this?' demanded Willie Rogers
angrily, standing in front of Richard's desk and slapping the front page of the English newspaper.

'What is it?' Richard asked, looking up. Willie Rogers appeared—the first time Richard had ever seen him thus—really
angry.

'This reservoir scheme! This plan to submerge the two
villages! Where does this come from?' Willie Rogers demanded,
quivering with indignation.

'D'you mean to say you've come right down from the Olympus
of the university to ask me that?' Richard asked, his relationship
with the Assistant Lecturer having always rested on a basis of
flippancy.

'This is not a time for joking, Richard. Where does this
abominable scheme emanate from?'

Richard studied him carefully. Willie Rogers was truly roused.
The fate of Sheung Tsuen and Ha Tsuen, announced in the Press
upon the favourable completion of the boring tests in the valley,
had touched the arrogant young lecturer's *côté paysan*. 'Sit down,
Willie. Have a coffee.' He put aside the file he had been reading.
'To be frank with you, I don't know how the scheme started. It's
certainly gone forward over my nearly dead body. But I've had to
give in.'

While the office attendant brought coffee, Richard wondered
at the strange self-identification that sometimes takes place in men,
causing them to speak, after a few months in a strange place, as if
they had lived there all their lives—a form of self-protection,
possibly, in remote, lonely surroundings. 'Have you a holiday?'
he asked.

Willie Rogers nodded.

'Then come out with me now. I'm just going to Great Island
to inspect the suggested sites for the new villages.'

'It's crazy, Richard! The villagers will never move!'

'Then they'll drown, won't they?' he replied emotionlessly. He

229

had been over the whole miserable business so often he was devoid of emotion. 'Let's go together.' He did not want to lose Willie Rogers' confidence, for Willie could be dangerous in the social game Sylvia and he were playing. Willie, unexpectedly, had been the first European in their old circle to welcome Sylvia back. Doubtless he dined out for weeks afterwards on his first dinner with them at The Heights, at which Sylvia, having drunk a happy mixture of no one could quite recall what, was so outrageous, and at the same time made Willie laugh so much that twice he had to take off his glasses and wipe tears off them, that neither of them begrudged it him if he did dine out on it. Willie Rogers, in fact, though he was probably unaware of it, was being used by Sylvia and Richard as a channel of communication between themselves and such arched-brow critics as Lady Mercer, Brenda Macpherson, Julie Holliday, and all the rest of them. Richard knew Sylvia would say he had gone out of his wits if he allowed Willie Rogers to slip from this convenient position. The present solution, Richard saw at a glance, was to make use of Willie's *côté paysan*, his odd self-identification with the simplest of country people. Let him identify himself, in addition, with Richard's aspect of the tragedy.

They embarked at the wharves around ten o'clock. It was a fairly cool morning, misty, blue, and calm, towards the end of September. Somehow they had weathered the summer with its battering heat, tropical and social. Sylvia had been amazing. A week after her return from America, the Club roused itself to sufficient righteous indignation to blackball him. Jenkinson had carried out his promise. Unable to break him officially, he set about it by the other means at his disposal. Sylvia's counterattack, when she and Richard found they were invited nowhere, not even to the private views of picture exhibitions and other minor invitations of the same social importance, was to turn up with him on the first open day of a show, having let the newspapers know in advance when she would be coming. They then had their photographs taken with the artist, bought a picture, and on one occasion Sylvia even made a short speech (by invitation) which the cub reporter of *The Bulletin* submitted for inclusion and was severely reprimanded for by the Editor, who was, of course, a member of the Club. Nettled at receiving no invitation to a British Council cocktail and private showing of a collection of high-quality British prints, Sylvia telephoned Eldon Wong

230

—'that nice clean innocent young man with far too many children already,' as she described him.

'What? Aren't you on the list, Mrs. Fairburn?' said the shocked Eldon. 'It must be a mistake.'

As they shook hands and passed the gaping jaws of the Winterleys on that occasion, Eldon was luckily the first person they saw in the room beyond.

'If anyone asks you, say you haven't the faintest idea how it happened,' she said as she passed him, after which they discussed the prints.

All in all, it had been more amusing than worrying, their process of rehabilitation. Mysteriously, invitations began to arrive from Chinese they had not seen for years, and it was only after several weeks that Frances Lau confided to Sylvia over the telephone that she had been ringing up a number of people whom she knew either Sylvia or Richard had helped in the past, telling them to be sure to invite the Fairburns next time they were giving a dinner party. If Frances could not help directly, she did all she could indirectly. Of such, Richard thought, is Chinese friendship. On Saturday evenings, as noticeably as possible, they dined and danced at the Ritz. Another newly developed friend turned out to be Beaton, the Police Superintendent, head of the Anti-Corruption Branch, who had come to know and understand better than most what Richard had been living through. True, they no longer circulated at quite the elevation they used to. But on a slightly lower, less brittle, grade they found several genuine friends.

In the launch, Richard explained to Willie Rogers his intention to approach the villages the back way, landing at O Mun, at the west end of the island, and walking thence up the hills and over into the valley from the landward side. In this way they could see the proposed new sites without being delayed by long discussion in Ha Tsuen—as would certainly be the case were they to come in the usual way, from the sea.

At O Mun, the market town, they met the Chinese surveyor from the Public Works Department who was to accompany them. Beside a stream, high up in the bare, grassy hills, they ate a picnic lunch, carried along for them by a messenger from the District Office; and in the middle of the afternoon, feeling hot, they reached the summit of the hills, from which they descended rapidly by a stone footpath into the valley, twisting and turning as they went. So sharp was the declivity that not even Chinese villagers

231

could take it without making a zigzag path, with many hairpin bends.

When they had dropped down considerably, being only two hundred feet or so above Ha Tsuen, the young surveyor stopped them.

'It's here, sir.'

Though the slope was less steep, it was difficult to visualize how a village could be set down there.

'The water level won't be very high, sir,' the surveyor explained; 'not more than a few feet above the tops of the houses in both villages, but it will spread right over the whole valley. We propose this site, rather higher than it need be, because this will meet the objections of the health authorities to having villages sited above the reservoir, with the danger of pollution.'

'There are adequate filter facilities in Victoria,' said Willie Rogers intolerantly.

'This is what the health authorities say, sir,' the surveyor replied patiently. 'It's because of the danger of nightsoil-polluted water running down into the reservoir. At this height we can construct water conduits which will carry all the water from the hill fields straight out to the beach, bypassing the reservoir.'

Richard looked round at the silent, monumental landscape, the flat rice-fields below, the towering mountains rising around and above, the sea calm and pleasant on the right. In the centre of the valley the grey, serried rows of houses of Sheung Tsuen looked like a small square platoon of strength, defying every comer from the sea. Ha Tsuen was hidden below the sharp fall of the hill they stood on. While he looked around, a mountain bird cried out, a pitiful, helpless sound in the great silence of the island. A cricket chirruped briefly, and was still.

'Sheung Tsuen,' the surveyor continued, 'we propose to rebuild over there, where the stream serving it can be diverted, and again reach the sea without polluting the reservoir water. I may say, sir, that the Medical Department calls this a special concession, because of the fact that these villages have been here quite a long time.'

Richard looked emptily at the nicely dressed young surveyor, with his recent haircut, new shoes, and tidy file of papers under his arm, and felt his temper rising as the neat English phrases were trotted out. It was Willie Rogers who spoke.

'Historically they can be traced back seven hundred years.

Actually, they have lived here since the beginning of time. It is *their* valley!'

'That may be, sir,' said the surveyor with a pleasant smile, 'but Victoria, as you know, needs water; and Victoria is a growing place.'

'How are they going to eat, you damned fool?' Willie Rogers demanded, his voice choked with anger.

'Yes,' Richard put in more quietly, lest the young chap lose confidence and tell them no more. 'How will they earn their livelihood up here?'

The surveyor faltered. Like every technical man, thought Richard, he had thought of everything except how other people were going to eat. For himself, he had a good little wife, no doubt, beginning to look out for him already in town as the shadows began to lengthen.

'They'll be able to grow terraced rice,' the young man said with a stammer.

'Not enough to live on,' Richard replied quickly, glancing round at the gradual steps amid the grass where, many years ago, terraced cultivation had been undertaken.

'And then, sir,' he added, gaining confidence again, 'I think this is tied up somehow with a vegetable scheme.'

'Don't talk to me about vegetables!' Willie Rogers said sharply.

The surveyor, sensing that he need only address himself to the District Officer, was unmoved.

'Yes, sir,' he said. 'I think I remember now. I heard it was the Government's intention that the people should live here primarily by growing vegetables.'

'Merciful heaven protect us!' Willie exclaimed in despair. 'Are the Government a collection of nitwits?'

'No, but it might be possible, Willie,' Richard said, 'provided there were transport, and provided someone could help them at the start.'

Willie Rogers glanced up at him contemptuously.

'Dear grief! You too? . . . It will *never* be possible for these people to grow vegetables!'

Richard looked down to where he stood, slightly below him in the sloping grass.

'That's what the village people themselves have always told me. Why not, Willie?'

233

The Assistant Lecturer, who an instant earlier had been pounding both hands on an imaginary table in his anxiety to be heard, became abruptly calm. Taking off his glasses, he let his curiously squinting blue eyes search weakly in space for Richard's body and expression.

'Women don't grow vegetables,' he said quietly, drying his glasses and concentrating on them.

Richard was uncertain.

'I—I don't quite get it, Willie.'

Smoothing his fair hair back, Willie Rogers put on his glasses and became once more his piercing self. Leaning upward towards Richard, he said incisively:

'You can't have babies and grow vegetables, my dear sir.'

'But the men can grow them,' Richard countered.

'The men!' Willie Rogers said with impatience. 'Have you ever seen more than one or two able-bodied men in these villages? All you find here are old men and small boys. The men earn their living as coolies or hawkers in the market towns. When they can't find a living there, they come back to the valley and catch shrimps, or work a stake-net off the rocks, catching fish, until they hear of a chance in town, when off they go again! They know nothing about agriculture, and never have. The only work they do here is repair the irrigation channels and help the women once a year, at the rice harvest. A few also help with sowing. Don't you see? All that keeps these villages from starvation is the fact that both sexes work, the women in the fields, the men in the towns. The Government talks glibly of the villages growing vegetables! Vegetables are not the same as rice. You can plant rice and leave it, deliver a baby, and be ready to work again before the harvest comes. You can't leave vegetables alone for more than a few hours. They have to be watered, and have nightsoil put round them, every day. If these two villages are to grow vegetables, the men will all have to come back from the towns to work these terraced fields. And what are the women to do, to make up the deficit? Go to the town and sell themselves as prostitutes? They're not beautiful enough!'

The Assistant Lecturer turned his face away towards the sea, the wind ruffling his hair slightly. The young Chinese surveyor fingered his papers nervously. The office messenger, a tubby young chap, smiled benignly as Richard looked round at him.

Why he looked round he couldn't think, unless perhaps he was

234

afraid that someone could see, from the shape of the back of his neck, that he was wondering how he could have been so crazy as to have plunged into the road project, or indeed any project altering the lives of men, when he knew so little. He recognized at once the truth of Willie Rogers' words. It was correct one seldom saw able-bodied men in the valley. It was correct that the men only worked in the fields once a year. What they did for the rest of the year, he had never worked out. Visiting the valley, one never saw the younger men. Consequently, one never speculated about them. Without asking, one could not have known there were any. When asked about village occupations, the older men discussed shrimps and stake-net fishing. He had always believed this to be the principal male occupation, and that when the young men were absent, it was because they were out fishing. He understood now why it was that the villagers could never explain their views about the introduction of vegetable growing. None of them were capable of explaining anything so complex. They would not know how to start. Instead, they said they could never learn, and let government officials think them obstinate and stupid. What alternative was there?

'You're right, Willie,' he said at last. 'You're perfectly right.'

'Yes, I know something about these people,' said Willie Rogers tersely. 'This scheme won't work. Has anyone inspected the valley behind us? There's plenty of water in it, it's uninhabited, and a reservoir would be just as easy to construct there as here.'

Having established himself as the superior intellect around the place, the Assistant Lecturer was relaxing, the tone of his voice becoming more reasonable. He even polished a finger-nail, a sure sign that he was feeling on top.

'Let's go on,' said Richard. 'I'm sick to death of it.'

In single file they continued their way down, passing through the area of disused terraced fields, after which once more the path became steep, twisting down to the bottom of the hills, and reaching the level of the valley rather unexpectedly, coming round the last sharp bend just beside Ha Tsuen, which up to that moment had been concealed by the land formation. As they reached this point, Richard paused, obliging the rest to halt behind him. He gazed across the valley at the line of scars made by the boring tests, and tried to imagine what it would look like with the valley a lake, with a huge reservoir wall running from one arm of the hills to the other, facing the sea, and with a huge pipe (bordering the new road, presumably) bearing the water away, along the south coast of the island and away, under the sea to Victoria. Barracks had already been erected near the shore temple for the workers who were expected to arrive in a few days, but at present there was a lull, between the boring work and the actual construction of the reservoir, which was being financed by a syndicate, in which several of the colony's largest business interests had allied themselves to Szeto, Lee, and their group, in order to raise sufficient capital for what was, by local standards, a very large undertaking.

Standing there absorbing the quietness and the first signs of approaching dereliction, he heard voices, not very far away, men's voices shouting angrily. Motioning Willie Rogers to follow him slowly, he proceeded down the path for a few more steps, to where it rounded a bend in the foothill, and Ha Tsuen lay before him, about forty feet below. The three rows of tiled houses, without windows, with nothing but an alley between each row, faced out to seaward, the rear houses having their foundations in the last square feet of flat land before the hills rose up behind them.

Seeing that something was afoot in the village, he sank sideways into the long grass of the steep hillside, lest he be seen. The others did likewise. A crowd had gathered on the long threshing-floor that ran along the whole frontage of the first row of houses. The group consisted of men only, although nearer the houses were some women too, watching from a slight distance. They had their black cowled headgear on, having only just returned from the fields.

The men were arguing amongst themselves, sometimes shouting at one another. They stood in a circle, in the middle of which was a single figure, a youth in a white shirt. Richard took his spectacles from his shirt pocket. The person in the middle looked like his young friend Fai, standing silent amid the shouting, with his head down. Meanwhile one man, more vociferous than the rest, laid hands on another older man, bringing the rest at once to separate them. The group gathered about the two men, the elder of whom wore black Chinese pants, naked to the waist. Richard recognized him. It was Fai's father.

In the movement to separate the two of them, Fai was forgotten. He walked slowly away, freed from the circle, to where a low wall ran along the outer edge of the threshing-floor. There he

236

stayed, looking away at the sea. The men, meanwhile, were moving confusedly in a bunch, those in the centre shouting and quarrelling, those on the outside watching and taking no part. Suddenly the group fanned out, there was a shout, and a woman came forward with a bamboo broom which the most angry of the men thrust into Fai's father's hand with the one word, clearly audible above the sea wind: 'Strike!'—that ominous word in the dialect, which could mean hit, or could mean kill.

With the father in their midst, the group of men turned towards Fai, who, sensing their movement, turned round to look at them.

'Strike!' came the command again.

'Strike!' they all shouted together, a deep, liquid note, followed by confused talking, as the father, holding the bamboo pole, walked slowly out alone towards his son. As he drew near, the talking died away. In silence, father and son faced each other, and for a moment it seemed as if nothing more would happen. Each stood motionless.

Then, with an awful cry, partly a groan, partly an aching laugh, the father swung the bamboo round and struck his son on the side of the body. The boy made no resistance. The weight of the blow knocked him sideways against a pile of medicinal roots the village had been collecting for sale. Before he could recover his balance, the father struck again, this time on the back. The boy was flung down on top of the pile of roots. When he tried to pick himself up, the father struck again, while from the rest of the men, and from some of the women, came a strange, low, breathy cry, increasing after each blow, dying away in anticipation of the next, like some weird animal achieving an orgasm.

'It's time we broke this up,' Richard said. Making to move, however, he saw that the office messenger wore a terrified expression.

'No, sir! Stay here!' he said.

Richard hesitated. It was difficult to know what to do. In Chinese matters one never knew quite when to interfere and when to remain an onlooker. He glanced down again at the drama on the threshing-floor. The bamboo pole had split, and Fai—it was too far off to see what state he was in—was slowly moving as if drunk, on his hands and knees, a small, white, bent figure, towards the edge of the cement floor and the path leading out of the village. As the bamboo split, the father threw it away and stood upright as if he had done enough, his chest heaving with the exertion. Then suddenly he roared like a frenzied animal, picked up a small four-legged stool, and crashed it against the boy's back. Fai crawled away faster, his body flung this way and that by a pounding succession of blows, as the father became like an insensed person, swinging the stool over his head and smashing it down again. The entire village, men, women, and children, had gathered on the threshing-floor, the men standing close to the father, following his every movement as he pitilessly drove his son out. Once off the cement floor the ground, a stone track, fell slightly, and the boy tumbled a few steps forward. The father raised the stool again, but missed him. Gropingly, the boy moved from stone to stone of the path. Gropingly, as if his eyes were full of sweat, the old man followed him. Once the boy fell completely. Once the old man tripped on a stone and fell heavily to the ground. The people of the village did not follow. Their strange murmurings ceased. In silence, from the edge of the threshing-floor, they watched the father and son make their uncertain, stumbling way towards the bridge. When he stood up, the father still wielded the wooden stool, but his steps were unsteady and his blows hit the air. Once he stopped, overcome by exhaustion. From where Richard stood, with wind rustling the rough, tall grass, it was just audible that both father and son were groaning. When he reached the bridgehead, the boy could no longer stand. Clutching the edges of the planks of which it was formed, he dragged himself and kicked himself along their surface till he was half-way across. When the father came to the bridgehead, he could go no further. Raising the stool, he flung it at his son. The legs, or some part of it, must have hit the boy's head. His hands rose to protect his head; his head dropped; the stool fell with a splash into the stream. The old man stood still. Then with a groan he lowered himself to the ground till he lay flat, his body on the stones, his head and hands on the boards of the bridge. Both lay still, the one at the bridgehead, the other half across, each in the same position.

'What's happening?' asked Willie Rogers. 'I can't see a damned thing at this distance.'

'I don't quite know what it is,' said Richard, turning round to face him, and as he did so his eye caught the happily smiling face of his messenger.

'The village people blame Ah Fai for the reservoir, sir,' he explained.

238

'Blame Ah Fai for it? What on earth for?'

'I don't know, sir,' he replied, grinning unredeemedly, 'but that's what the village people say.'

'May we please be allowed to carry on now?' Willie Rogers asked the messenger, with counterfeit deference.

'Oh, yes, sir!' he said, alert and serious again. 'But not by this road! Better we take the other road, this way.' He beckoned up the mountain.

Willie grunted, the young surveyor smirked, Richard looked back on the village. No one from the threshing-floor had moved an inch to help the father. Some of them were slowly dispersing into their houses. One man was putting on a Chinese jacket. At the bridge the old man still lay where he was, but the son had struggled across. His white shirt, torn to pieces, appeared beyond the rough bushes on the other side of the stream. He was moving away still further from the village.

Richard brought up the party's rear.

'From as much as I could see . . .' said Willie Rogers.

Richard paid no attention. He felt as if he had been looking upon an unsuspected pagan rite, savage and indecent. In his mind he could hear nothing but the father's laugh-like groan, the rhythmic breathing of the villagers, the grunts of the two in pursuit along the path, the dull, uninteresting sound when the stool hit the body. He felt, too, as always when reason gave way to violence, and when he himself was required to take some action, the series of internal conflicts haunting him throughout his life with the prospect of being an unsuccessful man. Beaton, without a second thought, would have strode down into the village and stopped the fight. Richard had preferred the advice of his office messenger. Partly because it was Chinese advice in a Chinese situation; but partly because it accorded with his own deep convictions concerning the privacy men must have in which to work out their lives without intervention. His own world, the Western world, admired the man who strode down and restored order. To that world, the man who watched from a height, sheltered by hill grass, was weak, repugnant. He and Willie Rogers were that type —well, Willie was as blind as a bat, in the first place. Yet, were he to live for a century, Richard knew he would never come round to believing in intervention in the personal relations of individuals, or in the affairs of cities and states. His road was an intervention. He had forced it on the villagers, forced it upon the Government;

239

and the outcome had been to set everything at sixes and sevens—
the same as it would have been had he intervened in the scene
they had just witnessed. In the West, to hold to such a belief
meant, in his view, an inescapable failure. In the East, even the
office messenger understood it. Richard's failure, as he saw it now,
was that he did not care for the office messenger's opinion, but
did care—yearningly—for the opinion of his own people.

They dropped down to the stream just as the District Office
launch, due to meet them, entered the bay. Crossing the stream by
stepping-stones, they rose to the level of the rice-fields and walked
quickly across the valley, toward the shore temple, as the day
cooled and the sky began to redden. The sea was exceptionally
calm, and the small rowing-boat, carried by the launch and rowed
by a Chinese sailor who never fully mastered the knack of conducting a boat (Western-style) backwards, entered the usually
dangerous cove mouth without trouble. It was decided that the
boat was too small to take all four passengers at once; the sailor
would take them in two trips. While the surveyor and the messenger were taken out through the cove mouth, Richard and Willie
Rogers sat in silence on the temple steps. After a time, Richard,
bored with waiting, stood up and mounted the steps to the temple
doors. As was customary by day, they were open. No one having
worshipped there recently, there were no tapers or candles within.
Leaning against the stone portal, he stared without interest into
the interior gloom.

He had looked at so many Queens of Heaven! With nothing
to do, he might as well look at this one also. Peering into the
semi-darkness—for the figure above the altar was generally small,
with a dark face—he became aware of something unusual below
his line of vision. Dropping his eyes into the shadows at the foot
of the altar he saw, spread out, a human body.

From what he had seen of people, at moments such as this men
involuntarily drew back, or caught their breath, or called a com-
panion to join them. Richard did none of these things, nor had he
any inclination to. He looked more concentratedly at the body. It
was face downwards, with arms and legs spread wide, the head
towards the altar. Black trousers, bare feet, a dirty white shirt—
torn. . . .

'Willie,' he said gently, 'the boy's here.'

Willie Rogers came up beside him and looked in, moving his
head from side to side as he did so, trying to see though his thick,

strong spectacles. Giving a short sigh of recognition, he crossed the raised threshold and entered the temple. It was a small edifice, and five or six feet brought him to the body, beside which he squatted. Richard followed him in, standing on the other side.

'Ah Fai!' Willie said in the dialect. 'Wake up and speak to us.'

There was no answer. Willie put his hands round the ribs, and nodded to Richard.

'He's all right. . . . Ah Fai! Wake up! . . . I don't think it's any use,' he added in a different tone, drawing back. 'He probably doesn't remember who I am. You speak to him.'

'Do we want to wake him up?' Richard asked.

'We can't leave him here!' Willie Rogers answered emotionally. 'He'll be killed if he goes back to the village! He's half-dead already. Where else can he go on this island?'

Acknowledging the truth of this, Richard too squatted down at the boy's side.

'Ah Fai! This is the Magistrate. Wake up and speak to me.'

Though the body did not move, the voice answered with vehemence that seemed to shake the little temple, with its gods and guardians, bell and incense-burners.

'Leave me alone, sir! Leave me! I must never speak to a foreigner again! Foreigners . . .' the voice faltered, clutching at a difficult word '. . . are my—my destruction.'

'Don't talk nonsense, Fai.'

'Sir! Please go! Go!'

The voice sounded vibrant enough, but still with no movement of the body. Willie Rogers looked across at Richard.

'I think we shall have to take him with us. Couldn't you put him up on Little Island?'

Yes, Richard thought, that did tend somewhat to be Willie Rogers' form of generosity. Nevertheless, what he had said was sound. The boy could not be left in the valley. In such a mood as they had seen in the village, he might well be killed.

'Fai, you're coming back with me, to my house on Little Island.'

'No, sir! Not a foreigner . . .!'

'Come on, pick yourself up. Can you stand on your feet?'

The boy simply moaned, a long brooding sound of despair, self-pity, revenge, helplessness.

There was nothing else for it. Together they lifted him up, each with a hand firmly beneath his armpit, while he sobbed, begging them not to take him, yet walking lightly between them, as they carried him away from the goddess at whose altar he had taken refuge.

When they reached the doors of the temple, the sailor returned to fetch them. Standing on the threshold and looking in, he was so frightened when he saw the three men that he all but ran away. Emerging into the dying evening sunlight, Richard glanced at the boy's face, a shapeless, broken statement of pain and exhaustion, at the lacerated, bloodstained shirt, the broken skin on the arms, the ripped knees of the black trousers, and below them the squat, strong feet, even they bruised and bleeding.

'It's all right,' he reassured the sailor. 'We're bringing him to the hospital at Little Island.'

'Yes, sir,' the sailor replied, still looking scared.

Meanwhile, the boy moaned and chattered incomprehensibly, and Richard pondered coldly, detachedly, after they had laid him in the bows of the boat; would it not have been wiser to have left him there, in the temple? Was not even this act of mercy an intervention?

The boat swung out into the bay, calm, serene, with Venus setting into an autumn evening sky. Supposing the boy could not return to the valley? Might he not be saddled with him—for a long time? That was the difference between a lecturer and an administrator. Willie Rogers was right when it came to the theory of it all, the way the village economy worked, and so on, but . . .

'What happened to him, sir?' asked the sailor, pulling the oars and nodding over his shoulder at the inert form behind him.

24

I T W AS going to be the coldest day of the year. Regularly, in the second week of January, in the twelfth moon of the Chinese year, the temperature dropped for five or six days, during which there might be frost. It never quite became cold enough for snow.

From early morning they had had a fire in their house on Little Island, and as he walked down the hill to meet the police launch he drew a pair of woollen gloves over his stiffening hands. It was a magnificent day, blue and cloudless, with the cold, buffeting north wind blowing, whipping white crests across the sea's deep winter blue, a dry wind, breaking the lips and chapping the skin.

The nightmare day had come, the day Richard had thought about, tried to plan for, dreamed about, dreaded, hated the thought of with all his heart.

'Good luck, darling,' Sylvia had said at the door. 'I shall be thinking of you.'

The two new villages on the hillside were complete, having been constructed without consultation with the people of the valley, because they had refused to be consulted. Now the day had come when the foundation works for the dam were sufficiently advanced to render advisable the evacuation of the lower village. There was no immediate danger to the village, but within about three weeks water from the streams would begin to collect behind the dam, a few fields would be flooded, and after a few more weeks the area under water would increase. It was not possible to say exactly when the water would reach the village. The land behind the dam being extremely flat, however, it might be that a large area would quickly come under at least a foot or two of water. The villagers had sent a string of petitions for the scheme to be abandoned. The Government had proceeded with its plans. It now proposed to evacuate the people of Ha Tsuen, and upon him, the District Officer who had promised them a road, devolved the responsibility for persuading them to leave their homes.

'I take it there may be some opposition.' It was the dry, authoritative voice of the Commissioner of Police on the telephone. 'Tell Hailey what support you need, and he'll see you get it.'

It was a piece of bleak encouragement.

'I suggest a small party of men,' he told the Assistant Commissioner. 'One launch should be enough, and no show of force. But I think there should be a hundred men on the island—they can stay out of sight behind the hills, and we should have an agreed signal for them to come down, if needed.'

'Make it two hundred,' the Assistant Commissioner replied, making notes on a pad.

'As you wish. We should be able to reach the valley, from the sea approach, by ten o'clock. The concealed force should on no

243

account land on the island before eight o'clock, or their presence will be known in the valley.'

'Wouldn't it be preferable if the people did know?'

'I think not. They'll never settle down afterwards if they remembered they were forced to move. We must try to obtain their agreement. That's the psychology of it. . . . And I need a really good interpreter.'

'I can lay that on, too.'

Richard had laughed at himself afterwards. He had sounded so confident, so like Napoleon at Austerlitz—and so too, he reflected, had Hailey. Confidence was an essential product when one entered the world of action. Whether it was genuine confidence or counterfeit hardly mattered.

The Commissioner had lent his own launch for the occasion, which, in view of the rough seas, was a blessing. Hailey, in uniform, talked as the launch rolled in the constantly changing angles of the waves. Here the angry Pacific met its first granite opposition after thousands of miles of freedom. Here it reared back with offended dignity, before bringing in a new assault.

Inspector Tung Sze-liang, from the Special Branch, was sick. So were several of the crew. Richard began to feel his head spin, but was not sick. Hailey and the coxswain seemed to be at ease.

When they entered the bay, the sea became very slightly calmer, but Richard still could not speak. He nodded as Hailey spoke encouragingly of other matters than the one in hand. Over the hills from Wireless Bay, the long, yellow scar of the cutting for the new road stood out sharply against the grass. Half-way along the south coast of the island, the line expired, becoming two rows of white pegs set out on the green slopes. The last of the pegs were visible in the valley itself, the scheme being that the road would pass the shore temple and mount to the top of the dam, across which connexion could be made with the new villages on the far side.

He glanced up at the superb mountain heights, pale purple in the fresh winter light. Great Island and its development had been his dream. He had deeply hoped to match with works of human greatness the noble beauty of this splendid landscape.

Nearing the shore, he saw in the hills the scarred sites of the new villages, the white houses with red tiled roofs, and the long, white building of the agricultural station where, ignored by the valley, cultivation preparations had already started under the direction of a competent and enthusiastic graduate from a Chinese university. True to his word, Jenkinson had spared no pains to bring to fulfilment the scheme in the impracticability of which he refused to believe.

The syndicate of contractors building the dam had constructed a temporary pier from the rocks, the narrow cove entrance being impassable by the larger craft. On a day such as this, however, no vessel of the size of the Commissioner's launch could approach anywhere near the pier in safety. When they came closer, a tough little motor launch put out to meet them.

The syndicate's chief engineer, an Englishman, met them as they landed, somewhat battered by the rough conditions, raising themselves up the pier steps, their feet pursued by the capriciously rising launch, whose impact against the pier might at any moment have broken their legs.

'They're waiting for you, Mr. Fairburn,' the engineer said in a thick, Devonshire brogue. 'I hope you can persuade them to move. We don't want a mass suicide on our hands, and we don't want any murders, either!'

This friendly voice of rural England warmed Richard. He felt less alone. Hailey could not deal with this; he did not speak the dialect. Tung could only help with a detail or two. His own interpreter, Leung, had become so unpopular in the valley that it was considered unsafe for him to set foot in it. The situation had narrowed down peculiarly till it became entirely Richard's. He alone knew these mountains, this island, the villages, their feuds and prejudices. In the way each man around him treated him, Richard knew that they too knew it. When he spoke, they were silent. When he suggested, they concurred. The problem was his. He was, of course, the senior District Officer, an expert in rural affairs. Yet their acknowledgment of the fact, on this blue, cold, gusty morning, begged the question of how much they knew. Did they know how profoundly this problem was his, and his alone? It was as if they did. It was as if they had come, these several persons, to witness in silence what they knew to be the downfall of all that he had hoped to achieve, as if they had come specially to put their thumbprints or signatures on a document marked FAILURE, with the name of Richard Fairburn at the top.

'Detach yourself from it, Richard,' Sylvia had said again and again over the past weeks.

How? In the future, maybe, he could remain detached; but

once attached, once personally committed, how to disengage without wounding the soul?

'Where are they?' he asked the engineer drily, his voice not entirely normal.

'Over there, Mr. Fairburn, beside the bridge over the stream.'

Richard gazed across the valley. So far, little had changed. Apart from the surrounding confusion of machinery, dwarfing the once lonely shore temple, and the meaningless pile of metal and stone stretching across the valley, the countryside still wore its customary appearance. Beyond the temple, in a cavity in the rocks, a cement mixer was making its distinctive, soft, shuttling sound—not loud, but it prevented one from hearing the cries of the birds.

'Right! Let's go,' he said, as he saw in the distance, on the far side of the valley, a group of men standing, as if waiting. The sight was in itself strange. When being visited, the Ha Tsuen people either waited in the village, or else the elders came down to the shore temple. They had never before waited at the bridgehead, as though they were defending it.

Defending it. The words rang in Richard's ears as soon as he conceived the thought.

'Surely,' said the Assistant Commissioner, walking behind him through the rice-fields, 'they're armed.'

Richard stopped.

'Good God! I forgot! They've got fifteen rifles.'

He glanced back at the seven constables following them, armed only with batons. Turning again, he peered into the distance. It did not seem as if the village people were carrying their arms. They were standing ordinarily, not in a position for firing. Yet, in that spot, this side of the bridge, they must be carrying them. Hailey's eyesight was better than his.

'I'm frightfully sorry, Hailey. I'd completely forgotten.'

'Don't apologize, old fellow. I keep the gun register. I should have remembered.'

'In effect,' he conceded, gazing out at the green landscape, towards the group he could only distantly perceive at the edge of the plain. 'You'd better remain here. I will go on alone.' As if listening to another person, he heard himself speak.

'Don't you want the interpreter?'

Tung Sze-liang came up beside Hailey on the bund between the rice-fields.

246

'Better I come with you, sir.'

Richard considered the clean-cut, honest face. It would be a relief if Tung could come with him. But if they fired, it would be at Tung they would fire first; and they were accurate with their firearms. In the affray with the pirates, they had seriously wounded three, sufficient for them to be captured.

'It will be wiser if I go alone,' he said. 'When I want you, I'll signal for you to come.'

'And if there's trouble?' asked Hailey.

Richard laughed drily.

'I won't have time to signal you, will I?'

With a wave to them and a damnation to himself for talking such histrionic rot, he walked on alone through the fields.

The sound of the cement mixer became distant and vague. The bird songs could again be heard. The wind, rushing over a high gap in the mountains, whistled round his ears in the otherwise serene blue sunny day. Why he was walking on alone towards fifteen armed men, it would have been hard to say. There was no real reason for it. It was foolishness. If he had advanced in a body with the police contingent, however, there was that much more chance that the villagers would fire than if he came towards them alone. Besides which, why should Hailey, Tung, and the rest be killed for his mistake? If anyone was to be killed, let it be he, and he alone. Why drag others into his personal downfall? They could stay behind, and, when it was over, go back to Little Island and break the news diplomatically to Sylvia. She would be surprised, of course. Both of them had forgotten that the village was armed. But she knew it was a day of crisis. She would be ready for anything. Afterwards, she would be free to marry someone else, a film star, a millionaire, somebody famous, who could match her wit with something of his own—fame, wealth, good looks, what did it matter? She would be free.

He too would be free.

Had he perhaps to admit failure in his marriage? She had been so sympathetic, understanding, accommodating, since her return from America that he could not avoid the sensation that she was making a sacrifice for him. He did not require such a sacrifice. It could do no more than disturb him. True, it did not seem like a sacrifice. It was only in his suspicions that the word arose. But the suspicion was enough to worry him profoundly. There was no answer to his married life except a writ. However one argued, however one dissimulated, the reality sooner or later asserted itself blatantly. He was the negative partner, the failure. Walking quietly towards the fifteen rifles, his pace easy, his footstep light, he found himself moving pleasantly towards the obvious answer. The villagers had come out to resist the approach of himself and his men. They would, when he was a convenient distance from them, fire. They would hit.

It would settle the matter. With Jenkinson and the civil service, for example. Jenkinson would be obliged to sign the civil service wreath and walk first in the funeral. Even the cricket player at the gramophone shop would have to say something like 'Well, I never expected it of him', and subscribe to a memorial plate in the cathedral. Brenda MacPherson would probably weep on Sylvia's shoulder, and Brian would be frightfully nice. The whole colony would come round to a new set of attitudes, by just one shot of a rifle, and everything would be solved.

He was unnecessary, after all. He had tried to do something in the world. He had tried to make his mark, in the shape of a yellow, dusty road, on the surface of the world. He had tried to be a husband to a woman who seemed to love him and to be willing to follow him. In all, he had failed. Pending failure, there was a reason for his existence: he might yet turn a corner and succeed. Failure achieved, there was no further use for him. A rifle shot might as well finish it. Sylvia would go on from strength to strength. Mourning his death, she would become overnight an even more dramatic figure than she was already. Dying conveniently, he could contribute to her, where now he detracted from her. People inevitably asked why she married him. They were unequal, and both of them—but she more than he—refused to face it.

Half-way across the valley, he paused to look up at the great heights around him, at the bare hills he had come to know and love. When he turned towards the north, the tune of the wind in his ears changed, assuming a deeper voice, more strident, less jesting. Slowly he gazed around him, up at the bright paint of the new villages, seaward to the untidy tops of ferro-concrete that lined the view and would one day be a solid wall holding in millions of gallons of water. The birds could be heard clearly now, the winter birds that descended from the cold mainland of Asia in search of warmer weather. The sun's heat had warmed the day sufficiently for him to pull his gloves off and stuff them in his knapsack.

248

No sooner had he paused, however, than he found he had done so with the motive of self-preservation. The villagers of Ha Tsuen, their rifles loaded, were watching him, waiting for him to draw near enough for them to fire. His action in pausing to gaze round the valley looked like a gesture of extreme nonchalance, as indeed —making it—he had, without thinking about it, intended. It might even disturb the villagers, making them wonder what to expect now. It would certainly make them say they were aiming to shoot at someone extraordinary. Yet, though he did it for these reasons, he only thought of the reason after he had done it. One should not tempt death. That was not a sacrifice; it was suicide. Reasonable precautions should be taken, because of the curious attitudes which people were apt to strike concerning suicide. One could be sentenced to imprisonment, for example, for unsuccessfully trying to commit suicide. His own reasonable precaution, thus, was to pause in the middle of the valley, and gaze around. Having done this, he poked the cold, hard ground with his walking-stick, bent down to examine something imaginary on the earth of one of the empty rice-fields, then, straightening himself up, resumed his gentle walk towards the village.

No, life must always be given a chance—the last chance possible. In the game of death one should play each card in one's hand as well as circumstances allowed, even though knowing the hand was weak, valueless. The world did not care for the player who threw in his hand at the outset, without playing the round. It had something to do with English ideas of sportsmanship, of which the effect on criminal law and international concepts of right and wrong was regrettable.

He could see the villagers quite clearly by this time. There was a more than usually large number of them. He wondered if the Sheung Tsuen people had come down to join them. They stood in a loose row along the raised edge of the rice-field basin, the last obstacle before reaching the bridge. All fifteen rifles were being handled. The men, standing very still, appeared to be silent.

At what point would it be wise to call out something to them? If they were going to shoot, the best moment for them to do it was before he reached them and could start talking. In what tone of voice should he call out something? A cry of false joviality might bring a sudden response of anger. As the incident with Fai showed, they knew they had their backs to the wall. They were desperate men, churning up from their collective past the most primitive instincts, prepared to defy anything and anyone—prepared to defy the water, or so they had said. A very ordinary 'good morning', in a completely neutral tone, without implication, would probably be best, not made till he was fairly near them.

Their faces were clear to him now, through his spectacles. Old Chan, Fai's father, stood in the centre of the group. For some strange reason, they had all put on their best clothes—or was it that the morning had been so cold they had had to cover themselves with as much as they had? If it was, he would have expected to see some men in woollen pullovers, or else standing as they usually did, wrapped up well around the chest and stomach, but with bare arms. Instead, each of them wore formal clothes, loose Chinese pants and jacket buttoned up to the neck, with wide sleeves. Most of them wore this attire in pale blue, a few in the dark brown that was more correct for the season. With this formality, rifles. No women were to be seen. The village must have found out from the dam workers that this was to be the day of ultimatum. What preparations seemed to be fitting had been taken. If the men were to die, they would die defending what their ancestors had won for them. It was thus proper that they should die in their best clothes.

It was not yet their turn to die, however. Someone else had to die first. The spark had to be ignited. When Richard came near enough to see Old Chan's face and expression, the old man slowly lifted his rifle. The dry click as he geared it to fire carried across the remaining fields between them. Richard found it difficult to walk. His legs felt as if their muscles had been drained of all impulses, as one section of his brain exerted all its power to prevent him moving forward. He seemed to be drooping forwards, like a lunatic or a drunkard, his knees sagging, banging against one another. He had to look down at his shadow, and at his shoes, to make sure that he was still walking normally, and had not given away to the villagers that he was about to break down, falling on the ground and sobbing out 'Shoot me,' because it would all be simpler that way and a true expression of himself. The heads of the mountains rose above him, rearing themselves, before bending down to crush him. The valley and everything in it were shaking and shivering, fluttering about in front of him, even the mountains fluttering. The danger was that he was about to burst into tears.

'Good morning,' he said, in the dialect.

The sound of his own voice—it seemed to be a very quiet voice right in the centre of his body—steadied him. The landscape became still again, and the faces of the Chan and Liu clans, their hard mouths and expressionless eyes, once more rested on him motionlessly. There was about thirty yards between them. Now was the time to shoot.

None of them moved or spoke. Apart from the elders, there were a number of others in the group whom Richard had never come across before. No one from Sheung Tsuen had come. In keeping with the everlasting grouse between the two villages, Ha Tsuen's day of disaster was no affair of Sheung Tsuen's. The fact that the same disaster would befall the upper village after a few more weeks was not an argument in the harsh context of a clan dispute. Each could go to the devil—but separately.

'I hope you're keeping those rifles of yours well oiled,' Richard said.

Again there was no response. There was no movement, either. Old Chan was fingering his rifle, but did not raise it. Evidently they were going to hear first what the Magistrate had to say. He came slowly up to them, took off his knapsack, and laid it on the bund he was standing on, letting his walking-stick balance on the top of it. Then he stuffed his hands into his pockets so that their trembling should not be observed, and was about to speak when he noticed that Old Chan was no longer looking at him, but into the valley behind him. Could Hailey be moving his men up? Richard dared not turn round to look. The instant he turned, they would sense his fear and strike him. He could only send out a silent thought to Hailey to, for God's sake, do nothing hasty.

'I see you all know why I've come today,' he said quietly, looking along the line of them, at the known faces and the unknown.

Old Chan opened his mouth to speak. His lips and tongue were dry.

'How many policemen have you brought with you?' he asked.

The extreme insolence of the question, a remark which, even in similar circumstances, good manners would have made it impossible for the old man to say had Richard been a Chinese official, reminded him with a peculiar assurance of the unusual relationship that subsisted in the colony between the country people and the officials, whom they respected, yet, because the officials were members of the white race, they despised and expected nothing of. They could hate a Chinese magistrate, and hate the government he represented. They could not hate a foreign devil magistrate, because he, like them, was of low class in Chinese society. He was their equal, or worse.

'Only a few,' Richard replied, his confidence growing. 'This is not a police matter. This is between us. I've come to tell you you've got to move. The water will not reach the village for several weeks, but in your own interests you should move now to the new village. Everything is ready for you up there. It's a good place.'

Old Chan gave a contemptuous grunt and looked down the line of his men.

'We are not going to move there.'

'Have any of you been up to see what's been done?' Richard asked, stepping down into the dry rice-field, where he stood head and shoulders below them.

'We're not interested.'

'What are you interested in?'

Old Chan nodded towards the dam.

'We want this work to stop.'

'It can't stop. The city has to have water.'

'We're not going to discuss this with you,' Old Chan said, turning away. 'We want to see the Governor.'

There was an indication that they were all going to follow Old Chan back to the village, leaving Richard alone in the field.

'I have been sent here today by the Governor,' he replied quickly, 'to tell you, with his regret, that you must move.'

Old Chan turned back to him again.

'We want to hear that from the Governor in person.'

'Will you be carrying your rifles when the Governor comes?' Richard asked with a slight smile.

'Why not? It was the Governor who gave us permission to have them.'

Some of the others were becoming restive.

'Don't speak to him any more,' Old Liu, the other elder, said to Old Chan. 'This is wasting our time.'

Again it looked as if the group might break up and go back to the village.

'Well, I'm going up now to inspect the new village. Will any of you come with me? There's one house up there for every family. Every one of you who has a house here will have a house there. I'm told the houses are good, much better than what you have now. I want to see for myself whether this it true.'

Because they had not killed him, he now had to cheat them into

252

doing what the Government wanted, cheat them into what he knew would be their ruin. Looking along the line of them he thought of Willie Rogers' explanation of how the village economy worked.

'I'm going back to the village,' said Old Liu to Old Chan. 'This is a waste of time.'

'Are all of you Ha Tsuen people?' Richard asked, looking at some of the younger men. They nodded, with just perceptible goodwill in their eyes. 'I've never seen some of you here before. You, for instance—do you live and work here?'

'They all live here,' said Old Chan, with a hint of menace.

'Really?' Richard pursued, still addressing the same young man. 'What's your occupation?'

'I'm a hawker, Magistrate,' he answered.

Concealing his growing assurance, Richard followed it up.

'A hawker? What, in the valley?'

'No, Magistrate. In the town.' He indicated over the hills.

'Yes. That's what I thought. You only come here occasionally.' Richard walked down the line of them. The personal touch, the magic to a young hawker of finding the Government taking a personal interest in him as an individual, and the fascination of hearing a foreigner speak the dialect: it all worked as it always did work, even on a bitter occasion like this. The younger eyes began to brighten; a smile flitted across an expression here and there. Then came the stroke of luck: a young tough—dark and swarthy —with curly hair and strong, square hands clasping the nozzle of his rifle. 'Good heavens! Ah Tak! What are you doing here? Are you a Ha Tsuen man, too?'

Tak grinned from ear to ear, unable to cope with gravity any more, when the personal situation was so much more exciting.

'Yes, Magistrate! I was born here.'

'Born here, maybe!' Richard answered with a laugh. 'Mr. Chan!' he said, calling back to the old man. 'This is the fellow I buy my bread from, every time I stay at O Mun! He's the best baker on Great Island, aren't you, Ah Tak?'

The grin expanded still further. The young man standing next to Tak nudged him. All of the younger men were happy and proud.

'You none of you stay here very much, do you?' Richard asked. 'I mean, if business is bad in the market, you come and sit behind a stake-net for a few weeks, pretending you're busy. . . .'

There was a laugh of agreement, during which Richard gave thanks to the benevolence that had sent Willie Rogers with him to the valley. Using his information, without having been able to check it, he found confirmation in the very laughter that followed its use. Willie Rogers was right about the valley and its people. It amused him, too, to reflect that Old Chan's cleverness in making the non-resident members of the two clans come and look convincing with rifles on the day of ultimatum had provided the District Officer with the clue to undermining his authority.

'Now, all you young people!' he said. 'You're the money-makers. You'd better come with me and see if those houses up there are fit for your old people to live in. Come on, Ah Tak, you're coming with me! Who else is coming?'

'It's a waste of time,' said Old Liu sourly for the third time, signalling to his Liu clansmen to return with him to the village.

But Richard's call to the young men had divided opinion; and Old Liu's call, following it, was ill-timed, serving merely to separate the village into its two clans: the old and faithful members of Liu following their Old Man; the Chan clan staying put; the younger members of the Liu clan uniting with the younger Chans in following Richard to inspect the new village.

'Let's go!' said Richard, picking up his walking-stick and knapsack. 'Come on, Ah Tak! Come along, you young people!' With which he started walking with a show of confidence alone up to the stepping-stone crossing of the stream, above which one mounted to the new village.

'No, Magistrate! This way is quicker!' shouted the young man who had nudged Tak.

Richard turned about. The lad was indicating the way over the bridge, which was in fact shorter, except that the elders were barring the way.

'Let's go and have a look, Uncle,' he heard Tak say to Old Chan.

The young men cleared a way for Richard along the bund. Slowly, unwillingly, the old men stood back to let him pass. Followed by Tak and his cousins from O Mun, Richard led the way through the narrow opening made for him between two rifles, and crossed the bridge.

'One day it'll be your village, after all, Ah Tak,' he said loudly as he reached the other side—loud enough for the old men of Chan and Liu to hear. 'You have to decide now what you want.

254

I believe you want to decide something that will keep you in agreement with the Government.'

'Quite right, Magistrate!' said Tak, following immediately behind him over the bridge. 'We want security in the future.'

'Well said!' he answered. 'This way you will have it.'

He started up the hilly path from the side of the village, mounting above the rice-plain. From the footsteps on the bridge, it sounded as if a fair percentage of the group were following him. He did not look back. Some of them, he could tell, still carried their arms.

'Ah Tak, it's up to you younger people to make the older folks see sense,' he said. 'You have to persuade them. You've been outside the village. You have more knowledge of the world. They're going to be as well off up here as they were down there.' He glanced back towards the shore. The police patrol had not moved. He imagined Hailey, sitting on the temple steps, smoking cigarettes and wondering what the hell went on. Rapidly they rose above the fields, some of the youths having to hop quickly up, owing to the fast pace set by Richard.

'I'm afraid the geomantic situation will not be suitable.'

Richard stopped at the sound of the voice. He had to check himself from turning round. It was Old Chan, following them in the rear.

'I have consulted three geomantic doctors, all of whom have given me their views on where, in general, is the best place to site a village,' Richard said.

'In general may be all right,' Old Chan muttered, breathing fast with the exertion of climbing. 'But for us Chans it may be different.'

'True,' Richard conceded. 'But it is interesting that all three doctors chose the same site, the site on which the village has been built. I have their written reports, which you can see when it's convenient to you.'

He felt easy in his mind. He had broken the village into its separate parts. One clan was following him; the other was not. The young were following him; the old, with the notable exception of Old Chan, were not. And when the old man mentioned geomancy, he knew he had won. Old Chan was interested in the problem. He had lost face with the entire village over his son. Somehow he had to recover face, become indisputably senior again to Old Liu. The new village provided the answer.

They would eventually move in peace. Richard had succeeded in cheating them. Up the hill, he was leading them to their certain ruin as a community. He felt silently exhilarated, like a merchant after selling for a high price a valuable-looking fake. His cheat had succeeded. Though they still carried rifles, the danger was past. He had put the sordid business through.

25

SEATED in a crowded bus, on his way home from the District Office on Chinese New Year's Eve, Interpreter Leung catalogued with composure how well everything had turned out. Wong Tak-wor had converted an enormous piece of land at Long Sands from agricultural to building status, without premium, in return for the free surrender of the strip of land required for the road, which ran for nearly five miles of its length through land owned either by him or by his concubines. On the land converted at Long Sands he was going to erect twenty-five holiday bungalows and a hotel. The one item in Wong Tak-wor's transactions which, in Interpreter Leung's view, might have led to trouble—the fact that he had bought, over a period of months, the entire village lands of Fa Ping—had surprisingly produced nothing but goodwill. Through his association with Wong Tak-wor, Old Fu of Fa Ping had been able to accomplish his revenge on the Chan clan of Ha Tsuen, by suggesting to the Public Works Department that Ha Tsuen was the best site for the new reservoir. As a result, cordial relations existed between the Fu clan and Wong Tak-wor, who would in due course ruin them, if he had not already done so. Interpreter Leung considered that Wong, in his relations with Fa Ping, had gone a little too far. The man was so expert at handling people, however, that he might be able to maintain the present happy state of affairs indefinitely.

As a result of these important transactions, and others in other parts of the district, Interpreter Leung had had a very fortunate year. His eldest son had entered the university; his second son was about to leave to take an engineering course in the United States. Various services rendered to the syndicate of contractors building

256

the reservoir looked like bringing in some more substantial sums in the year ahead. To do so well in a year of trade recession was exceptional.

Thoughts of the reservoir led him back to the interview he had given in the morning to Cow-neck Yeung from Wireless Bay. Interpreter Leung had already been over it several times in his mind, and he still could not understand what it was that the old boy had been trying to tell him. In a few days, doubtless, the other facts going to form the full story would come to his knowledge. At present, the interview puzzled him—worried him a bit as well. Cow-neck Yeung seldom came to the District Office. On the rare occasions when he did, it usually concerned a matter of importance to himself personally, a grudge against one of his enemies, a land transaction he wished to push through quickly. He had no public spirit, taking no part in welfare activities, and showing no interest in either Wireless Bay's school or clinic. It was furthermore extraordinary for him to come on New Year's Eve, a day when he would normally be at home, settling accounts and collecting rents.

Today's interview, like others in the past, concerned his personal affairs. It concerned his daughter, in fact. Only, what the fellow had been driving at, Interpreter Leung could not figure out. The old boy had arrived, as customarily, with three or four of his henchmen, who stayed as inconspicuously as they could at the far end of the office, near the safe. Cow-neck was one of those tiresome people who usually refused to explain the purpose of his visit to anyone except the District Officer, and Interpreter Leung was about to ring through to find out if Mr. Fairburn was free to see him when the D.O. himself passed along the corridor, saw Cow-neck, and made a sign to Leung asking whether Cow-neck wished to see him. When Leung signalled back, Cow-neck turned round to see who it was at the office door. Never friendly with foreigners, his reaction at sight of the D.O. was sharper than usual. He turned quickly away, his bony shoulders hunched up, and stared out of the opposite window. The D.O., not perceiving this, entered the office and patted him on the back.

'Hullo, Mr. Yeung. How's life treating you?' he said jovially.

Cow-neck grunted and said nothing.

'Come through and see me whenever you want,' the D.O. said, resuming his walk to his office. Cow-neck was an important person in the district, a person to whom it was necessary to give face.

'D'you want to see the District Officer?' Leung asked him, when the D.O. had gone.

'No!' the old man snapped. 'I've come to see you. It's a serious matter.'

Interpreter Leung read this unexpected reaction as a portent.

'What can I do for you?' he asked.

'My daughter is of marriageable age,' the old man said aggressively, his square mouth snapping open and shut like a piece of mechanism detached from the rest of his face. 'At that age, a girl's place is in the home—specially at the New Year.'

'I quite agree,' Leung replied, thinking of his own daughters.

'I don't allow her to run around in the city,' Cow-neck went on. 'She has to stay beside me till she marries someone of my choosing.'

'Yes, of course. Very proper.'

'That's the situation,' Cow-neck said firmly. 'I don't budge from it. I don't care who else tries to interfere. There'll be trouble for him.'

'Quite right,' Leung replied.

'That's the situation,' he said again. 'I wanted you to know. Now I have some other things to do.'

He rose to leave. The henchmen bestirred themselves in the distance as the old man, without saying goodbye or wishing Leung the compliments of the season, joined them, walking in silence out of the office.

Eighty per cent of the people coming to the District Office talked in riddles. The staff were accustomed to it by their years of experience. Country people spoke in riddles due to their mental inability to explain anything coherently. People like Cow-neck Yeung used riddles to cloak things they were embarrassed at explaining directly. Often, with one of the older clerks, the riddles were understood immediately. In difficult cases, inquiries—often elaborate—were needed before the meaning unfolded itself.

Interpreter Leung shrugged his shoulders as he rose to dismount from the bus. After the New Year holidays he would have to go into the matter. Crossing the crowded pavements, he mounted the dark stairway between two shops, which led up to his long, narrow apartment, the entire upper floor of an old Chinese house. In the main room within, his wife, carrying her eleventh child, was busy arranging things for the New Year celebration. The room was full of the small pale pink flowers of the Chinese New Year, branches of them planted temporarily in pots around the room. On

258

the balcony the dwarf orange trees were golden with fruit, and auspicious red paper decorated the doors and windows. He was sorry about his wife's eleventh child. She was too old to be having children, and women would be laughing at her. He could not afford a concubine, however, and there was thus no way out of it.

The telephone rang as he entered, and his five-year-old son ran to answer it. The children used the telephone far more than he and his wife did. He used to say caustically to his friends that he had the telephone for the benefit of his elder daughters' boy friends.

'It's a devil woman!' the little boy squeaked, taking the receiver away from his ear.

'Here! Give it to me!' Interpreter Leung said hastily. 'Hullo?' —and he made an angry gesture as his boy ran shrieking happily into the inner rooms of the apartment.

'Mr. Leung, is that you?'

'Speaking.'

'This is Sylvia Fairburn. I'm frightfully sorry to bother you like this on New Year's Eve, but I need some advice, and I don't know who else to turn to.'

He didn't like the sound of it. Throughout his career, he had always tried to have as little as possible to do with the wives of his District Officers.

'Yes. What is it, Mrs. Fairburn?'

'I'd rather not explain over the telephone. Would it be possible for you to come round and see me?'

Leung paused.

'Now?'

'If you could, Mr. Leung. It's—well, I'm not sure—it looks like something serious.'

'I'll come straight away,' he answered with a sigh, putting the receiver down.

No. One could not blame Mrs. Fairburn with not realizing how much inconvenience she was giving by telephoning on New Year's Eve. She did know; and it must be something important. Interpreter Leung had a cold bath, put on his best tweed suit, lit a cigarette, and strolled down to the street in search of a taxi.

Calling on Europeans, his style changed. He became less rushed, more leisurely and urbane. The distinguished calm of the houses above the city, with their gardens and tree-lined roads, infected him with its atmosphere. The secret pleasure of wasting a little money by taking a taxi—for there was no other way of reaching The Heights except on foot—made him feel like a plutocrat in a motion picture. He almost stopped at the tobacco shop to buy a cigar. The white and pastel-grey beauty of the Fairburns' apartment also affected him, as did being met at the door by Mrs. Fairburn, wearing an evening dress made of Chinese white embroidered silk. He felt very fine.

He had never really cared what Chinese said about foreigners. He had known many Europeans in his time, good and bad. The good ones always had the same effect on him. To visit their homes, spacious and well thought out, with carefully chosen Chinese porcelain and a colour scheme like the rooms in technicolor movies, made him feel rested and at ease—a little like going to hospital (some of the apartments were like hospital wards, everything so painfully clean and organized), but, apart from that, a pleasant experience.

'Mr. Leung, it's extremely kind of you to come. Have a glass of sherry.'

'Thank you, Mrs. Fairburn. Sherry's too sour for me.'

'This is a sweet one we keep specially for Chinese friends. Try it.'

When they had both sat down, he put the glass to his lips, but in fact drank nothing. He did not care for foreign wines. Drinking something was one of the encumbrances to be overcome when visiting foreigners. The charm of going to a foreign house was not connected with anything to do with food or drink. It was something far harder to define.

'You must think this is all very extraordinary, Mr. Leung,' she said, in a more serious tone of voice than he customarily heard her use. 'My husband has just returned home and is having a bath. As you see, we're expecting people to dinner.' She indicated the dining table at the end of the room, set with costly glass and silver, with napkins sticking up like palmyra trees. What a fuss English people made about their dinner! 'But I wanted to speak to you alone. This afternoon something very unpleasant happened. I've never had anything happen like it before, in my own house; and frankly I don't know what to do. You know my husband has allowed a boy from the district to use part of our servants' quarters to live in. He was thrown out of his village, for no fault of his own, they say, and had nowhere to go.'

Interpreter Leung nodded. He remembered the awkward moment when the D.O. had asked him to give Fai a job as an office attendant, and he had had to explain (after three hours taken plucking up courage) that the District Office could not employ anyone flung out of his village and community, as Fai had been. He himself was unpopular enough with the Sheung Tsuen and Ha Tsuen people, who blamed him for foisting the road on them, which drew attention to the valley and in its turn brought the reservoir with it. If the Office then employed Fai, all its influence in the valley would come to an end.

'So he's been living with us. Everything was perfectly all right —at least, I thought it was—until this afternoon, when I made my usual weekly inspection of the servants' quarters. I tried to open the door of the room the boy uses, but it was locked. I asked my old servant, Ah Juen, where the boy was, and she told me he was in the room. I knocked, and called to him, asking him to open the door, and from inside he began shouting at me in the dialect. You know I don't understand it very well, but I did understand it well enough to know that he was being extremely rude. He was making so much noise, attracting the attention of the other servants, that I thought there was nothing else to do but come back here. Later, when I'd cooled down a bit myself, I told Ah Juen to ask him to come in here, to see me and explain himself. After a certain amount of trouble, Juen says, he came. He was truculent and— well—menacing. I didn't really feel safe with him. He said he didn't see that I had any right to interfere with him, and finished by threatening to kill me if I complained about him to my husband. Well, I don't think one need take that too seriously,' she added quickly. 'People are always threatening to kill each other, aren't they? It's almost a form of words, isn't it? But I do admit I felt uneasy. He's never behaved like this before, and before worrying my husband about it, I thought it over and decided the best thing I could do would be to consult you.'

Interpreter Leung nodded again.

'Surely your Shanghai servant must know what it's all about?' he asked.

'I'm sure she does. But she won't say a word to me. I think he's threatened her, and she's too frightened to open her mouth.'

'Very probable,' he agreed. 'Should I have a word with him?'

'I'd be thankful if you would. Juen will take you through to the back. If I go out, trouble will only start again.'

He went through to the white, spotless kitchen—it looked, he thought with a shudder, like an operating theatre in a hospital—and out through the back door to where there was an iron gangway leading like a bridge over the courtyard to the smaller block of servants' quarters, built in a recess carved out of the rocky hill. The old maidservant would not go with him. In an angry, worried tone she simply said the number of the room, and left him to find it for himself. When he approached the door, he saw from beneath it that there was a light on inside.

'Ah Fai,' he called, knocking on the door. 'Let me in.'

The light was extinguished.

'Who is it?'

He told him.

'What reason have you for speaking to me? Leave me alone,' Fai's voice answered roughly.

'Open up, Fai! Don't be a fool. D'you want me to bring someone to break down the door?'

There was a pause, followed by the click of the lock. The door opened slightly and Fai came quickly out, holding the door against his body, so that by no chance could Interpreter Leung see anything in the dark room.

'Get back, unless you want your neck cut!' In the gloom of the gangway Leung saw that the boy was wearing a new white shirt, with a woollen sweater underneath it, blue jeans and soft basketball shoes. His face was drawn, as if for several nights he had not slept. 'Get back, d'you hear me?'

Glancing down, Interpreter Leung went cold, his body sweating in spite of the coldness of the night. In his right hand, the boy held a large kitchen chopper.

In the colony's murders a chopper was the weapon most frequently used. Leung leapt back to the open part of the gangway between the two buildings. Having him thus at a distance, the boy locked the door.

'What d'you want to talk to me about?' he asked, stepping a pace or two nearer to Leung, who hastily retreated some more. If there was one thing he hated and was scared of, it was physical violence. 'Well, speak up! What d'you want to say?'

A light from the courtyard illuminated the boy dimly. In his months in the city he had changed significantly. His way of speaking had become that of the youth gangs that had recently been disturbing the city's peace, his stance was arrogant, and he had had his hair curled in the manner fashionable among the younger thugs.

'I want to ask you why you've been threatening Mrs. Hui,' said the interpreter tamely, his voice shaking against his will.

'I will not have a foreign woman interfering with my life! I've promised to kill her if she tries to, and I shall keep my promise.'

He came a few more paces forward. Leung retreated till he was near the open kitchen door on the other side.

'Then you can hardly expect the Magistrate to go on helping you by letting you stay here,' he said nervously.

'Why not? The foreigners owe it to me! Without them, I would never have been forced to leave the village.'

'In that case, you must let Mrs. Hui inspect your quarters when she wishes to. It's her responsibility. You can't have it both ways.'

By this time, servants from other establishments were gathering on the gangways below, watching in silence to see if there was going to be a fight.

'No one is going to inspect my room,' Fai answered. He was by now half-way across the bridge gangway.

Leung was worried by the attention they were attracting.

'Ah Fai, put that chopper down, and come and talk sensibly to me in here,' he said quietly.

'No one is going to inspect my room,' he repeated.

'All right, all right. No one will inspect it. But put that weapon down.'

'Because you're a government officer, a running dog of the foreigners, you know how to tell lies. The foreign woman will inspect my room if she can. She wants to throw me out, and I'm not going.'

Interpreter Leung thought quickly.

'What have you got in that room that you're trying to hide?' he asked sternly.

'Yes,' said the voice of the old Shanghai servant, who was just behind him, busy with her cooking, 'that's the way. Get him to answer that.'

At the sound of the old woman's voice, the boy had a sudden access of rage. With a quick intake of breath, he dashed towards Leung at the kitchen door, the chopper raised in his hand. Juen screamed with terror and raced like a young girl towards the

263

living-room of the apartment. A saucepan lid clattered on the floor. Leung, yelling for help in the dialect, ran away from the boy, across the kitchen, nearly hitting the old servant as he did so, and slammed a door behind him with such force that the glass above it smashed and fell with tinkle and clatter. Together they tore down the short corridor leading to the living-room, where Juen, screaming hysterically, rushed to her mistress and buried her face in her breast, her upraised arms hammering against Mrs. Fairburn's bare shoulders. The door behind him opened immediately with a whirr of sound, the boy racing after him. Entering the brighter light of the living-room, Leung ran blindly towards where he remembered the front door was; but as he fumbled with the unusual lock the sound of the fleet rubber shoes behind him ceased. He looked back into the body of the room.

Fai had stopped dead in the doorway from the kitchen, the chopper still in his hand. In the centre of the room were the D.O. and another tall European, wearing black dinner jackets and each holding a sherry glass. Another European woman, in evening dress, evidently the wife of the other man, was beside Mrs. Fairburn, who was dragging the screaming, struggling servant off into the bedroom at the far end of the room. The unexpectedness of the scene, and perhaps in particular the black evening clothes of the men, which he had never seen before, had halted Fai out of sheer surprise.

The other European put his glass down and pointed at the chopper.

'Drop it,' he said in the dialect.

The boy did not move.

'Drop it, Fai,' the D.O. said. 'This is the Superintendent of Police. If you don't drop it, you will be arrested.'

The boy looked revengefully towards the retreating women. After sullenly summing up the physique of the Superintendent, with a defiant gesture he threw the chopper away. It fell against the wainscot, damaging the paint.

'Who is this boy?' the Superintendent asked.

'He's a boy from the district we've tried to help, with conspicuous lack of success.'

The misplaced generosity of Europeans, thought Interpreter Leung.

'I'm afraid all this is my fault, sir,' he interposed, his heart still thumping like mad. He was worried lest the Superintendent, whom he now recognized as Beaton of the Special Branch, arrest Fai and involve the D.O. and himself in a Court scandal. 'I was questioning him, and he lost his temper.' He was recovering his balance now, and his wits. He contemplated Fai's unnaturally curled hair. 'You're keeping a girl out there, aren't you?' he asked, in the tone of an accusation.

The boy did not move a muscle.

'Answer!' Beaton said to him.

Fai moved away to walk out of the room.

Beaton stepped forward and grabbed him by the arm.

'Is it true, Leung?' the D.O. asked.

'It must be, sir. He won't let anyone inspect his room.'

'Who have you got out there, Fai?' the D.O. asked.

Leung did not hear the boy's answer. His thoughts were racing back in time, till they rested on an afternoon two summers ago, when they had given Fai a lift in their launch to Wireless Bay. In the coldly adamant way in which the truth asserts itself, he recalled the strange, short interview he had had that morning with Cow-neck Yeung.

'Who is it, Fai?' he asked solemnly.

The boy did not answer.

'Is it Mr. Yeung's daughter—Mr. Yeung of Wireless Bay?'

The boy tried to wrench himself free of Beaton's hold.

'Ngau-keng?'[1] asked the D.O.

'Yes, sir,' Leung replied, adding with slow emphasis: 'He came to the office this morning to say that his daughter had run away from home and was somewhere in the city. I'm afraid she's in your servants' quarters.'

The D.O. walked in silence to the window. Beaton questioned Leung.

'Is she over the age of consent?'

'Yes, sir.'

'That won't mean a thing to Yeung Ngau-keng,' said the D.O. caustically. 'What are we to do? Could you put her up for the night in your house, Leung, and get her back as soon as you can tomorrow?'

He didn't have the courage to refuse what he knew would make old Yeung his life-long enemy, implicating him in the affair.

'I suppose I could, sir.'

[1] Cow-neck.

265

From the further room came the sound of the servant's continued sobbing.

'You're getting out of there, Fai, tonight—for good,' the D.O. continued.

'I've nowhere to go,' the boy answered sullenly.

'I don't care. You get out. And bring the girl in here to Mr. Leung. He'll look after her.' The boy did not move. 'D'you want me to bring her out myself?' he asked, taking his keys out of his pocket.

The boy swung away.

'I'll bring her,' he replied, and went.

'I'll get you a taxi, Leung,' the D.O. said, going to the telephone. 'You look as though you need a stiff brandy. Mix him one, Frank, there's a good fellow.'

'No, I'm all right, sir. I can't take brandy.'

The doorbell rang.

'Heavens! The other guests!' said the D.O., dialling a number. 'Frank, let them in, would you?'

Beaton went to the front door, to admit another European couple in evening dress.

'Come in! Come in! You've just missed the drama,' he said cheerily.

Leung was, quite unnecessarily, introduced to them. Mrs. Beaton returned from the bedroom. There were greetings all round, the D.O. talking on the telephone and shaking hands at the same time. Unnoticed, Leung walked out to the empty kitchen. It was full of a smell of burnt foreign food. Across the bridge gangway, he saw that the light in Fai's room was on, the door open.

'Hurry up, Ah Fai! The taxi will be here in a moment!'

There was no response. Alerted by the seeming quietness of the room, Leung crossed the gangway, came to the door, and looked in. A cheap quilt lay bundled in a heap in the middle of a wooden Chinese bed. A hand-towel lay on the floor. The room was empty.

26

I T WAS the third day of the Chinese year, the first working day after two public holidays. Richard opened his office door, and called along the corridor:

'Please tell Mr. Leung I can't see anybody!'

Closing the door, he leant back against it, and, with a long, deep sigh, realized that his career in the colony had come to an end.

It was noon. Sylvia was with him, seated beside his office desk, smoking a cigarette from a long holder. It had taken him the whole morning to reach this final realization. Shortly after nine-thirty Leung had come in, cackling and gleeful.

'Have you heard the news, sir?'

'What news?' he asked, absently. The third day of the year, with no callers in the office, was an ideal time for disposing of files which on busier days he had no time to read or think about.

'About Ngau-keng's daughter and that boy.' He was roving about the office with excitement.

Richard grew stern.

'What's happened?'

Leung chuckled, shook his head, and gazed down on the ground.

'They committed suicide, sir, together, on the site of the new reservoir.' With which he burst into a fresh cackle of mirth. 'A very romantic affair, judging by the police report. A suicide pact. Well, it's all right for the young folks. After you get married, you sometimes feel like suicide, but in that case you have to do it alone.'

Pleased with his humour, he giggled wickedly and sat down. He had recovered from his shock treatment on New Year's Eve.

'When did it happen?' Richard asked without amusement.

'The night after they left your place, sir. Where they spent that night the police don't know. But some time during the afternoon of the first day, when the ferries started running again, they went over to Little Island, where they could pass unnoticed. They had a meal in an eating-house (on her money, I suppose) and after that

267

took a sampan across to Great Island, where they landed near Long Sands. One of the road workers, not knowing who they were, came across them. He was coming back from a party by jeep, and had to be on duty that day. He took them as far as the head of the road, quite near Fa Ping, from which they walked the rest of the way after dark.'

Leung knew, by long experience of Court work, how to tell a story, putting the facts in the right order. In the office it was useful. At present, Richard found it only irritating. Leung's face expanded into its most revealing grin.

'They made love together first. The police reports never miss out these special details. Then they climbed up on to the top of the dam and walked along to a place where the water is already quite deep—deep enough to drown in, anyway!' he added with another cackle. 'They tied themselves together with a rope, twisted round and round their bodies, and threw themselves in. Well, at some stage, either before jumping in or when they were in the water, he strangled her.' He shook his head and opened his eyes wide. 'A very romantic story!'

Invariably, when listening to Chinese people telling about the misfortunes of others, Richard became nearly speechless with anger.

'Very,' he said icily. 'We'll discuss it later. I must get through these files.'

Leung took his *congé* with another giggle, and returned to his own office, oblivious that he had enraged his superior. What was the use, in any case, Richard thought, of trying to teach the staff not to laugh at tragedy? Unless they said what they had to say in their own way, one never reached the truth. With an effort of mental discipline, he reminded himself that Leung was as shocked as he was by the suicide: his laughter was evidence of that. Chinese and Westerners were just emotionally geared in different ways, that was all.

They had taken their last meal together at Little Island, avoiding Wireless Bay. They made love together first. Those were the details in police reports. They were also the details in laughing Chinese accounts of disaster. The West, with a solemn face and expressions of woe, tended to leave such things out—with the result that no one learnt the whole story. Like a body at a funeral, it was dressed up in a special way. He was not really angry with Leung, he concluded. He just felt sick.

Though he had long enough in which to do so, he did not identify his own part in the tragedy. Sylvia was due to lunch with him in town. She came much earlier than he had expected.

'You'll never guess who's been to see me this morning,' she said, as soon as she had taken a seat. He lit a cigarette for her.

'Who?' he asked.

'Dear old Chiu.'

'Chiu what?'

'I don't know his full name. You know him. He's the nice boy who works at Government House and always looks after us so beautifully.' Richard nodded. He could not remember what Chiu looked like, but let it pass. Sylvia never let a man's face slip out of her mind. 'He looked frightfully respectful, wearing his best clothes, and sat right on the very edge of his chair, with his hands on his knees.' Richard reflected that he was having a morning with accurate story-tellers. It was relaxing after battling with Chinese peasants incapable of explaining anything. 'He began, after platitudes, by saying did I know that his family came from your district, and that his ancestral temple was near Wireless Bay. He then asked if I knew Mr. Yeung. I said did he mean Ngau-keng and he said he thought that might be the one. He seldom visited the place himself and knew the names of few people there. Anyway, he was a retired Chinese Army man, so I said that's Ngau-keng.'

'Have some of our filthy office coffee?'

'Thanks very much.' He ordered it from the attendant, who was in the room collecting files. 'No sugar. He then made a terrible lot of apologies for coming, saying I mustn't think he was trying to make trouble for us. But he wanted to warn us both of what he'd heard from Wireless Bay, from his cousin, who visited him over the New Year. Incidentally, my dialect has improved, you know. I could understand almost every word Chiu said, and when I first met him we could really only say hullo. It appears that Ngau-keng is furious with you and has threatened that he's going to burn our house down on Little Island, with both of us in it. I said that would be rather hard to do, because we could easily run out into the garden, but Chiu said it was serious, and he asked me most earnestly—he's so attached to me, it's quite charming—not to go to Little Island, either of us, and certainly not spend another night there. After which, more apologies and platitudes, duty called at Government House—he says Lady Wellborough's terrible to work for—and the interview closed. What d'you make of it?'

Richard laughed. Though every Britisher in the colony might say the contrary, he had married the right person. He rang the bell for Leung.

'Have you heard anything about Yeung Ngau-keng wanting to burn my house down?' he asked, when the interpreter came.

Leung giggled, then looked serious.

'Yes. A man has just been in from Wireless Bay. It's true.'

'Is it serious?'

Leung looked grave.

'I think it is, sir,' he said. 'They say, actually, that if you go back to Little Island you'll not be safe.'

'There's a police station there. They can keep an eye on the house.'

'Ngau-keng has what amounts almost to a private army, as you know, sir. I think it's a risk.'

Richard drummed his fingers on the table.

'Thank you, Leung.'

He was so accustomed to the patchwork of threats with which the district was decorated that he found it hard to take a threat seriously, particularly when directed towards himself.

'Well, we needn't go to Little Island for a week or two, need we?' said Sylvia. 'This will probably simmer down. Why is Ngau-keng so angry, anyway?'

Richard explained about the suicide, leaving out the part about making love. Even he, he noticed, followed his own proper conventions—even with his wife. As he explained it, the identification grew stronger. He had taken pity on Fai, housed him, fed him, clothed him, tried to find him a job. Fai had tried unsuccessfully to marry Ngau-keng's daughter. Naturally, after Fai's expulsion from his own village, the old man would not consent. She had then eloped with Fai, who had brought her to the District Officer's town residence. The District Officer had known about it from the start, and tolerated it—at least, that would be the story. Fai was jobless and desperate. Instead of sending the girl back to her father, the District Officer had chucked them both out of the house after an altercation with the boy. They had then committed suicide. Seen from the viewpoint of Wireless Bay, and from the reports which had undoubtedly been disseminated by the other servants working at The Heights, it was not difficult to appreciate

270

that Yeung Ngau-keng might deem he had a case against the District Officer.

After twenty minutes, the door opened to admit Leung and the aged and valued correspondence clerk, Mr. Ng. Leung explained that Ng too had received reports from Wireless Bay.

'I assure you, sir,' the old man said, 'this is a real threat. You should not go to Little Island on any account. In my twenty-eight years of service, I cannot remember anything like this before. Please be very careful, sir, and Mrs. Fairburn too.'

They bowed and withdrew. Though short, the interview was portentous. Mr. Ng never entered Richard's office in the ordinary way. In two years this was probably the first time he had come, speaking gravely and sincerely, as he always did.

It was shortly after this that Richard went to the door and called to the attendant to tell Leung he could not see anybody.

It was the end—only it had taken him the whole morning to grasp it. Nothing on earth would make Yeung Ngau-keng believe that Richard was not responsible for the death of his favourite child, the child of his old age. His enmity, linked down the long chain from Wong Tak-wor to Szeto, Edwin Lau, the Chief Secretary, the Governor, could stretch far. Besides which, there was a positive danger in living on Little Island, close to Yeung's headquarters and surrounded by his henchmen. Even in Victoria he might not be safe. To have enemies as a result of one's actions as a government servant was one thing: to have enemies as a result of one's actions as an individual—and the case of Fai was very much an individual matter—was different, bearing more sinister implications, justifying revenge. By whichever medium he chose, through his henchmen or through his social and commercial connexions, Yeung could have his own way. His first reaction might be arson and murder. His second could as well be a calculated destruction by insinuation, denigration in the colony's high places. Either was, with determination, easy. Both could lead to the same thing—to the elimination of an enemy, to the satisfaction of revenge.

Later, when the wound had healed, or should Yeung not live much longer, Richard would be able to work in the colony again. For the present, there was nothing for it but to apply for transfer to another territory.

'You can't undo what is done,' he said slowly, leaning against the door. 'The thing develops inexorably. You can do nothing to

271

improve it. You cannot lessen your own involvement in it. If you remain in contact with it, even, your involvement increases, grows more complex, until . . .' He paused, his eyes on the window. ' "Be merciful," as Wen once told me the motto of a government official should be. Be merciful! To whom? To whom now?'

The thought of going to Jenkinson disturbed him. Jenkinson was still Acting Chief Secretary, no new substantive appointment having been made by the Colonial Office. Richard had come through it well with Jenkinson, and thus it could continue, so long as Richard held the best cards and never had to ask for anything. He had now to ask. In the first place, it would be impossible to admit that he was afraid of Yeung Ngau-keng. No one in the Secretariat would take such a thing seriously. The affairs of Great Island were of microscopic importance to them. Danger from some little Chinese living there would be nothing but a joke, Secondly, if he left out that side of it—and the people of Great Island were of so little interest to others that the suicide had not even been reported in the newspapers, so there was every likelihood that Jenkinson and the Secretariat would never know about the conflict it had brought him into with Yeung—there was the British side to be considered. Jenkinson and the Club would interpret his request for transfer as a triumph for them. They had probably been grinding their teeth with fury while, week by week, Sylvia sedulously fed the local Press with advance news about the filming of her book. She intended that they should. If the rumour should go about, as from Jenkinson it certainly would, that Richard was applying for a transfer, it would lead to another bout of unpleasantness such as he had experienced the year before. Nothing could be worse than the British colonials' cocksure crow of moral rectitude. His bad dream of dodging his fellow-countrymen among the streets and houses returned to him momentarily, making the pit of his stomach feel cold.

The telephone rang. It was the Private Secretary to the Governor. Would Mr. Fairburn please come and see H.E. at nine o'clock the following morning.

'Does H.E. want me to bring any files along?'

'He didn't mention anything about files, sir.'

'Thank you.' It meant a general discussion about the district and its problems. It had come at the right moment. He decided to use the opportunity to ask for a transfer. 'We must clear out of this colony,' he said quietly to Sylvia as he put the phone down.

272

After a second or two of silence, she sighed.

'Oh, dear! So they've won.'

He looked at her acutely.

'Who d'you mean by "they"?'

'Just "they"—things—the general build-up,' she said vaguely, with a gesture. 'I thought we might be able to make it. We haven't. We've been bulldozed. We've lost.'

The Governor's study was pleasant on a fine day. It was still too cool for the air conditioning to be needed. The french windows were open, but covered with plastic *persiennes* to keep out the glare of the morning sun. They flapped loosely against the window frames, while through their slats could be seen the dark green leaves of the magnolia tree.

Sir Wavell Wellborough, one of the Colonial Empire's most senior Governors, was a short, squat man, with close-cropped grey hair, a moustache, rough square chin, blue eyes, and spectacles that gave his eyes an intense look that was in keeping with his personality. He was a controlled, square box of mental energy. He never made imaginative remarks, and Richard had thus concluded that he probably had little or no imagination. He was a born chairman, capable of accommodating around him the most diverse intellects—and thus a successful administrator. He lacked the unexpectedly soft, artistic streak of Freddie Stainmore. Despite Richard's and Sylvia's friendship with Stainmore, however, it had been a relief to Richard when Sir Wavell returned.

He intrigued the British population of the colony by a device as simple as it was calculated. Among his lesser orders and decorations was a Companionship of the Royal Victorian Order, signifying that at some stage of his career he had rendered a personal service to the Royal Family. No one knew what this service was, and it provided, among the British, a subject of endless speculation. It was a matter on which everyone was free to hold opinions. Brenda Macpherson said with absolute certainty that Sir Wavell had accompanied the Duke and Duchess of York to Australia. No one could confirm this. Sir Wavell's entry in *Who's Who* made no reference to it, and he himself avoided mention of the subject. Maintaining silence on the matter was one of the subtle ways in which he maintained his *mystique*.

He indicated the chair beside his desk.

'I have received a report on the move of the villagers of . . . er

. . .' he glanced at his papers, 'Ha Tsuen and Sheung Tsuen, in which you are described as having demonstrated outstanding personal courage.' He glanced up over his spectacles. 'I am sending the report, with a commendation, to the Secretary of State. I congratulate you.'

The sparse words, the lack of emotion, the manner of a businesslike interview, gave Richard a peculiar pride. He pulled at his collar and cleared his throat.

'Have a cigarette,' the Governor said, indicating a silver box beside Richard's chair.

'Thank you, sir. I don't smoke.'

The Governor adjusted his glasses higher on his nose.

'You've been having a difficult time, I understand, in your office, and in the colony as a whole. You need a change of air. I've been offered a vacancy for one officer of about your age to be seconded to the Colonial Office in London for eighteen months. I propose, with your approval, to put your name forward. Have you any comment?'

Richard tried to stop his voice rising to a higher pitch.

'I can think of nothing better, sir. When would it be?'

'Leaving here in about a month. Could you manage it?'

'Yes, sir. Certainly.'

'I might add that I am recommending you against the general advice of the Secretariat,' the Governor said. 'Don't let me down.'

Richard rose.

'I shan't, sir.'

'No,' the Governor said, looking at him assessingly, 'I don't think you will. Thank you, Fairburn.'

Richard walked trembling to the door; his coldly perspiring palm slid along the handle as he pressed it down.

At lunchtime there was a telephone call from Edwin Lau.

'Frances and I are giving a small New Year party this evening at eight. I must apologize for the short notice, but we were wondering if you could both come along.'

Noting the speed and accuracy of the bamboo telegraph, Richard accepted without consulting Sylvia. In the distinctive way the social life of the colony worked, they had become respectable again—safe to receive and be received. For the next few days the telephone rang time and again as the news spread round. One influential Chinese after another invited them to dinners and lunches, the people who had for a year left them designedly in the

274

cold. A few Europeans phoned too, but within a day or so every evening till the day of their departure was booked up. There was nothing to do but suggest to various Chinese hosts who knew the Europeans concerned that they too be invited with them.

The hard core of opposition did not change, of course. Lady Mercer had not given her friends any signal that they might adopt a new attitude. As Sylvia said, the colonials had held the attitude so long, they had become stiff with it. They could not move so rapidly as the Chinese. Chinese had, symptomatically, bodies more lissom than Westerners. The fact expressed the mind within.

During the last week of their stay in the colony, the Great Island road rounded the rocks beyond Fa Ping and entered the valley of Ha Tsuen and Sheung Tsuen, as far as the beginning of the slowly, cumbersomely, growing wall of the great dam.

'This is your achievement, Richard,' croaked the huge bullfrog Szeto at a farewell dinner, 'and you should be proud of it! We are happy to have men like you in our Government, and the same goes for your accomplished and charming wife.'

There were plaudits, and the winecups were drained.

Amid a spate of social engagements, Sylvia managed to supervise the removal of their possessions from Little Island. The servants there were bequeathed to the next District Officer, while arrangements were made for Juen to follow them to London, travelling by sea. The apartment at The Heights was sublet.

Even Brenda Macpherson telephoned—three days before they were due to leave, when it was no longer sensible to issue an invitation.

'I've been fiendishly busy, darling, and I'm sure you have been too. We shall simply have to meet in London when Brian's on leave during the summer.'

'That would be delightful, Brenda,' Sylvia replied insincerely. 'Thank God,' she said, putting the receiver down, 'the woman doesn't matter to us any more.'

At the airport, on the day of their departure, between fifty and sixty Chinese friends came to see them off, not counting the senior members of the District Office staff. At least one half of the airport restaurant became a private cocktail party, in which the Jenkinsons, off on holiday to Japan by another plane leaving just after theirs, found themselves surrounded by people they knew but who had not turned up to see them, and became inextricably and most unwillingly involved.

275

As Richard and Sylvia, waving behind them, walked out in the muggy spring wind towards the waiting aircraft, Szeto's driver ignited a barrage of firecrackers and was promptly arrested by the airport police, who were, however, powerless to prevent the barrage burning to the end of its deafening and merry din.

'Did you pay for all those drinks, dear?' asked Sylvia, as they settled into their seats.

'Of course not! What can you do?' said Richard with a gesture. 'Edwin wouldn't let me.'

The air hostess came round with jujubes.

27

WILLIE ROGERS had come over to Great Island with Frank Beaton to attend the ceremonial opening of the road by the Governor. A large number of launches were berthed beside one another at the pier, from which the road started, and a speakers' platform and chairs for invited guests had been arranged at the pierhead where, as the front vehicle in an imposing line of jeeps, lorries, and one of Mr. Szeto's buses, the Governor's number two car, brought over specially in a tank landing craft, waited empty in front of a thick ribbon of red silk stretched from two white posts across the road, with a wood and paper decorated arch of welcome over it.

It was a brilliant, cool, blue afternoon, unusual for the season —the farewell cry of winter—and most of the city people were still wearing their cold-weather clothes. Wong Tak-wor, in a dark blue suit with a huge red rosette in his buttonhole, was making an honorific speech in atrocious verse, but as the country people were not critical of such matters and the Westerners could not understand what the speech was about, it did not make much odds. Seated next to him on one side was the Governor, in a grey morning coat, with Lady Wellborough next to him, a feathery woman edging towards plumpness, wearing pink, with a pink hat of two seasons ago with a grey feather on it. On the other side was Colonel Yeung, clad in black silk, again with a red rosette, and behind him in the second row sat his two concubines, looking very august, next to Mrs. Webb and the wife of the Director of Agriculture. About two hundred people had come over from the city. With them in the crowd was a still larger number of village folk from miles around, all the older ones wearing their best black silk, the younger ones in white shirts and Western-style trousers, some of the older girls from the Mission school wearing Western frocks.

Wong Tak-wor finished to mild applause, and put the table microphone over to the Governor. Press cameras clicked as the Governor rose. Those villagers who had been chattering became silent.

'Be ready to make a get-away,' Beaton whispered to Willie, 'as soon as he stops speaking.' Beaton, being on duty, had to ride in the jeep immediately following the Governor's car.

Together they moved slowly through the bystanders towards the row of vehicles. Going silently across, Willie shook hands with Professor Wen, patted the fat John Winnington on the shoulder, and bowed with a grin to the tall old general who was in the syndicate building the dam.

'. . . and it is important for it to be realized,' the Governor was saying, as the microphone drowned his voice in a high-pitched whistle and Wong Tak-wor, with his fish-like mouth wide open, craned expressionlessly round at the operator. With a mechanical effort, the whistle died away. '. . . multi-purpose!' the Governor's voice resumed, with emphasis that was unfortunately meaningless to the audience. 'Not only will this new road open up an important new area as a dormitory for city workers, but it will enable large and potentially fertile hill slopes to be brought within economic reach of Victoria's vegetable markets. Two entire villages have had to suffer the great inconvenience of being moved to new sites to make way for the large new reservoir, with which this road scheme is associated. But we have the satisfaction of knowing that this is going to be a blessing in disguise to those villagers. They possess hill fields already terraced for cultivation, and, with the help of the newly established agricultural station, they will be able soon to engage in intensive vegetable production, which will immeasurably improve their economy. The increase in vegetable production, in fact, all along the road, is one of its most significant features, capable of raising the tonnage of vegetables produced in the colony, and thus enabling us to cut down on the

277

amount of vegetables we at present have to import at high cost from abroad. I wish to congratulate . . .'

The speech moved methodically to a close. Webb, on Lady Wellborough's left, looked apprehensively about for Wong Tak-wor's little daughter, who was to present the Governor with the golden scissors for cutting the red silk. A moment later there was respectful clapping. The new District Officer having omitted to arrange for a Chinese interpreter to be present, none of the villagers knew what the Governor had said. Some of the women giggled to each other as they patted their podgy hands together.

'Stand by,' Beaton whispered, as the Governor was led out of the speakers' pavilion by Wong Tak-wor and old Yeung, neither of them able to say a word to him, but with Wong Tak-wor grinning fishily and saying 'ha! . . . ha! . . . ha! . . .' in various tones of voice, trying to make it sound intelligent. Plenty of men were present who could have acted as interpreters—the P.W.D. engineers, for instance—but with so many dignitaries present they had been swept to the rear and lost sight of.

The other guests were leaving their places to enter the jeeps, the lorries, and the bus, conversation had started again, and no one was paying much attention to anything except themselves and their friends. The Governor was first led to a large granite stone erected beside the road and covered with red silk.

'I have much pleasure in naming this road Wellborough Highway!' he said in as loud a voice as he could muster, while Lady Wellborough said something with a giggle to Mrs. Webb, who was wearing a hideous mauve dress of what looked like chiffon. The red silk fell away, revealing a carved inscription in English and Chinese recording the opening of the road and its name, which in the dialect read Wai Po Lo Sun Lo. As it did so, two long sticks of firecrackers suspended from the roof of the now nearly empty speakers' pavilion exploded in a steady roar, killing all other sounds.

The Governor was now standing in front of the silk ribbon. The little girl, in a pink dress, presented the scissors; the Governor turned back to the crowd, opened his mouth a few times inaudibly, swung about, and cut the ribbon.

Sticks of firecrackers concealed in the welcoming decorations immediately exploded on both sides of the road. In addition, villagers ignited smaller boxes of crackers, hurling them up in the air. Amid a pungent scent of gunpowder, everything and everybody was enveloped in dark smoke. The noise was deafening. Western women covered their ears with their hands, while Chinese boys and girls laughed, their laughter being a visual expression only, all sound of it lost in the terrific roar of the explosions.

Beaton gripped Willie Rogers by the elbow and pulled him into the first jeep. The smoke was so dense around them that all that could be seen of the Governor's car ahead of them was a dark shadow against the sunlight that opaquely penetrated the gloom. When a stick of crackers went off just beside the jeep, the explosions sparking out haphazardly in all directions, Willie Rogers began to feel nervous. With his poor eyesight he had the unpleasant sensation of not knowing what was happening. Beaton started the engine and moved the jeep forward, stopping with a jerk when he realized the Governor's car had not yet moved. The din continued unabated, an immense, strident sound of jubilation.

A few seconds later they realized they had lost the Governor's car. It had already started and disappeared in the smoke. Keeping in bottom gear, Beaton nosed the jeep forwards, uncertain where he was going, until, like a trick of photography, they were suddenly in fresh air again, the same sunny, tranquil afternoon they had just left. The Crown car was thirty yards ahead of them, the rear section of the hood lowered, and the feather in Lady Wellborough's hat was standing up in the breeze like the crest of a cockatoo going down in an elevator. With Beaton accelerating, the roar of crackers died away behind them.

When they reached the first bend, where the road headed up into the hills around the rice valleys of Wireless Bay, a new obstacle impeded their progress. One of the villages had brought out their unicorn, the huge, elaborately decorated head of a mythical creature, with lolling eyes like billiard balls and a big, flat red tongue in a mouth that opened and shut as the animal bucked and reared above the shoulders of the young man operating it beneath. Its long tail, supported by two small boys, darted and whisked about, as the beast lashed out proudly and angrily. A burst of crackers exploding in front of it, it jumped with delight, bending down close to the explosions. It then raised itself up gleefully, happy to receive so much attention. Beside the road were its attendants, a band of young men in yellow shirts and black trousers, beating cymbals, drums, and a heavy gong.

When the Governor's car stopped, the beast edged round to the side of it, nosing it, starting back in horror, and making feint

279

attacks at it, particularly at the person of the Governor himself. It appeared highly displeased.

But if the Governor was unprepared for this, Wong Tak-wor fortunately was not. Taking a bright red envelope of money from his pocket, he handed it to the Governor, who held it out towards the unicorn. It bucked suspiciously, put its head on one side, to consider the matter, then, bringing its head down almost to the level of the dust, it took a crafty look at the red packet from below, springing back delightedly after this inspection, while the cymbals, gong, and drum beat like fury and more crackers exploded. After hectically prancing about this way and that, thrilled with the prospect of something good to eat, it came abruptly to a motionless position. A sustained roll from all the instruments vibrated forth, while slowly, politely, as gently as a cat, it came forward towards the Governor's still outstretched hand, opened its mouth, stuck its tongue out slightly to take the red packet, and swallowed it. To a slow, rhythmic beat of the drums, the unicorn sat back contentedly, digesting its meal, cocking its head up each time a piece of food passed down its throat. This done, it reared and bucked happily, saluting the Governor with an obeisance. The Wellboroughs waved to it and its attendants, and the cars moved on.

In a few minutes they were up to the top of the ridge separating Wireless Bay from the southern valleys of the island, with a fine view of the expanse of rice-fields on either side. From there the road descended with several hairpin bends towards the sea, where it veered along the south coast, long, empty sand beaches on one side, the rolling, bare green hills on the other. Every time they passed a village, all the inhabitants, twenty here, thirty there, down to the smallest child able to stand up, waited respectfully for them, lining the road in their best clothes. The older people, in black silk, held their hands folded and bowed slightly as the Governor's car passed. At each hamlet more crackers were let off, usually no more than a single short burst, depending on what the clan could afford. The Governor raised his grey top hat; Lady Wellborough waved.

Of these bursts of crackers, the loudest occurred as they passed the seven grey stone houses of Fa Ping, where the Fu clan was celebrating its achievement, unaware that all of them were now technically landless labourers working for Wong Tak-wor. In this state they would probably be allowed to remain until Wong decided to build another of his bungalow estates there, after which they would be driven away—unless perhaps a few of them were smart enough to work as coolies for the new residents.

Within twenty minutes of slow driving, the cars drew up in front of the Ha Tsuen temple, where Old Liu of Sheung Tsuen and Old Chan of Ha Tsuen were waiting for them. They, too, were wearing black silk; but they had come alone. The temple was empty. There were no crackers. A gang of workers handling huge blocks of granite paused to gape at the Governor and Lady Wellborough. With a whirr, the cement mixer started.

Willie Rogers took in the subtleties of the situation, which the Governor, of course, would not perceive. For the two senior men of the two villages not to have come to meet the Governor would have been an insult. It would furthermore have been bad manners. They came down, therefore, from their new hill sites. To express their real feelings in the matter, however, they had ordered the rest of their clans to stay at home. The village people could easily have come down and exploded a cracker or two. Sheung Tsuen, too, had a unicorn. Though Fa Ping might not perceive the doom to which they were committed, Sheung Tsuen and Ha Tsuen did. They had begun to realize they had been cheated. The university graduate agriculturalist was doubtless doing his best, but what could he achieve? Women could not grow vegetables.

Willie Rogers sighed. Leaving the Governor's party, he mounted the wall of the dam and strolled along the scaffolding platform that ran along the side of it. It was a Saturday afternoon, and few people were working. After walking a hundred yards or so, he stopped. Water stretched untidily into the valley, covering everything nearby, but further inland only a field here, a field there, depending on the ground levels. Across on the west side he could just see the deserted village of Ha Tsuen. It was too far off for him to note any details, but Fai's cousin-brother had already told him what had happened. The houses were under about a foot of water. The roofs had been taken off each house, the tiles being useful for pigsties in the new village. Every scrap of woodwork had either been removed by the villagers or stolen by people from Fa Ping. Nothing but the bare shell of the seven-hundred-year-old home of Chan and Liu remained. They had moved there during the Mongol invasion of China.

Footsteps echoed along the platform, and the plank he was

281

standing on shook slightly. He looked back the way he had come.

'Ah, there you are! The elusive Mr. Rogers!' said Mrs. Webb, comforted by her own cleverness. 'What are you ruminating here for? Isn't this all marvellous?'

'Marvellous,' Willie Rogers conceded haplessly, looking at the extraordinarily wrong shade of mauve which the good lady had selected.

'Well, you can ruminate, if you like. But I can assure you, it's a great day for us—for Mr. Webb and me. They can call it Wellborough Highway, if that pleases them,' she said confidingly, her bare arm pressing slightly against his sleeve. 'My own personal view is that it should have been called Webb Highway. D'you know, Mr. Rogers, Mr. Webb and I look upon this road as *our* road. We've been in this from the very beginning. Mr. Webb was the first person to take the initiative, when he suggested making a road to Mr. Stainmore—I mean,' she said with mock pompousness, 'Sir Frederick Stainmore—though to *me* he was always plain Mr. Stainmore, just like anyone else. I can't see why people like him should be built up with titles and suchlike. It was Mr. Webb's initiative which led to this great reservoir. . . . Well, never mind,' she went on brightly, 'perhaps they'll call it Webb Reservoir—or Webb Dam!' she added, bursting into a peal of high-pitched laughter.

Willie Rogers made a polite answer. The subject of names, and the importance of names in Chinese, had drawn his thoughts far away from Mrs. Webb. The road would certainly never be called Wellborough Highway, except in official documents. The Chinese had already named it Suicide Road, and the dam Suicide Wall. Those would be the names that would stick long after the reason for them was forgotten, when Fai and Mui had entered the pantheon of local ghosts by becoming confused with one or other of the island's gods and goddesses. How typical it was, too, he thought, that the Governor should pay his one visit to Great Island to open a road called Suicide Road! It fitted so aptly the Chinese conception of foreigners. Being devils, they naturally associated themselves with death. In their rooms they placed scented flowers, only used by Chinese at funerals. When their friends were sick, they sent them flowers, such as Chinese would only send at a death. When they gave a present, they wrapped it in white paper, symbolic of death, and they slept in white sheets that were like mourners' clothes. When visiting the country, they ate long-dead meat out of tins, meat that no villager would dare to try. Chinese valued life above all, associating themselves with what was lucky in life. Devil people, being the opposite of Chinese, associated themselves with death and all that was unlucky. To the people of the island there would be a deeper significance than met the eye in the devil Governor coming in state to open Suicide Road.

'Shall we go back, Mrs. Webb?'

'Let's, by all means. I shall feel safer with you, Mr. Rogers,' she said in a coy way. 'You can catch me if I fall.'

28

THEY had gone together to Covent Garden to hear the latest cacophonous opera to be subsidized by the State. Sylvia, after the first harrowing five minutes, decided that, like most music subsidized by states, it was in due course destined to join its many forerunners in the limbo of the forgotten. Having reached this decision, she lost all further interest in the performance.

Richard appeared to be enjoying it. At least, he was paying attention. He had brought with them a nephew studying for a music degree at Oxford. Having drinks before the opera, the nephew had explained his intention of writing a sonata in the Dorian mode. Doubtless he too would, in the fullness of time, be subsidized by the State, which in its relation to art, Sylvia reflected, was like Henry Winterley on a large scale. Men, she further decided, watching the attentive expressions of Richard and his nephew in the soft light raying from the stage, were able to stand cacophony for longer than women—by which she meant feminine women, she added to herself, gazing round at the drab female figures near her, with their straight hair and sternly male faces, the one next to her leaning in a gesture of intellectual passion against the shoulder of a sallow young man with weak lips, large eyes, and soft, wavy hair.

Sylvia looked this way and that, wondering what to do. She would not be allowed to smoke a cigarette. Even chewing-gum would have been a consolation. After twenty minutes she became so bored and irritated by the noises emanating from stage and orchestra pit—it was not like Professor Wen's party: they had had to pay money to hear this—that she could not stand it any more.

'I'm going to the cloaks,' she whispered to Richard, rising to leave.

There were prompt expressions of 'Ssh!' from the devotees, and a sniff of contempt from the stern young woman next to her, whose clothes were not so pretty as Sylvia's. Women with pretty clothes should not come to cacophonous operas, she thought. The two do not mix.

As quietly as she could—but feeling she was escaping from things and people as inimical to her as the colonials had been to Richard—she left the auditorium, crossed the corridor, and pushed open the outer door into the ornate gold and red foyer, with its tall mirrors and restful Victorian atmosphere.

The female bar attendants were shocked when she asked for a brandy before the bar was officially open. They too, it seemed, were devotees of modern opera, but with the difference that they never had to listen to it, the padded doors around the auditorium closing as the curtain rose.

She sat down on a rococo settee, the uninteresting programme folded inside out on her lap. The peace of the foyer was only disturbed by the conversations of the barmaids—a quiet, domestic sound, conducive to thought—and by distant rumours of brassy orchestral squalls and the shriek of sopranos on notes at variance with what was happening below, which from time to time, at *fortissimo* points, penetrated even the two rows of padded doors, like a gramophone tuned down to nothing and accidentally left on.

The music, and Richard's earnest attention to it, brought back in flood the doubts which had unsettled her again and again since her return to him. She had found her road in life. Through a series of experiences, she had come to that sure instant of vision on her first night in New York eighteen months ago, when in loneliness she had faced herself, perceiving what she was and where she must go. Richard was still groping to find his road. Through every kind of experience he was prepared to grope, as tonight through the vocal and orchestral contortions of the new opera—groping, as the rest of the solemn-faced audience was groping—each seeking a road, a truth—unaware that the man whose brain evolved the

284

sounds they were listening to was groping too, unable to give them a single phrase of truth or inspiration.

It was true that human beings linked together in marriage could not always evolve at the same speed. One sometimes outstripped the other. If they thought they were evolving in unison, too often the thought signified that neither was evolving at all. Yet it worried her to find, at moments such as this, that she was ahead of Richard in whatever they did together. While he groped searchingly through the three acts, she had discarded the entire work after twenty minutes as a worthless noise, a waste of time to listen to. She knew, with the certainty of her own talent as a writer, that her verdict would be the verdict of the future. If only, sometimes, Richard could be ahead of her, could take the lead!

Only sometimes, though. There was nothing wrong in a woman being the more intelligent partner in a marriage, provided it was not everlastingly so. There would be dullness in that. A change in this pattern of things, however, could only come about if, in Freddie's words, Richard could find the fulfilment of his personality. She should have married Freddie. He would have tried to cow her, and she would have resisted him like hell. But that would have been a marriage. Her marriage with Richard was a company affair, with herself placed temporarily as the senior director, taking decisions in the absence of the opposition which at each meeting she hoped for.

It was a still, summer night, not warm by tropical standards, but sultry for London. She fanned herself with a Chinese fan. In the colony she seldom used one. In London, people expected one to use a Chinese fan. Was there anything in the world she could do, she wondered, to help Richard find his real road, his way to self-fulfilment?

A combined shriek by orchestra and singers brought the act to a close. Applause filled the tall old building. Commissionaires stepped forward to open the doors. The foyer was filled with an augmented din, the cries of the audience rising and falling as the principals, unseen from where she sat, appeared before the curtain and withdrew. In a few seconds the audience was walking smartly out to the bar and the sandwich tables, pressing notes and heavy cash at the black-and-white uniformed girls, harassed with fast arithmetic.

'You should have come back, darling. It was a magnificent finale!' Richard exclaimed jubilantly.

285

'I didn't like to disturb all those people again,' she lied, thinking of the intellectual frump who had been sitting next to her. 'Why! Mr. Hillary!'

'Mrs. Fairburn! How unexpected!'

The pedantic old sinologue, clutching a plate of sandwiches and a pile of coins, was retreating from one of the crowded tables, nearly treading on her toes as he did so. Dull old stick that he was, her heart warmed to him. Their meeting recalled what she had first experienced in the grey days after the Second World War: the affinity that existed between those few English people who spoke Chinese, who had penetrated another life, another world, another morality, and who, in the process of understanding it, partially lost the capacity to return to the life from which they started.

'Are you having a good time?' she asked—amid the noise of conversation there was little else she could say.

'I must admit to being entirely absorbed in the problem of food,' he said, munching his first sandwich with vigour. He then bent down close to her ear. 'I must also admit to being bored stiff,' he added in a deep undertone. 'I'm dragged to things like this by my wife.'

His wife, Sylvia knew, did not speak Chinese. She was a commonplace woman, who took coffee at the Colony Club at eleven o'clock each morning, with others whose company she found satisfying. Sustained by the music, apparently, Mrs. Hillary had no need of more substantial sustenance, and had not left her seat.

'How strange!' Sylvia said. 'It's my husband who drags me.'

As she said it, the question posed itself. Richard had undeniably taken the lead in bringing her to the Opera House.

'Where is Richard? I must congratulate him,' said Mr. Hillary, stuffing a second sandwich into his mouth and looking around him.

It was in keeping with Mr. Hillary's character that he should have scanned the minute print in *The Times*' publication of colonial honours, and observed that Richard had been awarded the Order of the British Empire, Fourth Class, in the Birthday Honours announced that morning. The two men shook hands and talked, their voices lost amid so many others. The student of the Dorian mode sipped beer.

'It's a work of profound significance, Sylvia,' he said, adjusting

286

a fallen lock of hair. 'You'll love the second act. I've seen the opera three times.'

She smiled condescendingly. She felt peculiarly alone, with only old Mr. Hillary to hold on to. He alone knew, in this concourse of people, all that she knew. His was the only word she could trust.

She wanted someone to trust. She was off balance. She wondered if she had been blind to Richard, if indeed he had already found fulfilment by taking on himself the burden of bringing to the people of Great Island the ill-conceived project in which he no longer believed, shouldering himself the responsibility of what he considered to be a tragic mistake. She wondered if—bringing it down to the present instant of life—she was wrong about the music, and Richard was right in bringing her to listen to it.

'Don't be so depressing about it, old man,' Mr. Hillary was saying, and swinging round towards her, he interpolated: 'I was telling your husband, the opening of the road was a howling success. It will bring nothing but that confused burgeoning of good and evil which men call progress.'

With which he laid another sandwich on his tongue and consumed it whole.

It was socially courageous of Sir Wavell Wellborough to have recommended Richard for an honour. In the colony, the award would arouse a great deal of criticism among the British. From the humdrum impersonality of his civil service life, the award, in some ridiculous way, raised Richard up beside her, and all the people could see him there.

For a month or so only, however. She thought of the manuscript, already over a hundred pages long, which lay on her desk at home, another hourly growing landmark in her career, another possible typhoon in her married life. Richard would have to build more roads, cheat more peasants, earn higher honours, if he was to keep up with her. It was a cruel calculation of fact, but a true one.

'Are you prepared for the ordeal of the next act?' asked Mr. Hillary, as the first bell rang. 'Personally, I like operas like *Rigoletto*, with some melody in them.'

'So do I,' she said faintly.

Mr. Hillary, in his ponderous way, understood her. Freddie understood her. It was only with the man she was married to that a hedge of uncertainty impeded the view.

'Come along, my dear,' Richard said. 'I know you hate it.'

She rose slowly and put her arm through his.

'Yes, I'm prepared for the ordeal,' she said to the old sinologue, who waved as he mounted the stairs to his seat in a less expensive balcony.

The nephew followed behind them, having hastily drained his beer glass as the second bell rang.

Richard had come back to her world, moreover, where she had told herself all would be well. Yet how lonely is the state that people call marriage! How distant, she thought, tightening her hold on his arm, is a woman from a man, a man from a woman!

———